T0359845

MODERN

Glamour. Power. Passion.

MILLS & BOON

JET-SET ESCAPE WITH HER BILLIONAIRE BOSS
© 2023 by Andrea Bolter
Philippine Copyright 2023
Australian Copyright 2023
New Zealand Copyright 2023

First Published 2023
Second Australian Paperback Edition 2024
ISBN 978 1 038 94553 2

CONSEQUENCE OF THEIR PARISIAN NIGHT
© 2023 by Michele Hauf
Philippine Copyright 2023
Australian Copyright 2023
New Zealand Copyright 2023

First Published 2023
Second Australian Paperback Edition 2024
ISBN 978 1 038 94553 2

MIX
Paper | Supporting
responsible forestry
FSC® C001695
www.fsc.org

Published by
Harlequin Mills & Boon
An imprint of Harlequin Enterprises (Australia) Pty Limited
(ABN 47 001 180 918), a subsidiary of HarperCollins
Publishers Australia Pty Limited
(ABN 36 009 913 517)
Level 19, 201 Elizabeth Street
SYDNEY NSW 2000 AUSTRALIA

Printed and bound in Australia by McPherson's Printing Group

Jet-Set Escape

Andrea Bolter

MILLS & BOON

Also by Andrea Bolter

Wedding Date with the Billionaire
Adventure with a Secret Prince
Pretend Honeymoon with the Best Man

Billion-Dollar Matches collection

Caribbean Nights with the Tycoon

Andrea Bolter has always been fascinated by matters of the heart. In fact, she's the one her girlfriends turn to for advice with their love-lives. A city mouse, she lives in Los Angeles with her husband and daughter. She loves travel, rock 'n' roll, sitting in cafés and watching romantic comedies she's already seen a hundred times. Say hi at andreabolter.com.

For my BAND group

CHAPTER ONE

"YOU NEED TO learn to relax, Jackson." Dr. Singh leaned forward in his chair, obviously trying to make his point. "When was the last time you took a vacation? Or walked on the beach, or even played a round of golf?"

"There are only so many hours in a day," Jackson quipped after pausing to reach into his pocket and tilt up his phone screen so he could get a quick check of the time. After his examination, Dr. Singh had asked him to step into his cluttered office, where they sat across each other at his desk. Jackson was already behind schedule, the doctor visit taking longer than he'd anticipated. "I'm swamped." Indeed, running the acquisitions company that became his after his parents died took every moment from him. Who had time for a vacation?

"Being busy doesn't exempt you from taking care of yourself."

With both of his parents dying much younger than average age, Jackson was screened regularly in the hope that any developing heath problem would be caught and treated early. But he'd scheduled a special appointment because the tightness in his neck and shoulders was becoming more frequent.

"I felt that muscle strain you're talking about. You're hard as a rock. You report headaches in addition to the occasional shortness of breath. Those are irregularities in a thirty-three-year-old man. We'll run some tests but I think what you're describing is chronically uncontrolled stress."

Jackson figured plenty of people lived to ripe old ages with lives that didn't leave time for golf. He tried to speed up the conversation with a short "Fine." At least Dr. Singh didn't think he was in immediate danger.

"I'm serious. It's long thought that lifestyle, and mental and spiritual wellness, greatly influence health. You need to rest, eat well, exercise. And take breaks from all of it every once in a while. Did your parents have pursuits other than work?"

"Are you kidding?" Jackson snarked. He thought back to his father and mother when he was growing up, both putting in eighteen-hour days, sometimes seven days a week like he did now. His doctor was stating the obvious, that Jackson was following in their footsteps. Which he knew in his gut to be true.

Still, the Finns weren't people with hobbies or sports or pastimes. They worked a lot and slept a little, plain and simple. That's how empires were built and maintained. Jackson's lean physique was the result of poorly digested meals eaten indifferently at desks and on airplanes more than from following a nutrition strategy.

"I think it's essential that you make some changes.

Carve out the time for yourself. You must find a balance or you're going to get sick. How about starting with a massage? That can be restorative."

Dr. Singh had no idea how ironic his suggestion was.

One, two, three, four, five stories, Jackson counted, eyes ticking upward as he studied the Sherwood Building across the street from where the driver dropped him off after his doctor's appointment. He owned that historic building, or that was to say that Finn Enterprises did. Which, of course, now came to mean Jackson and Jackson alone, as he was an only child. With his mother's untimely death followed by his father's, he was left with full ownership of their many assets. He hadn't seen the landmark Sherwood Building in a year, so long ago that while he knew it was five floors, he wanted to get a good view of the structure from across the street, counting the stories to reconfirm. He'd be spending time here now, remembered agonies notwithstanding. Jackson was on a mission.

New York's busy Tribeca neighborhood surrounded him. A syllabic abbreviation for Triangle Below Canal Street, the Lower Manhattan neighborhood was renowned. In the early eighteen hundreds the area's Washington Market was a central shopping hub for meat and fish, dairy and produce. In fact, upon completion in 1830, the Sherwood Building itself held dry goods merchants. By the end of that century many of the area's original brick buildings were replaced by factories, manufacturers and warehouses. Fortunately, the lovingly nicknamed Sher survived. In the past fifty or so years, Tribeca received a huge boon when film-makers, artists and celebrities began buying up property. Now a mélange of restoration, new construction, green spaces and a few remaining cobblestoned streets, it was one of the city's most unique enclaves.

Even with the typical New York swirl of hurried pedestrians, horns honking and the rattle of subways underground, Jackson's eyes stayed glued to his building. He'd really forgotten how dramatic it was, Italianate architecture with huge arched windows on the street level, and cast-iron front facades that were among the first of their kind in New York. He was proud to be such a grand old dame's owner.

On the street, businesses populated every available space. A boba café stood on one side of the Sher with a pet groomer on the other. The building's ground floor was leased to an art dealer and a couple of colorful abstract paintings hung in those front windows. Offices on the second, third and fourth floors housed longtime tenants. It was the fifth, and top, floor where Jackson had business today.

Some of those memories he dreaded ticked across his mind like a camera roll of still photographs. His awful debacle of a marriage had nearly shut down operations four years ago on the fateful fifth floor, which housed a day spa that had previously made every best-of list around the globe. Until Jackson's disaster. After that, it languished. Operational but underutilized. No longer buzzed about, true spa aficionados having long moved on to newer places. With a swallow, Jackson re-affirmed to himself that he was going to restore Spa at the Sher to the greatness it once held a reputation for. It was the least he could do for his parents. They wouldn't be there to see it, but Jackson would know he did it.

It was actually a paradox that the Finns owned a spa at all, given their all-work-and-no-play mode of operation, as Dr. Singh had just pointed out. It was only one business within their varied portfolio, but obtaining a landmark building in Manhattan was, in and of itself, a crowning triumph for his parents. Starting from an early age, they'd both worked three jobs a day to save up enough money to leave Ohio and start a life in New York. That they made it to the top, to own one of the city's most famous addresses, was truly an American dream. Jackson turned it into a nightmare.

It gnawed him alive that he had let their prized acquisition become irrelevant because of bad decisions. Meanwhile, other luxury spas pressed forward with beautiful designs and features, and both classic and cutting-edge offerings. With no new innovations, the Sher had lost its luster. Jackson himself had been isolating and living in hotels everywhere but New York, as if avoiding the city would make all the history fade away. Now he was finally back, as the spa's group of investors was gathering in a few weeks to vote on the fate of Spa at the Sher.

The spa deserved to be restored to its former glory, and Jackson was going to convince the investors of such. Lest they vote to back out of their shares in the business. He'd get rid of that cute fairy they'd hired as manager who they'd never given any power to. What was her name—Emma, Eden, Elsa? He'd hire a real spa director with a vision and give him or her the budget to implement it. Hopefully then the ache in the back of his neck that represented the past would subside. And perhaps he wouldn't wake up unable to catch his breath in dark hotel rooms alone in the middle of the night anymore.

Maybe he'd even take his doctor's advice and get a massage. After all, that was one of the services spas were best known for. There was a time when Spa at the Sher employed some of the best massage therapists on the planet, who came with their own client rosters and weeks-long waiting lists. He'd return it to those good old days.

He took in the majesty of the Sher one more time before retrieving that pixie girl's name from his phone. Up in the window of the fifth floor, part of the spa, Jackson spotted someone gazing down to the street scene. It looked like a woman. Was it that manager? For some unexplainable reason, a wiggle shot up his spine.

"My six-o'clock glycolic-acid-peel client canceled so I'm going home," Demi, one of the Spa at the Sher's estheticians, said to Esme, who was gazing down to the street from the large fifth-floor windows.

"Okay, see you tomorrow," she answered without turning. She didn't know why she was gazing down from the windows or what she was looking for. Well, actually she did. But she had things to do, so, with great effort, pulled herself away. She returned to her tasks, separating a large vase of colorful flowers into smaller ones so that she could place them on three different tables in the reception area. *He* was expected any minute now and she wanted to make the spa shine as much as it could.

After all, although the spa had no director, and therefore no direction, as manager she was running things with what she had to work with. Right down to repurposing a floral arrangement, or buying some new flavors of tea for clients to enjoy. Anything she could do so that guests had a memorable experience and would return. At that thought, she clicked her tongue against the roof of her mouth. *Not easy.* Not when there were incredible, unforgettable spas all over the world that offered so much more than the stodgy old Sher, which had seen better days.

"The Vichy shower is broken again," Esme's assistant manager, Trevor, announced as he came out from the main corridor and into the reception area. "Do you want me to call for repair?"

"Yeah. Get them to come as soon as they can. I don't want to have to rebook anyone because of it."

Trevor turned and ducked into a treatment room. Esme neatened up the front desk, putting away the sticky notes staff sometimes left for each other reminding them of things that needed doing. She didn't know why she was nervous. Maybe it was because owner Jackson Finn hadn't said why he was coming in as opposed to the typical email or phone call that was his usual method of communication. He rarely even scheduled a video meeting. Appearing after what Esme guessed was close to a year made no sense. Unless he was coming to fire her, having the decency to at least do that in person.

She again peered down to the street, as if she would recognize him in the crowd at this distance. When she'd seen him on video and a few times in person, she did notice how handsome he was, with his thick dark hair, impeccable in tailored business clothes and a devastating smile that made rare appearances. All of that was neither here nor there, merely observation. She reassured herself that he had no grounds to fire her. The spa wasn't losing money; they were afloat. It had lost its charm, though it was a perfectly serviceable establishment. The Wall Street crowd did still make their way up for deep tissue massages, sometimes booked at regular biweekly intervals to fit in with busy schedules. The Tribeca and SoHo art scene still trickled in for the ministrations given to battle the damaging effects of big city life. The Sher was still as much a part of the neighborhood as the dry cleaners and the pizzeria.

Esme remembered years ago reading about it in spa magazines. The historic building. The fifth-floor oasis of pampering and unfathomable luxury in Lower Manhattan. She'd read interviews with the professionals who worked here and had brought leading-edge everything from the online accounting program to the latest in skin rejuvenation. They'd all moved on now. Esme didn't know the full story of why the spa had fallen from its highest peak. When she was brought in four years ago, she'd heard gossip that Jackson's wife had been running things. Or that was to say, ruining things.

Esme was curious about what really transpired but was never privy to anything other than hearsay.

Doing her final walk-through before he was to make his return, she double-checked the side table that displayed those new teas. One large clear cylinder held cool water infused with cucumber and a second one was flavored with lemon slices. There were whole fresh fruits, nuts and dark chocolate to nibble.

With its palate of the palest lavender and sage accents against tan furniture, it was welcoming, pleasant although dated. All of the walls held photos, paintings or drawings of flowers. Again, pretty but not compelling. Likewise, the treatment menu itself was flat, nothing to offer those chasing the next new experience. There was nothing she could do to dazzle Jackson. A spa without a director, a direction and a budget to make it happen was stagnant.

Hearing the elevator doors open outside the spa's glass entrance door and catching sight of tall and formidable Jackson Finn meant that she was about to find out what brought him in. He opened the heavy door and entered, his dark brown eyes quickly scanning the foyer until they landed on her. "Esme Russo, right?"

"Are you okay?" Ooh, that was a bit personal but it popped out of her mouth. His shoulders were practically touching his ears, obvious even under the bulk of his fine wool coat.

"What?"

"Your shoulders are so tense."

"Yeah, I know. Everybody keeps telling me that."

He approached and reached out his hand to shake

hers. Which was strange to her. Spa people didn't shake hands. If you knew someone, you hugged and if you didn't, you weren't sure how they felt about touch so wouldn't want to invade their personal space until that was established. In any case, she'd forgotten that Jackson had a formality about him that was instantly out of place at the spa. Out of propriety she returned the handshake. His was firm and his hand all but wrapped around hers, an unexpectedly pleasant sensation.

"Can I take your coat?"

As he removed the garment topping a formal gray suit and handed it to her, she had this ridiculous impulse to bring it to her nose just to see what his smell was like. Of course, she resisted and quickly shook her head in surprise at herself. She hung the coat on the rack put out in the colder months so that clients weren't encumbered with heavy outerwear they didn't need in the warmth of the spa. When she turned around she saw that his eyes were directed at her, and she had the sense that he'd been watching every move she made. Please, please, please. Don't let him have come to fire her. With her considerable experience, it wouldn't be hard for her to find another job, but being fired never looked good on a résumé.

Jackson then scrutinized the reception area. Two sofas and the registration desk, with the relaxation room in sight to the right. "Was this how the front room was arranged last time I was here?"

Oh, no. She was sure she heard disapproval in his voice. "I believe so. We may have repositioned the sofas with a bit more feng shui."

He raised his eyebrows as if he didn't understand her. Was it possible he didn't know what feng shui was? She supposed, as the CEO of a multi-million-dollar company, he had underlings that handled everything for him including the harmony of environment. "Were you successful?" He caught her eyes so they locked with his. Wow, they were deep and soulful, brown like black coffee. She also saw pain inside them, and not just from the stiffness of the shoulders.

"Successful in what?"

"Improving the feng shui."

"I don't know if that's really measurable. It's just a flow decision."

"A flow decision?" Why did his tone sound like an interrogation?

After all, if he wasn't going to be involved with the spa enough to see it more than once a year, he didn't really get to be critical. Moving a couple of sofas around to create a more welcoming entry didn't seem like a change so big that she even needed to communicate it to her higher-ups. "Do you dislike it?"

He shrugged those stiff, broad shoulders slightly. "I don't have a feeling about it one way or the other." He was so tightly wound. He obviously didn't lead a spa lifestyle. Peering over to the beverage table in the relaxation room, he asked, "Are those cucumber slices in the water?"

"Yes."

"Your clients enjoy that?" Again he sounded like he had either just landed from another planet or thought she had.

Without waiting, she dashed over to pour him a glassful. "Try it. It's very refreshing."

He eyed it skeptically before taking a sip. Again she felt like her entire career now rested in that eight ounces of water as he weighed his decision. "Blech."

Failure! As if she'd just lost a contest.

Surprisingly though, he tried a second time. When he brought his full lips to the rim of the cup, she nervously licked her own. How did he make the act of drinking a beverage seem so...important? He didn't appear to like the water any more on the second sip.

"Would you like to sit down?"

"No."

"Is there something I could do for you, then?" She still had no idea what the true purpose of his visit was, and whether she was to assist him with it in some way.

He pointed to the computer at the reception desk. "Who has access here to your system?"

Wasn't that an obvious answer? "Staff."

"All of them?" What was he fishing for?

"Pardon me, I mean the administrative staff. Myself, my assistant manager, Trevor, and our two front desk supervisors."

"How often do you change access passwords?"

"I believe it's on our schedule every six months."

"It's very important." Esme thought he sounded suspicious. She felt a bit insulted by that. Maybe it was an attitude left over from what she'd heard were some shady dealings at the spa before she'd started working here. "I'd like to refamiliarize myself with the space."

She couldn't ask why. All she could get out was,

"Okay. A couple of the treatment rooms are in use—" she pointed down the corridor "—but otherwise, I'm sure you know your way around."

"Actually, I don't really remember the layout."

That was so unexpected she had to collect herself with a deep inhale through her nose and a slow exhale through her mouth. She hadn't realized she'd be giving Jackson Finn a tour of his own property.

CHAPTER TWO

JACKSON DIDN'T DOUBT that there were people in the world, New Yorkers even, who enjoyed a glass of water with mushy chunks of bitter plants in it. He just wasn't one of them and wondered what it would take to get that godawful taste out of his mouth. Perhaps a pastry from the Italian café down the block. Fortunately, there was a bowl of mints on one of the tables so he could grab a couple and pop them into his mouth immediately, which made an instant improvement.

"If you'll follow me, then." Esme pointed to the main corridor. He'd forgotten how pretty she was. She wore brown trousers topped by a sweater that was woven in varying shades of pink. Somehow the pink and brown complemented each other in a most unlikely combo that was unusual and upbeat at the same time. She no longer had what he'd thought of as a short pixie haircut; instead the brown locks had grown into a choppy shag with golden highlights that brushed her shoulders.

The sweater ended at her hip, and when she turned and gestured for him to follow, her most attractive behind swung a bit under the fabric of the trousers. Jackson checked himself. He was hardly in the habit of perusing women's bodies. Since his divorce four years ago he'd had intimate encounters with women, business types he met in bars around the world, when his mortal need for human contact had reached a crucial proportion and he had to have a release. The women were picked by their ability to understand that was all he was available for. He was exactly one and done when it came to relationships after the horror show known as Livia.

It was interesting that even Esme had noticed his shoulders were tight. Apparently, it was that obvious. Tension had become his normal state. Once he got the spa revamp underway, would all that he'd submerged release? He knew Dr. Singh was right that if he didn't manage his stress and modify his lifestyle he was surely on his way to the same early grave as his parents. Though in the past he'd dismissed advice to slow down and find ways to recharge, he acknowledged to himself that it had now become critical.

"This is typical of our massage suites." Esme pushed open a door to let Jackson enter. The room had the same cordial, if drab, decor as the reception area, referencing flowers as decoration. Dried stems in a collection of small vases adorned the side table while black-and-white photos of various blooms were hung four in a row on the wall. Meditation-type music played at a low volume. Regarding the massage table in the center of the room, she informed him, "We use Northstar tables in all of the suites. I think they're the best on the market. Made with a high-density foam that lasts a lot longer than some of the other brands."

"I wouldn't know. I rarely use spa services."

Her eyebrows bunched. "Interesting that you own one, then, isn't it?" He was taken aback—or was it intrigued?—by her bluntness yet it was something he'd asked himself. In his family, self-indulgence was not part of the regime. The Finns toiled; that's what they did. Spa was foreign to them other than profit/loss statements. Esme bringing it up merely added to the ludicrousness of the situation.

"My parents bought the Sher for its status as a landmark building. The spa was already established here so we figured we'd just continue with it. That is to say until my wife, my ex-wife, my then-wife..." Jackson tripped over his words. He still felt pure shame that he'd let any facet of this historic building into the hands of flinty Livia, who not only falsified business records for her own financial gain, but also cheated on Jackson with a man she organized the whole scheme with. His parents were furious at their son's lack of judgment in a partner.

Livia wasn't at all the type they'd have wanted him to couple off with in the first place. They were serious people. Never a couple. Never romantic. Never displaying love. Livia was loud and dramatic and liked the sound of her own voice. Jackson was attracted to the flash and fantasy, if only to offset what felt like an emptiness in the somber life he'd grown up in. His parents couldn't understand any more than Jackson could, really, why he was cut from a different cloth and needed more than the life they had created. He became enraptured, which led him to trust her, and that's how the trouble began. After the fury from the embezzlement, Jackson sensed a pervasive malaise grow in his parents, a disappointment in their son that he believed contributed to their untimely deaths, a stabbing guilt that he still carried. Which was why he returned. He couldn't bring them back to life but he could the spa.

Esme was probably completely unaware of the Finn family's problems when she was hired. He'd put his human resources team right to work finding a replacement for his cheating ex-wife, who he fired as soon as her ruse was discovered by a thankfully persistent accountant. They decided to bring in a manager, rather than a director. Someone who could just keep things running while they figured out what to do next. His HR people had picked Esme's résumé from a stack of others.

Unfortunately, Jackson's interest in the spa languished alongside his parents' weariness and their deaths. So much time had passed that his investors recently informed him they were considering pulling out of the partnership. The news lit a fire in Jackson he didn't know he could kindle. It was now or never for him to rebuild the spa's relevance or sell it off. Unfinished business whose time had come.

"It's an exquisite building."

Esme stopped his ruminating on Livia and those awful times. "Do you like it here?"

"Um, sure." She seemed thrown by the question and didn't know how to answer. He wondered if that meant that she didn't. Not an easy thing to say to the owner, especially not knowing him well.

She led him into another treatment room set up for facial work. "Here's one of our skin care rooms. We've got a separate sound system in each room—" she pointed to the speakers in each corner "—if the client likes particular music. We also utilize candles and aromatherapy."

"Is that what I'm smelling?" Jackson sniffed.

"That's actually the product we use in our pineapple facial."

"You use pineapple in the treatment?"

"It's the key ingredient in the products we use for the protocol. Pineapple contains a powerful enzyme, bromelain, that's great for the face."

"Pineapple. On someone's face. Not on a fruit plate." He didn't know why he was trying a little humor. Maybe because he was so out of place. All he knew about skin care was that he had to put sunscreen on after he shaved. "Why would anyone want to smell like fruit?"

She smiled, which he was glad for.

"I guess that might seem strange but in this case, it has a purpose. Scent can also be unwinding or stimulating, depending on what we're going for. A favorite smell can be transformative to the client during the fifty minutes or so that they're in the treatment room with us."

Jackson remembered how his doctor told him that he needed to find ways to relax. Although he couldn't imagine mucky cucumber water and sickly sweet smells as getting that done for him. He absentmindedly rubbed the back of his neck.

"May I ask, are you having some distress? I noticed your shoulders were tense when you came in. And just now I saw you self-massaging your neck."

He hadn't realized that he'd brought his hand behind his neck or that the motion had a name. "No. I'm not here for a massage." Despite whether or not he needed one. Esme's spine stiffened at the harshness of his tone. He hadn't meant to offend her. "Carry on."

He followed her farther down the corridor. "This is our wet room." It was as if the entire room she showed him was one gigantic shower, with floor-to-ceiling tiling, a large treatment bed in the center that had some sort of drainage below and a contraption above it that had seven water jets.

He had a vague recollection of receiving a very large plumbing bill to repair some sort of problem in this room. "What is this?"

"It's called a Vichy shower. The jets rain down on the client and we adjust the temperature and the water pressure to create a massage-like experience. Unfortunately, it's on the fritz yet again." Esme certainly knew what she was talking about, unlike him. After getting rid of Livia, he found less emotionally fraught projects to concentrate on. But it ate into his gut as a physical manifestation of letting his parents down. He wasn't born to a happy and demonstratively loving family. But his parents were good people and he discredited them by thinking he had to have the swirl of romance they considered a waste of time.

Esme continued her tour with the men's shower and locker room. "We've got a large whirlpool bathtub, steam room, six showers, two vanity areas and full-length cedar lockers. Another snack lounge, complimentary toiletries, hair dryers, lots of charging stations. I love our guests to stay for a lengthy visit with us, and take as much of a break from the real world as they can spare. And leave rejuvenated."

Rejuvenated. Interesting. Though he'd never thought of a spa that way. That it could become a personal oasis, a fee-paying club of sorts. He'd categorized it as a luxury for people with cash to burn, not unlike money spent on jewelry or expensive restaurants. When his parents bought the spa, there had been a longtime management team who'd spent over twenty years creating a top-notch, highly regarded establishment.

When the Finns bought it, that group took the change of ownership as an opportunity to move on, opening a few spas of their own in the Midwest. Then Livia came along implementing changes that didn't work, and willy-nilly eliminations of services that clients still actually wanted. Plus, in retrospect, even Livia's high-strung, reedy voice and fast, jerky way of moving never matched with what was supposed to be the vibe of the spa. Unlike Esme, whose lush voice sounded like the middle of a cool forest. One that he could walk through and feel a grounding he'd never even imagined. There was something unique about her.

He asked her solely because it popped into his head, "Where did you work before you joined us?" Obviously, he could have gotten that information from a résumé they must have had on file and she probably thought it was ridiculous that he hadn't. Or she might be wondering why he was inquiring after she'd already been working at the Sher for four years.

Nonetheless she responded, giving him the chance to hear her thick, luscious speaking voice again. "I held a supervisory position at a luxury hotel spa in Miami. Prior to that I spent two years at a Mayan spa in Mexico. And before that I did an apprenticeship in Denmark."

"So, you're not a stranger to moving around."

"Actually, I was born and raised in New York. In the Bronx. I can't think of anywhere I'd rather settle. New York is in my blood."

He let a smile tip up. He was raised in New York, too, although far from the Bronx. He grew up on Long Island in the wealthy suburbs. After Livia, New York was nothing but streets of regret so he stayed away. Although lately he'd been thinking otherwise. How long could he run, remaining a nomad of cold hotels and no roots?

The Sher's physical space was terrific; it was the lack of vision and keeping up to date that was needed. Weeks of work, not months, would be all that was required.

A couple of dangling pieces clicked into his mind. How much a spa director and a spa manager were different. He'd want a director who knew spas all over the world, who kept up on marketing, social media, human resources, client relations. Meanwhile, a manager would keep things running smoothly, supervising employees, and making sure what was needed for services was operational. Would he retain Esme as that manager? He supposed it depended if the still-to-be-hired director wanted her. His lips pursed at the idea of never seeing Esme again. Although he had no idea why.

What was Jackson planning? Esme wondered. He surveyed the spa as if he was a potential client inquiring about services, not the owner. Perhaps his online files kept him as informed as he needed to be. After all, he seemed disdainful of everything from cucumber water to enzyme scrubs. Was he on the premises to merely refamiliarize himself with the property and layout for the purpose of shutting the spa down? Would he repurpose the space entirely, into offices, shops, even residences if he had the required zoning? Although someone would have to be bonkers anyway to want to alter this gorgeous monument to the city's architectural history.

His personal questions continued. "What got you started in the industry in the first place?"

That shouldn't have been a loaded question but, in her case, it was. "I like spas, where people get taken care of."

"All right, so you could have become, let's say, a doctor or a nurse."

"True, but…" Did she really want to get candid with someone she barely knew and was unlikely to see much of? Still, she had nothing to hide. "I'm not from a family of means. Something like medical school would have been out of our reach."

"Yes, but there are scholarships and loans."

Why was he cross-examining her? "Is that how *you* went to college?"

"I'm very fortunate that my parents sent me to business school to manage our company someday, of course not knowing how soon someday was going to be." She remembered that both of his parents died, his mother not long after Esme had been working for them a year, and his father soon after that. There had been a lot of obvious strife in the Finn family and they had a black cloud over them, from what little she knew.

"Business. Was that your choice of study?"

"It made sense for our family as I'm an only child. The only one who could take over the company."

"Was that what you would have picked if you'd had a choice?" He glared at her, not actually at her, but into her, those luminous dark eyes suddenly fierce as a warrior.

After the awkward silence that followed, where Esme's fingers rolled on little bits of her sweater and he seemed to watch her do so, she realized she was nervous around this forbidding yet troubled man who held her fate. She'd offended him with her too probing question. She wasn't used to interacting with the boss man.

He broke the moment with defense. "Weren't we talking about *you*?"

"The truth is that there was dysfunction in my family and planning for my future was the last thing on my parents' minds." No, Gia and Matt were far too concerned with themselves to have ever put thought into their only daughter's future. "They'd have as soon had me never leave home, so that I could take care of them."

Jackson's expression flickered at her frank answer. "Oh." It was a lot to tell a total stranger. But she learned long ago that the more she threw past trauma out into the ether, into the universe, the less power it held over her.

An elderly woman emerged from the ladies' locker room frazzled and rifling through her purse. Esme rushed over to pick up a few things that had fallen out. "Sit down, Mrs. Lee. You're not at peace. Was something wrong with your treatment today?" She brought the woman to a couch.

"I lost my phone," Mrs. Lee lamented as they sat. "I can never find the darn thing."

"Let's do some breathing and then we'll figure out the phone. With me now, a deep breath in through your nose." She demonstrated and Mrs. Lee followed. "Then a slow exhale through your mouth. Do it again, in through the nose, out through the mouth. Two more times." She glanced up to see Jackson noting the interaction.

"That's better."

"Okay, now, when was the last time you saw the phone?"

"In the locker room. I was calling my daughter to tell her I was finished here."

"Should we have another check in your purse?" Within seconds, Esme located the phone. "There we go."

"Thank you, Esme." She helped Mrs. Lee to her feet.

"See you next time." As she walked the tiny woman toward the exit, Jackson dashed over to the door to open it for her. Hmm. To add to the enigma that was Jackson Finn, apparently, he was a gentleman as well. In the process, his arm brushed against Esme's, creating a shocking prickle down her arm.

"You were saying," he quickly returned after the woman left, "how you got into the industry." He peered down at his arm where it had touched hers as if he was expecting to find something there. The contact had affected him as well.

After she verified that there was, in fact, nothing on his arm other than her aura she answered, "There was a small spa near where I grew up. I got a part-time job there in high school. I mostly did laundry. You'd be amazed at how many towels a spa goes through in a day. I saw people come in colorless and hunched over, and walk out changed, standing tall, smiles rediscovered, as if their burdens had been lifted, even if only temporarily. And I liked that."

She wouldn't share with him the similarity to what went on at her home. Self-centered people having the attention and intention focused on them. That's what Esme was used to and what came naturally to her. Her father *needed* a pizza from Santini's. Her mother *needed* a hot bath drawn for her. Her parents weren't slave drivers; they were just endlessly helpless. Her father wouldn't have had a clue how to order a pizza or even understand how to walk into a pizzeria and wait for his order to be cooked.

They lived on money inherited from Esme's maternal grandparents, who died before she was born. The payout was dispensed monthly with just enough to meet expenses, so that didn't motivate her parents to go out and get jobs. They spent most of their time watching television. Currently, they did so in the ramshackle house that was left to them in Alabama, all they now had, their move allowing Esme to remain in New York and not have to be responsible for them anymore.

She'd always known that she'd get out from under their cloud of listlessness as soon as she was old enough. Taking care of people was the experience she could bring to the job, something she enjoyed as long as it was by choice. Washing towels, mopping floors and restocking products and tools was a start in a business she seemed born to be a part of. Now, at thirty-two, she'd been at the Sher too long, hoping she'd achieve her ultimate goal of becoming a director so that she could create the spa of her dreams. One that would claim her place in the storied history that dated back to medieval times when people would drink and bathe in mineral-rich waters to promote health and healing.

"The work comes naturally to you," he concluded. For reasons that she couldn't name, she wanted to tell him things she'd never told anyone. She wouldn't, of course, but she had never met anyone she'd ever had the urge to confide in. He'd figured her out right away. For a caretaker, the focus was always outward. What was going on with *her* was of no interest to others. Right? That was her role in the world. Except that Jackson was asking. About her. He was listening.

"I went to school to learn massage. I obtained a license in Western modalities and then later another in Eastern traditions."

"You're comfortable touching people you don't know?"

She chuckled nervously. Okay, so she had a one-second idea about touching *him* further than a handshake or a brush of his sleeve. He sure as heck needed to be touched, what with the rigidity in his body that needed loosening up. He was slim but powerfully built; she could see as much under his clothes. "That sort of goes with the territory, doesn't it? We do skin care and bodywork. It involves a lot of touching. And a contract of trust."

"You do the skin care part, too?"

"Yes, over the years I've gotten certified in everything in order to run a full-service spa. When I take time off from here, I go to conferences and trade shows and industry events. Though massage was where I started and it's what always had my heart."

"Impressive that you've taken it upon yourself to continue learning and growing."

"Have you ever had a massage?" Crazy that was a question for a spa owner but she was curious as he'd already declared that this was just another business to him and that it was the Sher Building that had interested his parents, not the spa.

He shrugged. "Here and there. Honestly, they're a waste of time for me. I don't relax. That's not on my agenda. Although..." He let his voice drift off. She was dying to know what it was he stopped himself from saying but it wasn't her place to ask.

"I hope you don't mind me saying so but I do see a lot of tightness in your neck and shoulders. Would you like to lie down or even sit in a chair and let me do a few acupuncture needles and see if I can help out?" At that his eyes froze. She knew she had immediately goofed; that had not been an acceptable offer. Okay, a big businessman does not need an employee to offer to heal him.

Taking care of people.

"Sorry, of course not. That was silly of me."

"Needles?" Oh, he was a needle scaredy-cat! So were many people until they tried it.

"Yes, acupuncture can be an immediate and powerful way to rebalance."

"Not in a million years."

"It was just a thought. My apologies."

"You're qualified to stick needles into people as well?"

"Yes. Acupuncture has been a respected discipline for over three thousand years."

"I'll take your word for that." He tried to chuckle it off. "I think I've seen enough today." He gestured toward the treatment rooms farther down, where, in his mind, sinister and painful things happened. He was quite a bit taller than her so she craned her neck back a little to study him further. Wow, was he gorgeous! Visible stiffness aside. He had smooth golden skin against that dark hair, and a jaw that seemed to catch light. She could detect the slightest five-o'clock shadow in his beard line, but she knew skin well enough to know that his stubble wouldn't have been coarse. Which had nothing to do with anything—he was just an attractive man who crossed her path.

She didn't do men, anyway. The last thing she needed was yet someone else to have to look after, to be used by, to take her attention off herself. No, thanks. Single spa professional was just fine. Which brought her back to the matter at hand.

"Jackson," she began, finally deciding to bite the bullet, "why are you here? Are you shutting the spa's doors? Have you come to fire me?"

CHAPTER THREE

JACKSON STOOD SLACK-JAWED at Esme's question as to whether he'd come to the spa to close it down, and to let her go. His inner staff knew of his plans but he hadn't specifically announced them widely or to Esme when he arrived. His agenda was quite the opposite. Her two-part question was a bit tricky, though. He didn't yet know whether she'd be remaining on staff. She'd held her lovely green eyes open and had boldly and bravely inquired about her future. She deserved a response. He had none for her. "To tell you the truth, I don't know."

"You don't know whether you're closing the spa or you don't know if you're firing me?" One hand moved to her hip in a stance of waiting for his next reply. Which was kind of sexy, her straightforwardness.

"I'm definitely not closing the spa. I'm revamping it. I want to take it back to the days when guests came from all over the world."

"What, you're planning to bring in all new people?"

"We want to attract practitioners who have their own client rosters. Each treatment room should be able to generate a lot more revenue than it is now. As to upper management, we're interviewing candidates."

"I see." There was a tinge of sadness in her voice. "When will you know?" Those eyes hooded a bit.

He intended to make the changes and get the new spa up and running quickly. In fact, he'd have to put it to vote with the investors in just a couple of weeks. That deadline was what finally provoked him. As he lay sleepless in bed in a five-star hotel in Croatia, his brainchild began to take shape. That he had to do it for his parents. And, if he was being honest, that he had to do this for himself. Or the stiff neck and shoulders and the chest pains were going to turn into something worse, as his doctor had just confirmed. While he never felt his parents forgave him for the Livia fiasco, they certainly wouldn't have wanted him to die an early death as they had.

He'd do this reimagining with a staff his HR team picked out. He didn't know about Esme's future. She was right to be concerned about her own employment status. "I'll let you know as soon as I can."

She inhaled such a long, slow breath that he could almost see her nostrils fill with air. Then she exhaled like she was blowing up a balloon. Just as she'd done with that older lady who'd gotten upset that she lost her phone. Was it some kind of spa breathing, perhaps meant to steady herself? He'd never dealt with any hirings or firings at the spa; that was left to HR. But he wasn't heartless and didn't need to know how to run a spa to know that people's livelihood was in large measure his responsibility.

"Great," she said, slicing with sarcasm.

She flustered him, a feeling he wasn't used to. *Just*

leave, he told himself. He really had nothing more to say right now. Everything wasn't going to be settled today. Something in him didn't want to go, but logic won out. He moved toward the exit. "We'll talk again soon."

"Great," she snapped again, clearly not saying words that were on the verge of spilling out.

With that, he went out the door and stepped into the elevator that was conveniently waiting. As the doors closed, his neck seized up. He felt bad leaving Esme with such uncertainty but he'd told her all he knew.

For a moment, he wondered what it was like for a client to leave the spa after a transformative treatment. Did they descend from the fifth floor in a euphoria that carried them into the busy, loud and abrasive New York City streets as if they were floating on a cloud? How long did the high last? He wouldn't know from personal experience because he never took a time out. Dr. Singh's words came back to him.

You need to learn to relax.

Maybe he'd get a massage soon, after all. Not from Esme, of course. That would be inappropriately intimate.

As he reached the street, late afternoon was falling to dusk and bustling Tribeca was shrouded by a gray-white sky. He wasn't as eager to leave the area as he thought he was. Instead of returning to his hotel and the many phone calls he had left to accomplish, he spotted the Italian café a few doors down from the Sher. A coffee and perhaps a snack could fortify him until he ordered dinner brought to his suite. The fall chill in the air was mitigated by the heating lamps that stood between every few tables of the café's patio, which was so inviting he sat down before talking himself out of it. He ordered a cappuccino, and then pulled out his phone to talk to his assistant, Kay, with his first question the most topical. "What sort of applications are we getting for spa director?"

"We've got a spa employment agency helping us evaluate. There was a candidate from a hotel spa in Philadelphia, nothing jazzy. A kinesiologist who worked in sports massage with a minor league baseball team. Okay, but she doesn't have spa experience." Jackson thought about Esme telling him that she was trained in both Western and Eastern massage techniques and had her esthetician's license in skin care.

"Are you finding that these people want to bring in their own support staff, like a manager or lead positions?" Again he thought of Esme's welfare and whether she'd be happy working under a spa director.

"Some do, some don't. We got a message from an entire staff of a spa closing in Brazil and they all want to come together but none of them have New York licenses so it wouldn't be easy. We're vetting everyone who applies."

"All right, keep me posted."

He tapped off of the call and stared into the middle distance as he took a sip of the warm cappuccino that had arrived.

Out of the corner of his eye, he spotted Esme coming through the Sher's ground-floor doors to the street. He couldn't help thinking how pretty her hair was, thick, with those caramel highlights. She was really quite beautiful in an organic way. He could imagine holding hands with her in a meadow of waist-high grass. Or splashing naked together in an ocean cove. Kissing under a waterfall. He could tell she was a woman who could make a man *feel*, something to be avoided at all costs. He'd felt enough for one lifetime already. Esme's attractiveness was of no consequence to him. Although it had been strange, the little jolt between them as they were helping that elderly lady out of the spa. Jackson didn't have much touch of any kind in his life. Yet in that moment he'd wanted more from her.

She stopped to button a violet-hued coat over her clothes and to wrap a multicolored scarf around her neck. For no logical reason he thought of the skin of her throat being protected by woven warmth, and the idea of that gave him a weird contentment.

He hoped she would head down the street in the opposite direction of the café, as they had concluded their discussion for the day. In fact, things had been left on an awkward and uncertain note. Instead, she turned in his direction and wasn't but three steps closer toward him when their eyes met. She nodded in recognition and as she approached the café's outdoor seating area, he felt both compelled and obligated to shout out, "Esme, join me for coffee?"

"Oh. Hi. Okay." She may have felt she had to say yes to the boss but, in any case, she took a seat and ordered a chai latte.

"Do you live around here?" he asked.

"No." She made small talk with, "How long will you be in New York?"

"For as long as this takes. Not letting the spa go to pieces—"

"Excuse me, Jackson," she quickly interrupted, "the spa is not in pieces. In the four years I've been there you haven't given me any upgrading budget or marketing or advertising. I'm doing the best I can with what I have to work with."

Her spunk fired him with energy. "I'm not arguing that, I assure you. What I consider to be our downhill slide began before you were in our employ. And it's my fault for not having corrected that. You've done fine for us."

Her latte arrived and she took a sip as she contemplated what he'd just said. "I just want to be clear that I refuse to be scapegoated for the spa's failings. If you do fire me, I would like to be assured that Finn Enterprises would give me a good recommendation."

Somehow, he already couldn't picture the Sher without Esme, but she was right; she had to think of her own future.

"Absolutely. HR has nothing but respect for you. We wouldn't be taking it lightly if we let anyone go." Respecting employees was something he took seriously.

"Besides bringing on new staff, what are you planning?"

He wasn't prepared to give a presentation although there was no reason to hide his overall plan. In fact, his PR team had already crafted press releases announcing the relaunch of the venerable old spa. Those would go out as soon as the investor group okayed his plans. "I want to know what's out there, what makes the world's best spas *the* best. What we can bring into a city environment. What we can offer that other spas don't."

All of that made sense to him in theory. There was so much to learn. He thought of his parents, who also knew nothing about spas other than that they wanted to own a piece of New York history. Until Livia, with her sleek hair and wandering eyes came along. A master manipulator who sensed that while Jackson was successful and wealthy, he was in need. The medicine he thought she fed him was love but it turned out she only used him, played him like a game. He'd never let that happen again.

"If I may say so," Esme started, then stopped.

"Go on," he urged, interested in what she had to say.

"I think it would be hard for someone who doesn't know spas to reinvent an already existing one."

"I couldn't agree more."

Her attentive eyes got big again. The way the little wisps of her shaggy hair blew this way or that was kind of like watching leaves rustle in the wind, both soothing and majestic. He'd never met anyone who gave off the same essence as she did. Especially while she was facing the possible loss of her job.

"What I'd suggest," Esme told Jackson as they continued sipping their warm drinks, "is that you physically go see some of the world's finest spas. There's only so much you can glean from photos and menus."

He nodded in acknowledgment. After he'd asked her

for any suggestions she might have, she was emboldened to share some. Suggestions, ideas, theories, plans, she had plenty of. What she hadn't had was the chance to implement them. She never thought she would at the Sher—her *babysitting* job was clear from the start. Yet she stayed for four years, having got a bit stuck in the sameness. Now the tide was turning whether she was ready for it or not. "I can help provide you with a list if you'd like. I mean, it's all subjective but there are definitely some obvious choices around the globe."

"The trouble is I only have three weeks until I have to take the whole prospect to my investors and get their approval."

"I guess you'd better leave soon, then." She tipped her mouth in a little grin.

Interesting what almost losing their job could do to a person. Instead of being intimidated by the powerful CEO she worked for, she figured she had nothing to lose by showing him how knowledgeable and experienced she actually was. He'd already said that no staffing decisions had been made. It couldn't hurt to dazzle him with her grasp of the industry. Besides, she knew with her contacts and work history, she could find another job. But she didn't want just another job. She wanted to step up. To move forward.

As night fell on Tribeca and they talked and talked, the sky changed from dusk to the indigo of night. Hot drinks at the café turned into two glasses of the house red. Which led to a cheese board, several varieties served on an attractive wooden plank with walnuts on one side and dried apricots on the other, olives and small slices of crusty bread. Once they'd polished that off, Jackson flagged the waiter to order a tiramisu with two forks.

She told him about special spas she knew, about everything from decor to equipment to marketing incentives. It was obvious he didn't know what extractions or fascia stretching were, but he did understand when she talked about promotions and loyalty programs.

"I certainly appreciate your thoughts. How is it that you know all the spas?"

In a flash, she wondered if he'd consider... *No, he probably wanted a fresh start... Although she knew she could...*

The conversation, explaining her world to Jackson, jazzed her up. The change at the Sher was a call to action for her. She couldn't stay in the same place anymore, with all new people above and below her, even if Jackson asked her to. It was time for a revamp of her own. As hard as it might be sometimes, like trying to walk through the molasses of her life, she had to take steps ahead now. The universe was shaking her up. It was time. This was good.

What if...? Could she be that bold...?

As to why she knew the best facilities, the answer was simple. "With my previous jobs and apprenticeships I was able to tour around. It's really a wonderful industry, great people who want each other to succeed. Everybody teaches each other."

"If only my ex-wife thought that way."

"There was a problem, which was why I was hired, right?"

"*Problem* would be an understatement," he let out with a bitter snort of a laugh. "She stole and falsified the books. Good heavens, do all of the staff know about that?"

"Nothing specific. I think everyone knew that the director had been fired for misconduct. Did people know you were married and then, subsequently, divorced?"

"Not many. She'd misled me into believing that she knew something about spas, having estranged parents who were hotel owners. Turns out she knew nothing but since I didn't, either, I was pretty easy to fool. I trusted her. Something I deeply regret."

Ah, so that's why the redo. He felt guilty for both believing his ex-wife was honest and for letting his parents' property devaluate. "Uh-huh," she uttered to encourage him to continue. It was interesting, though, to get the real story.

Esme even observed that between sips of the chianti and a lively volley of chat with her, Jackson's square shoulders settled down and were no longer grazing his ears. She studied that sort of thing in people. It's what made her good at her job. Checking in to what the other person was thinking, doing or feeling. Anticipating.

She had zero interest in men for fear that she'd end up with someone else to take care of, to put first, just as it had been since she was a child. Nonetheless, Jackson had awfully nice shoulders and it gave Esme satisfaction to see them release from their tight hold.

"I was preoccupied with other businesses of ours. I maintained total ignorance of the day-to-day running of the spa. But it gets worse."

"Sorry?"

She watched a series of reactions take over his face. First that jaw cut so exquisitely it could slice ice twitched several times on the right side. Then several blinks of his eyes seemed to further darken his pupils, really actually deaden them. And finally, he settled into a huff of stilted breath wherein she knew he was not going to tell her what *gets worse* about his ex-wife. Although, she was too curious not to try a prompt to get him to continue. "Is that why you don't partake in spa services?"

"I don't have time for spas. Finns work, that's all we do."

"Perhaps *relax* isn't a word that resonates with you. Self-care is essential."

"You sound like my doctor."

"Have you really acknowledged the emotional pain your divorce must have caused?"

"Acknowledged my emotional pain," he repeated as he swirled the last of the tiramisu around the plate with a fork, not wanting to leave anything behind. She liked that he enjoyed his dessert enough to finish it. Even though his tone in repeating her words was a little mocking.

"Have you?" she asked again point-blank. Heck, she was possibly about to be fired or quit; there was no reason to hold back. Something in her had an inkling that if she was able to help him see how restorative, how actually life-changing, a spa could be it might end up being both a good deed and a favorable reflection on her.

"Am I over my divorce? Is that what you're asking?"

"In a nutshell. We carry pain in our minds, in our bodies and in our souls. I'd imagine the body retains energy data for a long time after trauma such as divorce."

"Energy data?"

"Yes. Trauma."

"Trauma. Like the battlefield of war or a child's neglect?"

"Yes. Exactly." A child's neglect. Like her, maybe. Oh, yes, she'd consider herself traumatized.

"So you're likening a divorce from a dishonest woman to being in the middle of, say, a bombing?"

She sat back and folded her arms across her chest. Was this going to be his strategy, to challenge and, in fact, denigrate the work that meant everything to her? "I hear you, Jackson. You don't want to take what I'm saying seriously so you're making fun of it. Yes, people experience trauma from many different causes. It's okay to hang on to it if it feeds you in some way."

"I am not traumatized! I'm just divorced." His eyes shot into hers and she knew that while he was trying to shoo away her words, they had actually penetrated. He ran the back of his hand across his cheek in a motion with a certain tenderness that made her want to reach across the table and do it for him. In reality, he was just buying himself a moment to think. Then, he'd abruptly had enough and returned to an earlier topic, back to business. "I had intended to hire a spa consultant to help me redesign our style and our menu."

She could play, too. "And your retail, which could be

a big moneymaker for you, bring people into the spa, and keep them returning. Right now it's doing none of that. The retail shelves are paltry and ordinary, no products a guest couldn't get somewhere else."

"Okay, menu, look, retail, marketing, all of it."

"And I'd say again, you've gone as far as wanting to make all of those big changes, wouldn't you want to go see for yourself what's out there to compare to?"

"Where would you propose I go?"

"Let me think that all through. For certain, one stop would be Bangkok. Warm rain, juicy fruit, fragrant flowers."

"I take it that's a place you like?"

"What's not to like about Thailand?"

"I've seen the views from the thirtieth floor of a hotel."

She nodded. "I defy you not to enjoy an experience at Spa Malee." At this point she could only ponder his seeming refusal to have any fun at all. No wonder he was tense. She contemplated for a moment if his version of his divorce might be very different than that of his ex-wife's. Maybe she needed what he wasn't able to offer. He did mention she embezzled from him, though. There was no way that could come forth from a marriage of compassion and partnership. "What do you say?"

"I'll consider it." A smile spread across his lips as he removed his napkin from his lap and tossed in onto the table in obvious preparation for leaving. She hadn't seen a spontaneous grin from him. Whoa, when he wasn't trying not to, his smile could light up New York.

They stood and bundled back into their coats. She said a quick goodnight, mentally replaying that smile, as she turned away from him and left.

She called Trevor, her assistant manager, on the subway uptown to where she lived in Washington Heights. "If he invited you to dinner, he must like you."

"He definitely doesn't like me. In fact, I think I made him mad."

"How so?"

"Because I pressed him about whether or not he'd come to fire us."

"Please don't scare me. I have two kids." He and his husband, Omari, had just adopted twin babies. She had him to worry about, too.

"I don't know what he's thinking at this point. Let's don't borrow trouble yet."

CHAPTER FOUR

"I CAN'T THINK of a reason not to, can you?" Kay responded to the idea that Jackson just threw at her as they held their daily telephone meeting. An idea that Jackson knew was a little funky because he'd felt a sort of woggle in his stomach—or maybe it was lower on his body—when he'd thought of it last night, and the woggle returned as it crossed his mind several times already today. He wasn't sure that was a reason not to go forward, though. Or maybe it was. His brain was a little bit jumbled after yesterday's moonlight over Tribeca.

He'd spent such an unforeseen and interesting evening with Esme, his employee that he barely knew. He'd really never met anyone like her, someone who'd had so many obstacles to overcome and managed to make it through with a level head. Not to mention the fact that his brain had also lingered all day on thoughts of those almond-shaped green eyes that the golden highlights in her brown hair set off. And about the long, delicate fingers that picked at cheese and olives as they chatted.

"Do we have someone who can run things in her absence?"

"There's the assistant manager, Trevor Ames."

"I would just fly around the world with her for a couple of weeks?"

"If that's what you've decided to do. Like you said, go see some spas."

Jackson's wheels were turning. During dinner last night, Esme had mentioned Thailand, and also spa destinations in Sweden and Mexico that she believed were noteworthy. The thoughts of which made him feel a young man's rush about travel and adventure. Totally unlike him, the weary world trekker, lately burnt out on airports and hotels.

Kay intuited that something was going on. "So do you want me to make trip plans?"

"I haven't asked her yet if she wants to go with me." He sounded like a schoolboy inviting a girl to a dance, which made him giddy inside.

He arrived at the spa just before closing time again, not sure why he didn't just text or call Esme. He wanted to ask her in person. Or maybe it was that he wanted to see her today. In any case, she was surprised when he came through the lobby doors. "Oh, hi, Jackson. I wasn't expecting you."

"I have a proposition I wanted to talk to you about."

"I see. Are you firing me?" She said it with that cute lopsided smile so he thought, hoped, that she was kidding and knew today wouldn't be the day of her demise. Hadn't they already established that he didn't know yet whether her job was secure? A client came out from one of the treatment rooms, a woman in black yoga clothes. Esme turned her attention to her. "How was everything, Gwen?"

"Fine. Namaste."

"Namaste." He knew that was a yoga word. After the woman left, Esme turned back around to Jackson. "A proposition." That word sounded loaded coming out of her mouth.

"Can I buy you dinner again, or a glass of wine and we can talk about it?" If she said yes, they could sit down and have a leisurely discussion and lock down the itinerary.

"I'm sorry, I can't. I have plans."

Tightness clenched his gut. He hadn't even told Esme about Livia's betrayal of their marriage vows in addition to the money books. He met a woman he'd naively dared to have faith in. After two years of marriage an old friend informed Jackson that he'd seen her in a booth at a tony restaurant on the Upper East Side passionately kissing a flashy man. When Jackson confronted her about it, she didn't even try to deny it.

The whole thing set off a sickness in him, an acrid dry smell of jealousy and distrust. It kept him from getting close to people. It made him suspicious and skeptical. Irrationally childish, as a matter of fact.

His gut pulsed again. After Livia, he went back to his old self, the businessman who didn't let emotions direct his life. His parents had a marriage devoid of any romance or passion. Devoid of conflict as well, but it was a home run like factory machinery, the wheels on track and on automatic. Livia was a rebellion against all of that. Jackson thought he needed the fireworks that his parents did not. He got way more than he bargained for.

In any case, he needed to not let his silly disappointment show because Esme had evening plans. She was a coworker, nothing more. Although they'd talked last night about personal things, further than Jackson was used to.

"I wanted to get your feedback on something I'm thinking about. Can we at least sit for a few minutes?" He didn't want to schedule an appointment with her for tomorrow. Partially because he was excited about his idea and wanted to share it with her.

"Oh, so you *have* decided you'll fire me?" she asked in a slightly mocking way.

"Stop that." He grinned, again more open than usual. "I already told you it's too early to determine that."

Her smile matched his. He felt a connection in the merge. Like the smiles were reaching each other, like they were meant to. This woman was affecting him in a powerful way so he'd better keep his armor on. She threw him off balance, like the earth under his feet was shifting. The worst part about it was that he liked it.

"What, then?"

"Let's sit down." He gestured to the reception area couches.

"Oh, wow," was the first thing she said after he explained his plan for her to accompany him on the trip and show him the *what* and *why* of her favorite spas. Without too much more deliberation she jumped in with, "Thank you for the vote of confidence and the lovely offer. However, I'll have to say no."

Jackson's jaw slackened. A wave of defeat swept over him. Why had he been so cocky as to assume she would say yes?

She pulled the beige flowy sweater she'd been wrapped in even closer around her. When she focused on responding to him, she talked directly to him, making eye contact. There was something almost unbearable about that directness, nowhere to hide from it. "It's pretty simple. If we were to revisit spas where I've had the good fortune to know the owners and the operators, and they agreed to let you go behind the scenes if you will, that would be a lot to ask. Spa people are incredibly generous, but I can't abuse their comradery."

"I don't exactly follow."

She leaned back on the sofa and tucked her feet under her legs, like she was settling in to tell him a bedtime story.

"I have to look out for myself. Let's say I cash in on my contacts and they help you build out your menu. And let's say you hire a spa director for the Sher who lets me, and Trevor for that matter, go or I decide to leave. I may need to ask my contacts to help us find work, and to share their own connections with me. I'm going to have to hoard those favors for myself."

Jackson had to admire her foresight. He could see her as a scrappy teenager folding endless carts of towels or refilling massage oil dispensers. How she worked herself up through the ranks to a managerial job in Manhattan.

To the task at hand, though. It would be so valuable to have an industry veteran show him the possibilities. Not to mention the fact that something inside of him was telling him to spend more time with Esme. That she was good for him. Maybe it was his doctor's orders that he learn to replenish his well. Being in the same company as someone who brought that to people for a living could rub off on him. Also, there was something mesmerizing about her. He wanted to know her more. That last bit had nothing to do with the Sher but he acknowledged it, just part of the list of why he didn't seem to want to take no for an answer.

"Esme, there's no circumstance where you could do this with me? I can pay you a huge consulting fee."

"No. Thank you, but that still wouldn't solve my reluctance to overstretch my relationships with people I know in the industry."

They were at an impasse, both playing over things in their minds. "Hmm."

"Hmm."

"Hmm."

"Hmm," she repeated although hers seemed to sound like something was brewing. Then she relented, "Nah."

"What?"

"I do have one scenario in which I'd agree to this."

"What is it?"

"I know it wasn't at all what you were thinking."

"Let's hear it."

"My career goal is to become a director."

"Yes."

"I've been a manager for four years gaining skills and experience. I'm ready for it."

"I don't follow you."

"I'm ready to become a director now." She looked down, then lifted her eyes to meet his again, as if she'd had to summon the courage.

"Uh-huh."

"Are you ready to take a chance on me?"

"What do you mean?"

"If I take you on this trip and we redesign the menu, the style, the way we run the spa, you appoint me as the director and Trevor as manager. You call off your search."

He admired her bravery. "Without interviewing anyone else?" HR had mentioned some other candidates. Shouldn't he at least talk to them?

"I'm qualified. All I need is…opportunity." He wasn't sure why she hesitated for a moment. Maybe her bravado hadn't had a chance to display this much persuasiveness.

"You become the spa director?" He considered it. "I'd have to talk it over with my HR staff."

"You're the boss." That he was. If they'd been sitting in a corner office on the fifty-fifth floor of an office building and she'd just made that pitch to him, he'd hire her on the spot. In his estimation, people who wanted something badly enough did a great job of it. He got the impression she'd make a very fine director. "What do you think?" she asked him patiently.

Esme let herself into her apartment, still lightheaded from replaying the conversation she'd had with Jackson. Even though she'd met her friend Yina for the movie date they'd planned, her mind hadn't stayed on the screen. She'd wasted ticket money on a movie that may have been very good, may have been very bad and may have been just okay. She wouldn't know.

Plopping down on the sofa, she still couldn't believe that she had point-blank given Jackson Finn an ultimatum. That she'd take him on an odyssey to better understand the spa business and in exchange, if and only if, he'd name her director of the new operation. After all, if she advised him on what was feasible and desired by loyal clients, that would be within the purview of a director's duties, for which she was well ready.

She'd been lolling at the Sher. She well knew what a director did and could have been applying for that position at other spas after her first year or so at the Sher. She'd risen all the way up from washing towels, yet she'd stopped growing. Maybe she was just tired after so many years of hard work and keeping on a happy face, her adult personality miraculously mostly positive. Or perhaps she needed a boost of confidence beyond satisfied clients and cordial industry relationships. Beyond therapy sessions and self-care, the childhood slashes still hurt, crippled her. But now opportunity was roping her along. She was not going to let this pass by, which was why she'd surprised not only Jackson but herself with her steely determination. She had to at least try.

Jackson hadn't answered yes but he hadn't said no, either. She thought she did pretty well at pretending to be courageous when she proposed it to him even though her heart was beating so fast she could hear it in her ears. Of course, he left it hanging and didn't answer right away. That was fair enough. He needed to mull it over.

For now, she looked over to the clock and decided

to give herself fifteen minutes of pretending that he'd say yes, letting herself truly experience manifest destiny. Even if it was a fantasy, seeing herself in the role would create something like a memory, making it that much closer to real. She set the timer on her phone and closed her eyes. She saw it, herself welcoming clients to a spa that felt like hers, that she had a stake in, within the walls and under the floorboards.

Lying in bed later, she turned her thoughts from the decision she couldn't control to Jackson himself. His six feet plus of man was warm, strong and inviting with a smell of good soap. Making her feel something inside. Jackson Finn was intense. He made her think about things she'd forbade herself. Denied for her own survival. Even if she was lucky enough to have convinced him to let her have the position and she set off for travel with him, she needed to remember to protect herself first, as surely no one else ever had or ever would. Which meant no personal feelings for a man. That could suck her energy dry.

She and Jackson hadn't made any further plans to meet or talk but she figured the ball was now in his court, as the saying went. Therefore, it was both a surprise and it wasn't when he came through the lobby doors at closing time, as he had for the past two days. His navy blue shirt against his black suit was sexy and stylish.

"Ms. Russo, you drive a hard bargain."

"What?" She didn't want to assume she heard what she thought she heard.

"You drive a hard bargain, but okay. You show me

how you'd make this place something spectacular again and I'll give you the reins to it."

A nervous giggle emitted from her that she wished she'd been cool enough to hide. Instead, her stomach flipped over and then back again, and she was sure her face turned beet red. Luckily, she was able to stop from overdoing words and became überprofessional with, "Thank you. You won't regret your decision."

"I hope not. When can you arrange the trip and be ready to leave?"

Whoa, there was so much to do to make that happen. She had to see if Trevor could fill in and make sure her current duties would be covered. She had to make the arrangements with the spas she'd take him to. But she didn't want Jackson to have any reason to hesitate or change his mind so she quickly blurted, "How about the day after tomorrow?" Somehow, she'd pull it together.

"Good." He stayed to walk out with her, watching her go through the tasks of closing for the night. She turned off equipment, locked doors, set alarms and timers on the way out. As they exited, she fumbled to put on her coat. He reached a long arm to pick up the section of sleeve that was dragging and held it open so she could slip one arm in and then the other with ease. Something about the whole maneuver touched deep into her core. He'd noticed that she was having trouble with her coat. He took action to make sure she didn't go out in the cold without it. Someone caring for her. That was a new one.

First order of business was to impress, dazzle in fact, Jackson with her spa tour. She'd already thought of what she'd consider three representations of how unique and special a spa could be. Places that lingered in people's minds for decades, for a lifetime even. That made them dream of returning again and again, and of telling their friends and family about it. Jackson didn't know what would make a spa like that. She'd show him. After meeting spa professionals she'd been invited to visit, shadow and apprentice, she knew a lot of people. On top of that she kept up to date on spa news and had seen photos and menus for hundreds of establishments. Spa was her meat.

"I can tell you right away that we'll be visiting my friend Freja Olsson, who owns Spa Henrik in Stockholm."

"Right, Swedish massage. Even I've heard of that."

"Which wasn't even developed in Sweden but, yes, that will be our starting point for Western-style bodywork."

"Okay."

The last time she'd seen Freja was at a trade show in Las Vegas. Henrik was definitely a world's top pick. Freja was always very generous in giving back to the industry, so Esme was sure she'd be receptive. When she got home it was time to get cracking. It was the middle of the night in Stockholm so she'd fired off a quick text to Freja saying that she'd call her tomorrow but asking if she would be able to spend some time with her and her spa owner, Jackson. Demonstrations of traditional massage would be a good place to start with him.

Esme's mind spun with details as she lugged her favorite suitcase out of the back of her closet. She began unzipping the compartments when her phone rang. The number was not from her contact list. "Hello."

"It's Jackson." Hmm, she had assumed that their planning had been completed for the day.

"Oh, hi." He hadn't changed his mind about their agreement, had he? That would be devastating. "Can I…help you with something?"

"I was just calling to confirm that I'll have my assistant arrange the flights and book a car to pick you up and take you to the airport." His voice was lower over the phone or perhaps it was just evening. In any case, it was kind of sultry to talk to him over the phone. Seductive.

"Okay."

"You'll arrange everything with the spas?" Again, his voice was so resonant it was blowing through the phone like warm air, filling not only her suitcase but her entire bedroom. In fact, his tone prompted her to take off the sweater she still had on. She doubted he knew how magnetic he was. His charisma was something she needed to watch out for. She was not going to have a crush on the boss. There was too much at stake.

"Yes, I've already left a message for Freja in Stockholm."

"Send me all the travel bills, of course."

"So does your company have, like, a private plane?" She didn't really know much about Finn Enterprises on the whole.

"No, we're not at that level." His response came with

a laugh that was friendly not scolding. "I can promise you the first-class cabin on all the flights, though."

"And I can promise you the best spa services you're
ever likely to encounter."

"Wait. I have to receive the treatments myself?"

She smiled to herself. "Well, of course, Jackson. I
want you to experience for yourself how good and beneficial these protocols are."

"How about we do them on you and you can sort of
narrate for me?"

"No siree," she teased, remembering how resistant
he was to let her do acupuncture or even massage on
his tense shoulders. And what shoulders they were.
She pictured his long, lean body. She wondered if he
was calling her from an office or a hotel room. Was
he at a desk, or a sofa or...in bed? What was he wearing? She mashed her lips for a minute, hardly believing she was having those thoughts. So unlike her. She
forged on with, "Will you have the treatments I choose
for you? That's the whole point. Besides, your doctor
would approve, wouldn't he?"

She could practically see his thousand-watt smile
take over. "Oh, all right. What should I pack?"

That was a valid question as his fine suits and smud-
geless dress shoes didn't scream relaxation. "Do you
have casual clothes?"

"What kind of question is that?"

"You've said you're all work and no play."

"True, but I do business all over the world with all
sorts of people. Of course I have casual clothes."

"Great. Let's put them to proper use, then." And

in quick succession she pictured him in a ski outfit. In loose-fitting yoga pants. In just a towel slung low across his hips. Wicked musings that had no place in her dealings with him. Her tongue made a once-around her lips. She resuscitated herself with, "Stockholm in autumn will be colder than New York so you'll need outerwear, but Mexico and Thailand will be warmer."

"All right, I'll check in with you tomorrow."

"Good night, Jackson."

As she swiped off the phone she thought this could all go well or it could go horribly if Jackson wasn't impressed with the trip. It was a crossroads for her. A person didn't get many of those in their life. A way to turn the corner and cumulate the past into something that served the future. It was possible that Esme Russo had officially, finally, arrived.

CHAPTER FIVE

"GOOD MORNING." Esme greeted Jackson at the airport lounge before the flight as agreed. "Everything good?"

They hadn't talked yesterday after that flirty phone call the night before, just sent a couple of texts.

"Yes."

He gestured for her to accompany him down the jet bridge, onto the plane and into the first-class cabin, him flashing the boarding passes on his phone. He watched her take stock of their surroundings. The appointments were deluxe on this aircraft bound for Stockholm. A table between the two seats was set with a bottle of champagne and two flutes. It was almost, well...romantic. He was suddenly unsure about this strange journey that forty-eight hours ago he would have never imagined himself taking.

Not to mention the promise he'd made to her about the directorship. No sooner had he instructed his HR people to launch a search for the right person than he'd told them to halt the hunt, at least for now. It occurred to him, though, that had Finn Enterprises announced that they were hiring a spa director, perhaps Esme would have formally applied for the position anyway. He may have been saving time even if he'd acted uncharacteristically impulsive in saying yes to her. They'd both better be right as there was no time to lose before the investors meeting.

Once they were in the air, he tipped open his laptop and logged into the plane's Wi-Fi as soon as it was available. He'd work, slip into his cocoon for a while. Hours passed. He noticed Esme watch a movie from start to finish and then do something on her tablet. They chatted briefly about the food and drink they were served and that they'd both been to Stockholm before. However, neither knew the city well and there wouldn't be time for much exploring. At one point, the flight crew passed out hot facecloths, which he disregarded.

"This is always a nice touch," Esme commented. "Flying can be dehydrating to the skin."

"Good to know," he said, glancing over at her. Which there was no denying was a very pleasant activity.

Observing that he didn't pick up his hot towel she asked, "Why aren't you using yours?"

"I wasn't aware my skin was being dehydrated so it wasn't a crisis that needed resolving."

"Very funny. Remember, you're to pay more attention to your wellness."

"I do. It's a policy of distrust and jealousy that I rely on." Wow, that was sharp. Even she seemed taken aback. Who had he become, just a sarcastic and bitter shell with health problems? That was no way to live. Especially not at thirty-three. Esme's basic humanity and lack of pretension made him want to tell her more of what he had stashed inside. She'd told him on the phone that he'd be actually receiving the spa ministrations she thought so highly of. He didn't even know what had propelled him to call her at home. They'd laughed a bit about his aversion to therapies. Talking to her came easy to him. He picked up the hot, wet washcloth and brought it to his face. He wiped in big circles, a few times. He had to admit that it was pleasant. Not necessarily healing, as Esme would say, but nice nonetheless.

"See, not half-bad," she ribbed him sweetly. Her little told-you-so smile was adorable and sent a pang through him. "Distrust and jealousy, huh? Is that a blanket statement? Does that mean you don't trust me? Don't you think that if I was going to steal from you that after four years I would have done it already?"

"Fine. I didn't mean trusted employees, although—" he wasn't ready to share that one with her "—suffice it to say I'll never be in a personal relationship again. It clouds my judgment."

"I'll give you that—neither will I. But actively married to distrust and jealousy, do you know how toxic that is?"

"Toxic."

"Those kinds of emotions fire off your adrenal glands, which weakens your immune system and makes you especially vulnerable to autoimmune disease."

"And it's your position that you can just let go of that with a wet washcloth?"

"No, but finding techniques that give you a respite from all of that really does make a difference. There are thousands of studies on it. You've been working nonstop since takeoff. How about stretching your arms above your head?" She demonstrated and he followed. "Let go, and then arch your back. Rotate your neck. Little changes add up."

"I didn't tell you all about my failed marriage." The words were on the tip of his tongue until they just fell out. Was it the hot towel or the stretching that opened him up a little, like his lungs could take in more air? Or was it her, pulling him along? "Not only did Livia betray me with the spa finances, she didn't honor our marriage vows."

"What do you mean?"

"Forsaking all others. She didn't."

"You mean she cheated on you?"

"All over town." No wonder he'd avoided New York until now.

"Oh, Jackson, that's awful. Was it just once?"

"No, it went on for months until I learned of it." He had no idea what a relief it would be to say all of that out loud to someone. Not anyone, of course. Her.

"How did you find out?"

"A friend spotted her kissing someone at a restaurant."

"In plain sight?" She put her hand over her mouth, taking it all in.

"No regard for the decency of marriage."

"Then what happened?"

"Livia didn't even try to deny it. Although she didn't admit to the spa's bookkeeping irregularities that were uncovered at that time. Because she knew that she and whatever man she'd taken up with, her partner in crime, had committed illegal acts. We could have had her arrested but we didn't want to draw attention to ourselves, which we knew the whole mess would."

"Jackson, how awful." She looked at him with concern, or maybe it was pity. "Then what?"

"Very simple at that point. I had her out of the spa, changed the locking codes, took her off the bank accounts and so on." In his gut he wanted to keep talking to Esme even though he was embarrassed that he'd picked such a crooked person to marry. Esme had that way about her, like she was receptive and she could handle someone else's pain. She'd mentioned the neediness of her own parents shaping her into that caretaker she'd become and that she had parlayed it into a spa career. He hoped, in turn, she had people she could tell her secrets and hurts to. For reasons that made no sense he wondered if he could ever be that person for someone.

Not someone.

Her.

"You're having emotions about it now." Was she looking into his third eye or something?

"Frankly, the whole thing left me with my guard up, which is how I plan to stay." A way he thought was serving to protect him. In a moment of clarity, he realized how instead it was holding him in shackles. "I surely won't make the same mistake twice."

"At the expense of your health and well-being?" He was suddenly aware of her close proximity. He could almost feel her body heat. He'd bet her skin and her hair were as silky as they looked.

"What about *your* internal trauma?" he repeated, employing terminology that she'd used.

"You want to know something?" He surely did, ready to take the focus off himself. "I know all about jealousy. That was a little trick my parents used to play on each other. Fight for my attention and loyalty to make the other one jealous. I don't know what's worse, romantic jealousy or pitting your kid against your spouse." The heavy statement weighed like a brick and he ached for her.

Couldn't they both use a little fun on this trip? Doctor's orders, after all. Strictly professional, of course. Maybe he wasn't going to be as resistant to spa life as he thought he was. Or maybe something else was hammering at his walls, trying to tear them down.

"Ladies and gentlemen," came the pilot's voice over the sound system, "we have begun our descent into Stockholm's Arlanda Airport."

"I take it we're in Stockholm because the term *Swedish massage* is best known to people," Jackson asked as they stepped out of the taxi in front of Spa Henrik, their first destination.

"Yes," Esme acknowledged, "although there are some historical questions as to whether that namesake massage was really developed in Sweden or just popularized here. No matter, though, it's accepted as the traditional Western massage." The snowy and cold weather made their breath visible. The clean air of Stockholm was invigorating.

The spa was housed in a Gustavian building, the

city's classic architectural style, and they buzzed the intercom at the spa's entrance. Once Esme announced them, the door clicked and they entered a long hall of rooms with wooden doorframes and wood floors. She remembered from her visit years ago when she was doing an apprenticeship in Copenhagen that the min-ute she'd stepped into Spa Henrik, the outside world faded away. Perhaps it was the hush of the high ceil-ings combined with the thickness of the walls. She and Jackson moved toward the reception lobby. "See how this place just sucks you in. Makes you forget where you are. I'd like for us to be able to create that. En-velop people so they can leave their everyday lives at the door for a while."

Jackson took in the information. What she was ready to show him was her vision of a future for the Sher, something she'd thought about for a long time. He'd either be impressed enough with what she presented to him that he'd agree to implement it and let it rest in her arms or he'd reject everything she suggested and choose another spa director with a different perspec-tive. She'd decided that she wouldn't stay if she wasn't offered the directorship. Not after four years of being the manager. The humiliation of being passed over would be too difficult. It would be her sign to move on. This was the beginning or the end for her.

It was fitting that she was now walking the hallway of Freja's spa. When she'd come to Europe and taken the same footsteps years ago, straight after getting her first license, she was just learning the hierarchy of the industry. And now there was the possibility that a facility would be placed completely in her hands. To nurture like her offspring. Putting those hard-learned caretaking skills to use, with a spa baby of her own.

When they reached the welcome lobby she said to the receptionist, "*Hej.* Freja is expecting us." The young woman pressed a button.

"Esme!" The familiar voice called out as Freja appeared from an inner office.

"Freja! Gorgeous as ever."

Freja Olsson approached. She was a tall, thin reed of a woman in an outfit of dark leggings and a flowing white blouse with sandals despite the outdoor temperature. She moved swiftly with a kind of hips-forward gait that belied her age. Esme estimated she was in her mid-seventies. They embraced, Freja pulling her close and pressing Esme into the narrowness of her bony body. "I want you to meet Jackson Finn."

"A pleasure." Jackson put out his hand for a shake but Freja bypassed it completely and embraced him as well. Esme could tell Jackson was tentative and leaned forward for the hug rather than allowing his entire body to make contact with hers. He'd said he didn't have a lot of touch in his life, one reason he didn't like bodywork. He'd even initially pooh-poohed using a hot washcloth on his face during the flight.

But then, goodness, had he opened up, telling her buried secrets he must have been holding for years. He wouldn't recognize it yet but that was probably as valuable to him as the most penetrating massage. Plus, they had some inherent similarities, minus the cheating spouse for her, but finding those was cathartic to her, too, which was not unwelcome. She'd learned not to dredge up her past too often but, on occasion, the fellowship was reassuring.

"The spa was established by my grandfather in 1928. We've resisted modernizing and made as few changes as possible."

"Oh, I don't think that's so," Esme countered. "What about your cutting-edge skin care regimes?"

Esme's heart was in bodywork, but many spa users came through the doors for skin care. It was a huge source of revenue. "Jackson, Freja and I texted yesterday about giving you a massage and her men's facial."

"You'd be demonstrating the treatments on me?" He pretended to be in shock.

"Yes, darling," Freja answered.

"Wait, did we agree to that?" Esme could tell he was only halfheartedly protesting.

"We talked about it on the phone the other night," she reminded him. During that strange phone call when his voice crawled all over her. He shrugged and put his palms up as if in surrender. The three of them chuckled.

"You're in good hands," Esme promised.

"We'll begin with a massage," Freja instructed. "Do you prefer a male or female therapist?"

"Male," he answered at bullet speed. Esme knew that men were often uncomfortable being treated by women and vice versa. No doubt stemming from the seedy and inappropriate shenanigans that sometimes took place in what was incorrectly called a massage parlor. Esme, Freja and everyone they knew, had ever known, were absolute professionals. In her career Esme had never even heard of any improper behavior. Still, the reputation lingered and she'd had occasion to have to assure clients of their safety. In a spa setting, sometimes the client preferred the smaller, softer hands of a woman or the opposite, the strength and size of a man's.

Freja led them to the dressing room. "Use any of the lockers you want. Please take a robe. Generally, we prefer the access of a nude body, at all times covered with a sheet, but you're more than welcome to leave your underwear on if that makes you feel more comfortable."

"Jackson—" Esme wanted to check in as well "— we were planning to meet you at the massage table so we could talk about the session as it happens. To give you a sense of how we work. Is that okay with you?"

He definitely took a moment to digest it all and she couldn't blame him. He'd be naked under a sheet with an unfamiliar man's hands on him and two women watching. Spa people had a very clinical, medical view of it all but she was sensitive to the fact that he might not. Yet, anyway.

He nodded, "When in Rom— Stockholm."

"Anders will be your therapist today," Freja announced as a big strapping blond man entered the room. He wore a blue uniform shirt not unlike a hospital scrub that bore the insignia of Spa Henrik, a pair of hands joined together to resemble a heart. Underneath, he wore black pants.

Esme had never met Anders but she knew that Freja would have brought in one of her top people for this demonstration. "Nice to meet you," Esme said to him with a polite smile. Jackson watched her every move as she interacted with the man. In fact, he scrutinized Anders from head to toe before extending his own hello.

"If you'll lie face down on the massage table." Anders pointed. He helped Jackson lie down on the padded table and removed his robe at the same time as he covered him with sheets, leaving only his head and the bottoms of his feet exposed. "Are you comfortable?"

Jackson fit his face into the cradle of the headrest, a horseshoe shape that allowed the recipient to breathe fresh air while their head, neck and torso remained aligned. "I'm all right."

Anders brought his oils on a trolley next to the table. "Do you have any allergies?"

"No."

"Anders is asking that," Esme explained, "because he'll be using oils to lubricate your skin and facilitate his hands' movements on you. Some people are very sensitive to certain products or scents."

"I use a sweet almond oil as my base," Freja said. "Then I can add other oils for aroma or skin care properties. Almond is not the cheapest, that's for sure, but it's worth it."

Anders pumped oil from a dispenser and rubbed his hands together to warm it. "Let's begin."

"We start with effleurage," Freja began her narration, "which is the technique of using long gliding strokes along the curves of the body aimed toward the heart. This promotes relaxation and allows the therapist to get to know the client's body and where there might be tension. The oil gives us a way to warm the muscles."

Esme chimed in, "Also, we can learn if the client prefers light or firm pressure. A massage that uses heavy pressure is called deep tissue."

Freja continued, "The idea of calming the muscles manually is part of the Western style of massage, which looks at physiology and understanding of body mechanics. As opposed to the Eastern philosophies, which approach health by analyzing the life force, and flow or blockage of energy." As was proper protocol, Anders worked on a section of Jackson's body at a time, removing and then recovering parts with the sheet and uncovering others. He moved to each arm and leg and then his back to take inventory of Jackson's physique and where he was holding tightness or misalignment. "Next, we'll go to the technique called petrissage. Here we lift and knead the muscles and fascia to draw blood to the area, which promotes all-body release."

"How are you feeling, Jackson?" Esme asked, wanting to check in because he claimed not to see value in massage at all so she hoped this was helping to change his mind.

"It's fine." His voice sounded strained or maybe constricted. Esme hoped he didn't have his mind on work or on his ex-wife and the atrocity he'd told her about. Although he wasn't the easiest person, he certainly seemed honest so it was a shame that he put his faith in the wrong person. Although she understood plenty about not being able to count on people. Her parents took advantage of a child's innate trust.

Eventually, Anders explained the next phase. "We'll move on to tapotement. I'm sure you've experienced this rhythmic tapping. My hands are in what people call karate chop position. I move quickly up and down a large area to awaken the soft tissue after we've increased the blood flow. To create vibration within the body, which is profoundly restorative."

"With massage," Esme said, "we address muscles and tendons and ligaments and joints and connective tissue all at once. And the process reduces constriction to both the body and mind."

It was a lot to take in so after that they stayed quiet while Anders continued until he finished the session.

CHAPTER SIX

"How was that for you?" Freja asked after Jackson's massage demonstration.

Jackson didn't know what to say to these people for whom that question was of the utmost importance. *Fine* was not going to be an acceptable answer. Although, that's what he thought. It was soothing to have his muscles worked on by Anders, obviously a skilled professional who knew exactly what Jackson's body needed. But Jackson didn't feel like he'd had a monumental *aha* about it. That was okay. He found the details very interesting.

What he wished was that he hadn't winced to himself when Anders smiled at Esme for a little too long as they were introduced. He'd had a silly stab of jealousy at that, which was absurd on so many levels. First and foremost, he had no attachment to her other than as coworkers. She was an independent woman responsible for herself. Second, just because Livia had cheated on him didn't mean that every woman he got near was going to hurt or betray or double-cross him. His intellectual mind knew that. His mere acquaintance with Esme shouldn't be unearthing those demons. After all, he had many women in the company's employ. He hadn't exactly figured out what triggered him with Esme. It was a kooky yet instinctive response. Also, Esme had mentioned her parents pitting her against one another to make the other jealous. Which was sick and cruel and something she didn't need any more of in her life. He needed to nip his immature feelings in the bud right here and now.

As Esme had pointed out, he'd trusted her as an employee and that's all that mattered. He could trust her with the spa but not trust her with his heart. This had nothing to do with their personal lives. Which, in turn, had nothing to do with each other. Yet the mere thought of that made him sad.

"Marvelous," he answered Freja's question, not wanting to negate anything that had transpired.

"Would you like to do some inhaling in our salt room?"

Inhaling. Yes, he supposed he'd like to do some inhaling. So as not to die, that was. "What I'd like to do is eat."

"Wonderful. We have our spa café on the lower floor. Let me inform the chef right now that you're on your way down and she'll prepare a sample menu if that's all right." Freja drew her phone from her pocket and punched in.

"Jackson," Esme piped up, "why don't you stay in your robe and have that experience? Often people come to a day spa and spend hours there, keeping it fluid between treatments and their own leisurely pursuits. Many spas have extra features like meditation rooms, steam chambers, whirlpools, saunas and classes. Freja has a juice bar and a full-service restaurant for spa cuisine where it is absolutely acceptable, encouraged even, to eat in your robe and leave your belongings in the locker."

"Does *spa cuisine* mean I will still be hungry afterward?"

She chuckled, which was his intention. "People do tend to eat light and fresh at the spa. You can imagine that a massage might not feel as good on a stomach that was digesting a lot of food."

Freja said, "I promise to fill you with foods that will increase your vitality and be kind to your digestive system."

"Oh, so I'll certainly be hungry afterward," he said forcing his eyes wide open to make Esme giggle again. He couldn't think of the last time he purposely tried to make someone laugh. Maybe that massage had loosened him up some after all.

"Let's go." Freja led them down a flight of stone steps to the lower level, which was hushed with an almost echo. An enormous vase of yellow, gold and white flowers welcomed guests to the restaurant area.

"Beautiful blooms," Esme commented.

Freja pointed to a side door that led to another staircase. "Non-spa clients can enter here from the street. The restaurant provides good cash flow for us because people from the nearby office buildings and shopping districts come to the restaurant for lunch."

"That's not something we'd be able to do," Esme added. "I just wanted to mention what some people are doing to increase profits."

Freja spoke to the chef and then she sat them at a blond wood table with padded chrome chairs.

"Thank you, Freja," Esme said to her friend. Esme had such warmth about her, it seemed to emanate from every inch of her. He'd never been around someone like that. His parents were as cold as ice. Esme touched his heat inside. He wanted to wrap his arms around her as if he was a giant winged bird and could envelop her in his span. When she asked which was worse, being cheated on or being betrayed as a child, his heart clenched. As she'd said, she turned around the childhood of having to care for some selfish people to a vocation of taking care of others. Was she taking good enough care of herself?

At the Sher a couple of days ago, her eyes misted with tears after he'd helped her put on a coat that she'd been struggling with. Was she so unaccustomed to kindness toward her that even such a small gesture was a big deal? He was just being decent in seeing that she could use a hand. It was hardly a heroic act. While his parents were stoic, they were at least well mannered. And the funny thing was, after he helped her get her coat on he wanted to do more for her. He wanted to lay his own coat down on a puddle in the street so she could step over it. Or give her the imaginary gloves he had on to keep her hands warm.

He looked at her across the table. Yes, he'd like to keep her warm.

Then he blinked his eyes open. What kind of crazy fantasy had he just had? He needed lunch.

A waiter brought two glasses of water in goblets.

Jackson downed his in one sip. "Hmm. Room temperature?"

"We can request ice if you'd like. Freja thinks icy drinks are too shocking for the organs."

Next the waiter placed a small plate in front of each of them. "This is our farm-to-table quinoa beet bowl with fresh picked kale." As he'd feared, rabbit food. Kale was supposed to be a garnish on the side of the plate! "With an avocado goddess sauce." He had no idea what that meant but he liked avocado and there was definitely something goddess-like about Esme.

"Thank you." He'd give it a try.

The waiter stepped away and returned with two tall narrow glasses of a milky pink drink. "Our antioxidant berry lassi."

Jackson sipped it, a delicious smoothie that managed to be creamy, tart and sweet all at once. That wasn't as hard to get down as the kale. Wasn't Swedish food heavy and hearty, to combat the cold winter? He'd go get two dozen meatballs later.

Since he was stuck here for the moment, in a robe no less, as Esme gamely chewed her weed salad, he asked, "You and Freja began to explain about the variety of massage techniques. What are some other types besides Swedish?"

"I think we were explaining deep tissue. That's when we'll use more pressure. In doing that, we can better relieve pain or chronic stiffness and concentrate on one area of the body."

The enthusiasm in Esme's voice made him want

to keep her talking. He could listen to her for hours. "What else?"

"Well, there's trigger points where we work on one part of the body to assist another. For example, relieving pressure on the neck can help with the frequency and duration of persistent headaches."

He creaked his head to stretch out his neck in one direction and then the other. He had to admit that he felt more range of motion after that massage than he had in a while. "Interesting."

"I can see that your neck bands are more fluid," she said in response to his stretching.

"It amazes me that you can glean that from across the table."

"You have chronic stress, Jackson. I could tell from the minute you walked into the spa. What are you doing to relieve it?"

"I had been doing nothing. Now my doctor is warning me what could happen if I don't address it."

"What will you do?"

"I'm supposed to do relaxing things. Take more vacations. So, hey, this counts as a vacation, doesn't it?"

"Not based on how much time you spent on your computer during the flight."

"Do you have the magical, mystical work-life balance that everyone is so highly touting?"

"I don't know that it's so idyllic for anyone. But I take yoga and I practice mindful breathing."

"What's that?"

"Slowly breathing in through your nose and just as slowly out through your mouth."

"You were doing that with that elderly lady at the Sher."

"Try it with me. In through the nose." They both inhaled. "And out through the mouth." They exhaled.

"Okay."

"And you do it as many times as you need to. It will transport you, I promise." She took a few bites of her food.

He used his fork to isolate a couple of chunks of avocado and brought them to his mouth. "Tell me about other treatments."

"People have been using heat and cold as body therapies for thousands of years. A simple, non-messy and effective way we can deliver that is with hot stones."

"How do you use them?" He looked at his bowl while visualizing a big plate of bacon and eggs. "Are there twigs in this?" He scrunched up his face and got another smirk out of her.

She pressed on. "We place warmed stones on parts of the body where we want to open soft tissue and increase blood flow."

"Are there particular kinds of stones?" He managed another bite of the bunny food, fascinated by listening to Esme. He thought back to that first night with her in New York when a coffee at the Italian place turned into delicious wine and dinner. They'd shared a tiramisu dessert, a rather familiar act for two people who barely knew each other. Yet he'd relished it, hadn't realized how much he craved simple, honest conversation. A face across the table. He was a boss to many but friend to few.

"Really almost any smooth stone is fine but the industry standard is basalt, which is heavy and volcanic."

She was so truly passionate about her work. He loved that she'd found what she wanted to do with her life at an early age and was doing it. And that she was gutsy enough to stand up to him, to tell him that she'd take him on this trip only with the promise that if he liked her ideas, he'd name her spa director afterward.

"That sounds like it would be a unique sensation."

He sensed she was enjoying sharing her expertise with him. "Let's see," she continued. "Any spa session can be enhanced with aromatherapy." Thankfully, the waiter noticed that Jackson wasn't eating the garden in a bowl and brought another berry lassi and a plate of crackers and nuts. "We use scent to awaken the sense of smell along with everything else we're doing. For example, lavender is known to produce calm whereas citrus is a wake-up call."

"What about you, Esme? What's your favorite kind of massage?"

She looked at him as if no one had ever asked her that question. Which brought back his musings that if she was busy caring for other people, who was caring for her? Was she as complete as she fronted she was? He doubted it. Just like him. They were quite a pair.

"Thanks for asking. Actually, it's the Thai style. Bangkok will be our last stop on this trip so I'll have a chance to show you. It's a guided-movement practice performed on the floor with the recipient in loose clothing."

"What do you like about it?"

"To each his own but for me, the manipulation of my movements is so therapeutic."

He felt a surge of excitement, as if he'd never traveled to the ends of the earth which, in fact, he had. Never with her, though. Her spirit was infectious.

"Please," Freja said and gestured, "get comfortable in the facial chair." After lunch, it was time for Jackson's skin care treatment, which Freja was going to perform herself. He sat down and she used the controls to recline him and elevate his legs.

"This is like being at the dentist," Jackson said, "which, by the way, I hate." He snarled at Esme like a grouch. She gave him a thumbs-up signal.

"Some clients prefer to use earbuds and listen to their choice of music or spoken word, guided meditations," Freja said, "while they're having the treatment. Of course today, we want to talk to you about the protocol."

"Yup."

"We'll start with a thorough cleansing," Freja explained as she began. "I've got half a dozen cleansers here and I'll choose which one to use based on the client's skin type. Jackson, I can see that your skin runs a little dry so I'm going to use a product that I know is moisturizing. I'll blend that in all across your face starting with the neck and working my way upward. We want to completely clean the face and beard area. How does that feel?"

"Strange."

As she moved across his face she continued, "Skin

has a lot of impurities. I can see that you hold some deep grime, as we do in the cities. I also see patches of dehydration, which can be caused by a lot of travel and also from poor sleep."

"Check and check. You can tell that from my skin?"

"Skin works hard. It can become fatigued. It needs attention." She used wet disposable sponges to remove the cleanser. And followed that with a calming toner applied with cotton balls.

"Now she's going to use a polyhydroxy compound, which won't further dry out sensitive skin," Esme narrated. "What we need to do is exfoliate, meaning slough off the dead skin so that we can bring out the healthy cells underneath."

"Are you painting my face?" Jackson reacted to the small brush Freja was using to apply the product.

"As a matter of fact, I am."

"Would you like to see yourself in a mirror?" She didn't wait and grabbed a handheld mirror from the counter. She handed it to Jackson, who shimmied in disbelief that the so-called gentle exfoliator was... bright yellow, covering his face from forehead to clavicle, except around his eyes and mouth.

"I look like a lemon!"

Esme reached over to lay a reassuring hand on his arm. "What happens in the spa stays in the spa." She had to tell herself to take her hand back. It wanted to stay there.

"Now, we'll do the extractions." Freja pulled her wheeled work trolley over and began to position her lighted magnifying lamp correctly to view his face.

"This is often what clients find to be the most uncomfortable part of the facial and so they opt out of it. But there's nothing that replaces removing blackheads and other pollutants one at a time. May I continue?"

"I suppose, although you're scaring me," he answered with trepidation. After covering his eyes with cotton pads so the rays of her lamp didn't bother him, she used the magnifier to locate, and then used her metal extraction tool to scrape off the blackheads and clogged pores she found on his face. "Yikes," he commented immediately on his discomfort.

Esme couldn't disagree. But she wanted Jackson to understand the skin care component to the spa menu. "Very often clients book both facial and bodywork sessions for the same day."

"Are we done yet?" Jackson all but pleaded as Freja picked and picked until she was satisfied.

"Now we'll do a gel mask for hydration. It uses algae to firm, lift and brighten the skin."

"You're putting seaweed on me?"

"It's a nutrient-rich ingredient that yields fabulous results. Another thing I think would benefit your skin is microneedling."

"Does that have the word *needle* in it? I already don't like it." No more than he had liked Esme's suggestion of acupuncture the other day.

She showed him the penlike tool used for that process. "See, it has tiny needles. We brush the skin making minuscule punctures which stimulate the skin to produce collagen to heal them."

"Punctures. I'll take your word for that." He jumped out of the chair.

"Thank you for bearing with us." Esme wanted to hug him but he'd suffered enough, she laughed to herself.

After he showered and dressed, they decided to walk to their hotel despite the cold. They strolled through the Gamla Stan, Stockholm's Old Town, with its cobblestoned alleys and buildings of muted colors and carved wood. The air was filled with brisk flurries of snow.

One minute they were walking forward, continuing to talk about spa operations and then, really not meaning to, he took Esme's hand. Her skin was unspeakably satiny. He shot his eyes over to her for approval. She looked down at their entwined hands, as surprised as he was, like a force in and of itself had made the move, neither of them having anything to do with it. A bit like the energy wave that had passed between them at having brushed against each other at the Sher that first day. The thing was, it felt absolutely natural, normal and right. As if their hands had been searching for each other since the beginning of time. Like they had each been lost and finally found their way home.

A peace came across his face that he could actually feel, another move happening without him consciously instructing it to. He stopped walking, which pulled her a little closer to him. Still holding one hand, he took hold of the other to make their two spheres form a circle. And when his face drew just a few inches from hers, he kissed her. A quick wisp of a kiss, just letting his mouth make contact with the velvet that was her lips. His eyelids fluttered because he liked it so much, the smallness of the action becoming a still photo. His brain told him that the earth had, in fact, shifted. That there would forever be this instant. The timeline in the history of the world would now be divided between having not yet stood on the street in Stockholm in the snow kissing Esme Russo, and then time forever after it occurred.

He kissed her again, let his lips linger a bit longer, to feel the press of their mouths against each other. His tongue flicked a snowflake from her upper lip. One of his hands disentangled from hers in order to cup her cheek, downy, pillowy and cold at the same time. He brought her face closer, this time to kiss deeper, to kiss longer, letting himself swell with the desire to keep kissing her.

As the snowflakes fell, cascading them with powder, they kissed and then kissed some more. Until there was actually no weather, no sky, no Stockholm—there was only their bodies against each other, two as one.

Then, suddenly, after they'd been standing in that one spot for who knows how long, some kind of awareness took over Esme. She pulled her head back, creating an undeniable space between them, a chasm. The moment was over. Definitely and completely over. "Jackson, I don't..." She struggled for words, taking in one of her slow inhales and exhales. "I don't... With men... I don't really...date."

His mouth fell into a circle like a surprised child,

shocked by the kissing he'd instigated and even more shocked by her abrupt end to it. "Oh, was dating what we were doing?"

"And then there's lymphatic drainage, reiki, reflexology, shiatsu..." Esme forced herself to stop babbling as she and Jackson continued their walk.

"Uh-huh."

There weren't many people on the street; it was too cold. She knew she'd been talking a mile a minute as snowflakes whooshed around them. She was doing anything to avoid dealing with what had just happened.

He'd kissed her, with a fire that could have melted the snow around them for a five-foot radius. It had been a long time since Esme had been kissed by anyone. And she'd never been kissed like that, with a force and passion that she'd only seen in a movie or read in a book, nothing she'd ever thought was real.

It wasn't true when she told him that she didn't date. New York married friends always knew a great guy they wanted to introduce her to. The trouble was she never connected with any of them, never found any Venn diagram where their worlds overlapped. She wasn't interested in what they cared about and it appeared to be vice versa. Or worse still, they were needy and once her elemental competence was visible, they'd started wanting her to be their mother or at least their social director. In any case, it had been a long time since she'd even exchanged that with a man.

She decided to bite the bullet with Jackson, stop blathering about spas, and get said what needed to be expressed. After all, they were leaving for Mexico in the morning, and had the rest of the trip to get through and then a possible long-term working relationship. They had to get past what had just transpired. "So hey, you asked me if what we just did was dating? What did you mean by that?"

He glanced over to her as they walked, and then returned to facing forward so he didn't have to make eye contact. "I don't know. I just wanted to be clear with you. What just happened..."

"You kissed me," she jumped in. "Out of the blue."

"Did I? I can't remember how it started."

"What do you mean, you can't remember? We were walking and then we were kissing."

"Did I do something improper?"

"I suppose it could have been. I didn't regard it as such."

"So you were...as receptive as I thought you were."

She'd be lying if she didn't admit that she'd been thinking about him since he arrived in New York to make himself a presence at the Sher. Not only was he beguiling, but also he had a depth and a frankness that she was very attracted to. At this point in her life, she didn't need superficial encounters. And the way he asked her what kind of massage she liked or how he always held the door open were tiny moves that spoke volumes to her. But feeling good from the actions of a man, no matter how engaging and attentive he was, wasn't in her plans. Spontaneous kissing wasn't on the itinerary, either. And, most importantly, not with her boss! Her boss! She needed to be oh so careful that nothing got in the way of her big opportunity. To kiss him was to tempt the fates. "Yes, I was receptive, I just wanted to be clear that I don't think that qualified as dating."

"You don't pull any punches, do you, Esme? You tell it like it is."

"I can't afford not to. Whoever started it... Oh, wait, I mean that was you, which isn't to say that it wasn't lovely."

"And you want to agree that we'll never let anything like that happen again?"

"Right, I mean we're work partners now and maybe just being here in Stockholm in the snow was a little romantic." Well, actually, very romantic.

"Got it. Pact. We're coworkers and that's all we should ever be."

"Good, I just wouldn't want you to misunderstand my willingness to... When you kissed me and..." Then she yanked his hand to stop walking. And turned herself toward him, got up on her tippy toes and kissed him again. Was she crazy? Just after they'd made big proclamations that they weren't going to kiss again? His mouth felt so amazing that she couldn't help herself, kissing him in short presses. Soon followed by a not-so-short one that involved their tongues. That involved his tongue rolling along hers. Their mouths sealing to each other. Kisses that were hypnotizing, making sparks ignite that heated her on the inside. How could she feel so hot in the snow? "Oh, no." She stopped abruptly.

"Okay, that was definitely you, right?"

"I'm sorry. That really, really was the last time." The words came out of her mouth but she didn't mean them. She did want it to happen again. Right there on the street, or in more private quarters. She couldn't be blamed, could she? Those kisses were a kind of wake-up that made a person want more. Like a lifetime's worth, perhaps. Although she wouldn't do it again. She bore her eyes into his and told him so without words. His eyes were glassy as he returned the stare. With desire. His mere gaze sent blood coursing through her. This trip was quickly becoming very complicated.

When they came in from the cold and entered the hotel, a few people sat at the tables and chairs in the lobby as the front desk manager greeted them. "May I send up some champagne?"

Esme didn't ask Jackson before answering, *"Nej, tack."*

Things had become awkward and she just wanted to get away from him at this point to collect herself and regroup.

Jackson argued, "Not so fast. Can you send me up a plate of meatballs and potatoes?" he asked the manager. "What about you, Esme? We only ate leaves at the spa. Aren't you hungry?"

"Nothing for me. I'm ready for bed." Although she certainly took note that he'd asked whether she was hungry. Someone concerned if she'd had enough to eat. Hmm. How nice that was.

They ducked into the elevator. Exiting on their floor, they walked down the quiet and softly lit corridor until they reached their rooms, which were across from each other.

Based on those kisses that they equally participated in, Esme sensed that she'd only need to invite him in as a method of communicating that she wanted to take things further. On one hand, she did. Desperately, as a matter of fact. She was so drawn to him and imagined little snippets of what could be. How his kisses might land on her neck. How his big hands might feel on her bare skin. Would they be rough or gentle? Would they feel hot like his tongue?

She'd been intimate with a few men. A couple of encounters were one-nighters and a few more lasted for a couple of months until it was clear there was nothing going on to warrant continuing to see each other. She knew that she'd never been made love to in a way that stirred her center. That would make her replay the encounters in a dreamy haze for days afterward. The kind that touched all the way down. And the scary thing was, she was certain that would all change if she shared a bed with Jackson. Like he had all of that in him just waiting to burst up. The thought set off screaming red warning signals that taking things any further with him would put her in emotional danger. Not to mention the possible jeopardy of her career.

So, it was in great haste that she tapped the key card to her room, said a quick good-night over her shoulder and dashed through the door, waiting to hear the definitive click of the lock behind her before she could lean back against the wall and let out a sigh that was relief mixed with disappointment. Because maybe, just maybe, she had actually met someone who was showing her that what she thought she had all figured out, that living her life alone was the best solution, might not be so. This was new information. And unwelcome at that.

On the plane to Oaxaca, Esme and Jackson were served a lavish Mexican breakfast of eggs and chorizo topped with red salsa and cheese, accompanied by sweet bread rolls called *conchas* and spice-laden coffee. He'd ordered room service last night yet they both ate heartily. It was so yummy they didn't talk for a few minutes; all they could do was sensually indulge. More sensuality. His kisses at night and great food in the morning. She could hardly decide which was more decadent. Oh, that wasn't true. She knew which. Though she hadn't had much of that deliciousness in her life.

Lying in her Stockholm hotel bed last night, she'd felt everything change. That steely-eyed future she envisioned became not enough. She'd decided long ago against men and coupledom. That she wasn't going to devote all of her resources to someone else. There'd been enough of that. Especially when her journey had taught her that she could expect nothing in return. She was not going to spend her life repeating the same pattern. Of people taking but not giving. As a result, she'd never been in a relationship as she only seemed to attract the wrong sort of man. Until now.

Was it the way Jackson kissed her that was so earth-shaking? A give-and-take kind of exchange unlike anything she'd ever felt before? Whatever the provocation, her mental fog lifted and she saw the sky in a whole new way. How honest she and Jackson were with each other about their pasts and about how those pasts colored their lives now. There was something similar about their fear of betrayal, of trust, a trait hardened by their circumstances. She had this strange instinct that she could tell him anything and that he'd understand, and that she wanted to tell him everything. She had friends but she tended to keep things closer to the vest. When a child learns that information from one person can be used against another, it's training to keep their intimacies to themselves.

Now here, on this whirlwind trip with Jackson, she realized, and strangely for the very first time, that she was walking a very lonely road. It was a choice. And that there might be another one. A scarier one. But one that might have untold rewards that she'd never dared to dream of. Where someone wanted to know if she was hungry, and two people shared their ups and downs, hiked through the hills and valleys of a lifetime holding hands. It was overwhelming to consider what she'd never allowed herself before.

Once they finally slowed down on their gigantic plates of food, Jackson said, "I have to admit that I felt pretty good after that massage." His out-of-the-blue comment made her smile from ear to ear. Half in victory that she was getting him to understand the benefits of spa and half because it was so cute that he was admitting it to her as if he couldn't believe it himself. "Maybe my personal methods of self-care could use a makeover just like the Sher."

"Remind me again, what are those?"

"Barriers to ever being close to someone. Then there's living in corporate hotels so as to call no place home, spending as much time alone as possible, burying myself in work, always a screen in front of me, not getting fresh air. I think in your parlance you'd say I was *disconnecting* as best I could."

"Ooh, very good. Disconnecting."

He bowed his head as if accepting the accolade. "Thank you."

He reached over to steal an orange slice from her plate without asking. The familiarity in that made her heart ding though she pretended to protest with, "Hey!"

It was good that they weren't hashing over the snowflakes and hot sparks of last night. They'd talked it through, agreed it was a mistake. Now they were back to getting to know each other as colleagues with some kind of kindred spirits that would enhance their professional relationship. A good decision. No problem. If only she believed that herself. Because her insides were definitely replaying what had transpired.

"I told you," he continued, "my parents didn't value, or even understand, self-care. They worked day and night, coexisting in a world of numbers and flow charts and global predictions."

"And you've followed in their footsteps."

"I thought I needed more. Romance. Rapture. Exaltation. My one attempt to rebel was to marry a sparkly person who turned out to be made of smoke and mirrors. And now that's how I regard most everyone. As if I suspect them of something. In fact, after the whole debacle with Livia I did something I'll always regret."

"What's that?"

He hesitated before he committed to saying, "I fired the accountant who discovered that funds were missing from some accounts."

"He or she was who brought it to your attention?"

"Tom, yeah. I fired him in what I told myself was an abundance of caution. I found out later that he'd only reported on those accounts, he'd never had any access to them like Livia had."

"Couldn't you have hired him back?"

"He rightly didn't want to work for someone who thought that little of him."

"That's a lot to carry. You might want to unload some of this."

"What does that mean?"

"See a therapist, read a book about letting go and forgiving yourself. Hoping for an honest wife wasn't so much to ask for, or expect." Her words hung in the air. "Let's do some breathing. Inhale through your nose…"

He followed along but she could tell he was contemplating what she'd said. Finally he changed the subject to, "What's in store for me in Mexico?"

She shifted. "Cozumel and Luis's spa is very specialized. That's what I have in mind for the Sher."

"Give me a preview."

"I know so many spas with full menus of skin and bodywork. New York is obviously one of the magnets in the world for the finest in skin care. So what if we eliminated that entirely from our menu?"

"Huh?"

"Don't compete with those famed skin care salons. Focus only on certain kinds of bodywork. And build a reputation on that. Let's be the best at specific modalities. I want to show you what Cozumel and Luis are doing. That's what I'd like to model us on."

She could see his wheels turning. He was the boss, after all. That was okay. She wanted them to have a partnership where they both had a vested interest in the Sher's success. She'd need his approval. This was already a victory for her, being heard, allowed to show him her vision. His snow-flurry kisses, buried agonies of his past and her questions about being alone would all fall to the wayside. She hoped.

CHAPTER SEVEN

SECRETLY, JACKSON'S GUT was doing push-ups while he tried to keep his face neutral. He was all but sitting on his hands to resist the temptation to get another taste of what he'd gorged on last night. Esme's lips. He would never recover from those kisses that were the sweetest nectar he'd ever tasted. Not to mention the soft skin of her face and neck that his fingers had the good fortune to have stroked. All of which was very logically discussed and decided against, the same as an ill-advised business decision. Of course, the trouble was that he'd spent the entire night tossing and turning on those pale yellow Swedish sheets in bed alone with very contradictory thoughts.

"*Bienvenidos* to Oaxaca International Airport," the pilot announced over the sound system after they'd touched ground back on the North American continent. Jackson looked out the window at open sky and mountainous terrain, so very different than the Swedish vistas they'd arrived from.

"I hope you find this a special visit," Esme turned to say.

A driver took them a bit outside of Oaxaca City to

reach Spa Bajo el Sol, or Spa under the Sun. When they arrived, Esme couldn't wait and flung the door open to bound out of the car and greet a man and a woman who were seemingly waiting for them outside the entrance in front of a tiled fountain with a bountiful spray of almost blue water. Esme ran toward them calling out, "Cozumel! Luis!" When she reached them, the three exchanged hugs. Esme turned to extend a hand to Jackson and bring him into the circle with the Aguilars. "This is Jackson Finn, who I told you about."

"Hola," Cozumel greeted him. "Thank you for having an interest in the work we do here."

"With Esme's help I'm only just beginning to understand the scope of what spa really means." He brought forward a hand to shake, which Cozumel and Luis ignored, both bringing him into an awkward hug of their own.

After they disentangled, Cozumel said, "Here at Bajo el Sol we focus on ancient work regarding fertility and both male and female reproductive health. What we do is unique. We're blessed that guests have found us and have spread the word about our treatments."

Esme said to Jackson, "See, that's what I'm talking about. Rather than a general spa, they specialize and draw a clientele from all over the world."

"This is a place of love. Our bodies. Our bellies. Our babies."

"You must be hungry and thirsty after your journey," Luis said. "Let me show you to your casita." Esme had told Jackson that while Bajo el Sol wasn't a hotel spa, they did keep some accommodations for friends and family, and guests having sensitive treatments. They'd be staying in one of the small houses that faced out to a view of groves and mountains. The sunny skies and blustery breezes were quite a change from Sweden.

"Remind me, Luis," Esme asked as they walked toward the horizon, "what year did you establish the spa?"

"It's twenty-five years already." They followed him to the casita he pointed to. "The adobe walls of the buildings help keep the interior cool in summer and warm in winter. Come in." The small house was furnished and decorated with traditional Mexican design, bold colors in a rustic setting. Two bedrooms shared a bathroom.

"This is lovely."

"We are closed for the evening and there are no other overnight guests so you have the run of the property. Drop off your bags and then join us in the kitchen. It's the back door in the main house, or did you remember that, Esme?"

She'd told Jackson that she'd worked here for two years, staying in a spare room in the house, and credited Cozumel and Luis with teaching her many valuable lessons about both operations and treatments. "Oh, I remember the kitchen. How could I ever forget your Oaxacan cooking? Jackson, you're going to love Luis's food."

"As long as there's no kale."

They did as Luis suggested and freshened up in the casita, putting on comfortable clothes to suit the mild weather. Jackson had taken Esme's advice during that sexy phone call before they left and had packed lightweight clothes and canvas shoes. Esme looked angelic in a loose white dress.

In the large, open kitchen, Luis was stirring a huge cauldron over a fire, and everywhere Jackson turned there were pots and utensils that looked to be centuries old. "We have some *antojitos* ready," Cozumel said and pointed to the counter where an appetizer was sitting invitingly on a platter painted with the sun and moon around the rim. Beside it was a glass pitcher filled with a pale green drink. "These are *garnachas*," Luis said.

Cozumel jumped in with, "Small tortillas topped with shredded meat."

"And pickled cabbage," Luis added.

"And, to drink." Cozumel gestured to the pitcher.

Luis said, "That's a melon *liquado*."

They helped themselves to a more than ample snack. "Oh, my goodness," Jackson couldn't help but extoll, "these are divine."

After Luis attempted to stuff their faces into oblivion merely on appetizers, Esme wanted to go back to the casita before the main course. She plopped herself down on the couch. "I'm exhausted. I didn't sleep on the flight. I think I have jet lag."

"New York to Sweden to Mexico in just a few days can cause that." He cracked open the cap of a water bottle from the counter and handed it to her. "Drink."

"Maybe I'll take a little nap."

"Nope. The best thing is to get on Mexican time. Let's sit outside in the sun. That helps me sometimes."

"Mr. Finn, do I actually detect some knowledge about taking care of yourself?"

"Don't tell anyone." He put one finger up to his mouth for a shush. "I travel a lot. It's more like self-preservation." He stretched out an arm to pull her off of the couch.

They lay on the patio loungers that were on the patio. Esme lifting her face to the sun was unspeakably beautiful. After a while she said, "Hey, thanks for looking after me. I do feel better."

His mind was everywhere. How connected Cozumel and Luis were, practically finishing each other's sentences. Strange flashbacks about Livia, remembering the giddy feeling he had for a very short time in the beginning when he thought he was in love. How being a couple made him feel part of something he wanted and felt incomplete without. How it wasn't that his parents didn't care for each other, but they just didn't show it. For some reason they didn't think it needed expressing, or kindling, or romancing. In Livia, he was chasing that something different he thought he needed. Instead, all he came away with was hurt. And shame. Esme was right. If he was ever going to let go of the regret he carried in his body, he needed to let the shame go.

When they returned to the main house after it had gotten dark, Luis had finished preparing dinner. It was to be eaten under the stars at a table made from clear blue glass pieces that picked up bits of moonlight here and there. Just as Esme's hair did.

"When everybody thinks about Oaxacan cooking they think of our moles. There are many variations,"

Cozumel explained as she served Jackson a piece of grilled chicken onto which she ladled a dark sauce.

Luis jumped in with, "Mole contains dozens of ingredients and takes days to make. When Cozumel told me you were coming, I began this mole *negro* for you."

"You'll taste the subtle flavor of chocolate balanced with acidic tomatillos, nuts, tortillas, dried fruit, chili peppers. It's both savory and sweet."

Jackson took a bite and the richness and complexity of the sauce delighted his taste buds. "Thank you, Luis, this is beyond delicious."

Esme nodded emphatically in agreement.

Luis carried out a clay pot. "With it, we'll have black beans with epazote, an herb we farm here at the spa. We cook it with some onions and a little bit of bacon so it's herby but rich."

Next came a tray. "My goodness," Esme marveled. "This is enough food to feed New York City."

"*Tlayudas*, which are like our pizzas. We spread a tortilla with beans, *asiento*, which is pork lard, cheese and tasajo. Dried beef."

"And no kale whatsoever," Jackson said to no one.

After dinner Cozumel served them a small glass of mezcal, a spirit made from the agave plant, which had a smoky flavor. And a chocolate sampling on another beautiful plate, this one painted with sunflowers. "Chocolate is very important to us. It's used for all occasions and rituals. You'll see tomorrow we even use it in the spa."

"Cozumel, what treatments will we show Jackson?"

"I have a longtime client, Payaan, who I've seen

through her fertility issues. She's willing to have you observe our work together. Tomorrow, we do demonstrations. Tonight, we rest. Now, go sit by the firepit, take the mezcal and the chocolate with you and just be. Surrender to the moon." It was as if Cozumel knew him, knew that her simple instruction wasn't an easy one for him to follow.

Sitting on one of the circular stone benches that rounded the firepit, they quietly nibbled the chocolate and watched the orange flames tickle the night. It wasn't just the physical connection between them he couldn't stop thinking about. It was that all of his pronouncements and decrees about never getting close to a woman were melting like snowflakes in the firepit. He'd be all business with Esme, like they'd agreed. Yet his heart would know that it was her who had cracked his hard shell, giving him an inkling that being with someone heart, body and soul might be worth the risk of his greatest fear coming true, that he'd be betrayed again.

Eventually, he stood. "After such a wonderful meal, I think I'm the one who is going to fall asleep right here if we don't get to the casita." They got up and strolled under the moonlight and stars to their little house.

"Hard to believe we began our day in Stockholm."

"Let's go to bed." It was strange the way that came out of his mouth. As if they were a longtime married couple who always retired to bed together. It just came out that way. He surely wasn't speaking from personal experience. He and Livia had no bedtime ritual. He often stayed awake much later than she did, communicating with the rest of the world from his computer, some people beginning their workdays, some at the end. Time had no particular meaning to him and he hadn't considered it that much until this moment, when it seemed as if he and Esme and the black night sky were part of something connected, and last night in Stockholm they were part of something else. But perhaps his lofty musings were just those snowy kisses doing the talking.

"Here we are," Esme stated the obvious when they stepped into the casita and headed to the bedrooms.

His best bet would have been to walk straight into his room and close the door. Which he succeeded at. Except for one tiny detour. And that was over to Esme's face to give her lovely cheek just a peck of a good-night kiss.

Okay, he almost succeeded in that scenario, too. The kiss ended up on her sumptuous lips, which tasted like chocolate. And it was decidedly more than a peck.

"That kiss was your doing, right?" Esme pointed at him and played tough guy, but with a twitch of a smile.

"Yes. Not you. Me."

"Just checking." She entered her bedroom and shut the door, leaving him standing in the divide between the two rooms, frozen, stunned.

"Mayan abdominal massage, which is part of healing practices called *sobada*, has been around since Meso-american times," Cozumel told Jackson the next morning as they walked to the open-air massage plaza with its tentlike roof. A massage table was dressed with clean linens and a wooden cabinet with open doors displayed shelves of towels and products used for treatments. A small woman sat on the table under the shade. "Payaan, these are my friends Esme and Jackson who I told you about."

She made eye contact with them. Esme considered that it was very open of the woman to allow her and Jackson to observe her treatment. As if on cue, Payaan ran her palm across her belly.

Esme asked her, "Can I help you lie down?" She put out her hand and Payaan took it to help herself into position.

"We're being extra careful with Payaan. Although she has one beautiful daughter, six years old if I remember correctly," Cozumel said, to which Payaan nodded, "she's having trouble holding another pregnancy. We're going to try some techniques that have been used for centuries to aid in fertility."

"Gracias," the otherwise quiet Payaan whispered.

Cozumel began with a singsong chant in Spanish, blessing the elements that had joined them for today's journey. While she did that, she gently stroked Payaan's left arm from finger to shoulder and then her right. She did the same up the length of each leg from foot to hip. She rolled Payaan's skirt down from the waist, exposing the smooth brown skin of her abdomen, the soft center of her. "We'll set our intention to pour love into Payaan's belly, to send her the sun and the moon, water and fire."

"I will." Esme closed her eyes and brought those very images to mind, trying to use her own energy to penetrate into Payaan. She imagined her spirit traveling into the woman with every exhale. Afterward, she opened her eyes and shifted her gaze to Jackson. She didn't imagine he'd be spiritually trying to move his life force but nonetheless he was stilled by the uniqueness of the moment. And, after all, that's why they were there, to show him how transformative this specific care could be. Esme had this one chance to affect Payaan's reproductive health because tomorrow they'd be gone, and Cozumel would be on to her next client.

Cozumel washed her hands with the collected rainwater she poured from a pitcher, and dried them on a fluffy towel. She rubbed her palms together to warm them and then placed both down on Payaan's belly.

"Join me, Esme. If that's all right, Payaan." She nodded. Esme followed Cozumel in washing and drying her hands, warming them with friction and then placing them onto Payaan. The four hands moved to gently press into her belly, feeling for information. "Payaan, I sense some movement in you. Perhaps you are ovulating, either today or within the next couple of days." She began gently lifting and gliding along Payaan's stomach, moving with her fingertips in an outward circle. Esme did the same.

To Jackson, Esme explained, "With *sobada* techniques we can sometimes guide the uterus into the optimal position in the lower pelvis."

"How?" he asked simply. Esme was happy that he was taking an interest. She had wondered how he would feel about coming to Oaxaca to a spa that concerned itself mainly with fertility. But he seemed to understand that this was a very specialized practice, and Cozumel a very gifted practitioner.

"We can increase circulation to the area and break up blockage. That brings a better flow of oxygen and relieves stagnation."

"Esme has a beautiful touch," Cozumel said to Jackson. "She always has. She was born with it." Jackson caught Esme's eyes and smiled sweetly with what looked like pride. She all but blushed in return. A moment not lost on Cozumel.

No one but Esme knew the surprising gift of Jackson's touch. When he'd embraced her during those kisses in Stockholm. Even his impromptu palm at the small of her back when going through the airport was hypnotizing. His big hands were sure and powerful, teeming with energy waves. She was trying very hard to pretend that she didn't crave more.

Esme said, "The menu here can help with other ailments and maladies as well such as endometriosis, blocked tubes, fibroids, cysts, painful menstrual cramps, prostate health for men. And prenatal care, to ensure the mother and baby are comfortable and breathing easily."

They were quiet for the rest of the treatment, the rustling breeze their only sound. Upon completion of the session, Cozumel said, "Now we'll bring closure to our work together. That's part of the healing. We'll anoint Payaan's belly with cocoa oil and wrap her in a rebozo, a ceremonial shawl." Esme pulled the needed items from the cabinet.

After the session they reviewed. "I could see Payaan respond to you, Esme. You were a talented novice and you've become skilled in and out of the treatment room. I wish I could bring you back permanently. I'm too busy to take on all of the requests I get. Plus, my spa director, Itza, will herself soon take a maternity leave to birth her own baby and she hasn't decided if and when she'll return."

"My honor." Esme appreciated the praise. It was a transformative two years she'd spent here, learning from Cozumel and gaining the confidence her own parents failed to give her. Poignant that she was back here during this turning point in her life. In more ways than one, as she was here with this extraordinary man who was making her question all that she'd held sacred.

With the demonstration completed, Cozumel suggested Esme show Jackson the mud therapy. They changed into swimsuits and headed to the mud pavilion, another outdoor space on the property. As he walked a few paces ahead of her, Esme couldn't help admiring Jackson's sturdy back, his skin glistening in the late-afternoon glow. When they were in session with Cozumel, it was a thrill that he was so interested in the work that was done here. To understand this was to understand her. She'd never met anyone outside of the spa industry who had.

"Have you ever used a mud pool? We coat ourselves in the wet clay mud and then we sit out in the sun to let it dry. After that we rub it off, and then rinse with geothermal mineral water, which is one of nature's greatest detoxifiers."

Esme used hands full of clay from the well to completely cover one arm in a thin layer to show Jackson, who was quick to follow. "Slimy."

"It's food for your skin. The paste will nourish."

"Does my skin need nourishing?" he asked, getting used to the sensation and applying the clay to his chest.

"Yes, this is incredible restoration for your skin, another natural remedy that's been around for centuries. It stimulates your skin function. Did you know that skin is the body's largest organ?"

"I didn't even know that skin was an organ."

"The mud pulls out the impurities so they don't enter your bloodstream. It balances the skin, which can even have a sedative effect."

"And I didn't know that my skin needed sedation, either."

"Oh, that's a little thick on your chest. Let me." She reached out with a flat palm to spread out the too-heavy layer he had created. He took a quick intake of breath, making her realize that her hands were having an effect on him.

Just as his chest was having an effect on her hands. His solid muscles and skin so warm it was bringing the mud to a perfect temperature.

They looked at each other, a silent conversation that went long past clay. She wondered about being here in Mexico, about Jackson's dark eyes, heated skin and the penetrating feeling that she had been missing out on something central to the meaning of life.

"Do you want me to do your back?"

"Please."

He turned around, and it was almost painful not to

be able to see his face. She dutifully coated his back, whispering in his ear from behind, "It's easier when there's someone to help, isn't it?"

"I can see that now."

Once she'd applied the mud to the curves and planes of his extremely attractive back, he circled around. "My turn." It was a statement not an inquiry. She gave him access and his hands were indeed sent from heaven as they applied the clay to her shoulder blades, vibrating through her. In fact, she had to pull away because she was starting to feel so turned on and needed to put herself in check.

Fully coated, they lay on wooden reclining chairs. After a quiet time breathing the clean air and lost in thought she said, "Thank you for your suggestions yesterday. You really helped me with my jet lag."

"I'm glad to hear." He'd done something for her, and they both valued that more than she could express.

After a while it was time to begin sloughing the mud off. They moved to the cavelike rock formation where the spouts of showers awaited. "It's best if you rub as much as you can while it's still dry so there's less thickness to wash off. See?" She vigorously rubbed one area of her arm, watching the now-powdery clay fall from her skin. He did the same. Then they turned on the showers and let the rest of the mud glide down their bodies and swirl into the drain. "We'll finish washing up at the casita." Their time here was coming to a close. Tonight they were headed out on a late flight to Bangkok, onto the next, and last, spa.

CHAPTER EIGHT

JACKSON TURNED ON the casita's outdoor shower with its privacy and unforgettable mountain view so they could finish getting the mud off. He took a mental snapshot as he would remember this place for the rest of his life. This whole trip had already been an unexpected odyssey. What he was learning about himself as well as spa. He slipped off his still-muddy swim trunks and tossed them into the woven laundry hamper provided. Naked, he turned to Esme, aware that removing the small piece of fabric from his body actually presented a dilemma. He could tell that he'd aroused her by applying the mud, the way they'd talked to each other with their hands instead of words. And he certainly couldn't hide the physical effect she'd had on him. Was she comfortable being nude around him? There was no choice but to find out. She removed her bathing suit and he tried to keep from gawking at the parts of her he hadn't seen bare. Sort of. He was overwhelmed with a desire for the freedom, to take the action that his heart so wanted.

Unable to not, he guided them both under the showerhead and he took her face in his hands. He kissed her lips, lightly, then again until each kiss was slower than the last. He put his arms around her, hands stroking up the length of her back. The more mud that washed off, the softer she felt. He held her to him closely but not tight, just taking in the totality of the moment. Here, with her. It almost didn't seem real, this new life he'd stepped into the moment he returned to the Sher after his long absence. It was only the job of washing the mud off of her body that kept him grounded on earth. Otherwise, he might have floated up into the white clouds that dotted the bright blue sky.

"We're doing it again." He felt it necessary to label the moment, to make sure he wasn't coercing her.

"I want to make love with you, Jackson. Just once. We can handle that, can't we? We know what we're doing."

"I've wanted you every moment of every day since I came into the Sher." He kissed the lips that were glistening wet from the shower. "Yes, once, and only once, then we'll never taste the danger again." He had to have her. A promise of only once made sense. Then, with their itches scratched, they'd go on to a long and prosperous partnership. It would be a matter of will that they were both capable of.

He began wide swipes with his hands across her sides and lower, washing away every speck of mud until impulse had him move to the front of her. His hands held her breasts before his eyes did, round, firm, sized for a precious handful. The hiss of his inhale let her know she had his rapt attention. He'd dare not reach down between her thighs, not yet anyway. They had until late night to board their flight to Bangkok.

He was not going to rush this moment that they promised would be a one-time memory. He knew it would be his greatest treasure, forever.

His lips trailed to her neck and when he moved her wet hair aside to kiss and nip there, she let out a small moan of pleasure that gushed through him. His mouth traveled to kiss those inviting breasts, first with wisps down the outer side of one, then the other. Then his mouth longed for, and found, a nipple which he tickled with the tip of his tongue at least a thousand times. When his teeth returned to her throat, her head fell back to receive him again.

"Jackson," she barely murmured, "that feels so good."

"Thank you for telling me so." He did love making love even though he'd previously compartmentalized it as recreation with no emotional involvement. He'd barely witnessed any physical contact between his parents, who were always walking out the door to a meeting or some such. His father never sat him down and talked to him about anatomy or contraception, leaving that to the little bit of health education that was taught in schools. Nor did anyone ever talk to him about how to treat women. Gentlemanly behavior, yes, but not intimacy matters such as consent and consequences and attachments. He was left on his own with all of that. Perhaps a little more information in that regard might have helped him recognize who not to marry.

But by about age sixteen, when he was expected to participate in the family business, he found himself at functions and charity events where well-to-do women who were twice his age took interest in him and introduced him to sexuality. To some wild escapades, in fact. For example, making love on the rooftop of a forty-story building in Manhattan at two o'clock in the morning. Through being with older women who easily communicated their proclivities and needs better than less experienced younger women, he learned a valuable lesson. That sex was much more pleasurable to him if it was equally pleasurable to the woman he was with. He made up his mind to become a skilled and perceptive lover.

Those women, some married or divorced or career-focused, were as careful as he was not to form any taboo emotional involvements. He broke no hearts nor had his heart broken until Livia, who swindled him into thinking they *had it all*—the business, a passionate love and a genuine connection. How gullible he'd been, perhaps starved after all of those meaningless encounters with other women and the chilly home he grew up in.

Now it was Esme who was presenting him with a test to all of his rules and regulations. He felt something toward her that with Livia was only a facade. The pulling in his soul that told him he might want to actually be with her, to be a melded couple that moved through life together. *Together* together. Which was an unsafe place for him to be. He couldn't have his heart broken again. All of this traveling with Esme, seeing things as if through only one lens, natural partners in every sense of the word, was making him reconsider what he'd resigned to, whether he wanted to or not. He really didn't mean for this closeness to be developing between them, yet it was. Like destiny. Like fate.

His mouth captured hers again to merge under the shower into their fullest, most urgent kisses yet. She wrapped her arms around his neck and he ran his hands along the expanse, from her shoulder to her elbows to her wrists.

"Yes," she moaned. "Oh, heavens, yes."

A smile cracked his lips as his hand trailed down her side and slipped between her legs. She gasped. He held her in the palm of his hand, letting her sex press against it, finding what was good. She buried her face in his neck and her slow train of breath coaxed him to continue. His fingers started a gentle motion and found a groove for her, so he didn't vary it either in speed or in pressure, instead letting her do the moving against his hand, tuning it to her own comfort and pleasure. He himself became rock-hard in the doing. Once she was close to going over the edge, he added kisses to her décolletage until her back arched then she shattered into his hand with a long cry out.

He murmured into her ear, "Magnificent."

After sufficiently washing each other with soapy hands, he shut off the tap and handed her a big fluffy towel in the terra cotta color that was part of the spa's signature logo. "Jackson, I have to tell you something."

"Okay, please do." What did she have on her mind? Even though she'd said she wanted to make love, he wouldn't go any further if she had any hesitations.

"I've never…" Oh, was she going to tell him that she was a virgin? She'd mentioned dating although not having ever been in a serious relationship. He'd imagined that she'd had sex before. Not that he would have minded being her first as she seemed to be enjoying herself so far.

"Yes?" he encouraged her.

"I've never had real lovemaking before. The men I've been with were only interested in their own pleasure, and in achieving it as quickly as possible."

He brushed her hair from her face and smiled with what he hoped was reassurance. "Shall we change that?"

"I think we already have. The way you made my body quake just now was a first for me. I'm sorry I don't have experience pleasing a man, either. Will you tell me what feels arousing to you?"

"I will." He let her lead him into the casita and straight into the bed that had been designated as hers. She laid her naked body in the center of it. "I'll be right back," he said, remembering that he needed to grab protection from his luggage. He dashed into the other bedroom and back as quickly as he could. Then he climbed onto the bed, kissing and caressing her shapely legs along the way.

Hours passed although it seemed like days as he and Esme gave and received. Learning and taking chances. Bringing each other to unimaginable bliss. Finding themselves in positions that were not only unfamiliar to Esme, but were to Jackson as well. While he'd had some profound sexual encounters, ones that he revisited in his mind even years after the fact, those too, were nothing compared to what he shared with Esme in a wooden bed in Mexico with the scent of dirt and flowers wafting in and out of the open windows. Finding out what brought Esme to ecstasy was the most erotic experience he'd ever had. She was more than capable of igniting him without needing instruction. They rose and fell, danced and shook, penetrated, twisted, grasped, held and joined over and over and over again.

After the visit to the heavens and back with Jackson, Esme could see out the bedroom window that dusk was beginning to settle, which meant they only had a few hours left until they departed for Thailand. There was one more thing that she wanted to do before they left Spa Bajo el Sol, a place of such importance to her. Although it wasn't easy, she dislodged herself from Jackson's enveloping embrace and got out of bed. She turned to him. "Come on."

"Where are we going?"

They threw on some clothes and wandered into the main house where, no surprise, Luis was hard at work in the kitchen chopping vegetables. "Do you want to show Jackson where you stayed when you were here?"

"That's exactly where I was headed."

"Take a look at the photos we put up."

Easily remembering her way, she took Jackson's hand and led him through the common areas of the big house to the other side where the bedrooms were. Her old digs were through the farthest door on the left. The room was decorated as all of the house was, with traditional Mexican styling and open windows. A single-sized bed had a colorful blanket and pillows.

"This is it. This is where I slept when I worked here."

Jackson looked around. "Small, but I'm sure you had everything you needed." He noticed a gallery of photos mounted on the far wall and he moved to check them out. He pointed to one and beckoned her over. "Oh, my goodness."

As soon as she spotted the photo he was referring to, she put her hand over her mouth with a giggle. "Yup. Yours truly."

In the photo she was standing behind a seated Luis, her hands on his shoulders giving him a shoulder massage. Cozumel stood beside, squeezing oil from a bottle onto him, the three of them laughing uproariously. Esme even recalled that exact moment. The validation she'd gained here was invaluable to her.

Jackson actually reached out and touched Esme's face in the photo. "What a little beauty you are. How old were you here?"

"Let's see. I'm thirty-two now, so I was twenty-two."

She glanced at the other photos on the wall. They were of other young practitioners the spa had employed over the years, happy faces of every race, creed and color. Cozumel and Luis made it a habit to employ industry workers seeking experience. She used to joke that it was because they had no children of their own.

"You were just a babe." Jackson stayed focused on her picture.

"Yeah, but I was licensed by then."

"Could you teach me a little bit about how to give a massage? I mean, obviously it would take years to develop the skills you have, but would you show me how to do something simple?"

"Why?"

"It would be such a gift to make people feel transformed the way you do."

Oh, he'd made her feel plenty good just a while ago in the casita. What Jackson did to her very being. He lifted her to the spirits, taking her to a celestial high. It was a lifetime's worth of sensual information in only one encounter. Besides him having some sort of mystical skill at knowing her body, they had a desperation for each other that had to be fulfilled. Still, she'd bet he'd have a pretty fine touch for those basic massage strokes.

"Okay. Lie down face down on the bed." He stretched his gorgeous body out and she knelt at his side. "Even though you claimed you weren't that impressed with the massage in Stockholm, what do you remember about it?"

"That massage therapist was intense. I didn't like the way he looked at you."

"What? I mean about the work he did. How did he look at me?"

"Like you were prey."

"I doubt that." She'd barely paid attention to him, she was so busy trying to make sure Jackson had a positive session.

He considered her words, seeming to replay the session in his mind. "Well, in any case, I got a bad vibe from him."

"How about his skills?"

"He had some good moves."

"Name one."

"His palms along the sides of my torso. It was a kind of lengthening that was pleasant."

"Like this?" Esme demonstrated on Jackson's body. "It's called effleurage."

"Yeah. Can I try it on you?" The man who started off saying he didn't value touch wanted to practice some technique. Everything but everything seemed to be changing in the winds.

She had to admit this was fun. And of all places, in the house where she'd spent two years learning and growing. She gave Jackson a gentle push to make room for her on the bed and then he was the one to kneel beside her. He rapidly glided his hands along her torso.

"Okay, first of all you've got to slow that down." He attempted again but this time he was using the tips of his fingers. "Not with your fingers, use your palms."

She let him try a few more times, offering pointers with each attempt.

"This isn't easy."

"You see what we mean if someone has a particularly good touch. It takes hundreds of hours to master a protocol."

He kept trying, genuinely paying attention to her tutorial and improving with every stroke.

"That's nice, Jackson. What you have to do is learn from my body's response. Am I melding into your hand or are my muscles resisting?" He'd certainly gotten that one right at the casita. Was she really never going to have that with him again?

"It's so much more complicated than it looks."

"It is at that." Were they still talking about massage?

Eventually, they ended up lying next to each other on their backs, holding hands and staring at the ceiling, the sky outside now pitch-black. They might have slept there all night.

However, they had a plane to catch.

"Welcome to Thailand," Esme said, peeling her gaze away from the airplane window after she'd watched their descent into Bangkok. It had been a couple of years since she'd been in the country and she was looking forward to showing Jackson about traditions that particularly resonated with her.

She was also glad to be seeing Hathai Sitwat, owner of the world-renowned Spa Malee, which translated as *flower spa*. In fact, as soon as they made their way off the plane and to the baggage claim area, their host was there waiting for them. She was a curvy woman with lush black hair, wearing a vibrant print dress. After all the hellos and introductions Hathai said to Jackson, "I visited the Sher when I was last in New York. It's a magnificent building."

"Thank you. It meant a lot to my parents."

"Precious gifts," she added, "things that were important to family that came before us." Given that most of what Esme remembered from her parents was their selfishness, she could only raise her eyebrows at Jackson. He seemed to understand her with a reassuring single nod. Lack of modeling healthy and caring relationships was, unfortunately, a childhood similarity that they shared at this point.

They took in the sights and sounds as their host

drove them through a very lively and traffic-congested Bangkok. Hathai insisted that they stay at her house while they were in town. After turning down a street here and another there, Hathai entered the gate codes to access the front driveway, which was redolent with many colors of plants and flowers. Her home itself was a natural paradise.

Esme said, "This is incredible."

"I used to live in a high-rise apartment right by the spa," she explained. "It became unsustainable to never have quiet, to not hear a bird chirp. It was important for me to make the best use of my off time as possible."

"Yet you're still in the city."

"The best of both worlds. While I wait for grand-children." Hathai was divorced with two grown sons. Had Jackson thought about children and grandchildren? Esme couldn't help but feel that this trip with him had opened her eyes. That it wasn't just a strategic move to win her the directorship at the Sher. That it was bring-ing her whole self into the light. And she wondered if it might be doing the same for him.

They entered the large house and Hathai showed them to their rooms. While they nibbled some snacks, Esme couldn't take her eyes off Jackson. She'd watched him sleep on the plane, taking her time to indulge in studying his face. In repose he looked different than when they'd made passionate love, the feral, urgent burn in his hungry eyes so untamed she thought she'd orgasm from just gazing into them. As exquisite as his big dark eyes were, there was art in them asleep as well. His face took on a calm that she didn't see while he was awake. With his lips slightly parted and the tiny whoosh of air that accompanied every exhale, he was a sight not unlike one of the world's wonders.

She hadn't slept on the flight again, and was moving forward on fumes. That and the memory of the love-making she'd never forget. Esme had had sex with a few men, slipping out of bed when they were done, out the door before morning as she let her actions speak for her. That she was done. Although that kind of conduct would now forever be in question should she ever again think to have unsatisfying relations with anyone else, so mind-altering was her interlude with Jackson.

Her body quivered just thinking about it now as she picked one of the slices of mango laid out on a plate. She slid a slippery, ripe and fragrant piece through her lips. How she wished she could slip half of the mango slice into Jackson's mouth while keeping the other side in hers and let them take slurpy bites of the juicy fruit until their mouths met in the middle.

Fantasy aside, she was well aware that she'd been walking on a dangerous wild side when she'd told Jackson that she wanted to make love with him. Once. Of course, in fairness to her, she had no way of knowing that doing so would be so spectacular it would send her into a daze she might never return from. How was she going to keep her vow that she was allowed a one-time exploration and nothing more? Her second bite of mango was more of a frustrated chomp.

The car ride was quick to Spa Malee. "Oh, this is so much like the Sher," Jackson noted to Hathai right away, given that the facility was located upstairs in a commercial building in a tony part of town. Also like the Sher, the spa had a separate entrance, an unassuming front door that was either opened by code or through a phone app. There was a small elevator, same as the Sher.

"Well, here's where the similarity ends," he said when the elevator door opened.

They exited to a small foyer, just big enough to hold a wooden bench topped with a couple of colorful cushions. Ambient sound of rainfall made the space seem farther from the street than it was. It was a perfect nook for someone who needed to sit for a moment as a transition. A side table had a pitcher of water with a stack of small metal cups. Art on the wall was traditional.

Esme said, "That's what I was saying about the Sher. The elevator opens to a sleek and exclusive New York property. Instead, I'd like clients to have a total magical paradise as soon as they arrive."

"Agreed," Jackson said.

After they stepped inside that door, Hathai gestured for them to remove their shoes and place them in the cubbies provided. Jackson's eyes began a three-hundred-and-sixty-degree survey of the lobby. "My, my," he uttered. Long panels of intricately carved wood adorned some of the walls. Others displayed paintings of the sun, the moon and stars. There were clusters of teakwood furniture with pillows covered in brilliant-colored silk fabrics, deep blues and bright yellows. Succulent green plants and fresh flowers were everywhere, creating the most delightful scent.

"The bare floor with all the wood and greenery gives it such an open look," he said.

Esme was glad Jackson could appreciate what a stunner this spa was.

Hathai said, "Let me take you in. When a guest enters, we always greet them with tea or water." She discreetly pointed to a group of four women who were enjoying tea and laughter. "We have soundproof glazing on the windows so that in here we can disassociate from everything outside. And focus on being in a healing oasis."

"Hathai," Jackson asked, "when we were driving here through the city streets, and just like in New York, you see Thai massage businesses everywhere. With a sign outside listing prices, often much lower than for a spa. What is different about Spa Malee? I looked at your menu and of course you have high-end prices, appropriate for a luxury establishment like this."

"I think you answered your own question, Jackson." Hathai brought them to a semicirclular area of treatment rooms with more woods and silks. "In a street corner business, there are many people receiving massage in the same room. One next to the other. It's not at all private and it's not personalized for each guest. You could almost think of it as an assisted-movement class, comparable to yoga. Which isn't to say there's anything wrong with that. It shows us that this is medicine in Thailand, as it has been for thousands of years. It's part of a health care system for physical and energetic well-being. We advocate for those small studios. In fact, I own a dozen of them throughout the country where people who don't have the funds can receive treatment for free."

"What Hathai has established here," Esme added, "is the lavish secluded world of the day spa combined with a wellness center. That's what I want us to do at the Sher."

Ideas were solidifying in Esme's mind. Her concept for the spa she wanted. Something she'd mulled over for a long time but hadn't been in a position to execute. Bringing together all of these traditions from across the globe and creating a unique place like none other in New York. And the vision had now come to include Jackson, who had suddenly become her partner, her friend and one time, therefore, former lover. Everything seemed possible.

Hathai said, "We have chosen the finest of materials and furnishings for this spa, our flagship, and we hire only extensively experienced practitioners. Please," she invited and gestured with her arm to usher them into a treatment room.

"Welcome to utopia," Jackson said as he again took in the palatial surroundings.

"Please meet Aroon." A small man entered holding a big wooden bowl filled with flower petals and water. Esme knew right away that Hathai had called in this practitioner over another because he was small in stature, so that if he deemed to give Jackson the pressure technique of standing on his back, his weight wouldn't be a burden to bear.

Aroon put the flower bowl down on a small table that held a stack of white towels. He invited Jackson to take a seat in a cushioned throne-like chair. "At Spa

Malee we have a special welcoming ritual to let you know how glad we are that you are here."

Again, Esme thought of what saying those words to a client in New York might mean, that level of welcome to someone who was sick or had an ongoing health issue, or to someone who didn't have a lot of touch in their life, or even to someone who was just burnt-out and needed personal attention.

Aroon set the bowl of water and flower petals down on the floor in front of Jackson, and dropped to his knees. Gently lifting one of Jackson's feet, he placed it in the water and began to use his fingers back and forth to brush one foot with the water, and then the other. Esme and Jackson smiled at each other, her knowing he was as grateful as she was to be sharing this together.

CHAPTER NINE

JACKSON WAS DEFINITELY in unfamiliar territory. Esme's world of the healing arts wasn't anything he'd ever contemplated. The people he'd met in the past few days were truly remarkable. While Aroon rubbed his feet with flower petals, strange as both a sensation and the unfamiliar setup of this tiny man kneeling at his feet, he couldn't take his eyes off Esme, who was observing the proceedings as if she was judging the accuracy. Making sure he was being attended to correctly. More of her caretaking instinct again.

In Oaxaca he'd had a chance to show her that she could be the one taken care of sometimes. He was still elated to reflect back on the satisfaction he felt from her cries of pleasure and her tight grip that begged him to continue whatever he was doing, a request he was only too delighted to oblige. He tried to close his eyes for a moment just to take in the sensation of the water at his feet, but it was too agonizing to take his gaze off her. Something was rising in him that he didn't ask for but had arrived nonetheless.

His feelings for her were long past employee and employer, no matter how many times he proclaimed that, and even past two single people who'd decided to give themselves to each other for one coupling. No, Jackson was starting to settle in to Esme being a permanent presence in his life. One he wanted to have around him all the time. He could see them as both business and life partners, could visualize a life in New York where he stayed put and they moved forward step after step after step into a reality he'd never expected, especially after his divorce. He blinked his eyes a few times to try to come back to the moment.

He was so glad that before they'd left Oaxaca, he'd asked her to teach him a tiny bit of her considerable repertoire. It would be useful for him to think about the work from the practitioner's point of view as well as the client's.

"We work holistically," Hathai said from where she stood back to avoid interfering. "Some people know it as part of the Indian system of Ayurvedic health, or as traditional Chinese medicine, in which the energy lines in the body become blocked or diseased as opposed to having a healthy flow. It has also to do with acupressure points."

Esme added, "Aroon will move and stretch you in a way that is also known as assisted yoga."

With that, Aroon had Jackson lie face down on the mat on the floor. "Thai massage is done on the floor and with the recipient wearing loose and comfortable clothing. And we use no oils. Very unlike Western massage," Hathai said. Aroon began pressing Jackson's feet with his open palms. And then his legs and arms, which was to awaken his energy.

"It's thought that this type of bodywork might have originated with Buddha's own physician twenty-five hundred years ago, who learned from Indian medicine and integrated it into a regime for good health. The process helps with circulation, mobility, strengthening the immune system, even anxiety and headaches."

As they spoke, Aroon began pulling on Jackson's legs, grasping him with remarkable strength for a man his size. "The giver and the receiver become very connected during the treatment. Jackson, I can see your muscles releasing, perhaps because your body is following Aroon's instincts."

He stretched, then compressed, then rocked each limb, indeed putting Jackson's body into yoga-like positions. And there was more surrender involved when Aroon did walk on Jackson's back, steadying himself by holding on to an apparatus hung from the ceiling for specifically that purpose. Eventually, Aroon ended the session by pulling on Jackson's toes and fingers and ears. It was an unforgettable experience. No wonder it was Esme's favorite type of massage.

For someone who had little regard for massage, he'd undergone a metamorphosis. He hadn't had as much tightness as he had when he'd been to Dr. Singh's office. Although they'd been busy, it had indeed been a much-needed vacation from his usual grind. He suspected it had more to do with Esme's company than anything else. Nonetheless, his respect for these serious disciplines was profound.

"Okay, you sold me. That was incredible."

They decided to go out and enjoy some of Bangkok. Neither knew the city well.

Esme said, "I've never gone to the floating markets."

"Me, either. I know they've become more tourist attraction than anything else but I'd like to go."

Hathai recommended a famous one. Jackson knew that the floating markets used to be the main method by which food and other goods were transported along the country's rivers and canals. Because people settled near them, the culture of riverside shopping was essential to the city's livelihood. Nowadays, shoppers would find fruits and vegetables and a myriad of cooked food and sweets, also clothes, crafts and souvenirs. He quickly arranged for a private boat and driver, and they got to the riverfront and set sail.

"Wow, look at how many boats are on the river."

Indeed, dozens of vessels navigated their way in and around each other. "What do you want to eat? That was my ulterior motive," he said with a wink.

"They say Thailand has the best fruit in the world." She pointed to merchants on the riverbank selling fresh fruit. There was more of the ubiquitous mango, looking as inviting as it had on the platter Hathai served them earlier. Also on display were unusual fruits like mangosteen, with its dark shell and tender white segments inside. Rambutan, with its red spiky rind. The beautiful dragon fruit, white fleshed with black seeds inside surrounded by a vivid purple outer skin. And the famous durian, which was to be a love-it-or-hate-it item because of its extreme smell.

"What do you want to start with?"

"We'll have fruit after. Let's start with something spicy."

"Like you." He didn't necessarily mean to say that but it tripped from his mouth. The sun-kissed highlights of her hair glistened and her lips looked as juicy as the fruits vendors cut and sold in clear bags at the riverbanks. He followed his impromptu comment with an impromptu kiss, something he'd been working on holding back from all day at the spa as he didn't want to make Esme uncomfortable. Among the chatter and commerce of people in the boats and along the banks, conversing, bargaining, yelling out to each other, he kissed her succulent lips again and again, not able to pull away, as if his very life depended on it.

His hands lifted to hold her smooth cheeks, both their faces moist from the natural humidity. He wanted to find a way to join their bodies together, to become not two but one entity, the sum most definitely more potent than its parts. He glued his mouth to hers until they had to break away to catch their breaths and return to a stasis. Jackson noticed the boat driver had his head slightly bowed, which he was sure was in politeness to not watch the two of them kiss and to try to conceal the sweet smile that their display brought to his lips. Even a couple of vendors in boats alongside them giggled in approval.

"So. Spicy. Food, that is."

"I want to try boat noodles," she stated decisively. They saw the boats where pots of noodles were being prepared right on board. Their driver brought them close enough to one of the vendors to make a purchase and they could hardly wait to dig in.

"Oh, my gosh, these are scrumptious," he exclaimed after two bites.

"The broth is so flavorful with both the beef and the pork meats, the dark soy and the chilis."

"I want this every day. We'll have to find a place in New York that makes them well." *We'll* have to. Hmm, he was referring to that as if it was the most obvious thing in the world. *We*. Like they were a typical foodie couple who might travel throughout the New York boroughs in search of new tastes. Was that what was happening? He could no longer imagine a different reality. A New York without Esme. Kissing anyone else on the streets of Stockholm. Of making passionate, rapturous love after the mud bath in Oaxaca. Eating these very noodles on this very boat with someone other than her. Unthinkable.

"Okay, but we have to find somewhere authentic in Queens or somewhere. No fancy-schmancy."

Esme had opened up a door he thought was closed. He felt her in his bones. His priorities had changed. Her. It was her. Sharing boat noodles wasn't supposed to fill his heart. It was noodles, for heaven's sake. But everything with her made him stand up and take heed. He wasn't just pushing through anymore. He was awake and alive. A boat came by and the merchant was selling mango with sticky rice and coconut milk, a most perfect dessert after the strong flavors they'd just eaten. Esme bought a bowl and with her fingers, she fed him a piece of the ripe and luscious fruit. It was the sweetest thing he'd ever tasted.

* * *

Esme was sure she was in a dream, or watching a movie. This couldn't be fact. That she was kissing Jackson in a riverboat in Bangkok. Jetting around the world, visiting spas and kissing and now fitting in some tourist pleasures. Pleasures. After fantasizing about it, had she literally picked up a piece of mango and fed it into Jackson's lips? Her fingers tingled from the contact with his mouth, making her want to feed him all the mango in the world and lick the juice that remained on his lips.

He ran the tip of his tongue around his mouth after another bite of fruit. Was that just cruel, forcing her to witness that? Could a person be jealous of a mango? It got to touch his lips and tongue. Well, that was just it, she thought. She had no claim on those powerful lips, a mouth that had made her body shudder for hours. The mango didn't have to ask her permission for his lips. Still, she looked at the glistening orange slices and scowled at them. How dare they?

"Why don't we do an event for the investors when they're in New York for the meeting?" she said quickly, nudging her mind off of lucky mango slices. "We can do it big with some nice food and decorations and give them some mini-treatments. I can do a presentation about benefits and ancient treatments. It'll be great."

"I love how confident you are about this."

"I've been honing this concept for a while. I just didn't think my opportunity was actually coming right now. It's all presenting itself in my mind. I want to focus on women's wellness." She was more used to disappointment, so she didn't get her hopes up about things. Parents in the throes of a fight with each other had tried to bribe her loyalty with promises of a special gift or shopping money. Then once the argument was over and they were back to short-lived bursts of basic decency toward each other, the promises to Esme were forgotten. So she didn't know when her specific scheme for running a spa was going to come to fruition but now she knew it would be someday. Maybe simply saying that good things come to those who wait was real?

"An event is a great plan. The investors love razzle-dazzle."

Wasn't it okay if she gave him another kiss? Yes, she'd vowed to avoid a personal life and the potential hurt it could bring. But that thinking had become ridiculous and limiting. Was it possible that life had made a seismic shift for her? That by spending all of this time with Jackson she could understand just how good it could be to be a *we* under the right circumstances. That what she needed was someone to believe in her, who wouldn't drag her down and take more than they gave. Maybe she needed Jackson. To get her out of her rut and see herself through his eyes and with that, she could conquer the world. Jackson had enriched her life beyond measure, not stolen from it. Maybe *alone* had been a defensive mechanism that she didn't need to hang on to anymore.

She hadn't forgotten that when she was a young child her mother had told her that she'd once wanted to have a career, perhaps go to college. Then she'd met Esme's father and because there was just enough family money to live on, he talked her out of it. They soon had Esme and became nonfunctional, rarely leaving their apartment and teaching Esme to manage their needs as soon as she was old enough. Her mother never took even the smallest step to encourage Esme to pursue the dreams that she herself hadn't.

Could it be that history didn't repeat itself? Couldn't Esme make the jump? Break the mold?

She'd be lying if she didn't admit that spectacular lovemaking was part of the picture. Jackson had coaxed more sensation, awareness and sensitivity than her body had ever known. And she wasn't afraid to be impulsive with him, to do what felt natural and spontaneous, with her own lips, her hands, every part of her. Even though she said they'd satisfied their urge to explore each other and wouldn't do it again, she mentally tossed that rule over the boat and watched it float down the river in between merchants selling pad thai and T-shirts. Yes, she could let him in a little closer. Maybe she'd never devote herself to someone and the risk and obligations that might entail. But she could do this. Have this time with an accomplished and sensual man. She deserved the progress of it. She could keep that separate from long-term worries.

She leaned over and took one of his earlobes between her teeth. The sumptuous dark rumble that came out of him was electrifying. She opened her mouth to let her tongue trace his ear, enjoying that one small move to its fullest. "Jackson," she whispered.

"Yes."

"I have an idea of what I want to do with the rest of this mango." She gestured to the bowl she'd set down on the boat's bench.

"Is that right?"

"Mmm-hmm," she said with a kiss to the private spot behind his ear. "But I'm going to have to show it to you back at the house." Hathai had evening plans and wouldn't return home until late.

CHAPTER TEN

"Do you want to stop?" Jackson asked while taking off Esme's shirt when they got back to the house. They had dropped their belongings and purchases on the table and then crashed into an embrace, grabbing for each other tightly, as if their lives depended on it. Did they?

"No." She appreciated his little verification of her consent, but stopping was not an option. Not while his bites, one after the other, were making a line from her jaw down to where her throat met her shoulders. Her back arched at the sensation. His mouth was both commanding and questioning at the same time, wanting her to tell him more and more. She crooked her neck in the opposite direction to allow him wider access and a moan escaped her vocal cords when he took it. "I definitely don't want to stop."

He continued with his slow, erotic mouth for as long as she wanted him to. She remembered a time with a guy named Rob she'd been with for a few dates. It had actually been the first and one of the only times she'd really experienced sexual pleasure with someone. However, as soon as he noticed her responding to what his hands were doing to her, he pulled away, as if her enjoying it meant she was finished. With Jackson, it was a green light to keep going, and he seemed to relish doing so.

"Esme," he exhaled with a desperate gratification when she unbuttoned his shirt in return. It was equally exciting to know that she was arousing him, also not something she'd ever had validation of before.

And then their motions became like two flowers in bloom, her throat, his shirt buttons, opening, releasing, bending toward each other.

"We said we wouldn't do this again."

"Yup."

"Yup."

They issued their one-syllable protective thought but didn't halt what they were doing even for a second. After the kiss in Stockholm, they'd decided. In Oaxaca they changed that to a one-time license to be intimate. Now here they were, defying that rule, unable to keep away from each other.

How was it that, instead, she felt liberated by Jackson? Perhaps because of all the respect he'd shown her, relying on her professionally, making all that she'd been through to get to this point worthwhile. The quick trip around the world with him was the stuff of fantasy. They'd both had a rebirth and both were still forming, finding their new shapes. That fit into each other. She hadn't even realized how much she needed the affirmation he'd given her.

At the moment, though, after she'd peeled his shirt off his body, her mind was on a quick dash to the table to get the sliced mango they'd bought on the market

boat that she'd brazenly promised to continue employing in a private way.

"Oh, yeah, you said there was more about that
mango."

She took a piece of the fruit from its bag and held it
between her teeth. She approached him and wrapped
her arms around his neck to bring him closer. Then she
used the piece of mango to draw a line with its juices
starting from his Adam's apple and heading downward.
The journey was such a turn-on to her, painting him
with the mango, marking him, if only for the moment,
as hers. She moved slowly down his solid chest, still
gripping the fruit with her teeth. When she'd painted
that line all the way down to the top of his pants, the
task was complete. She coaxed him down into the chair
behind him.

"Now what?" His smoldering stare asked the question.

"It seems to be true that Thailand grows the sweetest
fruit in the world." She could hardly believe the words
coming out of her mouth, so sexual with a courage that
she was half faking but somehow believing that if she
acted that way it would become so. She leaned over
him in the chair using her hands to bolster herself on
the armrests so she could hover over him.

"Delicious. Yes," he graveled out, his voice husky
and sounding like three in the morning. She brushed
her mouth against his but then lowered herself to begin
to taste the sweet juice she'd just painted on him. She
sunk to the top of his pants and took her first lick there.
Indeed, the fruit mixed with the musk that was him

was an absolutely intoxicating combination that made her body undulate this way and that, moving to the music his body made her hear. She used the flat of her tongue to work up his torso. A groan forced its way out of him, a sound he didn't seem to have much control over. "Mmm, that feels ridiculously good."

"I want it to." The charge rattled through her again, him acknowledging that what she was doing was favorable to him. The more he gave back to her in that way, the more she wanted to keep doing it. A focused, long, thin lick up his very center made his head roll back, and his lips parted as his even louder groan filled the room. As did the sheer sensuality. The confidence did become real, her body swaying above him, a full-grown woman aware of her wiles. She felt a whole different person inside when she was with him. She didn't understand such magical powers but they were true.

Then as she covered his mouth with hers, she took the thoughts even further. That she was willing to risk for this. For him. That's what it came down to, wasn't it? Risk? She didn't have a crystal ball to look into the future. Maybe embarking on this partnership with Jackson, the personal one and the professional one, would be a total disaster. Maybe she'd give her all and end up jobless and brokenhearted. At least she would have done something. She'd opened up enough to try. Her heart knew it would be worth it and that if she didn't do it she'd regret it for the rest of her days.

Jackson placed his hands under her arms and pulled them up, kissing them into a lip lock. What was there in life without taking a chance? She, who'd thought it out so carefully, how to avoid being anyone's pawn, evading trust, never planning to relent. She'd grown a hard shell. She thought of it as her protection. But with armor, she wouldn't let things in and she would keep things out. Funny how that had seemed the right thing to do in the past, and now it made no sense at all. It wasn't who she was anymore.

He led them to his guest bed and pulled back the silk coverings. His gaze seared through, almost burning holes in her. But then he changed his expression to a majestic smile. Which said he was present, which might have been saying he needed to take a chance, too.

After they'd showered off the mango and all it entailed, Esme and Jackson were ready to go back out and have an evening before they boarded a flight home to New York the next day. Hathai had recommended a bar where they might want to get a drink.

"It's the famous ex-pat bar," Jackson said as they approached the entrance that was made up of six shutter doors, all open to let in the evening breeze. "The Federal."

"Hathai said it was where the Westerners who live in Bangkok met. Businessmen, volunteers, writers and so on."

"As long as I don't see one more mini-Buddha statue." They'd been bombarded with enough cheesy souvenirs at the floating markets earlier.

They entered and, indeed, they were all Westerners sitting apart from one another. Most of the men were dressed in white shirts and khaki pants as Jackson was, presumably the uniform for the humid weather. There were distinctly more men than women there. All eyes turned to Jackson and Esme when they entered.

"Toronto," one of the men called out to them.

"London," yelled another.

"Perhaps. Too well-heeled for the US West Coast," added another still.

"Or Chicago. But they don't look European." This was obviously a game of Guess the Strangers' Origin being played at their expense.

"Certainly not Aussie," the only man with an outback hat voted in.

"Good evening." Jackson called out, deciding that in good manners they should participate. "What are you basing your guesses on?"

"Nothing whatsoever, mate," said the man who had tagged them as not Australian but his accent suggested that *he* was. "We used to be better at it. We've been in Thailand for too long. The heat has made us stupid." That comment gained a couple of sniggers from around the room.

"We were always stupid, Callum," someone disagreed.

"New York," Jackson answered flatly. One of the men in back began singing about making a brand-new start of it.

"What are you drinking?" asked the bartender, an Asian man who spoke with a British accent.

"Whiskey," Esme called out.

"The lady dabbles in the dark spirits." The man with the Australian accent, Callum, leered at her as he said that. Which ruffled Jackson right away. Was that some sort of flirt? Jackson thought it was rude to comment when a woman walked into a bar with a man. Even more so if she was alone but, nonetheless, he bristled at the unexpected focus on Esme.

He lightly took her elbow, not wanting to seem too possessive, as they made their way in between some empty tables to get to the bar and retrieve their drinks. He sensed this was a pub full of regulars who drank together and were gruff but well intentioned.

"To the Sher." Esme tipped her glass to clink his, seemingly less aware of the vibes in the room than he was.

"To the Sher indeed," he toasted. That she so genuinely cared about the spa moved him.

After they finished their drink, Callum approached Esme, adjusting his hat on his head. Jackson wondered why he wore a hat indoors at all. "Buy you another? Or are you and Mr. New York together? In marital bliss even?" he rasped into Esme's ear, perhaps thinking he was whispering but the volume was well within Jackson's range.

This was getting ridiculous. Was this guy trying to provoke a fight? Maybe that's what drunk ex-pats did when they were bored. The equally boring habit of his jealousy and pessimism crept in. Between the parents that were so icy they'd never even notice the other one's interactions, to the wife that cheated on him with mind, body, soul and wallet, he didn't have much of an example of ethical relationships. He'd made a decision to never need that education, which was how he'd been living for years. Until Esme.

He looked at Callum as if from a distance, in an objective view. Sure, lots of men were going to be attracted to Esme. Why wouldn't they be? She was gorgeous but in a friendly way, wholly approachable. No wonder she was so well suited to the needs of clients. She was also smart and kind. Then he thought of *her* objectively. Even if he was to strip off those bandages that kept his hurt hidden from the sun, was she? After a childhood full of manipulation, she said she'd never take a chance on love. He had no reason to disbelieve her. Well, other than the last few days where they'd been as exposed as they possibly could. Something given openheartedly to each other. Somehow their barricades had been toppled over, despite their best efforts. Did they want to leave them demolished, or build them up again?

Was it only temporary? Were they going to zip up their coats along with their hearts when they got back to New York? Jackson didn't want to. While Livia had destroyed his hope, Esme brought its promise back. Esme was nothing like his ex-wife. He was sure that if she was ever in any kind of liaison with a man she'd be trustworthy and faithful to him, unless they had agreed otherwise. Without even answering the drunk stranger Callum's question as to whether Esme was together with Jackson, he said to her, "Let's go get dinner. Night, all." He laid some money down on the bar. Most of the men growled indifferently.

Jackson ushered them out because he surely didn't

want to spend their last night in Thailand, their last night on this globetrot, dealing with this Callum fellow or his own overreaction. While they'd been inside, it had started to rain. As they walked, he kept checking the expression on her face to see if she was appreciating the walk as much as he was. "Do you want to keep walking in the rain or should we seek cover?"

"I love it. It's refreshing. It's almost sticky on your skin." He wanted to touch her arm, or kiss it even, but they were walking.

"I hope I wasn't wrong in my assumption that you weren't interested in that man's attention?"

"No, but I'm not sure that was a battle I needed fought for me." Obviously, Esme was a very strong person. If she ever was to be with someone, she'd never be the little woman being overpowered by the big possessive male. Her fierce self-sufficiency, born of necessity, was something that was so compelling about her.

"Well, he bothered *me* so I wanted to get away before I provoked him."

In addition to learning about all of the amazing techniques and skills involved in the healing arts of spa, he'd never spent this much time with a woman. Full stop.

"What happens when we get back to New York?" He blurted what he only intended to answer in his mind.

"We put together a quick investor event. I've been texting and emailing with Trevor, and he's already got an event manager and caterer on call."

"I meant us."

"Are *we* an *us*?" They both chuckled at the pronouns.

He reached for her hand to hold as they turned a street corner and said hard things. He needed her palm in his to center himself. Motor scooters, bicycles and cars all fought for territory in the busy evening. "This time with you has completely caught me by surprise. I've told you all the things I had firmly believed were not for me."

"And now?"

He shrugged. "Now, it's a new dawn. This trip made it different. You made it different."

She focused her eyes forward; she needed a minute. He felt unwrapped, even though he hadn't made any declarations. In fact, his thoughts were a jumble as she asked the very thing he didn't know the answer to. "What does happen now?"

"Is that entirely my decision?" His answer was a bit short and he chided himself after he'd said it. But he was confused about what he should dream of. And what would never be.

"Fair point."

It seemed like neither of them were saying what had to be said. What did he really want? "I never imagined that I would care about someone the way I've come to care about you." He saw a flicker in her eyes. "I see now that I'm cutting myself off from too much if I keep myself closed and locked. Which would all just be a bunch of theoretical musings if I hadn't met you. You've changed everything for me. Now I want to explore my heart. I can't see going back to New York to a work-only situation."

"Meeting you has shaken all the pillars that I held

to be true, too. Nobody has ever made me feel so valued. That's a bigger deal than I'd ever thought it was. I assumed I'd be my only cheerleader."

And then he kissed her. In the rain. Their clothes soaking wet and clinging to their bodies. It had only been a few nights since Stockholm but it felt like a lifetime. He and Esme under the sun or the moon or the snow or the stars. Together.

CHAPTER ELEVEN

THERE WERE A million things to do as soon as Jackson and Esme got back to New York. It was good to be busy because everything that happened on the trip had her walking on unsteady ground. The Sher and her managerial duties, and planning the investor event, would keep her mind occupied. Elation propelled her every step but she still wasn't sure what was going to be with Jackson. During the plane ride home they'd committed to a sort of a let's-see policy as neither knew whether they could truly open themselves to the other in the long term.

They'd arrived in the evening and paid a quick visit to the closed spa just to make sure everything was okay. Which, naturally, it was in Trevor's capable hands. Once they turned off all of the lights, set the alarm and went out the door, Jackson voiced a dilemma.

"You know I don't actually keep an apartment in New York. Can I book us a hotel suite or…?" His voice trailed off, not sure how to finish, obviously inviting her to. They hadn't talked about the nuts and bolts of that we'll-see arrangement. Was he going to stay with her? As in day and night, work and…not work?

Instead of overthinking it, she was decisive. Terrified, but putting one foot in front of the next. "Why don't you stay with me? My place is tiny but we're going to be spending a lot of time at the spa."

The most charming grin came across his face, as if she'd given him a gift he'd really wanted. "I would love that." On the little landing outside the spa door, under the safety light that cast a wide glow across their faces, he reached over and wound her scarf around her neck.

"Here we are." The driver dropped them off at the curb in front of her apartment building and they took the staircase to the second floor. "I'm sure it's the size of some people's closet."

"I don't have a home so yours is, by definition, bigger than mine," he said as she opened her front door. He glanced around, at what she thought were tasteful, budget-friendly furnishings. On the wall she had hung two poster-sized photographs, one of rain falling in a forest and another of sunset over a beach. A small smile crossed his lips.

"What?"

"Nothing. These are just so you." He pointed to the posters. "Something to meditate on right up on your walls."

"Don't knock it until you've tried it," she mocksnipped.

They kissed softly and quietly. She rarely had anyone in her apartment, most certainly not a man. She thought his energy might feel oppressive but it was like he belonged. His essence filled the apartment, a kind of fragrance she could never get enough of. Was he a tree that could grow roots? Would he be able to stop chasing himself and settle into her? Would she, him?

She said as she shook her scattered head, "I'm whacked out again from the time change. How about I order a pizza and we can make some quick notes about what we need to do in the next few days so we can get right to it in the morning?"

"Sounds like a good idea."

After they ate and, in fact, outlined an action plan, she went into the small bedroom to put fresh sheets on the bed and lay out some clean towels for Jackson to use. By the time they collapsed into bed, it was the wee hours. Esme was unused to sleeping on one side of the bed rather than in the middle. At first it bothered her and her body tensed. It didn't need to be said that they wouldn't do anything other than sleep tonight, as they were exhausted. But while Jackson fell right to sleep, she kept her eyes glued to the ceiling for as long as she could stand it, and then rolled over to admire him. His gorgeous face was a work of art she could stare at endlessly, the way his features were so perfectly arranged. The long eyelashes, the elegantly sloped nose, the plump lips.

Was she going to play house with this man, and was it really playing after all? If so, it was a dangerous game. If she lost, she could lose big. If Jackson was to further break what was already broken, she didn't know if she'd be able to put herself back together. That's why she'd vowed never to let someone this close. And yet every fiber in her being told her that this would be worth it. *He* was worth it.

Although her musings kept her up most of the night, they had to hit the ground running if they were going to pull off this event before the investors voted on whether to stay involved in the Sher. Prior to their arrival, Esme had asked Trevor to rearrange her office and put a computer and desk in for Jackson so they could work.

"Will this do?" Trevor asked when they came in.

"Perfect, thanks. How are the twins?"

"Exhausting. Every second of it precious." He showed her a photo on his phone of the babies and Omari, whose smile said it all.

Esme and Jackson settled themselves in and began ironing out the details. The board president of the investors group was to come by in a couple of hours so they wanted to give him a mini-presentation of what they were planning.

"We're doing the cacao theme. Like in Oaxaca, everyone likes those tastes and aromas, and it has medicinal value. I can weave it into the food and use it in the treatments. I can even get some scented lotions and lip balms so we can do a gift bag they can take home."

A smile spread across his face. "In a million years I wouldn't have thought of something like that."

"I guess you're pretty lucky to have me around," she joked. She wasn't really joking but she voiced it with a laugh so that she wouldn't sound arrogant.

"In more ways than one," he replied in a flat voice that slid down her sternum. Although, there wasn't time for her to melt into goo.

"Continuing with the theme, of course we'll do a mole with lunch. Tamales would be good but they require a fork and sitting down. Let me think of something easier. I'll text Luis at Bajo el Sol. He'll have some ideas for me." Her mind filled with their time in Oaxaca, the *sobada* protocol, the mud therapy after which they made love for the first time. What a magical place that was. She wondered if Bajo el Sol would always be a touchstone place for her, the smell of the mountains, the almost supernatural treatments. It was perhaps the most unique spa she'd ever been to. She looked forward to the next time she could visit.

"Luis and Cozumel." Jackson smiled to himself, perhaps having a nice memory of his own.

"And we'll do a *tejate*."

"What's that?"

"It's a drink made from cacao and maize. It's high in antioxidants and tastes really rich. And we'll finish with a bittersweet brownie made with coffee and cinnamon or something like that to end on a heavily chocolate note."

"I have to concentrate on the financial prospectus I had my accountant put together. If you don't stop talking about chocolate, we may not have a spa soon."

Trevor's voice came through the intercom, "Brent Lloyd is here."

"Have you met the board president, Brent?" Jackson looked up from his computer screen to ask Esme.

"No, would I have had any reason to?" After all, she was previously only the spa's manager, responsible for things like schedules and supplies. She wasn't involved with investors or long-term planning decisions. Until now. She took a breath so long it started down in her toes and ended above her head. She was at the big table now.

"I'm just printing something. I'll be there in a minute."

"Hello, I'm Esme Russo, the spa director," she said as she approached Brent Lloyd in the reception area. Wow, that was the first time she'd identified herself out loud as director. The sound of it gave her a thrill. Proof that hard work and perseverance paid off. She was an unlikely success story. Who couldn't wait to pay it forward, to give someone else the break they needed to grasp their goals. She intended to start with Trevor. And then maybe her own children someday? Hers and Jackson's?

As to Brent Lloyd, did she perceive the tiniest wince on his face when he shifted his weight from one hip to the other? He was a salt-and-pepper-haired man, nice looking with aging skin, wearing a fine leather jacket atop his dress pants.

"Brent, if you don't mind me asking, are you in pain?" His body language all but announced that something wasn't right. She always pointed out observations like that and would continue to whether to prince or pauper or board president.

"How did you know?" he asked in surprise.

"I can see it in your stance."

"Can you? I have lower back pain. It's been worse lately."

"Do you spend a lot of time on a computer?"

"Yeah, hours upon hours. Seven days a week."

"Is it a stabbing pain or a dull ache?"

"Ache."

"I may be able to relieve the pressure a bit. Do you want me to give it a try?"

He rubbed his lower back, which caused him enough discomfort that his jaw clenched. "Sure. Anything would help."

She invited him to take his jacket off and sat him down in one of the chairs. She began some long strokes the heel of her palm to his lower back, the lumbar section, then used the tips of her thumbs to add more pressure.

"Tell me if I'm creating pain because that's the last thing we want to do." She pressed in but kept it gentle and could feel each small area she worked on loosen up. "There we go. Do you do physical therapy or get massages?"

"I used to. Then once I get busy, things like that just fall by the wayside."

She concentrated on a particularly tensed-up spot.

"Thank you, I can feel the difference already."

"So can I talk you into booking some treatments at somewhere convenient for you?"

"I live upstate but I'll have my wife make some appointments for me. I don't know why I stopped doing the thing that was helping." He let out a chuckle and she joined him.

"We all think we're too busy. Believe me, I hear that from a lot of people. Do you do any stretching?"

"Another thing I've let lag."

"Or applying heat or ice, or both?"

"Now you're making me look bad."

She smiled and glanced up from Brent to see Jackson standing in the office doorway as if frozen. His eyes bore into her but not in the sensual way they had been for the past couple of days. No, his look was equal parts fury and shock.

"Jackson, what's wrong?"

After a long day's work, Jackson and Esme decided to go for a walk. They ambled without talking through Tribeca up to Greenwich Village, passing shops, restaurants, galleries and all Manhattan had to offer. Jackson was agitated, not from the excitement of the city but because he hadn't gotten over what he witnessed earlier at the spa.

"Are you going to tell me what's bothering you so much?" Obviously, his mood was palpable.

"It's madness."

"So, it's madness. If it's real to you, it matters."

He loved that she said that but was he going to tell her things that he considered shameful? If he was ever going to change and be able to commit to her, he'd have to. And he wanted to. He did want to.

"You've been off the whole afternoon."

Did anything escape this woman? It didn't seem so! "When Brent Lloyd came in and you were touching him, I felt that jealousy I can't seem to control. Which I know is destructive."

"Are you kidding me, Jackson?" He could hear the annoyance in her voice. "I could see he was having some pain. I offered to help him out."

"That's what I assumed." His face became hot. He

was embarrassed. His ire had risen in Bangkok with the pushy Australian man at that pub. He'd even had a twinge in Stockholm when he felt that massage therapist Anders's eyes had lingered on Esme for too long. "Brent is a good guy, president of the board, I've known him for years. But when I saw the two of you…my mind just spiraled back to… I know it makes no sense."

"To what, specifically?"

"To my ex-wife. Not only that she had cheated on me both in business and with other men. The whole idea of trust. When I saw you with Brent it was like you had been deceiving me or doing something behind my back."

"Because I was touching a man in a professional capacity?"

"I told you. My suspiciousness is sometimes so fierce it feels like it could eat me alive."

He could tell by the set of her face that she was troubled, maybe even angry. This was really his moment of reckoning. The time had come. He knew he'd stay alone and bitter unless he broke free of the past. They walked at least three blocks again without a word.

Esme broke the silence with, "After my parents used me in their war games, I'm not playing anymore."

"You shouldn't have to."

Washington Square Park came into view, with its famous arch. NYU students gathered in pairs and groups, exuberantly talking and gesturing. Others sat alone, studying or typing furiously into their phones. People walked dogs. Older men played chess. Tourists posed for photos with the arch in the background. Jackson wanted to be part of this pulsing New York. To make a life in a truly great city with this magnificent woman. Could he possibly get out of his own way?

"Jackson," she began and turned her head to look at his face while they walked, "I want to move forward with my life. Going on the trip with you, our arrangement about me becoming spa director, the positivity heading me in the right direction. There's something I haven't told you."

"What's that?"

"I didn't need to stay at the Sher for four years before applying for directorships. After a year or two and all of my previous experience, I'd learned enough and I had the right ideas."

"Why did you stay?"

"Because while I project myself as confident, I got lost in doubt. I let myself loll. I was tired after thirty-two years of serving others. Even though I wanted to, I didn't really know if I could go further."

"What changed your mind?"

"I needed my confidence boosted. The old days were pulling me back down again. You gave me what I needed."

"Which you deserve."

"That's right, I do. If you care about me, don't hold me back, or let me hold myself back."

"That's the last thing I want to do." He had to do better. He owed it to Esme. He owed it to himself.

A group of young women rushed by, a cloud of squeals and perfume and colorful beanies.

"I'm willing to go further with you than I ever imagined I would with anyone," she said. "But I'm still fragile, and I always will be. I could shatter if injured. So if you can't do this, decide that now. Don't make me put myself in so much danger."

"Of course, I want to. I wish it was as simple as that. Just to have courage and faith."

"You want to start from a place of total *distrust*?"

They both laughed. "Because it's only up from there. Be patient with me." Two dogs barked at each other in greeting. Jackson gave Esme a kiss on her forehead. Horns honked and people walked by. He teased her with an overly dramatic raise of one eyebrow. "What, so you like that Brent Lloyd?"

She pretended to slap his shoulder. "Yeah, I gotta go. I have dinner plans with him."

"You rascal," he said as he pulled her in for a hug. "Seriously, what do you want to do for dinner?"

"Spend it with you being threatened by every move I make."

"That's a great idea. No wonder I named you spa director."

They walked the perimeter of Washington Square Park like tourists, pointing out buildings and trees. Students holding hands while lugging backpacks heavy enough to topple them. Two older men arm in arm as they slowly strolled. A pregnant woman walking alongside a man pushing a stroller with a sleeping toddler in it. Love was in the air in New York. Maybe it had always been, maybe not just in New York but everywhere. She just never thought it would apply to her.

"What do you feel like eating?" he asked as they ambled.

Even that, even him asking a simple question, made the world different. Growing up, she was never asked what she wanted to eat. She was lucky if her parents gave her enough money to get groceries for the three of them, always sending her with a shopping list to adhere to.

"Weren't we going to try to find good boat noodles here, like the ones we had at the floating market in Thailand?"

"Ooh, that sounds great. Let me look it up." He pulled his phone out of his pocket and began swiping a search.

It wasn't going to be an easy task, creating something solid and long-lasting with him. The business with Brent Lloyd earlier was almost more than she could handle. Jackson could see himself in action and explain his rationale yet he couldn't stop those old feelings from resurfacing. He felt some kind of certainty that she'd betray him in some way, trick him, further tarnish his dead parents' disappointment. She couldn't make his problems hers. Although, perhaps that was what a true partnership was, helping to hold each other's monsters.

If she let herself go down a certain path of thinking, it was actually touching that she arose jealousy in him. It was because he wanted her only to himself. Albeit unhealthy and unworkable, it was a measure of devotion. She'd surely never been protected before, which she had to admit was welcome in that bar in Bangkok with that aggressive Australian man. Maybe they could reframe Jackson's behavior into something positive while he hopefully *grew out of it* as time went on and he saw her as loyal. Or maybe that was asking too much of herself. Yet she knew she'd regret it for the rest of her life if she didn't try.

"I've got a couple of places in Queens." He showed her his phone. "Let's try this one tonight and we'll compare it with these others until we find the best one. I'll call a car."

They slid into the small wooden booth in the window of the restaurant. The smells alone were making her hungry. They ordered two different flavors of boat noodles. The server, who was also the owner, nodded approvingly at their ability to dig into the spicy cauldrons of noodles and broth without a flinch. They also ordered Isan chicken.

"We'll take the rest home and have it for lunch."

"What makes you think there will be leftovers?" He smiled and dug into a piece of chicken marinated and coated in spices, grilled to charred perfection.

They sat and shot the breeze, as the saying went. After all that hard stuff with Brent Lloyd earlier, they needed the casual quiet of a window seat and some comforting food in a low-key neighborhood. He'd been right that while their ravenous hunger was satiated, they still managed to pick at the savory chicken until there was none left to take home.

Home. Did he live with her now? It was only their second night back in New York but there had been no further talk of him going to a hotel. Nor did she want there to be. She wanted him wrapped around her. All night long. When they got *home* she washed her face and brushed her teeth. While he was in the bathroom, she turned down the bedsheets and put on some soft music. When he stepped out, she was there to greet him, standing on tiptoe to wrap her arms around his neck. They were finally relaxed, warm, with full bellies and a good workday behind them. She led him to the bed and guided him down. *He* was her new home.

If she could go the distance. As she lay in bed practicing her deep breathing before going to sleep, she made some decisions on her boundaries.

CHAPTER TWELVE

"I WAS GOING to put these out on the front tables," Trevor said as he put the finishing touches on the gift bags for the investor event. "But I think it's too easy for people to forget. I'm having someone taking and returning coats at the door. We could give one to each person when they're leaving."

Esme approved. "Good thinking."

Jackson stepped away from the tech setup he was working on with his marketing people. He came up behind Esme and wrapped his arms around her. "You okay?" he asked. She leaned back into him, knowing she had time for about a twenty-second hug and that was all.

"Yeah." She turned her head back toward him. "You?"

"Ready."

"Go." Lovey time was up. In fact, the first guest arrived, an older woman with white-blond hair.

"Yes, that's a longtime investor." He turned to her. "Millie Abernathy, please meet the spa director and visionary for what we want to do with the Sher, Esme Russo."

Millie's handshake was bony but firm. The woman moved on as someone else came through the door, another woman, this one probably in her forties, with dark hair and skin lacquered with a little too much makeup, in Esme's opinion.

Jackson made introductions. "This is Pia Bravo."

Before Esme could blink, a lively din filled the spa. Guests were served *tejate*, the famous old drink from Oaxaca that had been a refreshment for centuries. People who knew each other reunited while others met for the first time. Out of the corner of her eye she saw Brent Lloyd come in, the man with the lumbar issue that turned out to be a trigger for Jackson. Esme would try her best not to provoke Jackson, but after mulling it over, she wasn't going to be babysitting, or condoning, his behavior. That could only lead to resentment in the end.

"And that's why we invited you to join us today so we can give you a sense of how we see the Sher moving into a highly specialized place of healing that we hope will be cherished by New Yorkers and visitors alike for decades to come," Jackson spoke to the crowd.

Next it was Esme's turn. "Let's gather together and get centered with a simple breathing technique to ground us. Breathe in slowly through your nose," she said to the attentive audience, "and slowly out through your mouth. Concentrate on making it smooth and seamless. In. And out. Today I'm going to explain a bit about the Mayan traditions of *sobada* that we want to become foremost practitioners of." She gave her multimedia presentation, finishing with, "What we're going to do now is give everyone who would like a mini-treatment to get a hands-on sense of what we're doing."

The freelance massage therapists Esme had brought in who knew how to do the Mexican Mayan massages fanned out in the room and invited the investors into treatment rooms and a few makeshift areas they'd created in the common spaces. Of course, it would take years before a therapist could become an expert on a certain technique. This was merely a quick way to introduce the intention and spirit, plus the luxury of the rich and high-quality products used. She'd taught the staff to do a closing ceremony with each person, to wrap them in a makeshift rebozo shawl that they were able to approximate with some scarves Trevor picked up in East Harlem, an area called Little Mexico that had a large population of Mexican residents. They also concluded with a cup of raw cacao, which was thought to have highly medicinal properties.

As she surveyed the event, board president, Brent Lloyd, caught her eye and beckoned her over.

"I want to thank you for your therapeutic touch last time I was here."

"How's your lower back?"

"I wish I could say it was consistently better but it's not with my overuse."

"Can I have a feel?"

"Would you? I'd so appreciate it." She let her hands roam over Brent's lumbar area and inform her of his condition today. Indeed, his muscles were seized up, his body like stone.

"If you could even get one of those hot and cold packs from a local pharmacy, that might help."

He nodded.

Then, she felt it even before she looked up. From in between people mulling about, she sensed Jackson's eyes piercing into her. A lump in her stomach grew so big it almost burst. Because after all of their talk about recognizing negative patterns, where they came from and the relevance they did and didn't have, none of it amounted to anything when actions spoke louder than words.

The look she returned to him was one of anguish. Had all they'd said to each other just been drivel? She should have known that, in the end, they were like children playing dress-up. Despite them sincerely wanting to, the clothes didn't fit. She knew in an instant that they would both lose the match.

"Esme, is something the matter?" Brent noticed that her hands had gone slack, had stopped concentrating on his muscle pain. Jackson's face, contorted, threw daggers at her. The realization sent devastation coursing through her. But she had to keep herself together, with as much will as that took. That's what professionals did.

Yet she couldn't. All she could do was stare back at Jackson while he glared at her through arms holding colorful Mexican shawls. Perhaps both of them coming to the same conclusion. That nothing could work between them if she wasn't free to be herself. She'd thought maybe she cared enough about him to accept him, damage and all. Maybe someone who had herself come from a firmer base could have done it. In the end, though, she was too weak for him.

There was only so much she could do for him while still respecting the promises she'd made to herself. Which let anger slowly bubble up in her body. Because she'd thought they'd found a way to each other. But those seething glares of his were too much, not in their menace but in their sadness, both hurtful and hurt. Her anger quickly blended with sorrow. The notion that she could see his emotional issues clinically, and therefore not have them affect her this much, vanished. She was only human. He drained her. It could only get worse.

"Excuse me," she said to Brent as she stepped away, finding a quiet alcove down the corridor. There, one lone tear dripped out of her eye, which she quickly brushed away with the back of her hand. Two more fell from the other eye. She grabbed a tissue and mopped those with the same vigor, making sure none of the investors could see her.

Jackson knew in his gut. He couldn't put himself or anyone else through this again. Despite how much he wanted to, he couldn't pull himself out of his own wreckage. He'd vowed to never risk again and apparently, he was right to do so. As he'd stood watching Esme talk to Brent Lloyd, the same old thoughts took him over, a speeding train with him tied down on the tracks.

He supposed he'd made some progress. He knew enough not to think there was something untoward going on between Esme and Brent. Although that was only when he could force his rational mind to take the forefront. Because the child's mind, and the young husband's mind, remembered every shard of heartbreak and guilt as if it freshly cracked in him today. If it happened once, it could happen again. Esme would never be able to trust him to trust her. So there was nothing to fight for. It was about more than other men's attention. Their future would be him waiting for her to deceive him as Livia had. She could never tolerate that. Nor should she have to. His ears rang loud and clear to him the simple message that he was alone in the world and that's how he would remain. He was too volatile. He carried too much baggage.

He'd seen Esme slip down the corridor and he moved to find her. A passerby would just assume they were conversing about spa matters.

"I'm sorry," he said as the truth gushed through him like boiling blood through his veins. "I can't do this. I thought I could but I can't."

"I see."

Those sweet green eyes of hers hooded. He wouldn't subject her to him. To deny himself was better than to squelch her. That's how much she meant to him. She didn't need him, suspicious and prying, keeping tabs and not letting her fly free. No one needed that in their life, but especially not Esme, who'd already borne the brunt of other people's misconduct.

He'd let her think it was simple jealousy. That was easier for both of them. Neither having to face that those demons were a disease, a terminal illness. Never again make a bad decision that would let his parents' memory down. Never be taken on an emotional roller coaster where he'd end up feeling used. He wouldn't survive it again. He'd take the safer route. He might have been able to trust her with the spa. But not with his heart.

"It's better for you. And what's best for you is what matters the most to me now."

CHAPTER THIRTEEN

WHILE SOOTHING THE arthritic left hand of Mrs. Abernathy, Esme was determined not to lose her cool. As she worked the woman's joints, she gazed across the room and observed Jackson standing in a little conversational huddle with three other guests.

"Reducing inflammation can have a big impact," she said, her voice airy, not even sounding like herself.

"It feels better." The older woman's voice floated away.

Jackson looked wound up like a rubber band. His shoulders were up to his ears as they were when he'd first come to visit the spa a few weeks ago. She didn't wish him harm but if he'd just said to her in the corridor what he did and he wasn't affected by it, she'd be even more destroyed. If that was actually possible.

Yet he waved her over. She finished with Mrs. Abernathy's hand and joined him at his circle.

"Esme plans to also incorporate some ancient Eastern medicine techniques into our offerings," he told the group, gesturing for her to turn on the spa talk.

"Energy work has been practiced in the Eastern traditions for centuries and can be so powerful for overall health and wellness," she explained for probably the tenth time today. That voice that didn't seem to even belong to her came out as if she was in a trance.

Really, she was holding back the ocean of tears that wanted to burst forth from her eyes, drenching the room, drenching the building, maybe drenching all of New York. The words coming out of Jackson's mouth spoke to the investors of the Spa at the Sher's future. Esme was no longer certain if those plans still included her. Would she even want them to?

"We like what we see so far," one of the investors told Jackson.

Her zombie voice said to someone, "Thank you for coming."

"I'm so sorry," Jackson whispered in her ear as they ushered out the last of the guests.

Was he apologizing for what he'd said to her in the corridor or that he wasn't able to control himself for saying it during the event? She supposed his knee-jerk reaction to seeing her with Brent Lloyd again got the best of him and he lost his decorum. "Believe me, I came to the same conclusion when you again glared at me like I'd committed a crime. Because I tried to help Brent with his lumbar issue. Your board president, who is a nice man and who it might be beneficial to impress with the work we do here. You're right, Jackson, I can't go on like this."

"I know it seems twisted that not wanting to subject you to me is an act of devotion on my part."

"So you keep saying. Are you congratulating yourself?" All of it was riling her up and now that the guests were gone, she saw no reason to hold back. "Have you ever heard that expression about cutting your nose off to spite your face?"

"Esme." He reached for her hand. She pulled it away. "Esme."

"You're just going to be tortured for the rest of your life? You're so concerned with history repeating itself that you're going to bury what could have been a rebirth. Take the less risky road even though it might not be the one that could give you joy and fulfilment. And end up alone and with health conditions, just like how you started."

"I thought I could do it. I can't."

What would she do now? She wanted the spa directorship. And she'd known this was a possibility, that things wouldn't work out with him personally and that it could cost her the job. In fact, after all of this, could she work with him? Could he work with her? Either way, she'd forever live inside a shell of rumination, of what might have been with him. That she opened her heart once and it was swiftly trampled on. This shift was monumental. The world was suddenly a darker place, a lonely terrain. "You made me rethink everything, Jackson. I will forever regret that I wasn't able to do the same for you."

"No, it's not you. You are the finest person I've ever met."

"I know," she snapped.

"It's my albatross that I'll have to continue to live with."

"If that's what you choose."

The conversation was going around in circles. She absentmindedly began throwing out drinks and food that had been left behind. She wanted to go home. Jackson could book a room at the best hotel in the city. She needed to remove herself from this situation. While she had her hands full of plates, she felt her phone vibrate in her pocket. Once she put her armload down, she pulled it out to see the call she'd missed. It was Cozumel in Oaxaca, her familiar voice saying, "Esme, give me a call as soon as you have a chance. I have a question for you."

Jackson tapped his key card to open the heavy steel door of yet another hotel suite, as he'd done hundreds of times, one door indistinguishable from the next. Just a five-block walk ago, he'd locked up at the Sher and stopped to appreciate the dedication plaque on the door.

In memory of Beatrice and Wesley Finn

Today had been the launch of the newly revamped spa. All of the publicity his staff worked so hard on had paid off. Trevor kept everything running smoothly. It should have been a terrific day. The *New York Times* and the *Village Voice* came, as well as the spa industry trade publications. It was the signal of a new phase for Jackson. Although there was a gaping hole in the proceedings, one about five and a half feet tall with golden highlights in her hair.

He kicked off his shoes and moved to the thirty-fifth-floor window to look out at the city lights. What could have been one of the most transformative days of his life was dampened by the missing component. The piece that was the only thing that could complete him morning, noon or midnight, special days and ordinary ones, too. Instead, this day would have a different history. Of all that wasn't.

Good luck. Those were the last words she'd said to him. After he'd broken up with her, to use a common parlance. It occurred to him for the first time how powerful the word *broke* was. Because he indeed felt broken without Esme. Broken into shards, in fact. Too many to even count. Too numerous to ever put back together as one. *Broken up.*

Good luck. He was going to need it. Luck, or something. To survive losing her. She, who'd made him want to try again. She, who'd reminded him of what he was searching for all those years ago when he mistakenly found Livia. Esme seemed like she could fill the hole inside of him that was desperate for demonstrative love and excitement and passion. Someone to gush over. He thought he was in big, fireworks, trombone-salute love. One that energized him inside and made life worth living.

Good luck. That was three weeks ago. The investors had approved the launch. Esme had worked remotely with Trevor tirelessly helping get everything in order. They named Trevor as spa manager, which was a promotion Esme wanted for him all along. And Jackson returned to hotel life. Room service food that was never quite warm enough. Uniformed housekeepers tracking his packages of laundry.

Oh, how he missed the coziness of Esme's little apartment where he felt like a man at the start of his adulthood whose life was unfolding a little bit at a time. He missed Esme's mismatched coffee mugs. The one shaped like an apple, symbol of the city, had become his favorite. He missed her towels, always fresh and stacked high in the bathroom cupboard, encouraging an indulgent shower. Mostly, he missed being around her. She'd become his touchstone, his talisman, his password into the world. Nonetheless, despite her physical absence, the reopening came together. She'd been away from him for twenty-one days, each of which he counted with a check mark on his calendar. That was a lie because he really counted the time away from her by the hours. No, the minute. The second, if that was possible.

"Cozumel called me," Esme had explained to him over the phone the day after the investors event. "Remember she was telling us that their spa director, Itza, was going to take maternity time off and that she wasn't sure she'd return. She let Cozumel and Luis know that she wanted substantial time with her family and that they should look for a replacement."

"And of course, they thought of you."

"Yeah, I mean, we've always had a great working relationship."

"When we were there, Cozumel complimented your work with that woman who was having trouble with fertility. She said she'd love to have you back. Why wouldn't she?"

"By the way, the woman, Payaan, did get pregnant."

"That's beautiful." For some reason, a lump formed in his throat thinking about pregnancy and the desire for family. The continuum of life. What an amazing place Cozumel and Luis had created.

"They want you back. You are both a consummate professional and a true healer."

"It'll give me a start at that directorship I've always wanted. Luis plans to expand, open a second location. It's a great opportunity for me."

He knew her well enough to know that she wasn't saying everything she was thinking. "That's great." His lack of sincerity was audible.

"I'm doing us both a favor." She stopped. It sounded like she was slowing herself down, choosing difficult words. "We couldn't make something personal work. Why have the torture of running a business together? Let's cut each other loose, take the gains with the losses and walk away."

Why did she have to be so smart and logical? On the other hand, if she was swept with emotion and begging for them to keep trying, what would he do? No matter. Of course, she wasn't going to do that even if that was her impulse, after she'd been thoroughly rejected. She wasn't going to sign up for more.

"You'll find someone chomping at the bit to lead the Sher," she continued. "And Trevor is a gem. We did a great thing, you and I. We gave your parents' spa a direction forward."

"No, you did that. I bankrolled a quick trip around the world." Maybe she didn't realize that she'd also brought a dead man back to life. Changed his mental outlook in ways that would inform the rest of his life. *We gave the spa a direction forward,* he silently repeated the words into the recirculated air of the hotel room.

If he loved her, he'd let her go cleanly and completely. Wait. *L.O.V.E.* A word that might have been casually tossed around when he was with Livia but it wasn't until he'd met Esme that he began to even have a cursory understanding of its meaning. Yet he wasn't able to do what love demanded, to be fearless with no promises. It showed someone what was possible. If they believed in the best, giving what they took. He loved Esme. He was in love with her. Which was why she was telling him she was leaving and he was wishing her well. It was the greatest wish he'd ever have. For her to be well. In every way. Thousands of miles in another country or five blocks away. Self-love in action. She was taking care of herself, finally. She had to go, to fly with steel wings and make sure no one ever rusted her again.

"Good luck to you, too," his gravelly voice had creaked out.

He stared at himself in a mirror on the wall for a long while. Indeed, his shoulders were up as high as his ears. He didn't want to die. He inhaled deeply through his nose and exhaled slowly through his mouth as Esme had taught him to.

Finally, he picked up his phone and returned to the

website he had been lurking at for a couple of weeks now. A recommendation he'd gotten from Dr. Singh.

On the home page was a photo of tall trees and dirt trails. The graphic read, "Kendrick Washington, Psychologist. Is your past holding you back from what you want?"

CHAPTER FOURTEEN

THE MOON WAS so bright it provided light to what Esme knew were the wee hours. She didn't have her phone with her so didn't know the correct time. After tossing and turning in bed she'd stepped out of the casita and breathed in the cool air of night. She lay down on one of the lounge chairs by the firepit where just a few weeks ago she and Jackson had slowly sipped a mezcal in the mild evening. There were no sounds to be heard at this hour, just a maddening quiet that made her ask the moon a question. How would she clean off her wounds and move on yet again?

She'd spent most of her life fixing things. Placating her parents and compensating for their shortcomings. What would have become of her if she hadn't found her way to that local spa and all those towels to wash? Would she have ended up taking care of a man, repeating her childhood role? Or stuck at a job where she'd never found a passion or calling. Or, for that matter, she could have ended up homeless and destitute. Taking stock under the Mexican sky, it seemed, though, that she had let a man throw her off her balance. In spite of her better instincts.

Earlier this evening, she'd talked to Trevor, who

said the opening was a big hit although some of the guests wanted to know where the director with the good breathing techniques was. That made Esme smile, although with a double edge. Maybe she should have been strong enough to stay in New York and run the spa with Jackson, driven enough to put the romantic past behind them. The minute he pushed her away because his own scars hurt too much, she turned her back on him. She didn't stay to fight for the man she'd fallen in love with. The one who she'd never thought she'd meet.

Cozumel gave her a once-over when she came into the kitchen after falling asleep on the lounger. Luis was stirring pots on the stove and looked over. She said, "My, Esme, you don't look happy."

"I'll be okay," Esme said. "I won't let you down."

"I know that. It's you I'm concerned about."

How grateful she was that Cozumel and Luis had become friends, not just colleagues. She'd called Esme three weeks ago, on the day that happened to be the investors event, one of the best and worst days of her life. Taking over the Sher, and she and Jackson together in a way that really felt *together.* A dream she'd never dared before. Until he woke up and turned it into a nightmare.

"Does that handsome Jackson have something to do with it?" Luis asked while putting a mug of *café con leche* in front of Esme. "He was more than just your boss, am I right?"

Esme took a sip of Luis's creamy brew. "I thought he was. It turns out we're not a match."

"No," Cozumel jumped in, "I could feel it in my

bones. And see it in the way you looked at each other. You are each other's safe haven." Cozumel's words entered Esme's ears and she kept hearing them over and over in her head. *Haven.* She and Jackson were each other's haven. That was the truth. He wouldn't allow it, though, couldn't let her eyes guide him home no matter how hard she tried.

Had she tried hard enough? He knew what was imprisoning him. That self-awareness itself held promise. With her love, could he break free?

"I made a mistake in falling for someone in the first place. My first real relationship and I managed to choose the wrong person."

"You didn't choose him any more than he chose you." Cozumel shook her head. "Your destinies found you. Are you going to turn your back on fate?"

"That's exactly what I've spent my adult life doing." Anything to not become a statistic. Protecting herself. By denying herself. Never needing anyone no matter how much she was needed.

"You accepted our offer because it was an easy way out, is that it? We whisked you away from New York," Cozumel said. "And from seeing it through with Jackson?"

"Mi amor," Luis said to Cozumel, "maybe I think we made the wrong decision to keep Esme for ourselves. We're not going to stand in the way of Cupid."

"Wait a minute here. I didn't leave him. He's the one who cut it off." As always, she was the reed that had to bend with the wind. Always the teacher, always the forgiver. She'd had enough of that.

Yet she did need him. He gave her herself. He was the missing piece for her to become whole. By his side, she could soar. They'd be there to catch each other if the flight wasn't smooth.

Luis came away from the stove to give Cozumel a hug and kissed her face a dozen times. "When Cozumel and I found out we weren't able to become pregnant, we decided to share all the wisdom we'd gained in our own struggles by making the spa our baby that we created together."

"I predict you and Jackson will have many babies besides the Sher, although that's a good place to start," Cozumel said. "I have a few other people I can talk to about Itza's job. Go back to New York."

"It's too late."

"It's never too late."

"We don't need you hanging around like a sad yard dog," Luis added. The three of them smiled.

Cozumel was right to feel it in her bones. Esme did, too. Her body didn't align without Jackson; she was off kilter. Hiding from him was not the solution. And Cozumel and Luis had seen their vision come to fruition here. Esme couldn't be happy tagging on to their dream. She was finally ready to see her own. She'd gratefully take all Jackson had to give her.

Within hours, she was standing in front of the spa's tiled fountain with a suitcase by her side, just as she'd arrived. She gave Cozumel and Luis a final wave as she got into the car that would take her to the airport. The couple put their arms around each other as they watched her go.

Love conquers all was only a phrase Esme had heard. She needed that promise to be good to its words.

Once Jackson stepped off of the airplane and inhaled that fresh smell, he felt better. It was as if the flight took one hundred hours, so desperate was he to get back to Mexico and claim what was his. He didn't mean that to sound like a caveman but he wanted to try the image on for size. He liked the fit very much. His and hers.

Ah, Oaxaca. Where bliss had taken flight. The frozen kisses of Stockholm started it and Thailand's beautiful journey was the end but the warm skies of Oaxaca were unimaginably romantic. It was here he'd started to believe that everything was possible. Until he let the monsters wreck it. Just a few weeks ago, in the quiet night with Esme, he'd started to think he could throw his past into the firepit and watch it burn to ash. Turned out, he wasn't able to. That was then. This was now. With no chance of not getting it right. Esme was his. He was hers. End of story, or should he say beginning.

The airport was just as he remembered it, as was a particular smell of the terrain. He could recognize it with his eyes closed. He fantasized returning to visit here with Esme. That was if Cozumel and Luis forgave him for the tumult he was about to cause. Maybe this could become a special hideaway for him and Esme. Maybe they'd bring their children. Maybe their grandchildren. He enjoyed that thought. He wanted all of that old and gray stuff with her.

He carried his small bag through the terminal. He

hadn't packed much because they weren't staying long this time. He got a partial view of a woman walking toward him, her face obscured by other people. He craned his neck to see more. About her height and the same bouncy brown hair with golden highlights. Was he hallucinating?

Some people veered left or right so much that a space opened and they caught sight of each other.

"Jackson?" she exclaimed once he came into focus.

A rosy wash softly poured over him to hear her say his name. All was not lost. He hoped. "It is, my love." My love.

"What are you doing at the airport?"

"I came for you."

"You what?" She stopped a few feet before reaching him. Maybe to stake her own ground before entering his.

"I made a horrible mistake. I came to correct it." He advanced a few steps. "I can't live without you. And I won't."

"How was the Sher's reopening?" Oh, she needed to divert the topic. Okay, he had plenty of time to get everything said.

"The dedication plaque turned out beautiful. I can't wait for you to see it. I did what I intended to do. In my small way I made a peace offering for all the disappointment I caused my parents."

Then Esme took steps toward him, closing the gap. "You didn't disappoint them. Livia did. We've got to get you to forgive yourself."

"In any case, the Sher is ours now. We're going to

grow it from seed like two gardeners in the field." Her face lit up. "What did that make you think of?"

"Oh, just something Cozumel said about the Sher being our baby."

"Esme, in almost losing you I realized how much I am ready for you. If you'll have me, stumbles and wobbles and all." Finally, she stepped close enough that he could almost feel her. His breath quickened. "Wait a minute, though. Where are you going? Why are you at the airport?"

People passed by them, coming and going in every direction. A man walked through an exit gate and what looked to be his family rushed to hug him, the four of them running into a tight embrace. A couple deplaned holding hands, the woman wearing a sash that read Bride, both with big smiles on their faces. One young woman dropped her purse and its contents spilled onto the floor. A man about her age dropped to his knees to help her gather up her things and she smiled up at him. Jackson flashed back to the first day he'd returned to the Sher and Esme had been so kind with an elderly woman whose belongings had fallen out of her purse the same way. Lovers parted, after kissing until one had to hurry through the boarding gate. Tour groups and sports teams juggled carry-ons along with their coffees and electronics. Esme and Jackson were two people in the middle of the world, making rotations around the sun, most everyone doing their best.

"I was heading back to you, Jackson."

"I'm capable of evolving."

"We already decided…our starting place is total distrust." They both smirked.

"I'm further than that now."

"Are you?"

"You'll love the new version of me." He touched his own face with his fingers. "Look how I have a skin care regime now. I'm deep breathing. Kenji on our staff is fabulous at shiatsu massage. And I'm seeing a psychologist."

She brought her hand over his on his cheek. Explosions of joy went off inside of him. "I love you."

He wrapped his arms around her, lifted her up and spun her in a circle. "I love you."

When he put her down, she looped her arm through his. "Come on." They headed in the same direction, like they always would. "I heard about this job in New York I just have to have."

* * * * *

Their Parisian Night

Michele Renae

MILLS & BOON

Michele Renae is the pseudonym of award-winning author Michele Hauf. She has published over ninety novels in historical, paranormal and contemporary romance and fantasy, as well as writing action/adventure as Alex Archer. Instead of writing 'what she knows' she prefers to write 'what she would love to know and do'. And, yes, that includes being a jewel thief and/or a brain surgeon! You can email Michele at toastfaery@gmail.com, and find her on Instagram: @MicheleHauf and Pinterest: @toastfaery.

Also by Michele Renae

Cinderella's Second Chance in Paris
The CEO and the Single Dad
Parisian Escape with the Billionaire

Discover more at
millsandboon.com.au.

CHAPTER ONE

"ABSOLUTELY NOT!"

The woman who'd flatly refused Sebastian's proposal and shoved the engagement ring he had just shown her back in his face, grabbed the car door handle and opened it. She thrust out a designer-shoe-clad foot toward the curb and then turned to look over her shoulder to waggle a finger in his face.

"You, Sebastian Mercier, are a rogue. You don't want to marry me because you love me. You just want to control your family's company. And I will not be bought. Oof! Men!"

With that, she fled the limousine in a rage of silk and silvery sequins, a burst of fluffy white marabou fluttering in her wake.

Sebastian leaned back and closed his eyes. That had been his second failed proposal in a six-month period. And he'd thought finding a wife would be easy!

Apparently, a man with money, a luxe Paris home and social connections to everyone who was anyone wasn't motivation enough to entice a *yes* from a woman.

Well, he wasn't an imbecile. Women required an emotional commitment. A sparkly ring was not sufficient incentive.

He'd had to give it a go. He and Amie had dated for three weeks. Had seen each other every day. Had enjoyed great sex. As a fashion influencer followed by tens of millions, Amie had been a perfect candidate to step into the role of his wife. His family approved of her old money and fashion connections.

But...after a recent media leak, the competition between him and his brother, Philippe, was no longer secret. And such information tended to matter to some, especially if it affected their future. And their heart.

The refusal did not upset him as much as expected. He hadn't been in love. Nor, he suspected, had Amie. Theirs had been an affair of passion. Love must not intrude on such a cold business transaction. Love and the emotional attachment that came along with it must not interfere in his quest to find a bride.

Will you marry me and have my child so I can then take control of the family company?

Besides, what did love even feel like?

He'd try again when the opportunity presented itself. He must. Philippe must not win. He'd regroup and begin the wife search again after—well, after a good, stiff drink. A man did have a right to mourn his loss, didn't he?

Tucking the ring box away in his suit coat pocket, he leaned across the seat to grab the open door when a woman's shout—in English—called for him to hold the door.

A stunning vision sprinted toward the limo. A floaty pale pink dress dazzled with glints and sparkles. And wearing that lovely creation was a beautiful blonde with arms spread in a plea to wait as she neared.

Sebastian leaned back just as the blonde plunged inside the car, changing the very air with her arrival. He felt suddenly lifted, and curious. She shoved a heap of purse—and some sort of clothing—onto his lap, blew out a panting breath, grabbed the door and closed it.

"Drive!" she demanded of his driver with the pound of a dainty fist against the seat. "Please! He's chasing me!" She swiped a dash of wavy hair from her eyes and her panicked look took him in. "I'm so sorry, but could you...just drive me a few blocks from here? There's a man. He's after me."

Gorgeous, pale blue eyes surrounded by the lushest black lashes frantically met his. "Someone is after you? Whom do I have to fight for your honor, my lady?"

"It's the photographer. He took off after me because I kicked him in the—"

Still panting from what must have been a high-speed run, she patted her chest. His protective instincts in high gear, Sebastian glanced out the back window. No sign of the perpetrator. He nodded to the driver to pull away. Why not play along with this interesting insertion of feminine audacity into the evening?

Her huffing breaths settled a bit as she nodded and patted his hand. "Thank you. I'll get out soon. I just need to put some distance between us."

"If you are in trouble..."

"You'd fight for my honor?"

"But of course, mademoiselle. My limo is at your disposal."

"I'll take a rain check on that fight. But don't think I won't forget the offer."

"Anything for a damsel in distress."

Her worried moue crinkled into a smile. Freckles that dotted her entire face got lost in a few of those crinkles. Cute.

"This is your limo? Oh, dash it. I'm really sorry about all this."

"Don't apologize. I've never had the opportunity to rescue a damsel before. This one will look good on my résumé, eh?"

She laughed and shook her head. "Oh, it will."

"If I may ask, why the kicking of something or other and the resultant dash?"

"Well." She smoothed out the sparkly skirt. "My girlfriend gave me a princess photo shoot as a treat," she said. "Because of the breakup, you know. I dated Lloyd for six months. I thought for sure he was going to propose. So that night at the fancy restaurant I asked if he wanted to have kids and he laughed. Hated kids! Can you believe it?"

Sebastian wasn't sure if she was angling for an answer or some kind of affirming gesture. But he didn't have time to shrug as she continued her breathless ramble. It seemed her fear was streaming out in words, and he wasn't about to stop her, especially since she was already fearful of one man.

"And then!" she continued dramatically. "Lloyd confessed he'd slept with my flatmate, who was also my boss at the flower shop. Who—let me tell you—had the audacity to insist I move out of our flat while *they* were away on vacation." She paused, winced. "Sorry. Too much information? Probably. I'm frazzled. Anyway! I was so excited about the photo shoot. It was a means to forget about that awful breakup. And this dress is so posh…" She spoke as quickly as he suspected she must have been running. "And look at my makeup and hair. I look like a princess, right?"

He nodded, unable to resist a smile. A princess with freckles and looking more like an imp lost in a glamorous world that was perhaps not her natural habitat. But what did he know? If she truly had been in danger, he was just thankful she'd jumped into the back of his car.

Azalea was rambling! It was a bad habit that always swooped upon her when she was nervous. Or afraid, as the case was. Though her fears were reduced knowing they were driving away from the scene of the crime. And the man sitting next to her seemed quite gentlemanly. So handsome. His dark hair was short but looked as though it deserved a good finger tousle. A sharp jawline and the hint of stubble suggested an elegance that matched the fitted black suit. Was that a glint of diamond on his cuff links? His look said corporate raider with a softer touch of international jewel thief. She loved a good heist movie with a charming rogue robber. And his eyes held genuine concern. Offering to rescue the damsel?

Yes, please!

"I can't imagine a life without kids and family, you know? I love children!" Azalea added, because she didn't want the man to think she was totally off her rocker.

Just stop rambling, then!

She nodded to her inner thoughts. Yes, shut up. And perhaps they'd driven far enough by now?

"Children are lovely," he offered with a bemused tone. "You seem to have calmed a bit. I hope the photographer did not do anything untoward?"

"Well." She sighed heavily. "He made terrible, lewd re-marks. And he touched me! Not where a girl wants to be touched by a stranger, either. So I panicked."

It had all gone knees up when that sleazy photographer had slipped his mitts up under her skirt, insisting he was making an adjustment—and then he had gone too far.

Azalea had reacted. Her father had taught both her and her sister, Dahlia, if they ever felt unsafe around a man to kick first, ask questions later. And forget questions, actually. Just run. Which she had done.

"My dad taught me self-defense. My kicking skills are excellent. Got him right where it counts. Then I grabbed my stuff. And…"

She leaned back and blew out a breath. She'd made it away safely. Thanks to some quick thinking and maintaining her wits. Yet now the adrenaline rushing through her system made her jittery and she just wanted to go somewhere and cry.

No. She was stronger than that. Find a hotel to stay the night, and text Maddie about never recommending that photographer again, and then head back to Ambleside in the morning. The day had been a bust. No princess day for Azalea Grace, after all.

On the other hand, she had run into a rescuing knight.

"Tell me where they are and I'll take care of them both," Sebastian offered.

She shook her head. "I wish you had been around a few weeks ago when Lloyd broke it off. Oh, and now. I just… want to forget about this day." She grabbed her stuff from his lap. "Sorry. I've been rude. I'll pay you for the ride."

"No apologies necessary. What matters is that you are all right."

"I'm good."

"Can I drop you somewhere?" he asked.

"I…uh…was going to rent a hotel room for the night. My girlfriend and I spent the afternoon together. It was so good to see Maddie again. We grew up together. She headed to Paris the moment we finished our A levels. Anyway, she gave me a coupon for a hotel in the tenth arrondissement, I believe. It's in my purse somewhere." She began to dig inside her bag. "What an awful way to end what should have been a perfect day. I'm just…ooh, I need a drink, actually."

"I was just thinking much the same before you graced me with your presence. I have a proposal for you," he said.

"Yeah? Does it involve alcohol?"

"It could. It may also involve decadent treats and tiny hors d'oeuvres."

The way he said that, with a hint of a tease, made her smile. And nothing about him screamed lecher. The expensive suit—and his elegant manners—also made her want to hear more regarding this proposal. Instinctively, she felt he was someone she could trust.

She shoved her purse aside and leaned an elbow on the armrest "I'm listening."

"I was on my way to a party. Until my date…"

"I saw the woman leaving this car! I thought she was being left off by a cab. She was your date?"

"Yes, but no longer. We had…"

"A bit of a row?"

"Something like that. Heartbreak." He winced. Heartbreak could only mean they must have broken something off. Poor man. He needed a hug as much as she did.

"I suspect you want to forget your troubles?" he asked.

"I do."

"And while I sympathize for what you've just experienced, I wonder if a little dancing and champagne might lift both of our spirits?"

"I do like champagne. And dancing. And you mentioned tiny hors d'oeuvres?"

"I did indeed. I should not be so bold as to press you to join me. I am a stranger."

"That you are."

He offered his hand for her to shake. "Sebastian Mercier."

The warmth of his hand clasping hers sent a delicious shiver across her shoulders. Her rescuing knight even smelled good, like vanilla and cedar. Azalea had always prided herself on being a good judge of animals. Were they wild, persnickety, trusting or fearful? Judging people was a little hit-or-miss for her. And yet, there was nothing about the man that sent up a warning flag for her. They were comrades in broken hearts.

"Azalea Grace," she said.

"After the flower? It suits you."

"Thanks. My friends call me Lea."

"Would you like to spend a few hours with me in an attempt to forget our troubles? You are dressed for the soiree."

She smoothed a palm over her bespangled skirt. "This dress doesn't belong to me. I'll have to return it. Oh, how do I dare? I can't set foot in that studio again."

"I can see to its return. After the party. You've clothes here?"

She sighed and rifled through the tangled clothing on her lap. "Looks like I only grabbed my jeans during my quick getaway."

"No worries. I will make sure you are properly clothed before the dress is returned. But right now, there's the party."

"I thought it was a soiree?"

"Same thing. Basically. Are you in or out?"

As she let her gaze wander over his face, she exhaled, her shoulders relaxing. Sebastian was not of the same ilk as the man she'd just run from. He was a gentleman. He'd even offered to defend her honor. No man had ever done such a thing. And while she was not so stupid as to be won over by a handsome face and charming manners, the man was also heartbroken and probably felt as rough as she did. What terrible woman had been so cruel to break it off with this gallant knight?

A few hours at a fancy soiree? Her heart leaped before her brain could caution her.

"I'm in," she announced with an effervescent lilt to her tone. "Let's party!"

CHAPTER TWO

AZALEA WASN'T SURE what fantasy world she had entered since plunging into the back of the limo, but she was going along for the ride. Literally. And seated beside a sexy Frenchman wearing an impeccable suit, who kept giving her a smile and a nod? The smolder in his eyes was making parts of her shiver. And in a very good way.

The day had started well. She had been moping over the breakup with Lloyd for weeks, so Maddie had decided to grab her by the fetters and toss her back into life. Before the photo shoot, she and Maddie had done lunch, and then strolled the Jardin du Luxembourg, chatting about their jobs, men and life. Tears had fallen as Azalea had rehashed her recent breakup with Lloyd Cooper. She had genuinely expected him to propose that night at the ritzy restaurant. And to prepare, she'd determined that she must know how he felt about having children before she could answer such a question as a marriage proposal. She'd casually mentioned children over the first course. Lloyd's answer had stunned her. What sort of monster thought children wild and unsuitable for a proper lifestyle?

Then, her heart had crashed. Lloyd had shoved aside his plate and said he couldn't wait one moment longer. He had to confess. He'd hooked up with the woman who owned the flower shop where Azalea worked. The very woman who was also her flatmate! Lloyd had had the audacity to insinuate Azalea was unsophisticated. And she would never fit into his lifestyle, implying that she was a simple farm girl unfit for his important London friends. He and his new lover—her boss!—were headed to Greece the next day for a holiday. They'd insisted Azalea vacate the flat while they were away. So she'd packed her things and trundled home to Ambleside to stay with her dad on the family farm until she could figure out her next step. Finding a new job. And reclaiming her tattered heart.

Why did she always make the wrong choices? If it wasn't a haircut with a seventies-style fluff, it was a horrible spur-of-the-moment lipstick purchase. Why had she thought the eggplant would work against her pale complexion? And had she ever dated a man who hadn't wanted to change her in some way? Even Ralph Madding, the chicken farmer down the road, whom she'd dated when she was nineteen, had complained about her independence. Told her that he required a woman to cook, clean, and have babies with him.

She had nothing against cooking and cleaning. It was the *expectation* of such things that rubbed her the wrong way. Why couldn't men simply exist alongside women and allow them their space while also embracing them? Was that too much to ask?

A night in Paris with a sexy Frenchman she had only met moments earlier? Talk about busting out of her unsophisticated norm! She intended to end this miserable day with a bang.

This dress felt like fairy tissue sprinkled with stardust. The pale pink chiffon floated and was topped overall with a layer of silver-star-bedazzled mesh. Her long, wavy blond hair had been swept up and pinned with sparkling clips to match the stars on the gown. Her makeup was subtle and hadn't succeeded in covering her freckles. And the makeup artist had given her the perfect lip color. Hot pink. Who would have guessed!

Despite growing up on a farm and embracing her inner tomboy, she loved a girlie outfit and the chance to play princess.

She cast a sneaky glance at the seemingly very kind man who sat next to her on the back seat. He could turn out to be another sleaze. But no, she suspected he wasn't. How many men offered to fight for a woman's honor after knowing her for only a few minutes? She'd be cautious of his smolder, though. Those sexy bedroom eyes and devilishly coiffed dark hair melted bits of her.

She couldn't make two bad choices in one day. The odds must be in her favor!

The car arrived at a fancy building that featured an actual red carpet stretched from curbside and up a flight of stairs to the front doors, where neon lights flashed and music bounced out.

Funny, she'd always thought soirees were more refined, and possibly included tea.

"What kind of party is this?" Now a little nervous, she gripped the door handle. Paris was not her usual stomping ground. She didn't even speak the language. Hobnobbing with an elite crowd was not her style, but a rave or something wild like that would also set her off-kilter.

"A launch bash for Jean-Claude's latest perfume release. It'll be fun."

She liked perfume. And yet. "It looks fancy. Are there celebrities in there?"

Sebastian shrugged. "Probably." When he leaned closer, she inhaled the exotic vanilla and cedar. It tickled at her nerves and softened them. The man was teasingly edible. "I dare you," he offered.

What was it the French declared when taken by something wonderful? *Mon Dieu! Oh, mon Dieu*, this man's eyes. And his smooth baritone voice.

What had he said? Oh, right. He'd *dared* her to go into the party.

Much as whatever waited beyond the red carpet was probably far out of her league, and as unsophisticated as she might be, Azalea wasn't about to be taken down again today. This choice would not blow up in her face. And she wanted to get her mitts all over the promised champagne. And the food. She was hungry! And if opportunity presented, she wouldn't refuse a dance or three.

"Sebastian, right?"

He nodded. "At your beck and call all night, mademoiselle. It'll be fun. Promise."

A promise from a Frenchman wielding a smile that could lure her between the sheets was the most exciting thing she'd ever experienced. She took his hand. And he led her up the red carpet. At the door, a bouncer in dark sunglasses nodded to Sebastian and ticked something on the list he held. If Lloyd could see his little farm girl now!

The ballroom was vast and set in an old building that was tiled, columned, buttressed and everything else one could imagine from ancient architecture. Probably kings and queens had danced across the elaborate marble-tiled floor. The high, curved ceiling featured stained glass Art Deco designs. Mylar streamers, colorful balloons and shimmery fabric hung everywhere. The crowd was dressed to the nines. Diamonds and jewels dazzled.

And... Azalea noticed a lush perfume hanging like an invisible fog over it all. Must be the perfume being launched at the party. It smelled expensive and sweet, like candy.

Then she noticed the word hung overhead, dashed in bold pink neon. *"Câlin?"* she asked.

"It means a hug or something like a cuddle," Sebastian explained. "An odd choice, really, since we French are not keen on hugs. It is the name of the perfume."

"No hugs, eh?"

She imagined wrapping her arms around Sebastian's wide shoulders, fitting her body against his tall figure, and bowing her head against his shoulder, but a kiss away from his alluring mouth. He deserved a hug for rescuing her. As a balm to his own heartbreak. But she didn't want to scare him away—the French weren't keen on hugs?—so she offered up her pinky finger crooked before him.

His quizzical look made her giggle.

"Pinkie hug," she explained. "In honor of the perfume."

He twined his pinkie with hers. Could he contain that smolder that involved a sexy quirk up on one side of his mouth and a soft gaze, or was it a natural movement? "I fear we will both reek of expensive perfume even after leaving."

"It's very nice."

"Smells like something you could eat, yes?"

She nodded her head to the catchy music. "Yes, they must be pumping it into the air. Whew!"

Time to forget her troubles. Forget Lloyd. And the photographer wouldn't be manhandling anything but his private bits for a while. She was here to party.

"Would you like champagne?" Sebastian asked loudly so she could hear over the noise.

"Not yet. I need to dance!"

When she grabbed his hand, he followed her to the center of the ballroom. They insinuated themselves in a spot where they could get their dance on. Three or four songs passed while Azalea's energy soared. Movement always lifted her spirits. The man whom she had literally dragged onto the dance floor showed no signs of wanting to slow down. Undoing the buttons on his suit coat, he countered her moves with some surprisingly rhythmic moves of his own.

When had a man ever matched her silly dance floor energy? Certainly, Lloyd hadn't been able to deflate his pompous upper lip long enough to actually let loose. And despite Sebastian's fancy suit, the diamonds glinting at his cuffs, and what she guessed must be a ridiculously expensive haircut, he danced as if he didn't care what the world thought of him. He'd been dumped by the woman who had fled the back of the limo? Poor guy. They both needed this night.

Grabbing her hand, he twirled her a few times. They developed a dance language with some hip bumping, slides and spins. Azalea laughed and tilted back her head, lifting her arms to become the music.

When the music slowed, she spun and caught her palms against Sebastian's chest. The lights dimmed as the DJ announced a romantic interlude and they swayed beneath the constellation of glimmering party decorations. His cologne tangled with the sweet, perfumed air. Heady and delicious. She inhaled, drawing him into her pores. A girl could lose herself in a moment like this. And maybe she already had.

Something about the enchanting Frenchman reached inside her and tickled her battered heart. Offered some hope. Even a breathless dare to try again. Might she have a fling with a stranger? It sounded brazen and taboo to her practical heart. But it felt…like something she deserved. A one-night stand? She'd see where the evening led them.

"Are you having a good time?" he asked.

"The best!"

She held up her pinkie and he linked his about hers. "Me as well."

"You're not sorry you're here with someone other than the person you intended to bring here?"

"Not in the least. I've already forgotten her name. You are a spitfire of dance moves and freckles. I could fall in love with you, Azalea Grace."

She laughed, tilting back her head, and he spun her out. Twirling back to hug up against him again, she shook her head and said, "Fall in love all you wish. I would never marry you."

"No worries, my family would never—erm. Why is that?"

His family wouldn't approve of her. That was what he had almost said, but had realized his faux pas. Didn't matter to her. She knew they were not in the same social class. This was just one night. Nothing would spoil it.

She wiggled her shoulders, then shrugged. "Marriage isn't in the cards for me." Because—much as she craved a family of her own—she'd been hurt by expecting it to happen. And really? She, married to this fancy, obviously wealthy, man? A ridiculous dream. She must not be crushed twice. Or ever again. "But you know what my next goal is?"

"Do tell."

"Champagne!"

Hours into the party, Sebastian was on his third glass of champagne, as was Azalea. Lea was what she'd said her friends called her. He'd shortened her name to Zee. He was feeling the alcohol, but not drunk. His senses were sharp and acutely aware of every brush of her skin against his, each sweet smile she cast his way, and her bodacious laugh that seemed to birth from her belly and echo out and spread like the crystal stars suspended over their heads.

This night was multitudes better than he'd expected it to be. And he had expected to be engaged right now.

"Do you know all these people?" she asked as they stood, looking over the dance floor. Somewhere between dances they'd become comfortable with holding hands. It felt as though they'd been holding hands all their lives. "They all seem to recognize you and are so friendly."

"I do know most. It's a tight social circle. My brother was supposed to be here tonight, but I haven't seen him."

Of course, if Philippe had shown he'd have flaunted his latest paramour and inquired why Sebastian was here with an English woman. Not that his family was against the English. It was just that Sebastian tended to date closer to home.

"A Parisian girl will suit you," his mother, Angelique, had a tendency to remind him. *"Not too smart, but beautiful,"* she'd add. *"And don't worry about love, Sebastian. No one marries for love anymore."*

He'd almost blurted that awful statement about his family not approving of her. Uncouth. Yet she hadn't seemed to take it to heart or even notice. *Good save, Sebastian.*

While he hadn't the luxury to waste his time dating a woman of whom his family would never approve, this night wasn't about the competition between himself and Philippe. It was a means to get over tonight's rejection. And apparently, as Zee had spewed out in the limo, she had been rejected recently, too. Her boyfriend hadn't wanted children? And she'd been expecting a proposal?

She was a perfect candidate for Sebastian's win. He could not have placed an order for a more suitable wife. And he even had a ring in his pocket. But...no. He wasn't so heartless that he could bounce from one woman to the next over the course of a few hours. And he would not take advantage of Zee's broken heart and battered ego after he'd promised her a night of fun.

The live band sang pop songs that spanned decades. When they launched into an eighties' hit, Zee bounced giddily and turned her gleeful eyes to him. He didn't even have to ask.

He took her empty goblet and set it on the bar behind them. "Let's dance!"

Sebastian had never found a woman who liked to dance as much as he did. And who had the energy to keep up with him. Or who couldn't stop worrying about her hair or nails, or her expensive dress, long enough to simply let go and move.

He fit his hands to his surprise date's hips, and they joined a makeshift conga line. What a night! He'd never felt freer. And it was an easy kind of freedom that allowed him to be more intimate with her than he might have thought possible. She didn't mind when he clasped her hand and leaned in close to talk against her ear. She smelled like starlight. And that kind of romantic thinking was what tended to get him into trouble.

This was a one-night adventure. No reason not to enjoy.

After a few songs, he tugged her from the dance floor and to the opposite side of the ballroom. "Did you notice the life-size dioramas?" he asked her. "They're for photographs. Let's do some!"

Staged along the wall were makeshift rooms with props and colorful backgrounds for couples or groups to take fun photos to remember the event. Sebastian strolled toward the first, which featured a setting with paper palm trees. A tropical vacation called to him. A week or so to soak in the sun and forget the demands of work and family.

Suddenly he was jerked to the right.

"This one!" Zee called. "I want to hold the balloons!"

The scene featured a massive bouquet of red balloons set against a cerulean sky background. Zee stepped onto a stepstool and grabbed the balloon strings. Sebastian handed his phone to the assistant that manned each diorama. Then he positioned himself to grasp Zee's legs.

Photo taken, the assistant handed him his phone and Zee bounced up beside him to check the image. It looked as though she were floating away and he was trying to keep her grounded.

"I love it!" she announced, then flitted off again. "I want to do the one with the blossoms!"

Handing his phone to another assistant, Sebastian followed the bouncing woman under a massive paper tree festooned with pink paper flower blossoms. They fluttered everywhere and he had to admit the scene was incredibly romantic. Add to that the perfume that filled his nostrils—and likely all his pores—and he surrendered to the dreamy moment. They took a few shots smiling at the photographer.

Then, she stepped back to take in the overhead blossoms. "This is amazing. So creative."

Sebastian signaled to the assistant she might take a few more shots. He then took Zee's hand and spun her beneath the paper tree. "I'm glad you're having a good time."

"This is a bit of all right! Pinkie hug?"

"Pinkie hug." They linked fingers.

She sighed and tilted her head against his shoulder. Tendrils of her hair had tumbled from the upsweep and she looked tousled but more beautiful for the disarray. The warmth of her body and the press of her breast against his arm lured him to kiss the top of her head.

They met gazes. She smiled and her eyes dropped to his mouth. It felt perfectly natural to kiss her. Softly. Just a brush of his mouth over her pink lips. The sweetness of the moment teased at his emerging desires. When had he shared such a simple yet breathless moment with a woman? Whom he barely knew?

With a tilt of her body, she pressed harder into the kiss and threaded her fingers into his hair, teasing his surprise desires to alert. She tasted of champagne and the too tiny hors d'oeuvres she'd laughed over and then had popped into her mouth between dances. The warmth of her body melded against his as he slid a hand down her back. This dance move was subtle, reading her body, tasting her mouth. She electrified the air and his every desire.

This night could end one of two ways. Delivering her safely to a hotel or…taking her home with him. He knew which of the two he preferred. His inner rogue was not entirely tamable. Nor did he wish to tame it.

And yet something about this woman felt…remarkable. And so different from any woman he'd ever dated.

When suddenly she ended the kiss with a giggle, he turned her in another twirl and then she spun out in search of the next diorama.

The assistant handed back Sebastian's phone to him but muttered as she did so, "I switched to video. Seemed… special." With a wink, the woman turned to accept another phone from a partying couple.

Sebastian sought where his impromptu date had gone. He spied her snagging another tiny treat from a passing silver tray. "She *is* special."

Azalea clutched Sebastian's hand as they wandered along the edge of the dance floor. He'd spoken to so many people, in French, which she didn't understand, but he'd remained cognizant of her presence and those conversations had been short. He would often squeeze her hand and tilt down a smile at her. Gray-blue eyes stood out on his angular face beneath the dark brown, almost black, hair. So sexy. Handsome. A gentleman. A remarkable dance partner. And a hot kisser.

That kiss! What a way to get over a bad breakup. Might Sebastian be considered a rebound guy? Only if they went further than a kiss. And…that was not off the table as far as her desire-filled brain was concerned. A fling might make her feel better about men in general. Boost her confidence. At the very least, she'd leave Paris with a night to remember.

Not that this hadn't already turned into a memorable night. Hand in hand they wandered toward the exit, both in favor of some fresh air. Outside, the warm spring air swirled through her hair and restored her wilting energy.

After texting his driver for a pickup, Sebastian tucked away his phone and slid an arm around her shoulder. She leaned against him as if they were old friends.

Or new lovers. Could she?

Of course, she could. She wasn't that unsophisticated girl Lloyd had so rudely dismissed. Azalea Grace was a beautiful woman who could do anything, and have any man she desired.

"I've never had a better time," he said.

"Same. I sort of wish it wouldn't end."

"It doesn't have to." He saw the limo and waved that he'd seen him. Then he swept Azalea into his embrace.

The kiss was quick, passionate, and it said exactly what she had been considering: *we should take this to the next level*.

"I'm not a hookup kind of guy. But just one night…?"

He held out his hand and she glided hers into it. "Yes, just one night. I want that."

And she did.

CHAPTER THREE

AZALEA OPENED HER eyes to stare upward. The pale morning sky caressed pink-tinged, puffy clouds. With a twist of her head, she could just see the elegant Eiffel Tower in the distance. The two-story-high windows that curved over the bed she lay in captured the top of the city skyline and the dreamy sky. The bed sat on a wooden base, luxurious with sheets that boasted a thread count she was pretty sure exceeded the thousands. An ultrasoft comforter hung to the thick, plush rug spread on the herringbone-patterned wood floor.

Everything smelled like sweet flowers and candy. A hug? What had been the name of that perfume? Câlin. The scent certainly had followed them home. Good thing she liked the smell. But it was all so much.

Sebastian was so much. So much of a good thing.

Sebastian... Sebastian... What was his last name? He'd told her it, but she couldn't recall it.

Azalea suddenly remembered that she wasn't in bed alone. Clutching the sheet to her bare chest, she turned her head. Sebastian lay beside her, his eyes closed, pillow partially over his face and an arm wrapped over the end of it. A strolling gaze traveled from his square jaw with the hint of dark stubble to his broad yet smooth chest that displayed the hard muscles she had traced with her fingers last night. And down to his abs, well-honed and tight. And down farther... Oh, baby, what a night!

Never in her life had Azalea hooked up. Not with a complete stranger. She'd only known the man for hours before following him into bed! Yet from the dancing to the champagne, to the delicious sex, she didn't regret one moment of it. This trip to Paris had turned out to be an uplifting treat after all.

But now the walk of shame. Or rather, the day's journey back to her dad's cottage in Ambleside, where she must finally see to putting her life back together and reenter said life with a plan to move forward. Which entailed...

She didn't know what it entailed. But she did know it was time to stop moping over a failed relationship and get on with it.

Yet the thought of leaving Sebastian's side firmly tugged against the nudge to get up and move on. Maybe a few more minutes lying here, taking it all in.

The man was a dream come true. He ticked all the right boxes, including being a dance phenom, and she did recall at some point he'd offered to defend her honor. She'd loved every minute of the fancy soiree. And the dress had allowed her to easily fit in with the elite crowd. Perhaps being away from home and knowing absolutely no one had allowed her to let loose. Her inner wild child had jumped to the surface. What fun to find a man who enjoyed dancing, being a little silly, and embracing life. They'd pinkie-hugged into one another's lives. Their own secret handshake, of sorts.

Of course, she could have no clue what he thought of last night. Perhaps it was his manner? Hookups might be usual for him. In which case, he might expect to wake and find her gone.

Good plan. She'd gotten what she wanted—a night to remember.

It could never be more than one night. They'd both been burned in a relationship. Last night had been rebound sex. Nothing more. Certainly not if this stylish, big-city man ever learned she was but a simple country girl.

Right. She was out of her league here. Time to shuffle back home.

She carefully slid from the bed to seek out the bathroom. The spangled dress lay on the floor. Had Sebastian said something about returning it for her? *Yes, please.* She didn't want to face the photographer again. Though he'd been a creep, she had actually stolen a valuable gown from him. She'd leave a note with the name of the studio and trust the dress, along with the heels, would be returned. But that meant she had only her jeans and no shoes or shirt to wear home.

She wandered into a closet whose interior was the length of the bedroom wall. With the ceiling constructed entirely of glass, she could see the elegant suits, shoes and accessories neatly ordered. Each hung exactly two fingers apart. And all colors were arranged by hue in rainbow order. Someone had a bit of fashion OCD. Excusable. She wasn't going to judge a man who had given her, oh, so many orgasms. Had Lloyd even been capable of finding her *on* button? Not without some direction from her. Idiot.

Toward the back of the closet were folded slacks and a couple of neatly folded T-shirts stacked from neutrals to a soft heather tone. She plucked up a black one and held it against her bare chest.

"It'll work."

Grabbing her pants and purse, she slipped into the bathroom and carefully closed the door so as not to wake the sleeping prince who had rescued her from the lecherous villain.

Deciding against a shower because she didn't want to make noise, she splashed some water on her face and borrowed the comb that lay perfectly arranged in the side drawer.

Slipping on her jeans, she then pulled the T-shirt over her head. The scent of Câlin filled her nostrils. She suspected it might have to be sandblasted off her skin. At the very least, it did smell nice. And it reminded her of laughter, dancing and a kiss under pink paper flower blossoms.

Her phone vibrated, and, thankful it wasn't set to ring out loud, she quietly answered when she saw Maddie's name on the screen.

"How'd the photo shoot go?" her friend inquired cheerfully. "Must have been great, because I know what you did last night."

"You…know?" Meaning, the party? The man? The sex? How could she possibly…? "The photo shoot was a bust, Maddie. I had to run—"

"Run? What?"

"The photographer was handsy and a total sleaze. I took off. With the dress. Which I promise I'll return today."

"Oh, my God, Lea, I'm so sorry. I had no idea. I had heard good things about the photographer."

"It's…in the past. I got away from him. And…" Landed in a much more respectful pair of male hands. Who certainly knew how to push all the right buttons on her anatomy. Whew! Surely, that third orgasm had been worthy of her gasping shouts.

"And…" Maddie prompted expectantly.

"Well, you said you knew what I did last night. What did you mean?"

"Câlin," her friend pronounced as if declaring the name of the mysterious fiend on a late-night show.

"How do you...?"

"It's all over social media, Lea."

"You know I don't do social media. What are you talking about?"

"Seems you went to a fancy party last night. A perfume release by Jean-Claude? He's a Parisian icon, Lea. How *did* you manage that invite?"

"Well." Pausing to listen for sound on the other side of the door, Azalea sat on the toilet seat and explained everything from jumping into the limo, to the invite, getting her boogie on, and then landing in bed with the sexy Sebastian. "I'm in his bathroom now."

"OMG! When you get over an ex-boyfriend you really do it right. The photo of you and Sebastian is stunning. He's got you in his embrace and you are laughing. You look so happy. And he is the definition of sexy. Sebastian Mercier." Maddie sighed. "What a catch. But seriously, Lea, you don't want to get involved with that family drama."

Still stuck on his last name—she'd only heard him say it once last night—Azalea wondered why it sounded so familiar.

"Lea, are you listening to me?"

"I am. I wonder what photo that was?" From one of the diorama shots? Though, she did recall some shots taken in the crowd. Sebastian had slid an arm about her waist and leaned in to pose for a number of people. Had one of them been a reporter? "Why does his last name sound familiar?"

"L'Homme Mercier? Remember, Lea, we rented tuxes from them last year for my wedding?"

"Wow—the most famous menswear designer in Paris?"

"Yes, dearest, *that* Mercier family. They own an elite

atelier in the sixth and another shop in the Place des Vosges. And, apparently, you are not aware of what the poster wrote about that family's current competition."

"Competition? I don't understand any of this, Maddie. And I'm hungry. I need eggs and toast. With beans and tomatoes and a few of those curly onion bits sprinkled—"

"Lea! Focus. Listen to me."

Visions of steaming eggs set aside, Azalea nodded. "Right. Fill me in."

"So apparently your sexy dance partner and his brother are in a competition to win the CEO position of the family company. The first brother to marry and produce an heir wins."

Azalea's jaw dropped. Her sweet, sexy lover who could dance her into dreams both on the dance floor and in between the sheets was…looking for a wife? And an heir? As part of a competition.

Suddenly she wished for a toothbrush because the bad taste in her mouth stunk.

"That doesn't…" Sound like the man who had saved her last night. And had given her a taste of real, delicious passion.

But she knew nothing about him. So, he loved to dance. And make love. And was kind. An actual rescuer of lost, makeshift princesses. But had such amiable heroics been a ruse? The woman who had dashed away from the limo— Had he been trolling for a wife last night?

"Lea? Talk to me."

"I…thanks for telling me that, Maddie." This was a lot to process. "But don't worry about me. It was just a hookup. I'm not in the market for a husband. You know marriage is not on my list."

"Is that so? It was on your list. Your goal of having kids

and raising them wild and feral on a farm isn't going to happen without a man, Lea."

"That goal can be attained. Doesn't mean the participating man has to be my husband." Oh, how she lied to herself!

Maddie sighed. "Sebastian Mercier is worth millions."

"So? I'd never marry a man just because he's got money. You know me better than that."

"I do. And I believe that sweet, quirky Lea landed in the arms of a millionaire by accident and was swept away on a fantasy night of dancing and passion. And you know what? You deserve it. A night on the town. Doing as you please. With whomever you please. But it's a new day. What are you going to do now?"

"I'm heading home. I had my fun." And had made another wrong choice! Just when she'd thought she'd turned a corner on her bad decisions. Argh! "Time to get back to my life."

"Which means...? Are you going to find work in London and rent a new flat?"

"Well." Staying at her parents' farm provided a convenient hideaway from the real world.

"Lea. Don't let Lloyd's rejection bring you down any longer. You're better than that. And you don't have to go back to that flower shop. Find a new shop that's not owned by a backstabbing, boyfriend-stealing witch. You'll find something."

"I know I will." Pausing to listen for sound on the other side of the door, she was reassured by the silence. "I gotta go, Maddie. I want to duck out of here before he wakes."

"Oh, baby, you've had a night. Just don't trip and land in his arms again. That man could prove a real problem."

"No kidding. I'm not that stupid. At least, I'm not going to be that stupid about a man anymore."

"Hallelujah!"

"Talk later, Maddie."

She hung up and stuffed the phone in her purse. Then she faced the woman in the mirror. Hair tousled but still a bit wavy from the updo. She shook her head and exhaled.

"It was a fun night." No way would she deny herself that win. "But you need to dash before you do land in his arms again."

Because Maddie knew she had a weakness for a sexy man with pleading eyes and a heroic heart. What woman would not? But apparently this sexy man needed a wife and child. To consider such a fulfilling prospect—no. This wasn't her world. Azalea Grace loved her small life. It made her happy. Besides, a relationship with Sebastian would lead nowhere. How could it? He had a wife to find. A company to win! Better to walk away with her heart intact while the walking was possible.

With a firm jut of her chin, Azalea pulled on her metaphorical big-girl knickers—because in reality she was sans knickers—and snuck out of the best thing that would never happen to her.

Sebastian pulled up a pair of soft, jogging slacks and called out to Azalea. He assumed she was in the bathroom, though he didn't hear any running water. He raked his fingers through his hair.

The petite bit of freckles and blond hair had rocked his world last night.

They had danced like no one was watching. Laughed until his jaw had ached. Had sex. Really amazing sex. They needed to do all of the above again. Before she left and returned for home.

"Zee?" He wandered over to the bathroom door and

rapped with his knuckle. A twist of the knob, and he slowly opened the door… "Zee?" He scanned the penthouse behind him, not seeing any sign of her.

His gaze landed on the dress folded neatly on the vanity. The shoes were placed next to it, along with a note written on a piece of cardboard torn from a soap box.

Sebastian, it was an amazing night. I'll never forget it! Saw social media this morning. You're in a competition with your brother? Time for me to leave. Only good memories. Promise. You said you'd return the dress for me. Here's the address...

Sebastian cursed under his breath. She'd learned about the competition on social media? He rushed out to the bedroom and grabbed his phone to open the one social media app he used and searched for his name. A photo of him embracing a laughing Azalea popped up.

"So gorgeous," he whispered. "And happy."

And yet, after the night they'd had together she'd decided to sneak out without saying goodbye? Would she have waited and spent some time with him had she not seen the post? He would never know.

Sebastian looked out the window and ran his fingers through his hair. Had the best thing that had ever happened to him just slipped away?

No, it had been a one-night fling. In a few days he'd forget all about Azalea Grace. And her cute freckles. And her bubbly presence. And her delicious and surprisingly commanding kisses. Life would move forward. Back to the wife hunt.

He turned his phone over to peer at the social media post. Her smile was so effusive. Her entire face squinched and her eyes closed, drawing all attention to those remark-able freckles. He could hear her laughter even now and smell…well. *Mon Dieu*, that perfume had followed them home. They'd literally danced it into their systems. Despite its pleasantness, a long shower was in order.

Before tossing his phone to the bed, he recalled they'd taken some shots in interactive stages featured around the ballroom. Flicking through his camera files, he found the photos. In one, Azalea grasped a bouquet of balloons and stood on a concealed stool that made it look as though she were floating upward. Arms wrapped around her waist, he appeared to bring her back down as he looked up ador-ingly at her.

Sebastian smiled. Tapped the photo until it wobbled with a trash can on the corner of the photo. And then… he shook his head.

"No, I don't want to forget you."

CHAPTER FOUR

With the sun setting soon, Azalea found her bicycle parked behind the bookstore where she'd left it yesterday morning before catching a train to London to make the trip to Paris. She knew the store owner and had gotten permission years ago to use the rack. Everyone in Ambleside knew everyone else. It was a tourist town renowned for its hiking trails and beautiful scenery. It was one of many small towns in the Lake District that sat upon Lake Windermere.

Her dad, Oliver Grace, had texted her around noon. He and his girlfriend had left to catch their afternoon flight out of London to Australia. Would she be home soon to tend Stella? Yes, not to worry.

The bike ride was a pleasant meander along the paved roads and cobbled Ambleside streets to country lanes lined with mown grass and bright yellow buttercup and pale pink thrift. Inhaling the fresh air, she allowed the remaining sunshine to beam through her pores, reviving her muscles after the tedious hours of travel. Still, the perfume lingered on her. Most likely she'd left a scent trail on all the trains she taken from Paris to home.

One night in Paris? Well spent when she considered her sexual needs had been met. Big-time.

It was that pinkie hug from Paris that she needed to forget. And that smolder. The man was in a competition that required him to find a wife and have a child? Might Azalea Grace ever manage to pick a normal man?

Apparently, she was not meant to find a happily-ever-after sort of guy. At least, not the sort who could meet her expectations of what she wanted in her future. Country cottages and barefoot children, anyone? Yes, please. She'd meant it when she'd told Maddie marriage was off the table.

Maybe.

Dash it, her heart knew that was a lie. Her idea of the perfect life did involve marriage, and not living on her own, children or no children. But she would not marry a man simply because he'd rocked her world and needed her to win a competition.

"Forget about him," she muttered to her pining heart.

Once at the cottage, set in a dip beyond a sharp right turn and but a stone's throw from the lake, she parked her bike against the weather-bleached fence that had once kept wild rabbits from the garden but now tended to merely entice them to try their hand—or rather, paw—at wiggling through the wide gaps between slats.

She wandered into the cozy, brick-and-stone, nineteenth-century farmhouse that had been completely renovated two decades ago. In the kitchen, she filled a water bottle and walked out to the creaky yet comforting porch, where she sat on the steps overlooking a tidy and currently rabbit-less yard. Sunlight glittered on the wildflowers to her right and on the pond surface where a couple of wild ducks floated.

After a day filled with abrupt naps and rude awakenings—she could never sit on a train and not fall asleep within minutes—finally she had a moment to breathe.

She kicked off the cheap trainers she'd purchased at a tourist shop before hopping a train at the Gare du Nord and leaned against the porch railing. The wood was worn and smooth at her back because this was where she had sat all her life.

And soon it would be no more.

Her dad intended to sell the farm and cottage. Grace Farm had taken in and rehabilitated animals for almost three decades. Oliver Grace had started it along with Azalea's mother, Petunia. Now her dad wanted a new adventure. Which he had gotten with his girlfriend, Diane, a woman who defined the term *wanderlust* with a sparkle in her eye and occasional bits of grass in her hair and personal possessions proudly confined to but a rucksack.

Azalea was happy that her dad was moving on after her mother had divorced him three years earlier. Petunia Grace had told Azalea she felt confined. Needed to be free. It had been as amicable an ending as a thirty-year relationship could be. Her mom had moved to Arizona to start a crystal business with a longtime friend. A male friend who had read Petunia's aura and declared them soul mates.

So that was how freedom looked? Apparently.

The divorce had finally forced Azalea to move to London. Yes, she hadn't left home until she was twenty-two, being perfectly content to live on the farm and have no aspirations or ambitions other than to breathe fresh air and befriend any animal the farm took in.

London hadn't been so much a rude awakening as merely a much-needed rousing. Azalea had discovered a world beyond the confines of the country, and she'd enjoyed most of it. She'd stayed a few weeks with her sister, Dahlia, a lawyer. Dahlia had left the farm at sixteen, never to look back, compelled by the beck of the busy city and all its opportunities. She'd helped Azalea find a flat and a lovely job as flower arranger for a tiny shop tucked between a bookstore and a vinyl record shop. It had suited her. She had been happy. Much as Dahlia gently prodded her to aspire for something higher, more fulfilling, Azalea had never felt the need to enter the corporate rat race. She preferred a simple life, with simple things.

And though a tomboy at heart, she did have aspirations to become a princess. That childhood fantasy still held space in her heart. Not real royalty, but rather, well…last night had contributed to the fantasy. Fabulous gown, pretty makeup and shoes, an elite event filled with stardust and champagne. And a handsome knight.

Azalea inhaled the perfume that coated her skin and which had even imbued the T-shirt she wore. *His shirt.* She wished it smelled like him—sultry vanilla and cedar—but no such luck. A lovely parting gift to remember her one night in Paris?

Last night's fling had been amazing. Not a thing to complain about when viewing the larger picture. Sebastian had been perfect. Handsome. Kind. Fun. Even a little silly when they'd been dancing up a storm. An excellent lover. Obviously rich. But apparently in the market for an instant wife so he could gain control of the family company. That pesky detail could not be dismissed.

And he hadn't considered *her* a possible wife? He'd started to say something about his family not approving, but she'd forced herself to ignore it at the time. She had a right to be miffed at that exclusion. Even if it felt as if she'd dodged a bullet. So, like she'd written to him, she would remember the night, cherish it, but it was time to move on. More wrong choices to make, don't ya know?

A sneaky little devil landed on her shoulder and prodded her in the heart.

You liked him. A lot. Don't act like you wouldn't jump if you saw him again.

She sighed, catching her chin against her palm. Her heart did have a tendency to leap before her brain could stop her. Here she sat in a little piece of heaven on earth, undisturbed by the rush of the real world, and still Sebastian Mercier haunted her thoughts.

There was one problem. She hadn't given him her phone number and she'd not gotten his contact info. Though certainly she did know where he worked. L'Homme Mercier was a well-known Parisian brand. Maddie had mentioned the two ateliers. A quick browse online could easily locate them. She could make contact.

Yet, that felt like diving into something she wasn't sure was good for her. If he wanted to see her again, he'd find her.

And if she never saw him again, she'd have to accept that was how it was meant to be. Obviously, the man had a wife to catch. And she was all about not becoming a wife now.

Azalea sighed. Her relationship with Lloyd had broken her in a surprising manner. And one night with a stranger hadn't been able to pry the memory from her brain cells. Because of that breakup she'd developed a healthy fear of commitment. Marriage? Once it had been all she'd desired. Until Lloyd had reduced it to a condition of social status, and Sebastian had further cemented it with his emotionless quest for a wife. And while her parents had shown her that anything could be broken and still survive, she didn't want to touch the idea of an extended attachment with someone she didn't love or a man she might even eventually fall out of love with.

Yet her romantic heart still wanted love and a relationship. She wanted to be cherished, admired, and be a friend and lover. She wanted to be a mother.

Well. Wasn't as if Sebastian had intended to propose to her anyway.

Which left her here. Alone and unsure what her future held.

A moo from the barn clued her it was feeding time. Her dad, a bovine veterinarian, had taken in injured or sick cows for decades. He cared for them, tended their injuries and nursed them back to health before they were either returned to their owner or, if abandoned, lived in happiness on the lush acres of Grace Farm. Stella, a highland cow with a long brown coat and pearly white hooves, had given birth to a calf two months earlier. The little one was so fluffy it looked like a walking plushy. Her dad hadn't named the newborn, insisting he didn't want a reason to get attached when his plans involved selling them both before summer's end. In the few weeks Azalea had been staying here, she and the cow had become best of friends.

Stella wandered toward the wooden fence attached to the side of the barn and Azalea stepped down onto the grass in her bare feet.

"Stella!" she called. "You'll never believe the night I've had."

In a quiet office on the top floor of a 6th arrondissement building the Mercier family had owned for over a century, Sebastian leaned back in his chair. Two stories below, the atelier created bespoke suits for an elite clientele. The shop on the Place des Vosges carried their prêt-à-porter collection. Both shops drew clients worldwide.

L'Homme Mercier had begun in the 1920s as a tailor shop set up by Sebastian's great-great-grandfather and had grown exponentially over the years. It was a Paris icon. Their clients were rich and many. Yet the company prided itself on individual attention and exquisite detail to every piece of clothing it produced. Never mass-scale production. And marketing was tasteful yet sensual.

Philippe's suggestion that they integrate women's wear into their *oeuvre* was unthinkable. But his brother, just down the hall in his office, was moving ahead with plans, designs and clothing sketches. While their father, Roman, had not approved of the idea, neither had he rejected Philippe's ruse. That glint in Roman Mercier's eyes always indicated that he had set the parameters for the future of L'Homme Mercier. And those parameters would be controlled by whichever son first married and produced an heir.

A competition declared just weeks after Roman had suffered a stroke. It had only put him in the hospital overnight. The doctor had said Roman was very lucky in that his girlfriend had recognized the signs—one side of his face had drooped and he'd not been able to get his words out—and had immediately taken him to the emergency room. But that little brush with mortality had set Roman on a quest to secure his legacy.

Sebastian had never viewed the competition as silly or unthoughtful. Or even out of character for his father. It was what he knew. All his life he and Philippe had competed, be it on the lacrosse field, or attracting *Le Monde* for a feature article, or at boat racing at Marseilles. They earned their worth through their father's nod of approval.

And while this new competition would involve another person—and *creating* another person—his child—Sebastian set his heart to it as with all other competitions. And this time he must win. L'Homme Mercier would not be diluted by mass marketing and—by all the gods—a women's clothing division.

Did the battle require he be in love? Not at all. In fact, the idea of love equating to marriage was not a Mercier philosophy. Roman Mercier had four sons. By three different mothers. He'd never married any of the women. And while Sebastian knew there was something not quite right with that family structure, he also knew nothing else. Which did make the marriage stipulation a little strange.

Why did Roman insist on signed legal papers? Shouldn't an heir be enough? And really, was Sebastian supposed to put some woman's name on a piece of official paper that granted her half of everything he owned? That did not sit well with him. So he'd be sure to have a prenup drawn up.

Sebastian was very capable of taking control of the family legacy. He knew the company from bottom to top. He'd started in the sewing department when he was thirteen, learning the trade and taking pride in the occasional nod of approval from the tailors. Later, he'd moved up to promotions and design, and now he was in charge of the finances, shipping and suppliers. As well as sharing marketing duties with Philippe. Just last week he'd worked men's fashion week, which was held annually in Paris. It was always a whirlwind of fashion, celebrities, news media, interviews, parties and pressing flesh with all the right people. Philippe had missed half of it because he'd been in Marseilles schmoozing with an Austrian royal of the female persuasion. So, who was *really* devoted to the company?

Yet, during that exhausting week of fashion shows, Sebastian had struggled with distracting thoughts of *her*. Azalea Grace of the freckles and bubbly laughter. A woman who had leaped into his life, swirled him dizzy on the dance floor, and then dashed out as quickly.

But not without a pinkie hug. He smiled to think about that little gesture they'd developed between them within the short period they'd been together. The woman had dug up his fun side and he'd reveled in it. He hadn't felt so exhilarated and unguarded since he was a child. It was almost as if he'd been swept away into a fairy tale. Silly to think like that. Though she had mentioned something about feeling like a princess. And hadn't he been her rescuing knight?

A tilt of his head confirmed that bemusing thought. And yet. It had ended abruptly. Didn't feel right, either. Like Zee had left behind a hole in him with her sneaky departure. And that hole needed to be—well, he wasn't sure. Was it that he merely lusted after her? Or was there something more? The affection she'd given him so easily had felt genuine and surprisingly new. She hadn't asked for a thing in return, save another dance.

Had he seriously not gotten her contact info? Stupid of him. All he knew was her name and that she lived in England. Some village, or tourist town called Bumblebush. Or Anglewood. Or…he couldn't recall. He must remember the name. Because he wanted to see her again. Even as he'd schmoozed and shaken hands with the press and talked to all sorts at cocktail parties last week, whenever a beautiful woman had caught his eye, he'd looked away. Thought of Zee's springy blond hair. Those bright blue eyes that had reflected joy. And so many freckles.

And that kiss under the paper cherry blossoms. He'd

watched the video of it every evening, remembering the softness of her skin, the warmth of her sigh, the utter indulgence of her body melting against his. She'd gotten under his skin. Even more so than that blasted perfume.

Such nostalgic longing wasn't like him. Sebastian Mercier was a playboy. Just like his father. He loved women. Had found the process of frequent dating in his search for the perfect wife not at all taxing. And yet, for some reason, he hadn't hooked up with a single woman since the night of the perfume debut party. Quite out of character for him.

He toggled the mouse to bring his computer screen awake and decided to search for the name of the English village. If he could figure that part out, it shouldn't be too difficult to then find a woman named Azalea. He did have the photos of them from the party. He wondered if he could search for her that way. Might bring up a social media page?

His phone rang and, just when he thought to ignore it, a text popped up from his brother at the same time. Curious.

Sebastian answered the call, which was also Philippe, "What is it?"

"It's Dad. He's had another stroke."

CHAPTER FIVE

Months later

SO MUCH HAD happened as summer swelled. And so much had stayed the same.

Azalea's dad had called during week six of his vacation asking her if she wouldn't mind keeping an eye on things a bit longer. A few more weeks? Of course, that was no problem, she'd reassured him. And it wasn't. She loved the farm. She and Stella were best friends. And the half dozen chickens weren't too much trouble, save for Big Bruce, the cockerel, who had a habit of scampering off to the neighbor's farm and—well, she'd gotten more than a few rude phone calls pleading her to keep her cock locked up.

She'd gotten over the breakup with Lloyd. His loss. And with his lack of empathy, he would have never made a good father to her future children. Because, yes, children were her future.

And yet, the one thing that had altered in Azalea's heart lately was her need for companionship. It was more an inner blooming that pressed her to figure out her life. And to do it quickly.

Would she remain on this farm forever? No. It would go up for sale as soon as her dad returned. But where would she go and what would she do? London had been fine, but it had never felt like her place. Like a forever home. It was too busy. Too crowded. Too…just, too.

Even more, now she sought stability and comfort. Protection, even. In a sort of "man wrapping his arms around her and keeping her close" manner. Had she blown it by walking out of Sebastian Mercier's life?

She shook her head. Even if they had continued to see one another, she could have never been assured he wasn't using her simply for the wife and child stipulation that would have won him the CEO position.

Yet still, she was frustrated.

"Things have gotten complicated." She swore a bit more loudly than usual. Sometimes a well-intoned oath was required.

"Stella…" Azalea swept hay from the barn floor while the cow watched through the open gate at the end of the breezeway. "You and Daisy seem to get along well on your own." She'd named the calf. Difficult to keep calling her *little one*. And the little plushy did enjoy nibbling daisies in the field. "You think I can manage?"

The cow rubbed her cheek against the worn door frame, a favorite place to scratch.

"I am very capable of living on my own," she defended to no one but herself. Taking care of her own, she thought with a proud lift of her chest. "And I will find a job. I enjoy arranging flowers. There's a florist in Ambleside next to the ice cream parlor."

Yet it might never pay enough to ensure even the simple lifestyle she desired. She needed to get serious and figure out a means to an income to support herself.

Having been content on the farm for such a long time, she'd never considered pursuing higher education to enable her to get a nine-to-five job. Dahlia was the go-getter, the woman with a plan and a target. That target being becoming partner in her law firm and a million-pound home in Notting Hill. Dahlia knew her little sister was not so financially ambitious and had never tried to provoke her toward something beyond what she aspired to. Yet, Azalea was well aware she'd become complacent. Set in her ways.

Her parents' divorce had shaken her out of that complacence. Once located in London, she'd realized the only jobs she was qualified for were fast-food slinger—ugh; hotel maid—she did not like touching other people's messes; rubbish collector—seriously?—or simple yet creative jobs that she could easily learn, such as floral arranging. She didn't regret not furthering her education. The world was filled with self-starters, independent minds who made their own way. She just needed to make some life changes. Focus on her strengths. And…sooner, rather than later.

Because she'd taken a pregnancy test twice now. Both times it had confirmed the new life growing inside her. She'd only smiled about it since. Not once had she felt regret.

Honestly? Very well, anxiety had struck. And tended to wake her in the middle of the night. Could she do this? Could she actually be a mother? And do it alone?

What about Sebastian? He was the father, no doubts on that one. Should she include him? Did she want him in her life once the baby was born? Of course, the father should be allowed that option. But what if he insisted she marry him? He did, after all, outweigh her when it came to power, influence, and having access to hard-hitting lawyers. She barely knew the man. Might she risk getting trapped in his competitive plans for marriage? Plans that did not include love.

"Love is important," she muttered.

Stella mooed, as if in agreement.

"Exactly." She hung up the broom and slapped her palms across her khakis to disperse the hay dust. "I don't think I can tell him."

Stella's next moo was more admonishing. Azalea had debated with her nearly every evening when she went to muck out the stable. Should she or shouldn't she tell Sebastian?

Yet another moo and a curt dismissal as Stella turned to find Daisy. The cow left Azalea standing there with her hands on her hips. And her heart begging to be included in the debate.

"But there's no way to tell him," she insisted.

Another lie she told her heart. She'd already marked the GPS location of L'Homme Mercier on her phone. Flying to Paris and showing up at the atelier to announce Sebastian was going to be a father was not an impossibility.

"I don't know. I just…don't know how to do it in a reasonable and nonconfrontational manner. There will be a row. Loud words. Accusations. Questions. So many questions, surely. I've got enough to deal with in figuring out this pregnancy thing."

Put her indecision down to hormones.

Then she reprimanded herself for having normal doubts any new mother must experience. She was thrilled over being pregnant. Having a baby as a single woman hadn't been a choice she'd made in the moment. She and Sebastian had used protection. What was it she'd heard about a condom's failure rate? Something like two percent? She wouldn't even label it wrong. This baby felt right.

With or without Sebastian.

Wandering outside, she nearly slipped in the mud that curled around the barn but caught herself with a swing of her hand just dipping into that muck.

Swiping a palm over her thigh, she lifted one foot, clad in a mud-coated wellie, and the suction released her. Farm life. If she didn't end the day with mud, straw or some unidentifiable substance stuck to her hair, skin or clothing, it just wasn't a day.

"I'm going to shower, then take a walk in the field to collect some cornflowers for a bouquet," she told Stella. "You and Daisy might join me if you care to. Be back in a bit."

She strode to the back of the cottage, where a makeshift, outdoor shower fitted over a stone mat was useful for clearing away the mud. But before she could turn on the spigot, she heard a car. Driving *away* from the cottage? The property was in a neat little private area, sporting a long drive lined with hedgerows. Had someone been up to the front without her knowing? Possible. When in the barn it was difficult to hear beyond the back of the cottage. She wasn't expecting any deliveries.

Swinging around the side of the cottage, Azalea dodged the overgrown vines that she swore she'd tend soon and pushed open the creaky iron gate. A man stood on the fieldstone pathway curling to the front door. A smart black suitcase sat on the ground beside him. He was quite well-dressed. In a stunning suit—

Azalea swore under her breath. In an instant her heartbeat went from calm to freakout. She patted her frazzled hair, which she might or might not have combed this morning.

At the sight of her, he waved. Even at this distance his smile danced into her heart and giddied in her belly. He'd seen her! No chance to duck away and hide. To fix her hair. To—she studied her dirty hands—yikes, did she have mud in her hair, too?

How had he found her? Why was the sexiest man

in Paris standing before her cottage with a smile that shouldn't be there if he could get a good look at her?

"Zee!"

He could call her all he liked, but that didn't make her feet move forward. She was frozen in shock. And not because she must look a fright. Well, yes, there was that. But because—her hand went to her belly.

"Sebastian," she said on a gasp.

She'd gone over this moment many a time with Stella. How to tell him? *Should* she tell him? The answers depended on whether she'd see him again. And now here he was. Standing in her front yard. And she had not practiced for this scenario.

Seeing her frozen there, dumbstruck, Sebastian stepped carefully on the overgrown grass, and beelined around a crop of fieldstones that were supposed to be yard decoration but really her dad had tossed there because he didn't want to haul them to the back of the property.

When he stood before her, Azalea still felt like a statue that could barely breathe. Her insides were rushing, gushing and flip-flopping all at once. And the little tyke growing inside her had many months before it began to move about, so she knew it was nerves.

"I found you," he announced. "And believe me, it wasn't easy. But once I figured out that you lived in Ambleside, all I had to do was go around with your photo and ask—"

"You have my photo?" she dumbly blurted.

"Yes." He tugged out his phone and turned the screen toward her. The screensaver showed them in that silly pose they'd taken at the party with her flying away, balloons in hand, and him grasping to pull her down. "Everyone had a good laugh at the photo. They all knew it was you and where you lived. Though I must admit, finding a place 'just beyond the dip' was an interesting excursion."

"Yes, the dip in the road."

She gestured toward the road, realizing it was stupid to even converse about the condition of the old, winding road when the man of her dreams stood before her. Looking like a god who could conquer all of womankind with his smolder and a tug at his perfectly fitted suit. And she looking like the one who got trampled on by the masses as they rushed him for his favor.

"I'm sorry it took so long to come see you," he said. "I've thought about you every day."

"Same," she whispered more softly than her heart screamed. She must tell him.

Oh, heart, be quiet!

"After you left Paris, I was busy with fashion week. Which takes up a few weeks business-wise. And then my father had a stroke. Another one, actually. It was difficult to get away."

"Oh, dear, Sebastian, your dad? Is he all right?"

"Yes, he's recovering and dealing with some speech issues now. The old man needs to slow down. Take things easy."

And insist one of his sons get married and have a child so they could take control of the company? The thought shoved Azalea like a bully with his hands to her back, but she swallowed down a yelp, or worse, an oath.

"Is it all right that I've come?" he asked.

He took her in, his eyes gliding over her. Gray-blue irises caught the sunlight and toyed with her sense of personal space. Her newly acquired need to protect her growing family at all costs. And yet, all she wanted was to claim a hug from the man who had explained that the French simply didn't do that.

"You don't look pleased to see me."

Azalea exhaled and shook her head. "I am pleased. I think. I mean, well, it is a surprise, isn't it? I hadn't thought to see you again. Though…yes, I am pleased. Well. I feel a bit mussed right now. Been mucking out the barn. Would you like to come inside while I refresh?"

"I'd love to."

Sebastian had risked rejection jetting off to London, then on to the little village of Ambleside without having a means to notify Zee he was on his way. He'd gone from a café to a pub and, photo of Azalea displayed on his phone, had gotten lucky at the second stop. A young man around Azalea's age knew her from school and had directed Sebastian to take the west road for a distance, then turn right after the dip.

Surprisingly, the driver had found the place.

Now he sat at a round table graced with a bouquet of wilting blue flowers. The house was small and epitomized cottage core, with the checked curtains, cozy rugs, low ceilings and tidy cupboards. He heard a cow moo in the distance and the occasional crow of what he guessed could be a cockerel. That night at the party he'd guessed she wasn't of his world, but he'd not expected an actual farm girl. He was not put off but he also wasn't sure what to expect. He'd only ever dated city girls, women who'd given a care for their hair, nails and always the perfect outfit.

What sort of travesty had been those rubber boots covered in mud? And even more mud in her hair and on her face?

And yet, at the sight of Azalea—his Zee—his heart had

bounced. Almost like a dance he'd shared with her at the party. He'd found her. The woman who had jumped into his life and as quickly jumped out of it.

He'd had to make this trip. He wanted to get to know her. To see if this compulsion to find her was something more. But also, since his father's second stroke, the pressure to win the competition and take control of the company had increased. The risk that his father might have another stroke was high. And he might not survive the next one. L'Homme Mercier must be put in order before then, with the long-established traditions firmly in place without threat of change.

And if Zee had been on his mind so much, then, Sebastian had reasoned, perhaps he should entertain the idea of making *her* his wife? They both got along. And she had mentioned something about wanting a family and children. He'd come here to learn if she might be amenable to the idea. But even more so, he wanted to learn if he still felt the same way toward her. If they spent the night squabbling or couldn't find a common interest, then he'd mark the trip off as closing the door on a wonder that had prodded at his heart for months. On to the next potential wife. It was something he had to do for the company.

"Sorry to keep you waiting," she announced as she sailed down a curved stairway hugging a stone wall. "I didn't realize how much mud I had on me. It's Stella's fault."

"Stella being...?"

"Uh...my best friend."

The crinkle of her brow was so cute. Everything about her, from the tips of her now bare toes, up to her freckled knees, and the simple green checked dress to her button nose and more freckles on her checks. Her hair was fluffed and a little wet, and those bright eyes. The woman was simply stunning.

"So you found me." She stood at the base of the stairs, hands fidgeting before her.

Approaching her, unsure if she would allow it, Sebastian watched for a panicked look but only got a stunned blink of her eyes. Damn it, he'd been dreaming about this reunion for weeks. And it always started with a kiss. So he kissed her. And, thankfully, she didn't resist.

It had been too long. He'd thought about her kisses, her bare skin, the warmth of her body gliding against his. Her sweet murmurs as they'd made love that night, over and over. How the moonlight had glowed like pearls over her naked body. The two of them smelling like that crazy perfume and giggling about it. Now she was back in his arms. And a sweet murmur reassured him he was not overstepping any lines.

Something about holding Azalea Grace felt…fragile. Yet also a greedy desire prodded at him. He wanted the thing he wasn't supposed to have. And the little boy in him wouldn't allow any others to take it away from him.

When he pulled away to study her reaction, she nodded and said, "Yep, not a mistake."

"What's a mistake?"

"Nothing's a mistake. I was just remembering our night in Paris. It wasn't a mistake. That kiss reminded me of how real and fun it was."

"It was fun. And real. But too quick." He held up his hand, pinkie finger extended.

She twined hers with his. "Yes, too—well!" She quickly disengaged. "Now that you've found me, you must realize that I am a farm girl. Definitely not the type you're accustomed to dating. I'm not sure why you'd even bother coming to see me."

"Zee, I can't look at another woman without comparing her to you. I had to find you to see if the feeling I get every time I think of you was real. And well, it is real. I'm feeling those same flutters. Hell, it's like an animal pull to hold you, touch you, make love to you all over again. And I don't care if you're a farm girl."

"Yes, you do."

He shrugged, then chuckled. "There are certain odors out here, aren't there?"

She laughed. "But not me, I hope?"

"No, you smell like summer."

"And you..." She sniffed and then crinkled her freckled nose. "Do you smell of Câlin?"

"That perfume seems to have gotten into every fiber of clothing in my closet. I thought I'd aired it out but apparently not."

"That's crazy." She strolled to the sink, flicked on the faucet and grabbed a glass. Distancing herself from him? Not a good start.

"I wish you hadn't left without kissing me goodbye. But I understand. I'm sorry you had to find out about the competition from social media."

"I had to sneak out. I wasn't prepared to do the morning-after awkwardness. And the competition means nothing to me since we're not even a thing."

"We could be a thing."

"Listen, I'm not a fool, Sebastian. I'm so out of your social echelon."

"Oh, we're talking echelons now? Those are fighting words."

She laughed over a sip of water. "Be serious, Sebastian.

You asked that woman to marry you. She fled. You didn't ask me to marry you because I do recall you saying your family would never approve."

He should have never let that slip! "Do you want me to ask you? I recall you saying you'd never marry me."

"You got that right."

He clutched the back of a chair before the table. He hadn't expected this to be easy. "Still don't understand why this visit bothers you."

"It's just that, why waste your time on me? Surely you and your brother are in a race to win the prize. And with your father—oh, I'm sorry. I shouldn't make assumptions regarding his health."

"Assume anything you like. Philippe and I *are* in a race since Father's second stroke. It affected him more this time around. He can no longer go into the office. I've had to take over dealings with his special client list and Philippe has been traveling nonstop. We…" He shoved a hand over his hair and splayed it out before him. "Zee, can this just be what it is? I had to see you again."

"So you've seen me." She crossed her arms.

Not going to give him an inch? What had he done to make her so…disinterested? He'd thought they had parted on common ground, both quite pleased with their time spent together. Although she must've been miffed to learn about the competition. He'd give her that.

"Give me twenty-four hours," he challenged.

"What for?"

"To talk to you, get to know you." Find that crazy, silly happiness they'd shared with one another when they sailed around the dance floor. "I just want to be with you, Zee."

"Have sex with me, is what you mean."

"That would be ideal, but it's not a requirement."

She shook her head, then spread a palm over her stomach. "I don't know."

"You don't want to entertain a visitor for a while? Come on, Zee, give me a chance. Show me around. Take me into town. Introduce me to Stella. Can you tell me you haven't thought of me once since fleeing my home?"

"I didn't flee."

"You exited without saying goodbye, which is the definition of fleeing."

"Fine, I fled. And...very well. I'm not hating you being here in my home. My dad's home. I'm just watching the place until he returns from vacation."

"Tell me about it."

"Seriously?"

He spread out his arms. "You can't get rid of me now. I sent the driver away."

It took a while for her smile to blossom, but when it did her nose wiggled and her eyes brightened even more. She was so adorable. And he had just won the next twenty-four hours with her.

CHAPTER SIX

AZALEA OFFERED TO make a light meal, so a salad it was. Everything was fresh from the garden or field, even the mustard seed dressing. She and Sebastian sat out back on the porch, plates on their laps, wineglasses close to hand. Of course, she only had cherry-flavored sparkling water. In the background, a portable radio played her favorite station at a low volume.

Having combed her hair and gotten over her initial shock that Sebastian had actually come looking for her, she'd decided she would use this time to learn more about him. Her future, and the family she would create, required it of her. Because some day she'd have to tell her child about his or her father. What kind of man was he? Was he here to cajole her into marrying him to win that stupid competition?

Dare she let him into her life, allow him to learn more about her? It would be a cruelty if she ultimately decided against allowing him to participate in her child's life.

But that decision had not yet been made. And it was a big decision. One that needed all the supporting data she could acquire. Because no matter what, they would always be linked through their child. And that was an immense future to consider. Her wanting heart gushed and pleaded for her to invite him in and make him her own, while her logical brain put up a fit and insisted she ignore emotion and strive for practicality.

Stupid brain.

"It's peaceful out here," he commented as he set his plate aside. "Reminds me of summers at my grandparents' house south of Paris."

Pulled from the argument of brain versus heart, Azalea set her plate aside and rested her elbows on her knees, tilting her head to take him in. "Did they have a country place?"

"I suppose you would call it a château, but it was small and on many acres. Grandmother was the barefoot gardening sort who always greeted me with a spin."

"A spin?"

"She loved to dance anywhere, any time. She's the one who gave me a love for dancing."

"I don't think I've ever had more fun dancing than that night with you." Nor had she been more attracted, and downright sexually invigorated by his refreshing demeanor. Not what she'd expected from a man who knew how to wear an expensive suit. "Not many men care to loosen up like that. Especially one in such a fancy suit."

He brushed a trouser leg. He'd abandoned the suit coat, undone a few buttons at his collar and rolled up his white sleeves. Azalea decided it was his idea of comfort. "I'm all about suits, Zee."

"I suppose, since it's the family business. But with a little dancing included now and then?"

"Absolutely. I looked forward to those summers my mom would deposit me at the château to stay for weeks while she gallivanted off with her latest lover. My grandparents had a mangy dog and some chickens. And an insufferable goat."

"Goats are like that."

"They are. I even used to run barefoot in the grass." He eyed her bare feet. "So I'm not a complete slicker."

"You do earn points for that. But when was the last time your feet touched grass? I'm betting it hasn't been since those childhood summers."

"Is that a challenge?" He leaned in, tipping his glass against hers. "Because I'm all about challenges."

Yes, like finding a wife to give birth to his heir? Dare she spend the next day with him *without* telling him she carried his baby?

Oh, brain, just concede to heart!

"What's going on in there?" He tapped her temple and shifted to sit closer to her. "You're too serious for the fun-loving Zee I remember."

"You hardly know me."

"That's why I'm here. To learn more."

"Hmm, well, I do have moments that do not involve dancing wildly and tossing down champagne and tiny snacks."

"Oh, yes?" He paused, tilting his head to listen, and she noticed the sprightly song on the radio. "You know this one?"

At her affirmative nod, he stood and tugged her to stand on the porch. He spun her once under his arm, and they swirled into a few steps.

"Did your grandmother teach you this?" she called between bounces. She didn't know the dance exactly, but Petunia Grace had once been a competitive dancer during Azalea's preteen years.

"Of course! Grandmama loved the American dances."

With that he lifted her and twirled her around. Azalea thrust out her arms, her hair spilling out and a laugh gushing up. And when they whirled to a stop and he carefully set her down, he slid a hand along her cheek and studied her eyes with his beautiful, soulful, gray-blue eyes. From the frenzy of the dance to the sudden overwhelming *connection* of his gaze. She swallowed. Her heart resumed its swell in response. Tilting onto her toes, she kissed him.

A familiar place, this kiss. She didn't feel tentative or wary. Sebastian's heat coaxed her deeper and she reveled in the easy clash of tastes, textures and a hint of cherry sparkling water topping it off. As she leaned against his chest, her hands glided up and along his shoulders. Broad and straight. Her mighty rescuer in tailored armor. Her Parisian hero.

Breaking the kiss, she tilted her head against his shoulder and they swayed to the slower song that whispered behind them. The moment felt perfect, like something she needed to preserve in memory. So years from now she could tell the tale to her child.

"I'm glad you found me," she said without thinking her words through. It had been a confession. A true one. Her heart always spoke before her brain. "I missed you."

"I'm here now."

Yes, now. For less than twenty-four hours that she must wrap her arms around and squeeze out every moment. To remember forever. To tell stories about the man who danced her so silly they immediately followed it up with making a baby. Never would she have planned such a situation. However, this was not one of Azalea Grace's bad choices. And there was not a thing about it she would change.

If only she could blurt it out...*tell him*. But something kept her tongue in place. A worry that she might lose what little hold she yet had on him. Or more so, that he may want her for something she wasn't willing to agree to.

Behind them Stella mooed. The cow didn't need to be fed. And Azalea had no intention of listening to a cow's insistence she tell the man *right now*.

"Do you have a guest room?" he asked on a whisper.

Her dad called her old bedroom the guest room now. A hint that she should be moving along?

"It's my room."

His brow quirked. "I wasn't going to ask to sleep separate from you tonight. And it seems that we are both guests in this home. Shall we?" He hooked an arm and she glanced down at the plates and goblets. "We'll clean that up in the morning. Right now, I need to kiss your skin. Everywhere."

A quiet hush gasped from her very being. "Yes."

Hours later, both of them lying naked on the bed, with the sheets off and the open window beckoning inside a sultry breeze, Azalea turned toward Sebastian. It was dark in the room because there was no moon. One of the things about living in the country? No ambient city lights. She loved it. Though she would like to see his eyes right now.

Stroking her finger along his face, she followed the jut of his jawline back to his head and up to his earlobe.

"What are you doing?" he asked quietly.

"Memorizing you. You've got a sharp jawline. I like it." She trailed her fingers down his neck and along his shoulder to a bicep. "I'm guessing you do more than dance at perfume parties to get these muscles. Gym?"

"There's a weight room in my building. But I do run when I can."

"So, you could chase me across a field?"

"I'll certainly give it a go if the opportunity presents itself." He leaned in and kissed the base of her neck. His soft hair tickled her chin. "It's nice out here. So peaceful. Where will you go when your dad sells this place?"

"Not sure yet. I enjoy wide-open spaces. But I like the connection that London offers and sometimes all this rural charm really does annoy a girl. I mean, it takes some effort to pick up a few snacks."

"Sounds like you're stuck between the convenience of a big city and the peace of a smaller town."

"I suppose I am."

"What about Paris? It's a big city, but there is something less busy about it than London."

"Are you suggesting I move to Paris?"

"I wouldn't mind you living in my city. I'd get to see you more often."

"Sebastian..." She dropped her hand to the sheet. "What are you doing? This thing between us, you know it's only a..."

A fling? What *was* it? Because it felt big. Like something she could welcome into her life. Something she *should* welcome into her life. Into her burgeoning family. And yet... It could only ever be a dream. And wouldn't it be best to simply leave it as a dream?

"I don't want it to be a fling, Zee."

Neither did she. But she also knew what she didn't want. "I don't want to do a long-distance relationship."

"You could move to the French countryside?"

"Sebastian."

"What? I'm tossing out ideas."

"We've known each other for less than forty-eight hours. And yes, what we have when we're together is good. Really good."

"Feels soul-deep," he said. "I mean, I can just be with you, sitting on a porch, and that feels right."

Darn him for picking up on that intense connection. But thinking in such terms would only distract her from her staunch need to not settle for something that could never be real. Her mother had left her dad because she'd felt confined, stifled. How could Azalea possibly feel free under the thumb of a millionaire who wanted her for reasons that had nothing to do with love?

And yet, her fantasies of marriage and family had been recently renewed, treading right alongside the desire for a man who seemed too good to be true.

"Just because we're getting along well doesn't mean it will always be good," she said. "Besides, how will my living closer to you work when you have a wife and child?"

He rolled to his back and sighed. "I don't know."

That he didn't protest such a scenario meant it wasn't something he wanted to budge on. He had to find a wife. And have a child.

"I haven't seriously thought about that competition in weeks," he offered in the darkness. "I've been too focused on my dad's recovery and...you. Despite my busy schedule, I had to get away to find you. And now that I have, I question how to move forward. I want us to be a couple, Zee. But it feels as though you don't want it—"

"I do," she rushed out. A foolish outburst?

Oh, heart!

If she told him the real reason she wanted him, it would be as forced as his needing to find a wife. She wanted to be with Sebastian because she was falling in love with him, not because she felt beholden to him. Or because she was having his child and needed an official paper to give the baby legitimacy.

You want to make a real family. Mother. Baby. And father. You know you do.

He kissed the top of her head and slid a hand down to cup her derriere. "Let's sleep on it. Tomorrow is a new day. And I get to spend it with you."

He didn't say anything else. He didn't need to. She felt the same. Getting to spend time with him was a treat.

He would leave tomorrow, though. The idea of telling him she was pregnant suddenly felt manipulative. Like a means to keep him in her life. It wasn't like that. She'd thought about it. Debated the pros and cons with Stella. She was prepared to do the mother thing on her own. With the support of her family. She'd told Dahlia about it and her sister had offered to help her find a place to live and a job and day care. She hadn't told her dad yet. She would when he returned from vacation.

Now, to tell the man who needed a wife and child in order to secure his future that he'd already succeeded in meeting half that stipulation? Or to just step back and allow him to leave and have his own life in a world that she felt wasn't quite the right fit for her?

CHAPTER SEVEN

A DREAM-OBLITERATING SOUND woke Sebastian. He bolted upright in bed and muttered, "What the…"

It sounded again, long, obnoxious and…crowing. His entire musculature twinged tightly.

He swore.

The gentle touch of a hand to his back soothed reassuringly. He remembered where he was. On a farm. *Of all places.* But he was with her. And that made the next crow—still annoying.

"It's just Big Bruce," Zee whispered. "He's waking up the flowers. Lay down. It's early."

No kidding, it was early. Waking up the flowers? He didn't understand that. What did a cockerel have to do with—? Another crow crept into his spine and froze there.

The room was dark. He…couldn't exactly form thoughts beyond that. But the hand stroking his back chased away the chill and lured him to snuggle against the delicious warmth of Azalea. His Zee.

No obnoxious, crowing fowl could spoil that wondrousness.

Azalea rolled over in bed to find Sebastian smiling at her in the soft morning light.

"That cockerel is not my favorite part of this visit," he said quietly.

"Big Bruce is a noisy fellow."

"Agreed. Let's stay in bed all day and do what we did last night six more times."

"Six? You're awfully motivated."

"Too much? I'll settle for five."

She leaned in and kissed his nose and snugged her entire body against the length of his. Mmm, he was firm in all the right places. "Five, it is. But."

"But?"

At that moment, Big Bruce crowed.

"That," she said. "If I don't head out to feed the wildlife there will be a revolt."

"The life of a farmer?"

"I prefer rural princess, actually."

"Has a nice ring to it. Can I distract you for five minutes before you rush off to tend the animals?" He nudged the firmest part of him against her thigh.

"Absolutely."

After Zee left the bed, Sebastian showered and dressed. They'd only had time for two orgasms before she'd fled to tend the crowing and mooing menagerie. He'd claim the other three, or four, later.

The room was small but the bed had served as a cozy love nest. The entire place was minuscule compared to what he was accustomed to. But for the lack of maids who left his towels out and organized his fridge ingredients by color, he found he didn't mind the tiny home. Everything was an arm's reach away. He'd not had to walk across a vast closet to find anything.

The cockerel's crow tightened his muscles.

"Big Bruce and I will have words today," he muttered.

As for him and Zee, they had come together as if they'd

never been apart. Sure, she'd been initially awkward, but a dance and some kisses had reminded them both that what they had was magical.

"There you go again," he muttered as he wandered down the hallway, "thinking like a romantic."

He hadn't a romantic bone in his body. Truly. Hell, Sebastian Mercier didn't know a thing about romance and love. He'd not witnessed as much growing up. No heart-fluttering, gushing examples had filled his learning brain. Affection had been so fleeting he felt quite sure he was incapable of loving another person.

And yet, the fact he stood here in this tiny cottage, had been woken at dawn by an annoying bird, and now sought to spend the day with a sweet rural princess must allude to some part of his heart softening to the idea of love and romance.

Or was it that he simply needed a wife? A means to an end. And Zee offered an option.

When he thought of it that way, his skin prickled. It sounded so clinical. And certainly, Zee was not the sort of woman who would ever agree to become a convenient bride. Yet he could never give her the love and romance she deserved if he hadn't a clue how those emotions worked.

He'd thought to come here to see if they still had a connection. If not, he'd have headed home to pursue the next candidate for wife. Yet their reunion had been anything but cold and distant. The passion they shared filled him in ways that surprised him. Could he possibly convince Zee to marry him?

Down in the small room before the back door he studied a neat shelving unit that housed shoes, boots and various caps, hats and gloves. Ah, here was a tidy setup. The rubber boots on the bottom looked about his size. And they fit.

"When in Rome," he muttered. Make that *when on a farm.*

He gave a stomp to each boot. Not much for comfort, but they would serve a purpose. The mud-green color clashed terribly with his gray, checked trousers, but he'd not packed comfort clothing, so this look would have to do.

"They could be more stylish with a buckle and perhaps a leather pull tab," he decided.

L'Homme Mercier did not offer shoes in their line. Something to consider? If they ever went with a rustic line, for sure.

Stepping outside, he wandered across the tidy porch and stepped down onto a neat stone walk. The outdoor shower deserved a nod of approval. A few decorative pots of frothy grass rose almost as high as his head and gave off a lemon scent. The path veered in a curving fashion toward the blue barn. With the sun high in the pale sky he wished he'd worn a T-shirt or something lighter than his white button-up, but a roll of each sleeve provided some relief from the humid heat.

He could do rustic as well as anyone. Who would have thought? Certainly, though, his family would scoff to see him now. If it wasn't luxury, artisan-made, an original, or reeking of old money, it wasn't worth the notice. Cows and cockerels? The indignity!

His family didn't have to know about this trip to Ambleside. Nor did they have to know about Azalea. She was…

What was she, exactly? She had stuck in his brain for so long that he'd had to find her. And now that he had, he wanted to stay and never leave her side. Find a way to keep her in his life. Though he much preferred they be together in a less rural setting, he could manage for the duration of this visit. Which would be too short.

If he got involved with Zee, then what would become of his quest to find a wife? He couldn't have a lover and a fake wife. Or? Well? No. It just wouldn't do. He was not a French king or even the president of the country. Despite the press's tendency to label them careless, pleasure-seeking playboys, even the Merciers had their standards.

Might Zee consider becoming his wife? A name on an official piece of paper, who wasn't required to love him or receive love in return. But certainly, it did demand she give him an heir.

Sebastian scrubbed his fingers across the back of his head. He could never fake it with Zee. And not faking it would only complicate it all and confuse his emotions.

Then again, he was no man to back down from a challenge. Especially one that offered such a delicious prize as the freckle-faced rural princess. And the clock was ticking.

"Play it by ear," he muttered as he wandered toward the open barn door. "It's only been a day."

Yes, and things could change. His heart might simply be in the throes of a new and unique interest and passion. Everything cooled. That was a given. As his father had so often said to his sons, "The glow rubs off quickly. And then you're left with disinterest and the itch for something new."

Easy enough for Roman Mercier to say when he hadn't been presented with a win-it-or-lose-the-company ultimatum. There was nothing Sebastian wanted more than to claim the CEO position of L'Homme Mercier.

Not even Azalea Grace? his inner devil whispered.

Well. Which did he want more? Could he really claim attachment to a woman he knew so little? The CEO position meant more. It did.

"Zee?" he called as he entered the cool shade of the barn.

No reply. He wandered through and spied the blonde combing a rather monstrous cow with a long brown coat that flowed over its eyes and horns.

Sebastian had never been around large farm animals. He was rarely around dogs or cats, though he did favor a mellow, napping cat over the oft-rambunctious dog. Those stays at his grandparents' had only ever introduced him to one old dog who could barely wander from his bed to the feeding bowl. There had been the occasional turtles and snakes. Creatures that had fascinated his younger self. And heaven forbid he ever encounter another goat.

Slowing his pace, he cautiously approached, noting there was a smaller cow at the end of a fenced area, nipping at foliage that grew wild against a fence post.

"Why do you call me Zee?" she asked, keeping her attention on the midsection of the beast that she combed.

"You don't like it?" He winced at the scent of manure that rose from all around him. Yet it was topped with a sweet grassy note. He much preferred a perfume-doused room.

"I don't mind. Most friends call me Lea."

"Well, I'm not a friend." But what was he exactly? "Is this beast what you would call a bull?"

She smirked at him as he stopped a good five feet from the animal. He glanced back to the barn. Sprinting distance, if necessity required.

"Stella is a girl. Not a bull."

"*This* is Stella? I thought she was your best friend?"

"She is."

"I see." And here he'd thought her best friend would be a human. Well, he should have guessed, eh? "But she has horns."

"Girl cows can have horns. Specific breeds, that is."

"I didn't know that. She's…" He bent to find the creature's eyes but the long coat covered them completely. "How can she see?"

"Her coat moves when she walks. She knows where you are. She smells you."

"As I smell her." The beast snorted and bobbed her head. Sebastian took a precautionary step back. "Sorry," he provided. "I'm sure you smell lovely to other cows."

"I see you found my dad's wellies," Zee said.

"Do you think he'll mind?"

"Not at all. It's messy out here. Come closer. Give my girl a pat on the nose. She likes affection."

"Very well." Not about to appear afraid of an animal she was obviously comfortable to stand beside, he carefully approached, stretching out an arm until he was just near enough to gently pat her nose. It was…warm and had a soft leathery texture. The beast nudged against his palm. So he stepped closer and gave her nose a gentle rub. "She likes that."

"Stella is a flirt. She'll have you wrapped around her horns in no time."

"I'm not sure I like the idea of such a scenario."

"I didn't mean it like that. Like having you wrapped around her little finger. You know. Maybe you don't. It might have gotten lost in translation."

"Indeed." And yet, he was perfectly content should Zee wish to keep him wrapped about her pinkie finger.

The smaller cow now wandered over, its nostrils flaring as it scented him. Sebastian stepped closer to Azalea.

"She's only five months old," she said. "I think she's going to take after her mom. Goes for the handsome men, she does."

Patting the little one's nose, he was happy to note that

it stopped the beast from getting closer to him. "Do you have a lot of handsome men visiting your animals?"

She chuckled. "Nope. Well, my dad is handsome. And he babies them like they were his children. I think that's good, Stella. You look gorgeous." Zee wrapped her arms about the cow's head for a hearty hug.

"You don't worry about those horns?"

"I'm careful. So." She tucked the comb in a pocket of her overalls. "I'd offer you breakfast but I haven't had time to do grocery shopping. How about we head into the village for a hearty British brekkie?"

"If that means protein and eggs, I'm in."

"Great. You like to ride a bike?"

Sebastian strode after her as she headed through the barn, hanging up the comb as she did. "Bike? Are you serious?"

"Would you prefer we jog?" She chuckled but didn't reassure him that she was indeed joking with him.

And Sebastian swallowed to think that this trip to find the woman of his dreams might just challenge him in ways he never could have imagined.

They did not bike into the village. Azalea had been teasing. The look of utter horror on Sebastian's face when she'd suggested they might pedal in was probably the exact look she hadn't been able to see when Big Bruce had woken him before the crack of dawn.

Poor guy. Farm life could be tough for the uninitiated. But hadn't he said he was a runner? Probably he required fancy running togs and a dedicated path through a city park for such a venture.

Parking her dad's old car on a side street, she then led Sebastian down the quaint cobbled street to her favorite breakfast café.

* * *

After a huge breakfast of bacon, eggs, beans and toast, and a rosemary-seasoned blend of summer vegetables, she led Sebastian on a walk along the river that was hugged on one side by tight hedgerows. He snapped a few selfies of them standing before the Bridge House, then she tugged him down a pathway. The hiking trail was well worn, so the fact that he wore designer shoes without rubber treads wouldn't be a problem.

"It's beautiful out here," he commented as they paused on a hillock to look over Lake Windermere.

A corvid flew over their heads, frighteningly low.

"They're looking for food scraps," Azalea explained. "From the tourists. They come here for the hiking and scenery. It is a lovely place."

"A place you plan to stay in forever?"

He really wanted to nail down her future plans. He'd asked much the same last night in bed.

She leaned against a wood fence post and studied his profile. If she checked the entry for handsome in the dictionary, she felt sure to find Sebastian's picture there. With an addendum warning all women to proceed with caution.

"I fled London to lick my wounds after I broke up with Lloyd. I have a tendency to make bad life choices when it comes to men."

He flicked a concerned look her way.

She shrugged. "I'm not sure where I'll go after Dad returns from Australia. I don't want to intrude on his new relationship. He and Diane are quite smart together. She makes him smile again. And that's a good thing. Besides, he plans to sell, so I need to pack up and find my own place in this world."

And if they continued on this course of conversation,

she'd have to tell him everything. That information was not something she wanted to reveal with tourists wandering by.

"Tell me about your parents," she said. "Are they the sort who would welcome you to stay after a breakup?"

"Perhaps my mother would if she was staying in Paris at the time. My parents are... My father has never married any of his children's mothers."

"Oh. So you and your brother...?"

"Philippe has a different mother than mine. It's why we are only six months apart in age. And I just got a new set of twin brothers nine months ago. Another girlfriend for my dad. Good ole Dad is still single."

"I think they are called playboys. Or baby daddies."

Sebastian laughed and clasped her hand. "That is most definitely Roman Mercier. The man is set in his ways."

"And those ways involve pitting his sons against one another and forcing them to marry? I can dismiss his roguish ways, but really, Sebastian, a man who has never married is asking his sons to do so? I find that hypocritical."

"I try not to consider it too much. And since the strokes, I've noticed more urgency to his manner. He's tasted mortality. He wants to ensure L'Homme Mercier is in good hands before he leaves this world."

"I don't see why both sons can't work together."

"If you knew about the changes and direction Philippe wants to take the company you would understand. He wants to add a women's division."

"And you don't?"

"What part of L'Homme Mercier says women's clothing?"

"Nothing wrong with expanding, is there? The women's market must be much bigger than the men's."

He shook his head and scoffed. "We are a menswear company. Always have been. And should remain so. I'm not against taking the brand to new levels, keeping up with the trends, but there's no need to cater to the female clientele. So many other designers do it and do it well."

"I understand that." She tilted onto her toes to kiss him. A means to assuage what she guessed was a touchy subject that might have just raised his blood pressure a few digits. "I hope you win."

"You're just saying that because you like me."

"I do like you. You're smart. You're handsome. And you like to dance. We have fun together. But."

The fact that he'd tracked her down meant that he hadn't advanced his plans to find a wife. Or had he? Oh, bother.

"But?" He clasped her hand and pressed the back of it against his lips. Thinking something through? "Am I one of your bad choices, Zee?"

Damn. She shouldn't have put that one out there.

"Not completely. But well, what *is* this, Sebastian? You've already told me you wouldn't consider me marriage material."

"And you've told me you'd never marry me."

"I would not. I don't want to be a pawn in your family competition."

"I get that but… Zee, I like you. Very much. And that *like* puts a wrench in the competition."

"How so?"

"I'd much rather spend time with you than seek a potential wife. A woman I fully intend to marry only on paper. Show my father the male heir. Deed done."

"Sebastian, how can you say that? Much as I care about you, it offends me that you'd treat a woman like that. And use a child in such a manner."

"I don't know how else to do this, Zee. Unless the perfect woman falls into my arms, I will be forced to find a facsimile wife to win the company. And I must win because L'Homme Mercier must remain as it is."

He couldn't know how hearing that devastated her. Azalea bowed her head. She could understand his desire to keep the family business as he wished it to remain. That his father had set such a ridiculous requirement was cruel to both his sons and to the woman trapped in a loveless marriage, and the resultant baby.

And that made her even more reluctant to reveal her news to him. He didn't need to know. Well, he did. But he didn't need to be a part of her life. Nor she his. That was optional. A choice she mustn't allow to be wrong.

How could she possibly tell him she was pregnant?

"Let's walk back to town and try out the bowling green I saw in the little green square near a pub," he suggested. "I haven't played the game since I was a kid."

"Sure." She clasped his hand and he led them back to the trail. "You're a bit of a kid yourself," she decided. "You like to have fun. That'll be a good thing when you're a dad."

"You think?" He squeezed her hand. "I do enjoy when I see my little brothers. They're adorable. I will strive to be a much different father to my children than my father is to me and my stepbrothers."

That was hopeful to hear. But the idea of raising a child in the Mercier family of men who did not feel love was necessary to commit did not appeal to Azalea at all.

CHAPTER EIGHT

SEBASTIAN WAS SURPRISED at how the red-feathered hen had settled comfortably against his stomach as he held it. Trusting. Zee had shown him how to carefully pick it up, protecting its wings and cupping its feet. Now he stroked its head softly and whispered in French that she was pretty.

Zee sat beside him with another hen in hand. She winked at him. Her wavy hair spilled across her cheek, and if he had not had his hands full, he would have brushed it aside.

How to convince her that marrying him would make them both happy? Did he believe that they could be happy together? It felt as though happiness were a possibility. And really, if he had to marry, why not to a woman with whom he genuinely enjoyed spending time?

"You're a natural," she said. "Ginger is in love with you."

"Ginger, eh?"

"Yep. And this is Posh." She tousled the elaborate feathers that spouted bodaciously from the top of her chicken's head as if a cheerleader's pom-pom. "That's Scary over there with the missing tail feathers. And... Sporty is over there chasing Daisy. She's the most athletic of the crew."

"Where's Baby?"

Zee sucked in her lower lip and cast him a worried

glance. "Dad and Diane made coq au vin before they left for Australia."

"Oh." At that horrifying statement Sebastian could but hug his content fowl closer. Might he ever enjoy a chicken meal again after bonding with the sweet and snuggly Ginger?

"I know," she said. "But despite her name, Baby was getting long in her years. She wasn't laying anymore. She lived a good life."

"And you think *I'm* callous about this whole marriage thing."

"I would hardly compare eating a pet hen to faking a marriage."

"It's not—"

He wanted her to be wrong but she was closer to the truth than he was. How else *could* he manage such a situation? He wouldn't know love if it smacked him in the face. And that was what it was wont to do if it did occur and he had the audacity to insist on marriage.

"Let's not talk about that right now," he said. "I'm enjoying this moment with you. I like that we can sit together and be quiet."

She laid her head on his shoulder. "And hug chickens."

"It's a nice break from my usual hectic schedule. And the sunset is unreal."

Pink, violet and brilliant streaks of gold painted the sky. He'd not taken a moment to notice the sunsets in Paris. It was a vibrant masterpiece. Just like Zee. And Ginger. The colors made him think of the first time he'd been introduced to embroidery work by one of the tailors. It wasn't utilized in suit-making but had been a hobby. The old man had crooked a finger, urging a young Sebastian to follow him into the back room at L'Homme Mercier. With a gleeful flash of his eyes, he'd then opened a sewing box to reveal a rainbow of embroidery threads and shown him the various needles. Sebastian had run his fingers over the silken threads, in awe. Perhaps that had been what had cemented his true interest in the creation of fine clothing, from the very basic stitches to the elegant fabrics and quality craftsmanship. It beat out machine-made factory clothing by everything.

He hadn't worked hands-on creating a suit in years. But there were days he wished the old tailor with the sparkle in his eyes was still around. Sebastian would like to explore his collection of colored threads and create something.

As CEO of L'Homme Mercier he would take on more responsibility, yet at the same time he might be able to delegate to others some of his current duties that were tedious. It was his life. He honored hard work and talent, but he also appreciated this trip that allowed him to relax and not think about shipping schedules or clients or vendor complications.

"I don't want to go home," he blurted.

"I was wondering when you were going to leave. You said you would stay twenty-four hours. That's right about now."

"Do I have to leave?" he asked himself. Then he looked to Zee. "Do you want me to leave?"

"I want you to stay as long as you like."

"Then I'll stay. Because leaving you doesn't feel right. Don't you agree, Ginger?"

The chicken cooed quietly. Content. As he felt. Sitting beside Zee felt right.

"You don't have work to get back to?"

"I can manage another day," he decided. Maybe two? "I have a meeting on Friday with a supplier that I mustn't miss. He's traveling from Dubai."

"That gives us two more days."

"My stay won't be unwanted?"

"Honestly? I wish you could stay all summer." She kissed him and in the process her chicken squawked and made a fuss so she set it free. "How about I go in and make us something to eat."

"I'm quite hungry after our adventurous day."

"Great. I'll make chicken!" She got up, leaving Posh on the ground by his feet, looking up at him with a worried fowl stare.

"I'll protect you," he said to the hen. He scanned his gaze around the yard, sighting the other two birds. Stella wandered near the fence. "Should have done a head count on the poultry earlier."

On the other hand, if Big Bruce were sacrificed, he would not argue the quiet.

The next afternoon they hiked out across the hillocks and stones of the countryside along the bank of Lake Windermere.

Azalea chose a spot next to a low stone wall and laid out a plaid blanket near a crop of wild poppies, while Sebastian snapped some shots of the glassy blue lake and the lush greenery hugging it. It truly was as gorgeous as the tourist advertisements made it look. And it smelled like the real world, so verdant and full. And as luck would have it, she'd led them onto an unmarked trail that only the residents knew about, so unless some tourists got curious, they'd have this cozy little patch to themselves.

She'd packed a simple lunch of sandwiches, fresh fruit, cheese and bottled water. Diane had made cream cheese cookies before leaving on holiday and had left them in the freezer. Azalea had been judiciously thawing but one a day as a treat. Today, she'd packed four.

Taking the stone path carefully, Sebastian returned to sit on the blanket beside her. "You say people come here to hike the mountains?"

"Yes, it's a big tourist draw. I mean, I don't know if the summits qualify as mountains but they give good exercise."

"Have you hiked them?"

"Yes, all around the area which is the National Forest. I can start out in the morning and not be seen until after sunset. There are sweet surprises all over, like tiny stone bridges, or enchanting tree-covered paths, and the Stagshaw Gardens. There's a waterfall that way in the Stock Ghyll woods. It's a lovely way to while away an afternoon. Oh, and there's the champion trees. It's a pretty walk among hundreds of different types of trees. My favorite is the sequoia."

"You're a real nature girl. I understand now why a big city does not appeal to you."

"And yet, a big-city man does offer appeal." She handed him a bottle of water, and he took her wrist and pulled her closer to kiss her.

Feeling like a heroine from a nineteenth century novel, Azalea decided the flutter in her chest and the warmth enveloping her neck was a genuine swoon. The man could own her with his slow and deep kisses. And that was a dangerous realization.

He bowed his forehead to hers and tapped her lips. "I'm glad your heart is not determined to find a rural lover wielding a pitchfork and wearing wellies."

Recalibrating her malfunctioning common sense, she sat up straight and lifted her chin. "Nothing wrong with

that type. They are dependable, hardworking..." And yet...
the one she had briefly dated had wanted her barefoot,
pregnant and subservient. "Though I feel sure my princess inclinations would not be weathered well by such a
hardy rural man. I do like to dress up and do the city life
once in a while."

"You balance between the wilds and the urban," Sebastian said. "Princess one day, cow whisperer the next?"

"Works for me. But what about you? I don't fit in with
your lifestyle, do I? I mean, Lloyd said it best when he—"

Another kiss made her realize that she had been about
to spout nonsense and silliness. Lloyd was her past. The
comments he had made about their differences were just
his perspective. Common sense wasn't always fun, nor
should it ruin a perfectly lovely picnic.

Sebastian said, "We are different, Zee. My grandmother
used to read me a story when I was little. Something about
a country mouse and a city mouse?"

"I think that story was more about one's ambitions and
desires. Each has their own comfort zone. Of course, I believe it was the city mouse who lived in fear of the cat all
the time. The country mouse was quite content to return
home after a brief adventure in the big city."

"You think my ambitions are too much?"

"If they involve marrying a woman merely on paper to
achieve a position?" She busied herself with unwrapping
the sandwiches and cookies. It had just come out. It was
the truth, to her. Even Sebastian had said as much.

"You think I should concede to Philippe in order to
avoid a moral misstep?"

Who was she to tell him what he had the right to do or
how to live his life? She couldn't even come to terms with
how to proceed with her own life!

She handed him a sandwich and shook her head. "I think you should be true to your heart." And her heart performed a double beat in response to that statement.

Listen to me, it seemed to beg. *Are you being true to your heart?*

He nodded, taking a few bites. "I'm not even sure what my heart's truth is right now."

"My heart has a tendency to think before my brain does. It can sometimes be annoying. And I regret the things I do. But later, it always seems as though it was right."

"Even when it was a bad choice?"

"Even so." He wouldn't let that one drop. Sebastian Mercier was not a bad choice. Well, not as bad as some of her choices had been. "My heart speaks my truth. I just have to learn to listen to it and stop arguing for something different."

"What arguments have you with your heart right now?"

If he only knew. The one where she wanted to wrap him in her arms and never let him go. Tell him she was pregnant as a means to keep him in her life. Win the man she adored.

Stupid heart.

In this particular situation, her brain knew better. Nothing good could come of such a relationship because her heart could never really know if Sebastian's feelings for her were true or just manufactured to obtain the CEO position.

"Wow." He brushed breadcrumbs from his pant leg. "There really is an argument going on in there." He pointed to her chest, there where her heart pounded to be heard, to be acknowledged, to simply be followed. "Is it about me?"

She smirked and leaned back on her palms, stretching out her legs. "You know it is."

"I am honored to have found a position in your heart. Though it saddens me that it causes you internal struggle."

"Sebastian, you are a charmer. But we both know this can't go anywhere. So why not just enjoy what we have right now?"

"Then walk away from one another and proceed as if it didn't even happen?"

"Oh, I'll never forget you."

"Nor I you." He took her hand and pressed it over his heart. "My heart developed this weird little hole the morning I woke up and found you had snuck out, never to be seen again. And since then, it's been wanting to fit you into that hole. Someway, somehow."

Such a confession kicked her own heart, trying to convince it to comply. To be honest with her needs for her future. But her brain held her back. So much to consider now with the way her life had begun to unfold.

Shrugging, she offered him a treat. "How about a cookie to fill that hole?"

With a smirk, he took one and bit into it, turning to look across the lake. And Azalea knew that with or without him in her life, he would always be a part of her world.

She couldn't decide whether that was good, bad or ugly. But mostly, she just wanted her heart to get its act together and win.

They walked back through Ambleside just as a city parade was coming to an end. The streets were packed with tourists and residents and so many children.

Sebastian noted they carried wood frames covered with flowers and long weedy leaves. "What did we miss?"

"It's the annual rush-bearing festival. Celebrates the cleaning out of the rushes from the churches. I guess it's become so commonplace to me I didn't even think to ask if you wanted to watch. Those wood frames are rush bearers. And the leafy things are rushes. They used to place them on the floors in medieval times as rugs and to keep things cleaner. Seems to me they might have been more of a big mess."

"Interesting." He paused at the edge of the crowd, taking in a crew of bustling children dashing about with rushes and flowers in hand. One of them ran up to him and with big, beaming eyes offered him a white flower.

Sebastian bent and took the flower. "Thank you."

The little girl, no more than five or six, winked at him, then performed a twirl and spun back into the procession alongside her friends. He stood and sniffed the blossom.

"You are a lady killer," Zee muttered. "But that was also the most adorable thing I've ever seen."

The look she flashed up at him landed in his heart like a warm beam of sunshine. It felt like admiration, perhaps even pride. And Sebastian had never felt more worthy of a woman's regard in his lifetime. Wow. It wasn't an overwhelming feeling, yet it seemed to flood his system with a knowing warmth, a quiet joy. The noise of the parade faded out and he smiled to himself, sinking deeply into the moment. It needed to be honored, recognized. And enjoyed.

Azalea Grace had a power over his heart that should frighten him, but instead he wanted to sway toward her and allow her open access to it. To him. To anything she desired that would see that look of pride beaming at him again.

"Sebastian?"

Surfacing from the feeling with a tilt of his head that allowed back in all the ambient noise of life, he gripped her hand and gave it a squeeze. Tucking the white flower into Zee's hair, he kissed her forehead.

"Back to the farm," she said, unaware of his incredible journey of emotion. "You've got a train to catch."

After witnessing Zee in her natural environment, Sebastian realized what he wanted was not something he could have. They were two different people. Living in two very different places. With two different focuses. And while millions of couples all around the world obviously made similar situations work, he sensed Zee's reluctant to give it a go. She pulled him to her while at the same time pushed him away. Such inadvertent machinations had the potential to drive him mad.

So he must be done with it.

All the proud, admiring glances in the world would never change their situation.

If she wasn't willing to give this thing they had a try, then he must set back his shoulders, chin up, and walk away from her. Much as he adored her, if she couldn't see a future between them, then he must stop trying to prod the dead horse, so to speak.

Thinking of animals, he thought of Zee, out in the barn tending Stella and Daisy.

He paused in folding the dress shirt he'd packed and peered out the window. He'd called for a car, which would arrive soon. And then he would leave. Never to see her again?

He stuffed his shirt and trousers into the suitcase, not caring if they wrinkled. Perhaps he had one last chance to woo her, to convince her that they could be more than just a brief fling. Should he take it? Would he wound her by further involving her in the mess of a future life he must create to win the prize?

"One more try," he muttered.

CHAPTER NINE

AZALEA PRESSED HER palms against the wood fence behind the barn. With a few deep inhales, the wooziness she'd felt passed. Morning sickness. It had occurred two or three times in the last month. And not necessarily in the morning. A quick online search had told her it could occur at any hour. She hadn't vomited yet. But the nauseous feeling rose so quickly all she could do was focus on her breathing until it subsided.

She could be thankful it hadn't attacked when in Sebastian's presence.

By her calculations she was three months pregnant. When she'd taken the test a month earlier, she'd surprised herself with her reaction. No tears. No regrets. She'd been excited to know a new life was growing inside her. While she'd not come to a decision regarding whether to tell Sebastian—that nasty competition spoiled everything—she did realize she was strong and independent. Women did the single mother thing all the time. She could manage.

"Really?" she scoffed. "How's that going to work without a job or home?"

Sure, she could stay here at Grace Farm. But her dad intended to put up the For Sale sign when he returned from Australia. And she was quite sure she couldn't tag along with him and Diane to their next location. If they even bought a permanent home. The twosome planned to travel for a while before settling down. Azalea would not be a third wheel, even if one of the other wheels was her dad. Especially so.

She needed to find a home and a job within the next few months or she would be left homeless and sporting a baby propped on her hip. Not the way she wanted to begin life as a mother.

She could ask Sebastian for help. But that would mean revealing all to him.

Sebastian had disconcerting views about family and children. The family he created in order to gain control of L'Homme Mercier would be fake. And the idea of even considering them as a couple, possibly married, didn't sink in right. She might never know if he were marrying her because she was the mother of his child or because he wanted to win a competition.

And even if love were involved, she would never force a man to marry her just to make things look right. The world had changed. Single mothers were no longer ostracized or sneered at. And forcing a man to be a father, simply to make a family, could go the wrong way and the child could suffer because of it.

Though she wouldn't mind a little financial assistance from him.

"What to do?" she asked Stella, who currently rocked her head against the fence for a good scratch. "I have to tell him. It's only fair. But I don't want him to feel coerced. Or to take advantage of the situation. How am I going to do this?"

He was leaving soon. An important meeting tomorrow morning required he return to Paris. She couldn't guess how he would react to her news. She didn't want it to turn into an argument or a sob-fest or, worse, an obligation.

She stroked the cow's side, giving her a firm pat. "What do you think, Stella? The next step I take is going to steer my life. I just want to make the right choice this time."

Rain seemed appropriate for his departure. It began fitful and heavy, then settled to drizzle. The air smelled like ozone and flowers. It really was a kick to notice that unadulterated scent.

According to the tracking on his app, the car he'd called for would arrive in about twenty minutes. His suitcase sat near the front door. The wellies he'd borrowed were cleaned and placed neatly in their cubby. And Zee... She'd been strangely aloof since they'd returned home following the rush-bearing festival. When he'd suggested they have sex one last time she'd said she needed to feed the cows.

Really?

He suspected she might be feeling the same way he did. Parting would tear out his heart. As much as he wanted to stay forever, though, it wasn't possible. She'd drawn a line. He must respect that. And remember that for one amazing moment he had earned that look of pride from her. A look he would never forget.

In the kitchen, the white flower blossom gifted him by the little girl sat in a small glass vase on the table. He heard the back door swing shut on its creaky hinges.

"Zee?"

"Right there! Just washing the mud off my legs."

When she wandered into the kitchen, she was barefoot, wearing a simple floral dress that was a little wet from the rain. Her hair hung in loose wet waves over her shoulders. A beautiful mess.

"You're ready to leave? I'm so sorry I lost track of time. When does the car arrive?"

"Soon." He set his coat on the suitcase and took her in his arms. He swayed, sliding a hand up her back. "One last dance?"

Hugging up against him she followed his slow steps, her head against his shoulder. They didn't need music to find their rhythm; they'd been in sync since the moment they'd met. Every move, every glance, every shared smile felt meant to be. Fated? He'd never thought much about fate and destiny but it did feel special.

And yet, he noticed her careful separation from him, the sudden absence of her head from his shoulder, the mis-step as she turned the opposite direction he'd intended.

Sebastian blurted, "You've been avoiding me since we returned to the cottage."

"I…" She exhaled and stepped from his embrace, nod-ding. "Sorry. This is difficult."

"I feel the same. But I thought you had decided this wasn't possible?"

"This?" She blew out a breath and rubbed a hand over her belly.

"Well, us, of course. Have you had a change of heart? Zee, I know this whole marriage thing isn't fair to you. But I need you to understand that you are set aside from that. That's an odd way to put it. You—I care about you, Zee. I think I could fall in love with you."

She tugged in her lower lip and winced.

"Please don't make that face. I'll take it personally." He held up his hand, pinkie extended.

She sighed but didn't return the pinkie hug. Oh, the un-bearable weight of rejection.

"I'm sorry. It's just the love thing," she said. "You only think you're in love. Or could fall in love. You can't say, with certainty, you are in love. I know it's complicated.

Oh, Sebastian. There's something I need to tell you. And I've been sitting on it since you arrived, unsure how to reveal it."

At that moment a car rolled up the drive and honked.

Sebastian took out his phone and texted the driver that he'd be five minutes. "What is it, Zee? When I say I think could fall in love, that's it exactly. I'm not sure I've ever been in love before. And God knows it's not a thing I've ever gotten much of in my life. This is a new feeling for me. Allow me some measure to figure that out?"

"You weren't in love with the woman who fled the back of the limo that night we met?"

"No. Amie and I had dated for only three weeks."

"Why did she run off?"

"Because for some reason she was offended by my proposal." He knew the reason. Amie was not stupid. Love was an important ingredient to marriage. Or so he suspected. She'd made the right choice. "She tossed the ring at me and left. I was honest with you about that situation. It's the past. Has no bearing on what's going on with us. Zee, we can make this work. Paris isn't that far away—"

"Sebastian, I'm pregnant."

"And I can— What?" The heartfelt argument sluiced from his brain like a flood. What she'd just said. Had he heard her correctly? "You just said…"

Zee splayed out her hands. "I took a test—two of them—and I'm pregnant. It happened that night in Paris. I haven't been with anyone else, so I know it's yours. Promise. And I know what this means in the competition sense of things to you. But it can't be like that. I won't allow it to be."

He took her by the upper arms. Big blue eyes peered up at him. No freckles caught in the crinkles though, because she wasn't smiling. Was that sadness in her irises? Why was she not bubbling over with joy? Did she not feel the same, sudden intensity of emotion that he did?

"Zee," he breathed. His heartbeats raced. Every muscle in his body wanted to follow that race. What a rush of emotion and— "Do you tell me true?"

She nodded.

"But that's…"

What was that? He was going to be a father? That sealed that part of the competition—but no. He mustn't react that way. It was… Not right. Unfair to Zee. Unfair to his own feelings.

What *were* his feelings about this unexpected announcement? Besides the fact that he felt as if something inside him were actually bubbling. Was it joy? It felt akin to the feeling he'd savored while they'd stood watching the parade.

"Really?" A smile wiggled on his lips and he didn't fight it. This news felt…not wrong. Though he wasn't sure if it was quite right, either. At least, not to judge from her lack of enthusiasm. "Zee, I wish you had told me about this sooner. We could have talked about it."

He'd given up on asking her to marry him after seeing her thriving in her natural habitat, but with this news… might he have asked her after all?

"There's nothing to discuss. I've decided that I don't want to involve myself, and this baby, in the Mercier family drama. I just thought it was only fair to tell you about it. You are the father. You have a right to know. I'll be fine on my own. I'm not going to ask anything of you."

"But you must. Ask me for everything! Zee, this is *my* baby."

The car honked.

Sebastian cursed. He stuck his head out the doorway and gestured for the driver to be patient. "I can't believe this. I need to process this. We must discuss what this means. Zee?"

"I know. I apologize for saving this for the last minute. I think this is as cruel as I've ever been to a person. And I'm not proud of that. But I was scared of your reaction. That you might want to use me and the baby to win the game you're playing with your brother. Even though I do desire family and...finding someone who cares about me."

"But—"

She thrust up a palm to stop his desperate plea. "Just accept that I have to do it this way."

He nodded, though it wasn't a means to agreement. It was merely a reaction to—such a surprise. Processing it would take some thought. Never would he have expected her to reveal such a thing as... "I'm going to be a father?"

She shrugged. "Well, it's your sperm. I'll be doing all the mothering and childcare."

He didn't like that she put it that way. It relegated him to the side, to not being a part of the baby's life. Did he want that? He needed a child. But that was a need created by his desire for career advancement. For the very thing he most wanted in life.

Another honk annoyed him, but he reacted to the rude prompt—and Zee's seeming indifference to his heart—by grabbing his suitcase. "We have not discussed this properly. You owe me that much. Promise me, when your father returns, you'll come to Paris so we can talk about this like adults. Zee?"

She nodded. "Of course. It's only fair."

She was so resigned. His heart broke. No joyous bubbles. Just utter ache. Was he not worthy of her recognizing him as the father of her child? Did she not want him in her life? And here he'd made plans to attempt to woo her one last time...

"At the very least don't you want to come to Paris to see me again?" It felt like a childish plea, but he was at odds, unsure about anything right now.

"I do, but... This is just so big, Sebastian. I need time—"

"I do, too. But I also need us to handle this. Together." He opened the door. "When will your dad return?"

"A few weeks."

"Then...here." He took out his phone and started a text. "I'm sending you my address...along with all the digital entry codes. As soon as you can, come to Paris. If I'm not home, you walk right in. My place is yours." A tap of his finger sent her the information. With reluctance, he lifted his head and nodded. "I'll see you in a few weeks?"

She nodded and managed a weak smile.

A kiss would be most appropriate, but something held him back from leaning in to claim that delicious connection. Things had changed between them. So suddenly. And he honestly didn't know whether to label it good or terrible.

No pinkie hugs this time. He'd lost that connection. Or rather, she had indicated it wasn't what she wanted.

Turning and taking the cobblestone pathway to the waiting car was the hardest move Sebastian had ever had to make. Raindrops spat at his skin. He put his suitcase in, slid into the back and closed the door, and the car rolled away. Away from a woman who dazzled him. A woman for whom his heart beat. A woman who allowed him to see the world in a new way, or rather, reminded him of a simpler time when he'd been a child and had enjoyed life.

A woman...who carried his child.

"Mon Dieu," he muttered as he rubbed a temple.

Was he doing the right thing? Walking away from her right now? The meeting could—well, it was important. But he could reschedule. The client was flying in from Dubai but he could put him up in a hotel for a day or two...

"No." Zee had asked for time to think about this. As well, he needed to think about it. A few weeks before her father returned?

This was going to be the longest fortnight of his life.

CHAPTER TEN

OLIVER GRACE AND Diane had returned to the farm a week ago. After Diane left for town to pick up groceries, Azalea decided it time to tell her dad she was pregnant. He'd looked surprised but had immediately pulled her into a hug and kissed her forehead. Motherhood, or rather nurturing, had always been her true calling, he'd declared. Then he'd asked if the baby would call him Grandpa or maybe Pops?

That had been much easier than how she'd expected the talk to go. Even the information about Sebastian, and his family competition, had been listened to with a quiet nod from her dad.

"You've got to do what feels right in your heart," he said now as they sat out on the porch steps. "I'm here for you, Lea, you know that. And I agree that London isn't the place for you. But..." He sighed. "You can't hide here forever."

"You posting the For Sale sign out front yesterday was a very obvious clue."

"It's not even that, Lea. If you wanted to stay here and we could work out a means for rent, I'd be behind that."

Yet she knew he needed the sale of the land and house to finance his future. A future of new dreams and adventure that Diane had been detailing since they'd returned. Next stop? The United States, starting with New York City!

Diane had already booked a room and purchased Broadway tickets for October in hopes the property sold quickly.

"But speaking as a man," he said as he clasped her hand, "Sebastian does deserve more than the quick five minutes you gave him before he had to leave."

The manner in which she'd told Sebastian, as the driver waited to whisk him away, had been cruel. She'd panicked, prolonging the reveal for far too long. He would have stayed if she'd asked it of him. But the moment had felt like ripping off a plaster. She'd just wanted to toss it aside and not look at it, so seeing him off had been all she could manage at the time.

"Go to him, Lea. Talk to him."

"I will. I just..."

"No more excuses. Stella will survive without you. In fact, I spoke to Burke the other day." The owner of the farm on the opposite side of the lake from Grace Farm. "They lost two of their calves to sickness last winter. He's interested in buying ours. As pets," he reassured when she almost protested that the neighbors tended to butcher their cows for the table.

"I know a trip to Paris is necessary. I do want to see Maddie again."

The air felt heavy with things she should say, truths she wanted to confess about how she felt about her baby's father, emotions that rose when remembering how they simply seemed to belong with one another.

Her dad smoothed a palm over the back of her hand. "Is he so terrible, then?"

"Sebastian? No. He's possibly the most wonderful man I've ever known." She knew what her dad alluded to: then why avoid him? "He didn't ask me to marry him. And I didn't expect him to. Nor did I want him to, knowing what

it might mean. And after how things went with Lloyd…
And Mom deciding to leave…"

"Oh, Lea, you mustn't believe the divorce was anything but meant to be. We talked about this. It was a mutual parting."

"I know, but Mom said she felt confined. And you know how I love my freedom. But also…" Now she was just grasping for excuses. Her heart would never give up the dream of having family.

"Marriage is different for everyone. Your mother and I shared thirty wonderful years. People change. They grow apart. That doesn't mean you should never give a person a go on the off chance the same might happen. Life is meant to be lived. Live it without looking into the crystal ball and asking about your future. Take a chance!"

She sighed. "Maybe my heart was waiting for that proposal from Sebastian after hearing about the baby. Just so I know it was something he would have considered."

"He's being smart. Maybe even cautious of your heart. If he had asked you right away, I would have been suspicious. Like he was only trying to do the right thing."

"Maybe." What was so wrong with that? Well, everything. At least, as far as she'd decided. "Oh, Dad, this is difficult. I should be focusing on finding a job and a place to live. In less than half a year I'm going to be a family!"

"I can't wait to welcome my grandbaby! Heaven knows, Dahlia will never make me a pops. I think we're going with Pops, yeah?"

"Sounds perfect, Pops. I'm glad you're excited about this. It makes everything feel a little easier in the grander scheme of things."

"Raising children is never easy. It's messy, emotionally

trying and downright frustrating at times. But it is also wondrous, joyful, and so worth it."

She tilted her head against his shoulder. "I love you, Dad."

"I promise to love the heck out of my grandbaby. I might even save some space in my heart for the tyke's father, too."

"Sebastian takes up a lot of space," she started to say, but swallowed and couldn't bring herself to finish the last part—*in my heart*.

Her dad pulled her into a hug. "It'll all go as it should, Lea. I promise you that."

Days later

Azalea had asked the taxi driver to drive to the L'Homme Mercier atelier and home office in the 6th arrondissement. She'd considered being dropped off out front, but then she'd decided that walking in with suitcases in hand, looking like the last woman the posh Sebastian Mercier would ever involve himself with, would be bad form. She couldn't do that to him, so she redirected the driver.

A small corner hotel offered an available room. It was literally just a room, like in someone's house, with a basin and a bed and a window that looked toward Notre Dame. She plunked her suitcase on the lumpy bed and went to freshen up in the closet-sized bathroom. The lavender soap made her dizzy, so she tucked it away in a drawer.

She hadn't texted Sebastian to let him know she'd be coming to Paris. He'd texted her over the weeks since he'd left the farm. He hadn't asked after the baby, just sending notes to let her know he was thinking about her.

You are in my thoughts.

I miss your bright eyes.

We dance well together.

She appreciated his careful distance. But it also put dread in her heart.

A very rich and powerful man now held a claim to her unborn child. If she didn't go along with whatever he wished, would he take it away from her? It was a dramatic scenario, but she'd played it over many times. Sebastian had been brought up by a father who had many children, all by mothers he'd never married. Could this baby be the first in a collection that Sebastian would grow just as he'd witnessed his father do? After all, he'd known nothing else.

A terrible thought. But something she needed to have answered while here in Paris.

To look on the plus side, she felt great. The morning sickness had passed, though her aversion to smells had grown. Her appetite had also increased. As had her gut. Though she'd yet to pop out with an apparent baby bulge. So far, her middle had thickened, overwhelming what had once been a slender waist. Not the most appealing shape. She'd begun to wear looser clothing—today a spaghetti-strap sundress—to accommodate the weight gain.

Checking her phone, she vacillated between going for a walk and calling him. Sebastian had given her his home address, which was in the 6th arrondissement. The entry codes, for gosh sakes! But it didn't feel right walking in and making herself at home. Much as part of her felt a certain right to do so. Carrying the man's child, anyone?

That did grant her some clout. But no. She wasn't the sort to expect anything of him.

Yet why not? And really, *shouldn't* she expect something? And if not from Sebastian, then certainly she must figure in her own expectations for this strange but curious affair of having the rebound man's baby.

"Such dramatics," she muttered. A chuckle was necessary. She was a rural princess, not some wayward romance heroine desperate to claim her baby's father.

"Maybe a little," she then whispered.

And her heart remained hopeful in response to that realization.

Since it was early, she decided to ring up Maddie. Her girlfriend was hopping a flight tomorrow for Berlin, so they arranged to meet at a café in half an hour. Starting this trip with some friend time was what Azalea required to bolster her courage.

Finding the café with ease, Azalea crossed the street. Maddie, seated at an outside table, waved, gold bracelets clinking. She stood to kiss Azalea on both cheeks as she arrived. "I can't believe you're back in Paris. I wish I'd known sooner. We could have spent more time together. So, what's up?"

Azalea sat and took a sip of the water already at the table. "A lot, Maddie. Are you ready for this?"

Her friend wiggled on her chair and excitedly said, "Always!"

CHAPTER ELEVEN

JUST AS HE was leaving the office for the evening, Sebastian received a text from Zee. She was in Paris. An utter explosion of relief loosened muscles that he hadn't realized he'd been holding tight for...possibly weeks. He texted her back that he was on his way to pick her up.

He'd given much thought to the idea of becoming a father. While it hadn't been something he'd planned, it was also something that he'd sought. Weirdly enough. He'd thought of his baby every day since learning she was pregnant. Most of the time he smiled. A few times he shook his head. Was he even ready to become a father? How to be a good parent when all he knew was...well, it was what he knew.

And now he'd been gifted with the very thing that could catapult him to the win.

But a softer, more caring side of him admonished that he couldn't very well take the baby and run, while seeking another woman to marry him. Azalea did not deserve such cruelty. Yet if she wouldn't marry him, what was he to do? If he made the wrong choice, he could very well lose not only the CEO position, but as well, the only women he desired.

How to have both?

He hadn't come to any sane means to obtain Zee's hand in marriage without offending her morals. Kidnapping, threatening and coercion had only been temporary, ridiculous thoughts. He wasn't that man.

Gently wooing her might work. Could it?

For the first time in his life, he struggled with his feelings for a woman. And that was remarkable to realize. Was this, in fact, for the first time in his life...love?

He'd told Zee he thought he was falling in love with her. But at the time he hadn't known for sure. And he wasn't even sure now. The idea of love excited him. And it worried him.

Love might spoil any plans of gaining control over L'Homme Mercier.

Half an hour later, Sebastian collected Zee and her things, and whisked her off to his place. Now she stood before the massive wall of windows, looking out over the city. The sun wouldn't set for hours, but the hazy day cast a shadow over the sky and silhouetted her before him. He felt as though she were untouchable and yet so down-to-earth. A princess of quaint and chickens but also a goddess of beauty and frolic. Yet he couldn't forget when she'd told him she wasn't sure where life would next lead her. He had a few ideas. But he cautioned himself from overstepping with her. She was skittish. And rightfully so.

Since returning to Paris from Ambleside he'd had opportunities to date and had refused them all. No woman interested him like Zee did. The idea of proposing to anyone but Zee didn't even fit into his brain. And now there was another reason for him to invest in their relationship.

He agreed with Zee on one point: he did not want his child to be a tool to lever his position in the family drama. That was unfair. And reeked of his own childhood. Not an unpleasant upbringing, but even he could understand it wasn't normal, and most certainly was not in Zee's range of comfort.

"How are you feeling?" he asked as he pulled a bottle of sparkling water from the fridge, then poured them both a glass. "Am I allowed to ask?"

"Of course, you are. We are still…friends." She swallowed.

Unsure about that title? It wasn't what he would label them, and it poked at his heart to hear her declare such. On the other hand, who was he to claim something more? How to navigate this delicate balance between them?

"I'm feeling good. I assume you're asking baby-wise? I had a little morning sickness for the first few months but it's gone. It's just odors that bug me now. Although you smell great. Very subtle. I like it."

"Thank you. I finally got the last remnants of Câlin out by hiring a cleaning crew. Remind me never to attend another perfume party."

He handed her the glass and kissed her cheek. He wanted to hug her and never let her go, but she'd flinched when he'd met her at the hotel. Keeping a bit of distance between them? That killed him. He daren't offer a pinkie hug either. She'd not responded the last time he'd tried that. He'd react to her cues.

"I still can't get over how beautiful Paris is," she commented. "It's a cloudy day and still the sky looks like a painting. Is that Notre Dame over there, with the scaffolding climbing the structure?"

"It is. Under repair following the fire a few years ago. Though soon it will be complete."

If she intended to pussyfoot around the subject that he'd not been able to stop thinking about the past few weeks, he would pull out his hair. But he reminded himself to give her some measure, and to allow her the lead.

"I'm sorry it took so long," she said. "I mean, to come here. Dad got back a few weeks ago and I told him about the baby. He's over the moon to become a grandpa. Pops is what he's decided the baby will call him. Diane, his girlfriend, is excited as well. She's been doting on me."

"Doting is good, yes?" Some things got lost in translation.

"It involves lots of stories about when she was a mother, shopping for baby things, and stories about how to breastfeed properly and select the best pram. So, yes, very good." She set down the water and splayed her hands before her. "So. We need to talk."

"I don't intend to make talking to me a hardship, Zee. Are you so against the idea that we now have a connection? You called us merely friends. I thought we got along so well."

"We did. We do. It's just…everything has changed." She sat on the sofa that faced the windows and patted the cushion beside her. "First tell me how things are going for you at work. You had a meeting you had to get home to? How did that go?"

"It was for next year's spring line. All signed, sealed and sent to the tailor. And work is always a pleasure for me."

"I know that about you. That's why I also know how important it is that you win the CEO position."

He sat next to her and took her hand, kissing the back of it. The softness of her skin brought him instantly back to her farm, sitting on the porch, watching the sun beam across the pond. With chickens. An odd moment to remember, since it should be the very last thing that he cared to repeat, the country retreat part. And yet, if Zee were beside him, would he be comfortable spending the rest of his days living such a scenario?

"I don't want to talk about work, Zee. I've done a lot of thinking these few weeks. About us."

"I don't think there can be an us."

He turned abruptly to search her gaze. She looked down, avoiding his nudging desire to find the truth in her eyes. "Zee?"

"It all comes down to that stupid competition. I won't be a part of it. It's unfair to me."

"First, I haven't asked you to marry me. And second, I'm not so insensitive. You mustn't believe I would use you in such a manner, Zee. You mean too much to me."

"That's lovely to hear, but I will never know if you're saying it because it's what I want to hear or if it comes from your heart."

"It comes from my heart. I know we haven't known one another long, but you should know that I am a man of my word. I do not tolerate lies."

"I think I know that." She sighed and leaned against the cushions, closing her eyes. The hazy light emphasized her freckles. "I can do this on my own. I just need to find a job. Get a little place in London—"

"But you told me London is too big and noisy."

"It is, but it may be the only option. And Dahlia has already started scoping out potential flats for me."

"A London flat is expensive. And you have no income. Zee, I don't want you to sacrifice your comfort for the necessity of earning an income. And who will take care of the baby?"

"I'll hire a sitter. Day care is also an option. Both are… well…" She winced.

"What you can't say is that they are expensive. So you'll

work to pay someone to watch our child while you work…
to pay for childcare? Sounds like running in circles to me.
You don't want to do that, Zee. I know you. Your best
friend is a cow. You thrive when you are wandering the
grass barefoot and dancing with the flowers. I can't imagine you'd want to raise a child in London."

She shook her head. "Not really. But it's a place to start.
I can find a job at a florist, or maybe a supermarket."

He cringed. "You, a supermarket clerk? Absolutely not.
Such a menial job would extinguish your bright light."

"A person can find joy in any task if they look for it.
Even shelving canned tomatoes. Sebastian, I'd do anything
for my baby. I want to give it the best life."

"The best for our baby is to have its mother there for it.
As well as its father. I want to be a part of my child's life,"
he insisted. "I need to be a part of his life."

"His?"

"I'm sure of it." He smiled. "I have a feeling. But I won't
force you to allow me into his life. I don't want to be that
man who controls people with his money. I want to be in
his life because you want me there. And Zee, I will take
care of you. No matter what you decide. I'll find a place
for you to live. Or you find the perfect place and then I'll
finance it. You'll never want for anything. You simply
need to enjoy being a mother."

"No matter what I decide? Like I have options? Sebastian, this is one choice I know isn't a mistake. I'm having
this baby."

"Of course, you are. I'm sorry, I didn't mean to imply
there were any other options."

"I didn't plan for it, but now that it's here…" she patted
her stomach "…inside me, I'm actually excited about this
little bean. Boy or girl, I'll be happy either way."

Sebastian wished she could be as excited about inviting him to share in the baby's life. But then, he hadn't given her any reason to do so. Proposing felt wrong. She'd flee, insisting he wanted to marry her to become CEO. It wouldn't be like that. Maybe a little like that? If he wasn't even certain himself, then he could hardly be certain with her. But he could understand how she would think. So taking care of her was his only option.

For now.

To win her over and change the course of his future was the question. Because winning Azalea and his baby meant forfeiting the CEO position.

He kissed her cheek and nuzzled his head aside hers. Raising a hand to place over her stomach, he stopped before touching her. "May I?"

"Uh…yes." She took his hand and laid it over her stomach. She didn't appear pregnant, though perhaps she'd filled out a bit? "The baby doesn't start noticeably moving around for a few more weeks. I read about it online. I'm about four months according to my doctor."

"I'm pleased you've seen a doctor. I'll cover all your medical bills. Will you allow that?"

"The prenatal visit was free, and most of the rest is, including the midwife, but there will be expenses…"

"I'll make sure you get a card to use for any and all expenses. Medical, baby supplies, food, anything, Zee. You've only to ask."

"You know you can't buy my baby with the slash of a credit card."

Sebastian gaped at her. "How can you say such a thing? I would never."

A curious anger forced him to stand and stride into the kitchen where he grabbed the bottle of sparkling water. He was not buying her baby because—it was *his* baby, too! How dare she use such an accusation to repel him? He had as much right to watch their child grow up as she did. Why was it the woman always got the key role and more say in what would happen with the baby? It wasn't right.

He was still embracing this news about being a father, but more and more he was excited about it. And he wanted to share those feelings with her. He wanted to hear the stories about the best prams and how to survive the sleepless nights that would come with fatherhood. He wanted to be there for his child's first smile, his first words, his first toddle across the yard.

"I'm sorry," she said quietly. "This is an unusual situation to navigate. If not a little weird. Don't you think so?"

He took a swig directly from the bottle. "I do think it's out of the usual. Though not by my family's standards. It would be easier if we were…" At the very least, in one another's lives. In the same country. On the same page. "Am I to believe you don't want to be my girlfriend, then?"

"I…wasn't aware that title was on the table. I've only ever considered us lovers. Friends. Sebastian, I don't even live in Paris!"

"But do you live in Ambleside? Not for much longer."

She shrugged and gestured dismissively. "I will probably have to move before the leaves drop from the trees."

"Which is fast upon us. What about a cozy little town on the outskirts of Paris? Something wooded and with cobblestones and cows and chickens?"

She laughed, then looked up at him, as if realizing he was not joking. She had her dreams of being a princess; he could dream, too. Yet he wasn't quite sure what the dream of his future looked like. He was winging it. Trying to please her and not make a wrong step.

"So that's a possibility," he boldly decided. "Good to know. As I've once said about you, you teeter between village life and big-city life."

She agreed with a nod. "A happy medium would be perfect."

"At the very least, will you stay in Paris for a while? Grant me some time with you? Let me romance you as I've wanted to do every day we've been apart."

"I do like how you romance me."

"I think you're talking about the sex part."

"All your sex parts are quite lovely."

Was that a blush he felt heating his neck? "I'll work half days so I can spend all my time with you. We'll have a grand time."

"Until?"

He wasn't sure what she wanted him to say. He didn't know where this relationship was headed, or how it would get there. But if he could win another day, week, or more with her, then he'd snatch it and honor it as something precious.

"Until you need to seriously start wife hunting," she said.

Sebastian clutched the neck of the bottle. That was a sticking point she wasn't able to get beyond. Something that he should not overlook. Life had delivered him an interesting curve. He could follow it and see where it led him or try to straighten it back on course.

He wasn't at all sure which was the better choice. And really, what *was* his course?

"Should we make a deal not to talk about wife hunting or baby heirs?" she asked. "Just have some fun for a few days?"

He nodded. But it wouldn't be simple fun. It could mean the start to something grand.

Or the beginning of unbearable heartbreak.

CHAPTER TWELVE

Days later

THE LIMO PULLED to the curb and Sebastian leaned over to kiss Azalea. "Ready?"

She inhaled and said, "Give me a minute."

"We can sit here as long as you like. Are you nervous to meet my friends?"

Yes, she was. She had spent the afternoon shopping for the perfect dress to wear tonight. Not too fancy, not so country bumpkin as her favorite floral dresses were. She'd landed on a simple white linen dress that did not have a tucked waistline. Red sandals were a necessity since lately her feet were swollen. So much for doing this pregnancy gracefully. Everything was growing larger. Puffy. Although she'd take the swollen breasts since they did now make her look like a B-cup.

She was confident she looked passable, but the key now was to not come off as uneducated or a farm girl. Lloyd's words had embedded themselves into her soul. She wanted to ignore what he'd said, but right now it was hard not to feel those words wrap around her like a bold red flag. Surely Sebastian's friends were rich and elite and maybe even snobbish?

"A little nervous?" she offered.

"You mustn't worry. They will love you. And they are not pretentious. If anything, they laugh at me when I have a model on my arm. They are always telling me to find a woman of substance and elan."

"And look what you've come up with. The chicken lady from England."

He laughed heartily. "That's a good one. I will have to tell them that one."

"No, don't! Sebastian, please, I just want to make a good impression."

He kissed her. Each time they connected, no matter how briefly, it fortified her courage a little more. "The only one you have to impress is me, and you've already succeeded on that front. Come on. You'll be surprised at how down-to-earth they are."

She nodded. Just the fact he'd arranged for her to meet his friends had to mean something. Had he told them about the baby? She hoped not. It was too big a topic to get into with people she didn't know. Right now, she just wanted to get through the evening. And perhaps learn a little more about Sebastian in the process.

They got out and entered a cozy restaurant walled with black steel and blue furnishings. A circular fireplace at the center was viewable by all the tables. Sebastian held her hand firmly, and when they arrived at a half-circle booth, three men and two women greeted her warmly.

"Azalea is not fluent in French, so tonight we will speak English for her, please?" he asked.

"Of course!" they all chimed.

An hour into drinks—nonalcoholic for Azalea and Sebastian—and a round of appetizers and desserts, Azalea had relaxed and was laughing along with everyone else as they went round the table telling tales about their adventures with Sebastian. From boating excursions in Marseilles that resulted in a broken-down engine that left them stranded for hours, to college lacrosse days when he'd led the team to a championship. They genuinely cared about him, and he was right when he'd told her they were not pretentious. She did not feel as though they were judging her. And she relaxed even more, her thigh hugging his, her head tilting onto his shoulder occasionally.

The past few days had been adventurous, visiting the Paris sights, afternoons wandering lush city parks, and evenings spent making love and staring out the window at the city lights. As well, carrying the weight of the situation between her and Sebastian, which had begun to sink in deeply. There was no easy resolution to what they'd created between them. She was thankful no one had brought up "the rebound baby." It was still her and Sebastian's secret.

When she yawned, she tried to disguise it behind her hand, but Clemente, the gorgeous redhead with silver dangle earrings, noticed and suggested that they end the night. "I'm as tired as Azalea looks," she said sweetly. "How about we split the tab?"

"No, I've got it." Sebastian gestured to the waiter to bring the check. "It's been a marvelous evening. *Merci, mon amies!*"

"And thank you for going out of your way and speaking English for me," Azalea added. "That was very kind."

"Not a problem." Charles, who worked for Sebastian's competition as a marketing exec, said with a pat to the back of her hand. "You're adorable, Zee. We hope to see you again, and soon."

"*Oui*, very soon," echoed out as everyone rose and began to leave with kisses to cheeks.

Consumed by a whirlwind of cheek busses, she finally

stood in Sebastian's arms out front of the restaurant. "I like your friends." She sighed and sank against his chest.

"I'm glad. They very much liked you."

"Thank you for not telling them I'm pregnant. I'm not sure how to deal with that announcement yet."

"No worries." He held up his hand, pinkie out.

She met his hug with her pinkie, glad for the secret code that meant to her that they did care for one another and no matter what happened, she trusted he would treat her well.

"Shall I also keep it a secret this weekend when we do supper with my family?"

"Your family?" Suddenly Azalea's throat went dry. Her heart pounded. "Oh, I don't know about meeting the family, Sebastian."

"Why not? We get together once a month, all of us, including all of the moms and girlfriends and kids. They'll love you as much as my friends do."

"But I thought you said your family wouldn't approve of me?"

He winced. "That was a crass thing to say. I regret it. I realize it doesn't matter to me what my family thinks of anyone in my life. All that matters is how I feel when with you. We're not trying to impress anyone, are we? Let's go and have a good time and you can meet Philippe and my dad. Roman has been working with a speech therapist. He still has trouble enunciating words but he has a manner of getting his point across."

"I'm glad to hear he's recovering. But seriously, you may not think it a big deal, but this is going to be my first impression on them. I might need something different to wear."

"You have the card I gave you. Buy what you need."

"It's generous of you to give me whatever I want but I could take advantage and buy a car or something."

"If it makes you happy, it makes me happy. Besides, what good is it to have money if you do not use it to buy things you enjoy?"

"Oh, mercy, you will corrupt me."

"And I intend to enjoy every minute of it."

Making love to Sebastian was the best feeling in the world. Besides taking off her bra after a long day. Nothing could compete with that feeling. But she'd never tell him he had competition. And that her mind wandered to silly things like undergarments after she'd just climaxed—for the second time—bothered Azalea.

Because after the bra she started thinking about his family. She didn't want to meet the family! Did she really have to? But of course, if she was to have Sebastian's baby, she should probably assess the relative situation. On her side the issue was easy enough. One grandpa and grandma and their respective partners. On Sebastian's side it was the one grandpa and…how many grandmothers? She'd lost count. And would they be called step-grandmothers?

Kisses to her spine stirred her from her mad-making thoughts and she rolled over to snuggle against Sebastian's chest. Heated vanilla, cedar and saltiness scented his skin. She nuzzled closer and licked him. "You are a talented man."

"And you are a vocal woman. I love when you climax."

She smiled against his skin. "You're not so quiet yourself."

"Fortunately, I own the whole top floor of this building, so we can be as loud as we care to be."

With that permission, she let out a long and bellowing call that ended in a giggle.

"Is that so?" He tickled her ribs in punishment.

Her laughter turned to shrieks and kicks and then she collapsed in a huffing sigh of relief as his tickles turned to kisses from neck to breasts, to stomach. Gentle and reverent, he took his time covering her entire growing belly. Then he pressed his ear against her stomach.

"Can I help you name him?" he asked.

She'd not yet given thought to names. Hadn't any favorites. And how he guessed it was a boy was cute, but she'd not gotten confirmation during the ultrasound on the sex.

"Of course, you can. As long as it's not Clifford or Harry."

"What's wrong with Harry?"

"That would remind me of my lost love," she said with a dramatic tone.

"Do tell?"

"When I was in primary school I intended to marry Harry Marks. He once gave a report on how he wanted to be a prince when he grew up. At the time I didn't realize you had to be born into the title. Anyway, you know about my aspirations to princess-hood. Alas, the last I heard, Harry works as a bartender in the West End."

"Alas," he mocked gently.

"Oh, come on! I could have been a princess."

"You already are a rural princess, Zee. And I'll fight Harry any day to win your regard."

She assessed him in the pale beam of moonlight that shone across the head of the bed. "You did offer to punch the photographer that night you rescued me. You must be quite the brawler."

"I did punch him."

She gaped at him. "What?"

"I brought back the dress and made sure he understood he'd done wrong."

"Seriously?"

He shrugged.

"Wow. You're my knight in shining menswear. Your suit is your armor."

"I suppose it is." He kissed her belly and tugged her against him, her back to his chest, and nuzzled his face into her hair. "I'm falling in love with you, Zee. And I'm not using the word *think* this time around. This time I can feel it right here, in my entire being."

His words sounded so real. Just what she wanted to hear from him.

"Don't be mad?" he added.

"Of course not." And yet, she wasn't happy.

And why she wasn't happy astounded her. Because the man of her dreams had just confessed his love to her. Or almost love. And he wanted her to have everything that would make her life, and the life of her child, perfect. She should be dancing with joy. Over the moon. Wearing that princess crown with pride.

Yet how to get over the self-imposed caution that would not allow her to believe Sebastian was only in this for the CEO position?

CHAPTER THIRTEEN

TEN DAYS HAD passed since Azalea had come to Paris. Puttering around the neighborhood, slipping in and out of the trendy shops, and browsing Sebastian's home while he was away at work felt like the most normal thing in the world. There was plenty to keep her busy, from exploring the parks and cafés, to exploring the elegant suits in his closet and laughing over his meticulously ordered fridge. Yes, there were hues of wine and each bottle was arranged in order from pale to dark. As well, the cheeses were in alphabetical order!

She'd not even considered when she would return to Ambleside. Though she had thought about finding a job. She could look into teaching English as a second language, or even apply at one of the florists on the main strip hugging the river, using her English as an attribute considering all the tourist business that must demand a command of the language.

"Possible," she muttered as she scrolled through a website that sold baby furniture and clothing.

She preferred the plain pinewood furniture and simple clothing that wasn't frilly or the declarative pink or blue. Her toddler would amble through the grass barefoot and chase butterflies in whatever color inspired her that day.

"He has to," she said with the dream swelling in her

heart. "That's how I want to raise a child. Free and wild. Respectful and prone to common sense."

She would definitely homeschool. But that was a lofty dream for a penniless, pregnant woman who had no home or job.

Sebastian's offer to pay for everything was not to be disregarded. Which was why she'd accepted the credit card he'd handed her. She wasn't going to refuse it on some arrogant moral ground that she was too good for charity. Heck, he was the father. He could chip in to raise their child. However, she did want to make her own way as well. A happy medium must be achieved. Because while she was living it up, enjoying the luxurious life in a swanky Parisian penthouse, eating at exclusive restaurants and buying fabulous clothes, she didn't want to take advantage of Sebastian. Nor did her aesthetics require such swank. Not all the time, anyway.

Simple things. A simple life. With a side of Weekend Parisian Princess added to the mix?

The thought made her smile.

"How to incorporate Sebastian Mercier into my simple plan?" she murmured. "And at the same time give an inch and occasionally slide into his world?"

Could she incorporate him into her life in a meaningful way that would allow her to accept his need to keep a wife? No. If he married, or even if he dated someone else while keeping her on the side as his family, the way all the Mercier men seemed to keep women, Azalea was absolutely sure she did not want a part of that.

But convincing him *not* to go for the CEO position would be unfair to him. He wanted that job. He had plans, dreams for the company. She couldn't deny him that win by insisting he not marry another.

It could be as simple as telling him they should get married. It would give him the win. Could it ever be a real marriage?

Maybe?

"I only want it if it's real."

"Hey, Dad, how's it going on the farm?"

"Casual, as usual, with a side of packing and tossing all the junk we don't need. How's it with you and Sebastian? Are you working things out?"

Azalea bit her lip. She never lied to her dad. And really, even she wasn't sure they had worked things out, so a straight yes or no couldn't apply.

"Lea, sweetie, you've got to get things straight with him."

"I'm not sure what is straight for me, Dad. I'm still working this out in my heart, if you can understand that."

"I do. You don't want to be treated any lesser than what you deserve. Nor do I wish that for you. You know Diane and I will support whatever decision you make."

"I know you will. So, what's up?"

"I just called to let you know we've had some offers for the property."

"Dad, that's wonderful."

Was it? Azalea's heart sank. Such good news would allow her dad to take the next step. But she felt some panic in that it felt as if her life, her very roots, had just been torn up and were dangling like dirt clumps above a hole in the earth. Her escape to the farm would soon be gone. Then where would she go?

"What about Stella and Daisy?"

"They sold two days ago."

"What?" He'd just up and sold her best friend?

"You knew I was selling them, Lea. The neighbor is going to pick them up in a few days. He's promised not to eat them, I swear."

That sounded so not reassuring.

"The hens are…" He exhaled heavily and she knew that meant he and Diane would be feasting on chicken for the next few weeks. "It's going well, sweetie."

"I'm glad for you, Dad. Though I wish I could be there to send off Stella." She slid a hand over her not too round belly. Still, she was proud of it. "I have a feeling no matter where life takes me and this little one, it may involve a cow."

Her dad laughed. "Sure you don't want to buy the farm from me? There's still time."

Not that she could afford such a thing. Would it be possible? No, it wouldn't be fair to her dad to work up an arrangement to keep something that she loved, yet also felt would keep her from moving on. She needed to forge her own life.

"If you're selling at fire sale prices, sure."

Another laugh. "Let me know when you've plans to return. I'll drive to London to pick you up."

"Thanks, Dad. I'm not sure how much longer I'll stay. I'll ring you when I do. Love you!"

She hung up and tossed the phone to the comfy sofa and walked up to the window to look out over Paris. The sun was bright and tendrils of some vine twisting about a nearby tree snaked toward the window. The city of lights was so pretty. And here in Sebastian's home, it felt not quite so busy and hustling as London had to her. Still, it wasn't exactly her style. Even if it was home to a man she couldn't imagine pushing out of her life.

Sebastian's trajectory and hers were not aimed toward

one another. His life was here in Paris. Hers was…not here. And there was nothing left for her in Ambleside after the farm was sold.

The door opened and Sebastian breezed in, as was his habit. Even after a full day at the office he always seemed light on his feet, his smile seeking hers. If a person's eyes could speak his screamed happiness. It was difficult to sulk when in his presence.

Azalea sailed toward him and he swept her into an embrace that suddenly turned into a full-on, dance-floor dip. She let out a hoot, and he pulled her upright to kiss her. Her Frenchman's five-o'clock shadow tickled her skin, perking her nipples and zinging desire through her system. As their kiss deepened, they swayed to an unsung melody backed up by the timpani of their heartbeats.

When she came up for air, she asked, "What was that for?"

He shrugged. "The best part of my day is coming home to find you here, smiling at me."

"I was thinking much the same."

"Another dip!" He spun her before the window and when she swirled back to him, he bowed her low. "Do you think we could qualify for that dancing show on the TV?"

"Why not?" He spun her upright and she landed in his secure embrace and they kissed again.

Everything was perfect. And everything was wrong. His kisses only managed to distract her from the more serious stakes.

"Can we make this work?" he asked.

"I'm not sure."

"Do you want to make it work?"

"Honestly? I want to, but I'm also cautious because I don't want my heart to get broken."

"I would never do anything to hurt you, Zee. Or our baby." He spread a palm across her stomach. "I think you've got a little belly?"

"Don't remind me. It's not so much a belly as a full spread. I feel like a lump."

"A beautiful lump." He bent to kiss her stomach. Feeling him there, paying respect to their child, made her question if she were being too protective of her heart. Should she give him a chance?

"Are you ready for tomorrow night? The dinner with my family?"

"Oh." Her consternation switched to panic. "I haven't found a dress yet."

"We'll go shopping in the morning. Don't worry, Zee, I'll hold your hand." He clasped hers and kissed it. "It won't be so terrible. Dad is more quiet than usual. The girlfriends are all a bit materialistic and focused on fashion and jewels. Like those housewife shows on the television."

Azalea laughed. "And your brother. Will he have a date?"

"Not sure. I haven't spoken to Philippe for a few weeks. But we do try to show up at these family soirees with a date."

"To show the other you're committed to the competition?"

"This—us—is not competition," he said. "I've found the perfect woman. And she's already told me she won't marry me, so I must suffice with merely adoring her for the rest of my life."

"Don't be foolish, Sebastian. You wouldn't give up the CEO position to stare at me as I grow fatter and my fingers and toes swell to sausages."

"Honestly? It's something I wrestle with daily."

"I hope the CEO position wins."

"Really?" He studied her with that perceptively delving gaze that always brought her to her knees. "You don't want me to choose you?"

"I want you to be happy. And the CEO position would make you happy."

"It would. But *you* also make me happy."

"You can't have both."

He sighed. "No, apparently not."

"Besides, don't you know happiness is an inside job? Only you can make yourself happy. And if you're not happy on your own, then it doesn't matter if another person comes into your life and makes an attempt to create that happiness."

"Profound," he said. "Are you happy?"

"I am. Mostly. I would be much happier if I had definite future plans, but I feel as though things will work themselves out."

"So you don't require me in your life to be happy?"

Answer truthfully, her conscience nudged.

Azalea shrugged and shook her head. "But you are a nice bonus."

"The bonus guy. How utterly romantic."

"Don't take it the wrong way. I adore you, Sebastian. And... I really do hope things can work for us. But I'm not going to make plans for something that I feel isn't a sure thing."

"What about life *is* a sure thing?"

"Not much." Her father had said much the same to her. *Life is meant to be lived. Go off and live it!*

"Well, we'll see how things go, eh?"

Yes, they did like to dance around making a final decision on this situation. And she was fine with that. Because

Azalea sensed any decision would result in heartbreak for one, if not both of them.

"No matter what happens between us?" he said. "I am going to create a stipend for you and my child. You'll never want for anything, Zee. I promise you that."

"Oh. Well." That was very generous beyond the credit card he'd already given her. But not so surprising, knowing Sebastian for the kind and generous man he was.

"Tell me you'll accept?"

It would help her in the interim until she could really figure things out, decide what the future looked like for her with a child, and maybe or maybe not the child's father.

She nodded. "Thank you. But I only need a little help until I get my life on track—"

The kiss he often employed to stop her from rambling senselessly never failed to be successful. And to shift Azalea from brain mode to soft and accepting heart mode. Could she seriously imagine life without Sebastian's kisses?

"You'll have an account forever, Zee. That's how it's going to go. Like it or not. Now, I ordered food on the way home. I'm going to wash up. If the bell rings, answer it!"

He strolled down the hallway, leaving her feeling floaty from his kiss, but at the same time she could feel the chain tighten about her ankle that bound her to the floor. His floor. His chain. His money. She'd become one of those women his father collected, mothers of his children the patriarch wasn't willing to commit to.

Would Sebastian feel he could direct her future, and that of her child's, because he was financing it? She didn't want that.

Had accepting his offer been a mistake?

She shimmied off a creeping tightness in her shoulders and shook out her hands. "No, it'll work. It has to."

While Zee was in the shower, Sebastian washed the dinner dishes. Night hugged the windows with a glint of moonshine across the glass and an ambient pink glow from the city's neon. The neighborhood was old and quiet, but the heart of Paris was always present no matter where one lived or stood within the city. Lights, river, history. This was his home. He loved it. Couldn't imagine living anywhere else.

Now that he was to become a father, he had some hard choices to face. He wanted to see his son raised in Paris, or at the very least, France. His child must speak French, and of course English. He would know his family and their history—with some careful edits and alterations regarding what a family really was. And that meant he should consider going traditional and marrying his child's mother. Bring him up in a nuclear family surrounded by those who loved him.

Yet how to convince Zee of that? Surely she must want the best for their child? And she couldn't believe denying her son his father would be for the better. He knew she didn't believe that.

Was he ready to make the commitment and propose to her? He'd twice already made a proposal. Hell, he even had the ring. But those times had meant nothing more than winning a competition. They hadn't been based on love, respect or even like.

It was different with Zee. As much as she teased that he couldn't possibly love her—and perhaps he was mistaken, for the only kind of love he knew was that which he'd experienced from his family—he did feel a deep respect and attachment to her. And what better basis for starting a family, something formed from friendship, laughter and passion? All of which had nothing to do with the competition. He didn't want it to be associated with the infernal contest. Because that detail was the one thing that kept Azalea from seeing him.

Could she ever see him for his own man? Someone who had not followed in the footsteps of a pleasure-seeking rogue who could not commit to his children's mothers?

Dinner with his family would either cement Zee's opinion or change it. And he wasn't feeling very positive about which way that pendulum would swing.

CHAPTER FOURTEEN

WATCHING THE SUNRISE from the balcony that wrapped around Sebastian's penthouse, a soft blanket wrapped about her naked body, Azalea felt as if she existed inside of a dream. She had crept out of bed, leaving Sebastian sprawled on his back, arms out and legs wide, still asleep. The guy was a master at the unconcerned sleep. She loved it.

Now she leaned against the ornate wrought iron railing. The city was quiet, and a foggy heaviness sweatered her with the heat of August. It felt like a hug from Paris. Seeming to rise from the dash of rose light that hugged the horizon, the Sacré-Coeur Basilica, far on the Right Bank, pierced the gold sky with its bleach-white spires. Closer, wearing scaffolds like intricate lace, Notre Dame announced to all that she would not be taken down, no matter the strife she endured. Below on the sidewalk, a woman in sleek jogging wear ran by, earbuds depriving her of the peaceful morning.

It wasn't like rising to Big Bruce's call and then wandering through a meadow barefoot, each step stirring wild and earthy scents, but Azalea wouldn't neglect this moment. This was the Paris she could manage in her life. Quiet, beautiful, something out of a postcard. But give it a few more hours and the rush and hubbub would change her mind.

Dinner with the family tonight. A dreadful clutch at her heart forced a swallow. But really, she was a grown woman. She could do this. A few hours seated before the eyes of a klatch of snooty girlfriends, a virtually speechless and likely judging father, and the brother who viewed Sebastian as his greatest competition?

What could possibly go wrong?

Smirking at the disaster scenarios that deluged her brain, she shook them all away. This night would go well. And she did want to meet the family that had influenced Sebastian's life. They were going to be her child's relatives. Whether or not they were included in that child's life was a matter for another day. First, she had to gather basic intel and check out the gene pool.

"Zee," Sebastian called from the bed. She'd left the balcony door open. "Come back to bed."

"It's perfect out here." She remained by the railing, despite his wanting moan that seemed to vibrate through her erogenous zones.

A glance over her shoulder saw he'd rolled to his side, back away from the morning light, derriere exposed. Now, that was a sight she couldn't resist. And it gave fun definition to the word *manhandling*.

Enough city-gazing. Time to put her hands on that.

Sebastian tugged at the violet silk tie that added some color to his simple black velvet smoking jacket and trousers. From last year's summer line, the violet silk was tied in a trinity knot. The single button on the jacket was a Louis d'Or minted in the sixteenth century. The gold coin added a touch of flair to the look. He felt comfortable. On trend. Fashionably right on the mark.

Roman Mercier appreciated his sons' attention to even the smallest fashion details. Rather, he expected such diligence. Sebastian could recall, as a child, watching his dad dress and being tutored in the correct arm length for the various dinner, smoking or tuxedo jackets. Proper shirt styles for all suits, jackets and occasions. How to pair shoes with trousers, and what colors went with what seasons. Styling the perfect suit was like breath to Sebastian. It was his second language, even before English, which he got to use so much lately with Zee.

Another tug wasn't necessary to loosen the tie, but rather readjust it slightly. It was being stubborn. Hmm... Ties never gave him bother, so why...

With a wince, he realized he was nervous about tonight.

He'd wanted to accompany Zee on her afternoon shopping adventure to select a suitable dress, but a call from the office concerning an emergency fitting for a visiting celebrity hadn't allowed such. And when she'd asked him if he didn't trust her fashion sense, those big blue eyes had lured him to tell her of course he did.

He hadn't lied. Maybe a little. But he'd also the sense to encourage her to be herself. And she had found the perfect dress. This evening his rural princess teased big-city casual chic.

Flicking off the lights and spinning out to retrieve his date by the front door, he took the elevator with her to street level.

Now, sitting next to him in the back of the limo, Zee smoothed at the white fabric splashed with florals. It was cut just above her knees and hugged her figure with a sweetheart neckline. Her soft blond hair was done in loose waves that framed her face and the red lip matched the flowers on the dress. Sweet yet elegant.

Now, if he could just get his head straight on how to handle the situation of her pregnancy. It could mean the win to him. If they married. That was the calculating way to look at things.

Yet a softer, more heartfelt, side of him simply wanted to do right by her and make her happy. And to be a father to the baby that he had helped create. He couldn't imagine not being involved in the upbringing of his child, unplanned or not. But that way also looked exactly like the path of Roman Mercier. And that did not suit him either.

Realizing she'd given his hand a squeeze, Sebastian then noticed the limo had stopped. "Right. We're here. You ready for this?"

Her nervous nod told him so much. Honestly, he shared her butterflies. His mother could be judgmental at times. *Merde*... All the time.

"I've got you," he promised. "We can do this together."

She exhaled heavily. "Yep. Together."

The Mercier family met monthly in a private top-floor room at an elite four-star restaurant in the 8th arrondissement. The owner was a former lover of Roman Mercier's, though she'd not produced a child and therefore didn't qualify for the family dinners. Sebastian had lost count of all the women who had passed through his father's life over the years. It would be madness to try and keep a tally.

Once out of the elevator, they were greeted by a friendly hostess, and he accepted a drink from the waiter who offered wine and champagne. He suggested sparkling water for Azalea, and the waiter dashed off to get that.

"Ah! There are my baby brothers." He walked up to greet them.

"Sebastian, so good to see you!" A woman in an elegant black silk gown walked alongside the nanny dressed in plain black linen, who toted a baby on her hip. In a stroller sat another rambunctious baby.

She bussed Sebastian on both cheeks, then eyed Azalea. "And who have we here?"

"Elaine, this is Azalea Grace. My...girlfriend." He smiled at her and she affirmed the label by returning the smile. "Zee, this is Elaine Desmauliers. And this here—" He bent to the baby in the stroller. "Is Henri?"

He got a nod from the nanny that his guess had been right. The twins were only nine months old and were always dressed identically. Tonight, they sported black onesies with a designer logo in leather applique across the bellies. Who could tell the dark-haired sprites apart?

"Hey, Henri." He waggled the baby's toe, clad in matching designer socks. "How's my little brother?"

"So nice to meet you," Azalea said to Elaine and offered her hand to shake.

Elaine leaned in and bussed her cheeks. "Lovely, *cherie*. What a pretty dress."

Sebastian picked up on the snide tone and returned his attention to Zee. He slid an arm around her waist and tugged her close. "There's never a moment Zee is not the most beautiful woman in the room."

Elaine's elegantly tweezed eyebrow lifted. He had seen the bills come through the L'Homme Mercier accounts that authorized twenty thousand euros monthly for the woman's coiffure and wellness spa expenses. "Well, well. Have you found the one?"

Sebastian smirked. "I'll leave Zee to decide whether

she has successfully captured me. But we must get on to the dining room. How is Father tonight?"

He hooked his arm in Zee's and led her as Elaine took up his other arm. Behind them, the nanny followed, pushing the stroller.

"He is doing well," Elaine said. "His inability to get some words out frustrates him, but he is easier to understand every day. He's changed, Sebastian. You will remark it, I'm sure."

"Changed? How so?"

"He's softening. More so even than he did following the first stroke." She patted his hand and looked up at him.

He read the success in her eyes. She would love to be the one woman who finally procured a ring on her finger from Roman Mercier. Sebastian doubted that would happen, but he wished her luck, if only for Henri's and Charles's sakes.

They entered the dining room through elegant Art Deco stained glass doors. Zee's grip on his arm tightened as they stopped before the long dining table. The rest of the family was already seated. All looked up to take them in.

Sebastian leaned in to whisper at Zee's ear, "Ready?"

"As I'll ever be."

After introductions, and some initial questions from each of the family members regarding Sebastian and Azalea's relationship, everyone seemed to settle and sniff at their wine and poke at the hors d'oeuvres.

The room was amazing, featuring more of the Art Deco stained glass, lots of dark woods, gold flatware—was it *real* gold?—and a bottle of champagne so large Azalea wasn't sure anyone would even be able to lift it to pour.

Her nerves did not settle. Maybe her upset stomach

was more baby-related than nerves. She hoped not. Now would not be a good time to start delivering on the vomiting she'd avoided during morning sickness. So she sipped water constantly, then realized that must look suspicious. Pushing the goblet forward on the table she clasped her hands on her lap.

Roman Mercier's girlfriends were all glamorous, and there wasn't a single one of the three of them—Elaine, Angelique and Cecile—who did not look artificially enhanced with breasts that defied gravity or cheekbones and lips that plumped just a bit too unnaturally. But on the surface, they were kind and, beyond catching their assessing gazes of her perfectly plain dress—spangles and rhinestones seemed *de rigueur*—Azalea didn't feel like a piece of overcooked meat that none of the elites wanted to touch.

Yet.

Philippe, the brother—son of Cecile—who shared Sebastian's dark hair and gray-blue eyes, but was stockier and more built with thick biceps, eyed her suspiciously. He also had a girlfriend sitting alongside him, not as uber-plumped but certainly working the sequins and glamorous hairstyle, and with eyebrows that defined perfection. He kept a keen eye on Azalea. Was Philippe sizing up his chances at being first to the marriage stipulation of the competition? What might it do to him if he learned his brother had successfully completed the "produce an heir" portion of the race to the win?

And the fact Sebastian introduced her as his girlfriend both annoyed and excited her. They hadn't agreed on such a designation. Sure, they'd spent the last days with one another as if they were in a relationship. Had chatted with his friends as if they were a couple. *Did* that make her his girlfriend? She loved the *idea* of being Sebastian's girlfriend.

Though certainly carrying the man's baby did give the girlfriend label some credence.

Oh, Azalea, stop analyzing! Just try to enjoy this night. The sooner it will be done.

And then later at his place they could discuss the way they would label their relationship. Because it did need a label. For her sanity.

The woman seated on the other side of the table from her, next to Sebastian's father, was Angelique, Sebastian's mom. Dazzling in pale pink beaded chiffon, the woman eyed Azalea covertly through long false lashes. Wicked red nails caressed a champagne goblet. Sebastian had to have told her a little about his date. Was the woman musing that Azalea was just a country bumpkin and how dare she insinuate herself into her son's life? Most likely.

When the main course was served, Azalea took some solace in being able to eat and not make eye contact with anyone. Sebastian reached under the table and gave her thigh a squeeze. He leaned in and whispered, "Still good?"

She nodded. Yes, as long as he was by her side, she was good. So far, none of the women had scratched out her eyes. Not that they had reason to. It was the competitive brother who worried her. And at that moment, Philippe stood, gesturing for everyone to silence.

Azalea met Sebastian's gaze and he shrugged, indicating he had no idea what was to come.

"Family," Philippe began, "I have exciting news I must share before the desserts arrive. I want to announce that Colette and I are engaged to be married!" He bent to kiss the exuberant Colette as everyone gasped. Then the girlfriends all clapped and cheered. Roman, who used his words sparingly, tapped his spoon on the side of a goblet in applause.

Azalea did not miss the wink Philippe directed at his brother. Yet beside her, Sebastian raised a goblet and said, "*À la nôtre!* To a good life!"

All echoed the toast and drank.

Colette extended her hand to reveal an acorn-sized diamond ring. "I didn't slip it on until just now," she said. "We wanted to surprise everyone."

"It's lovely," Cecile cooed. Philippe's mother walked around to hug the couple and congratulate them.

And Azalea noticed Roman's expression as he quietly observed. There was not so much a proud smile on the father's face as a curious moue. He cast his glance between both of the sons he'd pitted against one another. Was he reveling in the competition? One had already achieved half success. Or was he plotting something else? It bothered her in a way she couldn't quite label.

And then she realized how this must make Sebastian feel. She slid her hand under the table and clasped his hand. A good squeeze brought his attention to her and she kissed him. "He hasn't won yet," she said.

"Doesn't matter," he murmured. "It…really doesn't. What matters is the way you look at me."

With that, Sebastian stood and made another toast to the couple's future and the entire family.

Once desserts were served it was Roman's turn for a speech. He stood and thanked them all for their support. According to Sebastian's whispers in her ear as he translated for his father. The family had been speaking both French and English through the night, but Azalea would not expect the patriarch to employ English when he already had difficulty with speech.

"Family means more now than ever," Sebastian translated. "He is happy."

Dear old Dad having a change of heart about family? Interesting? And she hoped, for Sebastian's sake, it would develop into gentler, less aggressive expectations of his sons. But still she felt uncomfortable about the whole thing. Something was brewing inside Roman Mercier's brain.

After desserts were cleared and the champagne was poured with elan by the sommelier, everyone chatted quietly. Philippe was showing off his fiancée's ring to his dad and Cecile, explaining how it cost two million but he'd got it for half that thanks to his connections in the jewelry industry.

"Sebastian," Angelique said over a sip of champagne, "you look so well. I don't think I've seen you since Roman was in the hospital. What is it that's got your eyes so bright, my love?"

"Well, isn't it obvious? Zee here is the one who makes me happy."

Eyeing Azalea over her goblet, Angelique made a dismissive noise. Red nails rapped the crystal. "Interesting. Not your usual type."

"Mother," Sebastian admonished.

She shrugged and Azalea felt that the woman would not be dissuaded from what felt like a venture into villainy. Likely she'd been waiting for just the moment to toss out a few comments.

"She's rather unkempt," Angelique said. "And so thick around the middle."

"Mother!" Sebastian remanded with a pound of his fist on the table that alerted everyone to hesitate in their conversations. "That thick middle is a baby."

Everyone at the table turned their full attention to Azalea.

Sebastian, not seeming to notice he'd silenced the room, continued, "*My* baby, Mother."

Now gasps swept up like a violent wave that crashed against Azalea's skin and flooded into her heart. Philippe swore. Roman tilted his head, and then nodded in what looked like approval. Elaine cooed, saying *"Ooh, la, la! Another Mercier baby!"*

The heat that rose in Azalea's throat to circle her neck felt suffocating. Why had he announced that? They'd agreed not to tell anyone tonight. When she felt him reach for her hand she tugged away and stood. "Excuse me. I need some air."

She fled the table, leaving surprised gasps, remarks that she was rather touchy, and someone congratulating Sebastian on having secured one half of his success.

CHAPTER FIFTEEN

AZALEA MADE A beeline for the ladies' room. Thankful no one was inside, she aimed for the last of the three sinks and leaned over it. She wanted to splash water on her face but thought better against ruining her makeup. The oval mirror showed no black mascara smears from the few teardrops that had escaped as she'd rushed away from the dining room.

What Sebastian's mother had said about her had been cruel.

But Sebastian announcing to all, in a boasting manner, that she carried his child, had gone beyond. How dare he? It hadn't been his place. They had agreed not to tell anyone tonight. This was her body, her baby. And if Sebastian thought to use it as a means to gain control of L'Homme Mercier, he had another think coming.

It had to have been a slip of the tongue. He wouldn't throw her under the bus like that. Or maybe he'd simply needed to feel some pride at that moment? Some small win after Philippe's engagement announcement.

Wrapping her arms across her chest she paced. She studied her stomach in the mirrors as she passed before them. Thick in the middle? Why couldn't she have a baby bump instead of this full-middle swelling? It did look like she'd gone a little too hard on the sweets and carbs. Maybe she had been enjoying Diane's homemade crumpets a little too much lately. With blueberry jam. And lots of butter.

Azalea Grace was definitely not one of those glamorous women sitting out at the table. As nipped, tucked and contoured as they were. Not...sophisticated. So how had she even caught Sebastian's eye in the first place?

Right. She'd taken him by surprise by commandeering the back of his limo. And then they'd spent the best night together. And since, whenever they were together, she really thought they enjoyed one another's company. Had amazing chemistry. She was happy that if she were to have a child, half its genes would be from the smart, sexy, adorable and terribly funny Sebastian Mercier.

But if she had to raise that child within the family sitting out in the dining room?

She shook her head.

The door opened. Azalea turned to the vanity and made it look as though she were checking her hair. Angelique sidled up alongside her, sequins hissing with her movements, and studied her reflection in the adjacent mirror before speaking.

"Sebastian says I must apologize for calling you thick. Apparently, truth is not always welcome. I am sorry."

What an apology. So genuine. Not.

"You are unlike any of my son's previous girlfriends," she said to Azalea's reflection. "They were all very stylish and..."

"I'm sorry, Angelique. I don't meet the standards you have set for your son. I know the Mercier family is rich and has style and a certain social standing. It's not my world, and it never will be. But his abrupt announcement about the baby—"

"Ah, that is the bright side to this startling evening, *oui*?"

Azalea turned to face the woman who granted her a bright smile quite opposite of the treatment she'd just served her.

"You are going to have my son's baby! He is already halfway to the CEO position. You've only to marry him and he wins."

Azalea's mouth dropped open. Tears again threatened, but she held them back with an act of willpower. The woman was truly lacking in empathy.

"I would have chosen a different mate for him," Angelique continued, unaware of her stinging words, "but it gets him what he deserves, so I will go along with it."

Go along with it? As if the woman had any say over any of this!

"You will marry him?"

"He hasn't asked." Why had she said that? It didn't matter! She wasn't going to insert herself further in this messy family drama. "Besides, I wouldn't marry your son. And he knows that."

Angelique's expression remained the same. Because everything on her face was unnaturally tightened. But Azalea suspected she would frown, if she could.

"Just because I'm carrying Sebastian's baby doesn't mean he gets to jump in and assume control. I have choices. And I'm not going to marry a man just to help him win some stupid family competition. It's so cruel that his father subjects him to such a thing!"

"You mustn't speak of Roman like that. He simply demands the best from his sons. His expectations are exactly the reason why Sebastian and Philippe have done so well. They are highly respected by their peers in the industry.

Both are millionaires. And how dare you suggest you will keep my son from his child's life!"

No, she could never do that, but— Walking into this crazy argument had not been on the books for tonight. The past few months Azalea had felt emotionally fragile, and as if she were walking uncharted grounds. And speaking with Sebastian's mom only lifted that fragility to the surface. She couldn't hold it together much longer.

"I don't want to argue with you about something that should be between me and Sebastian."

Angelique grabbed her by the arm. "Sebastian is my son. And…" Was that an attempt at a frown? "I don't want him to be like his father."

Her desperate confession startled Azalea. Had the woman empathy after all? Of course, who would want their child to be a man who collected women and sons as if prizes? And now that she thought about it, she realized Sebastian was doing just that! He had emulated his father's example. He'd offered to pay her expenses for a lifetime. Just as Roman had done for his sons' mothers. And she had accepted!

What a fool she had been to allow herself to get sucked into the Mercier family drama.

"I know that as his mother, you think very highly of your son," Azalea started, "as you should. He's amazing. Talented, smart, kind and so funny. We seem to get one another despite our differences. But I could never marry him, even if he did ask. If it was simply to win a competition, then it could never be real. I don't want to live like that."

"Has Sebastian told you he loves you?"

"Well…he has." At least, he'd said he was falling for her. "But…"

"But what? If you know my son as you think you do, you know he does not lie."

No, he did not. Azalea couldn't imagine a lie coming from Sebastian's mouth.

"So, if he has told you he loves you, why do you believe that is a lie?" Angelique challenged.

Because there were too many other conditions distorting that truth. And maybe she just needed to step back from this crazy family to see it all clearly.

"I know he wouldn't lie to me," Azalea replied. "And I do believe I love him. But it feels wrong. This. Your family. It's…crushing in on me. I'm sorry."

With that, Azalea fled the bathroom, but waiting outside across the hall from the door stood Sebastian, hands in his pockets. He straightened, pleading with his soft yet devastating gaze.

Azalea put up her hand. "I don't want to do this. Not here. I'm going home." Dash it, she couldn't flee. Home to her right now was Sebastian's place. "I just need to get away from this drama."

"I'll text the driver to pick you up and take you back to my place," he offered.

"Thank you." When he made to take her hand, she shook her head. "I need some space, Sebastian."

Angelique strolled out of the ladies' room and took her son's arm. "I tried," she said to him. "She's not got the Mercier dedication to family."

"Mother, enough. You were only to apologize to Zee."

"She did," Azalea said. "And there are some things your mother and I agree on."

Angelique lifted her chin proudly.

But there had been no agreement on the definition of family.

"You are a good man," Azalea said to him. "I have never believed otherwise." She wandered toward the elevator. "I'll talk to you later. Please, just give me an hour or so to myself."

"I can do that. I'm sorry, Zee!" he called as she stepped onto the elevator.

Before the doors closed, she saw Sebastian with his mother standing beside him, clutching his arm like the protective yet unknowingly wicked mother who could never unfurl her tentacles from around her child. Azalea felt terrible leaving in such a manner. It didn't reflect well on Sebastian. And she didn't want to hurt him.

But this was all too much to process.

The man had once offered to defend her honor. What had happened to his valiant promise? Did his family stifle that individuality, his genuine impulse to do right? It seemed like it. They loved him but they wanted certain things from him, and he had unknowingly fallen right in line.

CHAPTER SIXTEEN

BEFORE SEBASTIAN ENTERED his home, he leaned against the wall and took the ring box out from inside his suit coat. It had been nestled there all night. He opened the velvet box. Inside sat a 10 carat diamond ring surrounded by sapphires as pale as Zee's eyes. It wasn't the same ring he'd utilized two times previously. He'd returned that and purchased one that was fitting of Zee's beauty, her soft innocence and her bubbly nature. He'd intended to propose to her after a successful family dinner.

Now? He'd blown it. Everything felt wrong.

His mother could be cruel in her forthright manner. Angelique was a judgmental person but also honest. Yet he hadn't expected her to treat Zee with such open disdain. He should have never allowed her to go into the ladies' room to apologize. After they'd watched Zee's exit, she'd told him Zee had threatened to take the baby and never allow him to see it.

He couldn't know if that was true or an exaggeration. He suspected the latter. It was Angelique's habit. What was it that she and Zee could have possibly agreed on? He should have asked his mother, but he'd wanted to get away from her as much as Zee had. They had returned to the dining room. He'd hugged Colette and Philippe, congratulating them both. To Sebastian's surprise, their engagement didn't bother him at all. He didn't feel as though he'd slipped in the race to the prize. And yet...

Tucking away the ring box, he blew out a breath. He should have never blurted to all that Zee was pregnant. In that moment he had felt pride and exhilaration to make such an announcement. But at the sight of Zee's sad expression, he'd immediately known he'd done wrong. He should have asked her permission to make the announcement. And...when he was really honest with himself, the first set of eyes he'd met after breaking the news had been Philippe's. His brother's gape had pleased him. He'd successfully created an heir! Halfway to the prize. He and Philippe were still on equal ground.

He swore and caught the heel of his palm against the doorframe. Was he so callous as to use Azalea in such a manner? To gain the CEO position? The baby hadn't been planned. It wasn't as though he had plotted his way to the win. But any proposal of marriage now could only be seen by Azalea as his final step to securing that position.

And maybe it was.

That his father had patted him on the back and told him, "Good job," had again bolstered his pride. For a few moments. And then he'd surfaced from that false emotion and realized that Azalea didn't see any of this in the way his family did.

Or maybe she saw it for exactly what it was.

He was following in Roman Mercier's footsteps. Because if he did propose, Zee would surely run away from him. And that left him only with the option of providing for her, financially taking care of his family. Just as his father did for his sons and girlfriends. Sebastian hadn't even seen it coming. It had obviously been ingrained in him all his life. But that was no excuse. It couldn't be.

Damn this stupid competition!

There was no way to erase the damage it had inflicted on his and Azalea's relationship. And they did have a relationship. He cared deeply about her. He loved her.

Or was he telling himself he loved her because it felt like what was expected? He couldn't know if it was because his heart hadn't taken the full jump or rather if it was all this family stuff that was deflecting any real emotion from fully forming.

Again, damn it all!

He knew this was difficult for Zee. And that she was pregnant on top of all this had to compound her stress. But it was hard for him, too. He didn't want to mess this up. But he wasn't sure how to make it right. And…what was right?

Inside his home it was dark save for ambient city lights beaming through the wall of windows. Was she already asleep? She needed to rest for the baby.

He tiptoed through the house, leaving his suit coat on the back of the sofa and taking his shoes off before slinking into the bedroom. The lamp by the bed was on and Zee stood beside it in the red silk negligee he'd bought for her.

"Hey," she said.

"Did I wake you?"

"Nope. Can't sleep."

"I'm sorry. I wanted to give you some time."

"Thank you for that." She sat on the bed and patted it beside her thigh. "Let's talk."

He noticed her pallor. "Are you feeling okay?"

"My tummy was a little unsettled after dinner. Might have been that taste of octopus."

"Or the judgmental mother?"

She smiled and clasped his hand, tilting her head onto his shoulder. "Angelique is an interesting one. But she's your mother. And I can see that you both love one another. I don't want to do anything to change that between the two of you."

"You wouldn't and you haven't. Angelique can be abrupt and has a tendency to speak her mind. She wants the best for me."

"I know that. And I realize that, no matter what happens between the two of us, those people I met tonight are forever going to be my baby's aunts, uncles and grandparents."

"Henri and Charles will have a niece or nephew close to their age with whom they can play."

"It was nice to see you interacting with Henri. You really like the little guy, don't you?"

"He's my brother. And he's silly. Loves when you blow on his toes. You should hear his giggles. Charles, on the other hand, is a sober bit of pudge and baby goo."

"The fact that you notice such defining traits in them makes me believe you would make the best dad, Sebastian."

"You think so? Better than Roman?"

"Well, I don't know your dad at all. And I shouldn't judge him on the one quality alone. But he does seem to want to pit his sons against one another for reasons that are—" She sighed. "I just can't see you doing something like that to your children."

"I would never." And yet…here he was. Committing much the same crime against the family structure as his father had.

"And your mother…well, Sebastian, she's quite dependent on your father, isn't she?"

"He does finance her entire existence." As he had offered to do for Zee? *Mon Dieu*, why had he not seen that one for what it was?

"And is that how you wish me to be? You offered to pay for things, and—I shouldn't have accepted. I'll give back all of it."

"Don't do that, Zee. I don't want you to be dependent on me. You won't be. You'll get established with the baby and then find a job that suits you so you can feel as though you are making your own way."

She frowned.

"Or not?" he added with a shrug. He didn't know how to read her mood. Whatever he said would be wrong, no matter if it sounded right to him.

"I won't become another kept woman like those girl-friends who sat around the table tonight."

And he didn't want that for her, but his offer would do just that. How to allow her the freedom she obviously desired but also provide her the help he knew she required to survive?

"Despite it all," she said, "your mother loves you and she only wants the best for you and your family."

"Is that so terrible?"

"It isn't."

"As for my dad, I sometimes think the competition and race for the top is all he knows. His father was the same. Roman was one of four boys who eventually won own-ership of L'Homme Mercier after much the same sort of competition. Except my dad had to produce an heir *without* marrying. My grandfather didn't want the woman involved in the family wealth. Which is why he's never married."

"That explains some things. Yet I wonder why he's in-sisted now his sons marry?"

"Might have something to do with his brush with mor-tality. The first stroke is what served as catalyst to this competition. On the other hand, Dad is always energized to watch Philippe and me compete."

"So odd. But again, I shouldn't judge. Sounds like the only lifestyle he's ever known. I find it interesting that he still keeps all his sons' mothers in his life."

"Kind of crazy, eh? Roman does love family. In his manner. And if he had refused my mother to be a part of my life, I may have hated him for that."

"I suppose. You are not a playboy like your father."

"A man can't work in the fashion industry, surrounded by beautiful women, and not have his roguish moments." He clasped her hand and kissed the back of it. "Not anymore. I honestly have no desire to date any other woman, Zee. And it's not even about the fact you're carrying my child. I care about you. I want you in my life."

"I want the same."

"You do?" He searched her gaze, smiling a little. "Then why are we at this crossroads that feels as though one of us is going to turn in the opposite direction and leave the other standing alone?"

"You know how I feel about us marrying."

"Fake. Which it wouldn't be, Zee. Not to me."

"That's where your mother and I agree. We both know you are true to your word. When you tell me you feel as though you are falling in love with me, I know you are speaking from the heart."

"I am. And I promise you nothing about a marriage between us would be fake."

A kiss was necessary to his wanting heart. Their connection did not cease to make his world feel right. Even if in reality it was not right. He caressed her hair and she sank into their kiss. He didn't want to lose her. He didn't know how to keep her. He'd never been more at odds in his life.

"My father has made this difficult," he said when he pulled away. "I don't want to blame him. It's all on me. Where I'm standing right now. The situation life has presented to me." He stroked her cheek and she leaned against his hand. Her quiet acceptance both filled his heart and broke it at the same time. "I don't know how I could have made a different choice, Zee. You did hijack me."

She smirked. "Guilty. But you did invite me to the party, and your bed."

"You could have refused."

"I couldn't have possibly refused the sexy Frenchman who danced into my heart."

"Would you stay with me if I asked?"

"Here in Paris?"

He nodded.

"That's just it. I don't know. I can use the excuse that Paris is another big city that makes me feel uncomfortable, but the thing is, I feel comfortable wherever I am as long as you're holding my hand."

He pressed her hand to his lips. Losing her felt inevitable. Because at the moment, this—whatever it was they had—felt more forced than right. As if they were both avoiding speaking the truth. But he didn't know his truth. *Did* he love her? He'd been speaking the word, but had he a grasp on its true meaning? How to know what love really was when all his life it had been expressed through expectations, challenges, boasts and achievements?

"I love you, Sebastian."

His heart thudded and then dropped. It felt too tremendous and too small at the same time. Because if he replied in kind he wasn't sure if it would be accepted in kind.

"But I don't think we can make this work," she said. "Not the way your family wants it to look."

Now his heart dropped to his gut. A swallow tasted of acrid heartache.

"Can you tell me it can work?" she challenged.

"I don't know what you want to hear, Zee. Rather, I do. I know what your heart craves from me. But…right now? I feel like I'll break your heart no matter what move I make. And I don't want to be like Roman. I can't be. Someone has to break the cycle."

"I'm proud of you for recognizing that."

He closed his eyes. Yes, and he'd only just made such a realization this evening.

He hadn't swept Zee off her feet and given her good reason to surrender to a future with him in it. Because that ring box in his pocket out in the living room was not the thing to make it all better. He needed to win her heart, soul and trust.

If he'd ever had her in the first place.

"I'm returning to Grace Farm tomorrow," she said. "I think it's best. I need to spend time on the farm before it's sold and gone forever. It holds a lot of memories for me."

"I don't want you to leave me, but I understand. Of course, you'll need to send off Stella and Daisy."

They sat in silence for what seemed a lifetime, though he suspected it was only a few minutes. Zee laid her head on his shoulder and snuggled against his arm. How was it possible she could smell like summer when the moment felt like winter? Was this the end? Were they breaking it off forever? He didn't want that. But he didn't know how to ask for forever from her.

"We've come to a certain agreement about the baby," she said. "I will accept the financial help you've offered. If it's still on the table."

"Of course, it is. I would never rescind that offer."

"Thank you. Sebastian. But I won't take your money forever. I promise I'll figure my life out and get a good job sooner rather than later. I'll be able to support myself. And eventually I won't need your assistance. Because it feels like we'd be perpetuating your dad's…"

Yes, his father's ways. And his father before him. What a legacy the Mercier family flaunted.

"There are some aspects of what we have that feel different than Roman and his girlfriends. It does to me. I mean, the emotional part of it all. With hope, you'll realize that as well. I will never stop supporting you, Zee."

"I…" She sniffled and tears rolled down her cheeks.

That she hurt so deeply tore apart his bewildered heart. He felt that sadness as much as she did, but he didn't know how to express it. So he settled for ignoring the shards of his heart that seemed to crackle and fall.

He pulled Zee into a hug and kissed the top of her soft, sweet-smelling hair. "Things will go as they should," he said.

It was more of an encouragement to his own heart. It was all he could manage without crying himself.

She would leave him. Take his baby with her. And he might never see her again.

No. He wouldn't allow that. And not because he was some rich bastard who could have anything he wanted with the wave of his wallet. No, he wanted Azalea in his life—baby or not. And there may yet be a way to win her.

"Will you go with me somewhere tomorrow morning?" he asked. "It's someplace I want you to see before you leave. I'll put you on a private jet back to England after."

"What is it?"

"Just something I want you to see. I promise there will be no Mercier family members there."

She nuzzled her head onto his shoulder. "Sure. One last trip together, then."

Such a final announcement. Now Sebastian had to tilt back his head to staunch the tears from falling. He was so close to losing her.

CHAPTER SEVENTEEN

AZALEA HAD NO idea what to expect when Sebastian pulled around the front of the building in a blue sports car. He'd told her he kept it for summer driving and hadn't yet had it out this year. Now they cruised out of Paris to a destination he said was an hour's drive away.

Anything to spend a little more time with him before she left for home. Because while she knew going back to the farm was best for her, she hated that decision in equal measure. Leaving the one man she loved couldn't be right. Was it pregnancy hormones screwing with her mental reasoning? Possibly.

Her life had suddenly become so big. She was swimming in new experiences and yet grasping for something solid and familiar. It was hard to process the entirety of it all. So she decided to take it one day at a time. And do it with pastries. Sebastian had kindly pulled over in front of a patisserie and she'd bought croissants and chocolate-stuffed rolls. But when he'd given her the side-eye as she started to pull one out of the bag, she'd said she'd wait until they stopped. Didn't want crumbs on the leather upholstery.

Now he drove down a quiet country road lined with thick emerald grass that wavered in the breeze. Tall birch and lush maple blocked the sunlight for a second, then a dash of warmth hit her nose again. Rolling down the window filled the car with fresh air.

"You know that Pierre Hermé in Paris delivers pastries on subscription?" he said as he pulled into a driveway before a medium-sized, stone-faced château.

"Really? I wonder if they'd deliver to England?"

"I can look into it."

The offer was too rich to accept, but on the other hand, when pregnancy cravings nudged... "Go for it."

With a kiss to her cheek, he leaned over and opened her door for her. "I appreciate that you don't argue the simple things, Zee."

"When life offers me a party, I party. And when it offers pastries, I am no fool. Where are we?" she asked as he swung around the back of the car and met her as she stepped from the car.

Before them rose a château that could almost claim quaint cottage-ness for its size, were it not for the tall windows on the two floors and so much slate tile on the roof. The yard hugging the gravel drive was overgrown, the grass as high as their knees. Oak trees dipped their boughs over the front doorway where pink flowers bloomed and designed an elaborate trellis.

"Oh my gosh!" Azalea rushed toward the frothy pink blooms. "Do you know what these are?"

Sebastian shrugged. "Flowers?"

She plucked a bloom and tucked it in her hair, spinning to declare, "These are azaleas!"

"Really? Then this adventure was meant to be."

"Whose place is this?"

He shuffled in his pocket for a ring of keys. "It used to belong to my grandparents on my mother's side. When they passed away, the property went to me. I haven't been out here since I was a kid who got dumped with Grand-père and Grand-mère every summer while Mom and Roman took a vacation overseas. Or Mom and whomever she was dating at the time. Though I did stop in a few years ago when it came to me. A grounds crew and cleaning service stop in twice a year. Let's go inside."

The house was cool and bright enough to navigate without switching on the lights. The electricity was kept shut off, he explained, as well as the water. Sturdy white canvas dust covers hugged the furniture in the front sitting room. In the kitchen, counters were also covered and glass-faced cupboards were bare. The place had been cleared of the smaller things and decorations, leaving behind only large furniture and appliances. He led her toward the back of the main sitting area, which opened to a stone patio overgrown with weeds.

"It needs some love," he said as he walked out onto the grass and weed-frothed stones. "Maybe a cow or some chickens?"

"Are you asking me or telling me?"

The air smelled so good that Azalea felt compelled to spin, eyes closed and head tilted back. This felt like her dad's farm. Safe and cozy. And the sun beaming on her cheeks made her forget about last night's debacle.

"I'm asking."

Suddenly he twirled her and they did a little dance. It was always easy to find their silent rhythm. Kicking off her shoes, she shimmied her hips and plugged her nose, performing the dance move that he mirrored. Then with a grand flair, he spun her under his arm and performed their patented dip that activated her libido every single time. When she rose in his embrace, he kissed her deeply.

Kissing Sebastian always felt right. Like something she

deserved. They knew one another in an intimate, silent way that said more than words could ever begin to define. Safety in his embrace. And excitement. An exhilaration of discovery and a confidence of ease. There was no one else in this world she'd rather be kissing. And she could kiss him for the rest of their lives.

That thought made her pull back.

"Why did we come here?" she asked. "Did you want me to see where you were most happy as a child?"

"That and... I want you to have it, Zee."

"Have what?"

"This place." He dangled the keys before her. "The property. It would be perfect to raise a little boy, yes?"

"Well, yes, but..."

"You like a farm, but you still prefer to be close to a city," he pointed out. "I know it would mean you'd have to move to France, but...will you accept? I promise it's not like I'm tucking you away out here to keep you for myself."

Now that he brought it up... "That's exactly what it sounds like, Sebastian."

"I..." He exhaled heavily. "I wrestled on the drive here with the whole 'tucking away the girlfriend and her child' scenario. It might look like it, but it doesn't feel that way in my heart. I'm not Roman Mercier. At least, I hope that I will not follow in that most egregious of his traits. I so desperately want to be different, Zee."

She could see that in him. She wanted it to be that way if that was what he truly desired. But could he rise from his conditioned ways to forge a new path?

"I want you to have this place to do with as you will," he said. "A place that will make you feel safe. But also, I want to be close so I can visit my son. You will allow me to do that?"

"Of course, I wouldn't forbid you from being a part of our child's life. But. This is a very generous offer, Sebastian. This home holds memories for you. How can you give it away?"

"Maybe I want to put new memories here to share with the old ones? And as I've said, I haven't used it since it came to me. It would be a shame for it to sit empty when there's a bright soul who could bring happiness to its walls and grounds."

"It's a lot to take in. I mean, it's beautiful. And it would require a lot of work…"

Which would keep her busy. And she'd start with this patio, plucking out the weeds and maybe planting some rosemary along the borders for fragrance. And wouldn't a birdbath painted in bright colors be a lovely addition?

"The grounds and cleaning crews can come in this week and polish it up for you," he said. "You can select a decorator to do up the inside. Or do what you like by yourself. It's completely up to you."

Oh, baby, what fun she could have making the place her own. Could it ever be her own coming from a man who struggled with doing the right thing and who may eventually revert to his father's ways? Then, the place may become like a cage to her and her child. Oh!

"I have to think about this."

"Of course, you do. You only jump into things when the door is open and you're being chased."

She smirked at his reference to their first night together. That was the night her heart knew Sebastian was the man for her. Yes, even when her brain continued to insist he was not.

"Here." He took her hand and placed the key ring on her palm. "Take these with you. I'll text you the GPS coordinates for the property. You can come here whenever you like. Move in. Do what you wish. But please accept this from me, Zee?"

"I..." She dangled the key ring from her fingers, thinking how much fun it would be to decorate the place and make it her own.

To make a life for her new family.

It was too generous. But that was simply Sebastian doing what made him happy. And what a perfect place to raise her child. "...will take these keys and give it a good think. How does that sound?"

"I can't ask for anything more. Well, I could, but I don't want to push you into anything. Now, let's get you to England."

"You want to be rid of me so quickly?"

"No, I want you to stay with me." He slid his hands down her arms. His touch always served her a good shiver. Was it her heart responding to his heart? Nah, it was base and wanting, completely lustful. "But I also want you to do things your way, in your time. And I did arrange for the pilot to meet us at the airport in about an hour and half."

"Then let's get going."

Azalea locked the door and clutched the keys to her breast the entire ride to the airport. It felt like she held her future in her hands. And within her body. Yet beside her sat a piece to that puzzle that didn't seem to orient itself to fall neatly into place.

CHAPTER EIGHTEEN

Weeks later

STELLA AND DAISY, carefully loaded on a livestock trailer, rolled down the driveway and away from Grace Farm. Azalea waved, and—dash it—sniffed back a few tears. It was silly to get so attached to a farm animal.

"Hormones," she muttered. That was her story, and she was sticking to it.

Oliver Grace returned from the front gate, having pounded the Sold sign into the ground earlier this morning. They had two weeks to vacate the premises. Both her dad and Diane were ready to go, with most of their possessions packed. They weren't taking any large furniture. Only clothing and necessities. Because they intended to travel the world for a few years before—if even—settling somewhere.

"Where do you think you'll ultimately land?" Azalea asked as her dad wrapped an arm across her shoulders and they stood before the cottage watching the trailer disappear down the road.

"England will always be my home. I'm not sure I could ever leave it completely. Diane thinks Greece."

"Beautiful water and the sun." She tilted her head against her dad's. "Sounds like a dreamy place to stay for a while."

"How you feeling, Lea?"

"Great, actually." She smoothed a palm over her belly. "Finally this extra weight is turning into some semblance of a baby bump so I don't just look fat."

He laughed. "Your mother was the same way with both you and Dahlia. When are you due?"

"February."

"Then we'll plan to be in France after the New Year."

Yes, France. Because she'd spent the last few weeks muddling, creating scenarios, mentally arguing, and then finally deciding that, yes, she would move to the château south of Paris. She would be a fool not to accept such a generous offer, especially since her desire to go job hunting never seemed to match her need to take it easy. To honor her changing body and heart.

Besides, this farm was no longer her home. And she couldn't be a rural princess in a low-rent London flat.

She looked forward to the adventure of it all. And while she could never know if Sebastian would be a common fixture or an infrequent visitor, she had talked herself into accepting whatever he decided would work best for him.

Did she want him to live with her? To help her raise their child? Yes. And…she knew she could do this on her own, if need be, but…yes.

"You going to be all right, sweetie?"

"I am. Off to adventure! And with Dahlia helping me move in, I think I'll have a great start."

Her sister had vacation time and planned to stay with Azalea for a couple of weeks. Painting, weeding, decorating and lots of gossip, was how she'd put it. And shopping for baby things.

Her dad kissed her cheek and then mentioned Diane would have supper ready soon.

* * *

It had been days since Zee had texted him. Sebastian stood in the office before the window. The sun had set, and the coffee his secretary had brought in earlier was cold. The instant his phone buzzed he spun and picked it up. His heart fluttered to see a text from Zee.

I'm at the château. Here to stay. My sister is helping me move in and make it a home. Wanted you to know I think of you every day. Want to see you. But give me some time?

She'd accepted his offer to stay at the château. That was immense. He would give her all the time she needed. It wouldn't change the way he felt about her. Now more than ever he had to win her heart. Because being CEO of the company wouldn't matter if he didn't have Azalea Grace in his life.

"That turned out much better than I thought it would," Dahlia said of the bedroom wall that they had dry-brushed with shades of maroon, violet and pink. "Gives it some warmth in a rustic kind of way. Not my style, but I think it's you, Lea."

"I love it." Azalea tilted her bottled water against Dahlia's wineglass. "Thanks for helping me with everything these past few weeks. The baby's room is adorable."

They'd found simple pine furnishings for the small room next to the main bedroom. It was a sunny room with a balcony, so Azalea could sit in the rocker on warm summer nights.

"I'm excited about this," she said with a smooth over her belly. "I feel like this little guy is eagerly waiting to come into my life."

The doctor had accidentally revealed the baby's sex after a sonogram and Sebastian had been right. A boy. Azalea hadn't cared whether it was a boy or girl. She was simply ready to hold the little tyke and mom the heck out of it.

"You do have that proverbial glow, sis. You know I'm not the motherly sort, but you almost make me want to have one, too."

"Do you think Clyve would make a good dad?"

Dahlia's boyfriend had proposed last year but they hadn't set a date. They were in no rush, both working in the legal sector and having eighty-hour workweeks. Who had time to say vows?

"Maybe. I don't know. It wouldn't be fair to a kid with our work schedules. That's what I love about your situation. Your man is taking care of everything so all you have to do is be a mom. How perfect is that?"

It could be more perfect. Like having that man in her life to actually be a father to her son. Not being relegated to the cottage where she had her own life and he had his in the city. She tried not to overthink it. Sebastian had gifted her the world with his generosity. And if that meant she'd be just another girlfriend sitting around the monthly family dinner, she had to accept that.

But did she really?

"You're thinking about it again," Dahlia warned. "I shouldn't have brought him up. You always go all melancholy on me when I do."

"I love him, Dahlia. This château is a dream, but it's not the perfect dream."

"You need the father in the picture rather than floating around the edges."

"Exactly."

"Do you think Sebastian would make a good father?"

"I actually do. The little I've seen him interact with his baby brothers makes me believe he would be a kind and gentle dad. But then, what do we ever know about how well we can parent before we've even given it a go? I just hope I can be the best mother and raise a boy who is respectful and kind."

"You will. And if his dad does more than float around the edges that would be ideal. Maybe you should ask him to marry you."

"Can I do that?"

"Heck, yeah. But I get the struggle you have over that stupid family competition debacle. You'd never know if he married you for love or money."

"His brother is engaged right now. There's always a chance Philippe could win. But I really want Sebastian to win. Oh, why am I being like this? I can help him to win something he wants more than anything."

"At what price? Your heart? Your trust for him? Standing in line next to the other girlfriends? I can't see you getting a boob job."

Azalea sighed and settled onto the floor before the bed. The fake fur rug was soft and dark pink to match one of the colors on the wall. "Tell me what to do, Dahlia."

"I think you're doing it." Her sister sat next to her. They each slanted a foot toward one another, touching toes as they'd always done when they were kids. "You're capable of doing the single mom thing. It'll be much easier with financial help than not. And you've got a dream home. What more is there?"

"A dream man."

Dahlia sighed dramatically. "Give me the bloke's address. I'll stop in to Paris to have a word with him."

"You will not. Sebastian will...*we* will make this work. One way or another."

"Fine. But I'm not going to promise to babysit once the little man arrives."

"I wouldn't expect you to, especially living as far away as you do. But you will have aunt duties."

"What will that involve? I don't think I can bring myself to change a nappy."

"How about throwing a baby shower?"

"Oh, I can do that! Let's go online and shop for baby stuff!"

When, within five minutes of introducing himself to Oliver Grace, the man asked Sebastian to help him out back, he agreed eagerly. A means to ingratiate himself to Zee's dad? And to get to know him better. He'd flown over specifically to talk to the man. What better way than to do it within Oliver's comfort zone?

Apparently, comfort meant mud and hay. Donning the rubber boots once again, Sebastian helped Oliver heft a dozen bales of hay that had been dropped off by a neighboring farmer to store in the overhead loft of the barn. They were heavy but not overly taxing. After a few bales he got into the swing of it, and it felt good to work up a sweat. Even wearing a dress shirt and trousers.

When they had finished and Oliver invited him to stand at the back of the barn where it opened to the fenced field, which was absent any cows, Sebastian had to ask. "Where are Stella and her baby?"

"Sold them."

Right. Zee had mentioned something about her dad selling them. She had been heartbroken. He'd seen it in her expression. A woman and her cow were not so easily separated by the heartstrings.

"Then why the hay?"

Oliver shrugged. "I bought those bales this spring. Forgot about them. They'll be good starter stock for the new owners."

"When do you move?"

"Few days. We're headed to the States for six months. Diane wants to tour all fifty states. Not sure we can do it all in that time, but we'll give it a go."

"Why the time limit? If your intent is to travel, then why set a schedule?"

"Exactly." He smirked. "But she's the one with the schedule in her head. You must know how schedules work. Big-city businessman like you."

"I do, but I've learned to be more lenient thanks to your daughter."

Oliver nodded, but Sebastian noticed his tight jaw. He could guess what the man must think of him. So he'd end the torture.

"I had to talk to you face-to-face," Sebastian said, "because your daughter is important to me. I love her." He waited for Oliver's reaction, but the man merely inclined his head. Listening.

Yes, he did love Zee. He'd created his definition of the word, and it felt right in his heart. It was that immense feeling he got every time he saw her blue eyes crinkle and her freckles dance. The feeling that all things were right.

"I know she'll be the best mother."

"Yes, she will. But what about the father? What does he intend to do?"

"That's why I'm here. Monsieur Grace, I want to ask you for your daughter's hand in marriage. I love her. But

I don't want to ask her to marry me without your permission."

Oliver stood from his lean against the barn wall, crossing his arms over his chest. Defensive? Not a good sign.

"I'm sure she's told you about the competition with my brother."

Oliver nodded. Swatted at a fly.

"It's why I haven't felt right about asking her to marry me. But I intend to tell my dad I'm out. I love Zee too much to risk losing her. And if that means I have to step out of the competition, then I will."

"Won't marrying my daughter make you the winner?"

Sebastian exhaled heavily. "It would. But it wouldn't be right. Not to Zee. I know she would always wonder if I asked her to marry her out of love, or if it was to win a competition. I can't do that to her. It must be real with her. The one thing we value most between us is truth."

"Noble. But…"

Sebastian met the man's gaze. Same pale blue as Zee's eyes. But not so fun-loving and perhaps even cynical right now.

"Lea's told me that winning that CEO position would make you a happy man."

Sebastian nodded. "It would. I believe L'Homme Mercier should remain true to its legacy by continuing its attention to menswear, but my brother has different plans. Much as I hate to see the company add a women's department under Philippe's control, stepping out of the competition is a sacrifice I am willing to make."

"Not for my daughter you won't."

"I…don't understand."

"I don't give you permission to marry my daughter."

"But—"

Oliver held up a hand. "I understand that you love Lea. It fills my heart to know my grandchild has a father who will love him and his mother. Even if he isn't in their life."

"But I want to be—"

"You asked for my permission? Well, you've got your answer. I won't have you marrying my daughter if it means sacrificing something that would make you happy. It wouldn't be fair to Lea. Happiness is an inside job. That saying about making another person happy is nonsense. Only you can make you happy."

Zee had once said much the same to him. The apple hadn't fallen far from the tree.

"And then?" Oliver continued. "Once you're happy? Then you can find another person who complements that happiness in their special way. But if you think you're doing something noble by walking away from a job you desire to prove your love to Lea? Nope." Oliver shook his head. "Not going to happen."

"I intend to tell my father I'm out of the competition," Sebastian reiterated. "No matter what."

"That's your choice. But if you're serious about my opinion on the future you may have with my daughter? You've heard my say."

Sebastian nodded and bowed his head. The man had a point about making himself happy. But he hated to hear that. That meant he'd have to continue the competition.

He wasn't about to lose Zee, though. There had to be a way to make this right. Which meant, his happiness first, and then he could begin to imagine embracing his family.

Family? Yes, that was the key to all of it. He had to talk to his dad. And he knew what had to go down. Truths must be honored.

"Can I get you a bite to eat before you go?" Oliver offered casually. As if he'd not just torn out Sebastian's heart.

"No, I'm... I just came to ask that one question. I should be on my way."

He started to walk through the barn. What had just gone down? He didn't need Oliver Grace's approval for a single thing. Because that man's approval did not make him feel like a smile from Zee did. Her smile gave him such pride and he felt respected by her, seen. That was all he needed.

And yet, Oliver had a point. Could he truly stand as head of a family if his heart were not made happy by his work? What sort of example would that set for his son? He'd grown up watching his father flit from woman to woman, never committing, and—

It had to stop! It would stop. With him.

"You seem like a good man, Sebastian," Oliver called after him. "I know my daughter loves you."

That small comment landed right in his heart. The Grace family had a way of gifting him respect in a manner he'd never experienced.

Sebastian paused in the open end of the barn and turned back to Oliver. "I'll make it right. I promise."

CHAPTER NINETEEN

DURING THE SHORT flight from London to Paris, Sebastian pulled out his phone. The screensaver was the photo of him clasping Zee around the waist so she wouldn't be carried off by a bouquet of bright balloons. That had been a hell of a night. One that had changed his life.

He opened the video that had been taken moments after that photo. He and Zee had marveled over the display crafted entirely from paper. It had looked like a Japanese cherry tree, spilling blossoms from its slender branches to the ground. They'd stood in the middle of it all, posing for a few photos, and then...their first kiss.

At the time, Sebastian hadn't been aware the photographer had switched his phone to video to record. Afterward, when she'd handed him back the phone she'd apologized, but had said it was a moment she'd thought worthy of capture.

Indeed.

Now he watched as he kissed Zee. They'd both been exhilarated from dancing and getting to know one another. Like two magnets, they'd instantly clicked. Her freckles had dazzled him. Her bright smile had seeped through his skin and flooded his system with joy. And he realized now he was watching himself as he lost his heart to a woman he had only known for hours. At the time it had felt as if they'd been searching for one another all their lives. Their souls had finally found one another.

A silly thought? No. It had been real. And that beautiful soul now carried his baby. They'd made a new soul together. They belonged together. And not in some weird arrangement where he kept Zee on a farm and visited her on weekends because they weren't married. Or even married because he wanted to gain the CEO position. Their souls wouldn't survive with anything less than true, real connection. No conditions attached.

His heart ached. He'd thought it a noble gesture to fly in and request Oliver Grace for his daughter's hand. He'd never expected a no. But if Sebastian were in Oliver's position, he would have delivered the same answer. And while it wasn't binding, and wouldn't keep Sebastian from doing as he pleased...he would honor that *no*.

Until he could make it right.

Roman Mercier was recovering slowly but surely following the second stroke. With the use of a cane, his gait touched stability. He'd initially refused the cane, but when Elaine had presented him with a stylish walking stick, he'd ceased argument. It was his voice and his ability to speak fluidly that still troubled him. He could speak but his words were jumbled together and sometimes he chose the wrong word. Aphasia, a condition of the stroke. A speech pathologist worked with him three times a week. Elaine made sure he did not miss the private, in-home sessions. She'd told Sebastian she wanted her twins' father to be able to communicate with them. As well, she'd mentioned her plan to win his father's softening heart by convincing him he should marry the mother of his latest sons.

Sebastian had wished her luck. And he truly hoped she would be successful, if not for his youngest brothers, but for the Mercier family overall. The toxic sins of the father had to be redeemed.

And today Sebastian was taking a step to do just that. There was no time to dally or hope for change. Action must be taken. His future would look different than his father's past.

Sebastian found his dad in the conservatory, which overlooked the narrow garden against the ancient limestone wall that separated their property from the neighbor. Roman was going over some paperwork for L'Homme Mercier. Sebastian realized that even though their patriarch had been felled by the stroke he was still an able and important part of the business. He had connections, a certain trust built up with their oldest and some of their largest clients.

But the man also had two capable sons. It was time he retired or took a smaller role.

Still, Sebastian did not see Philippe as the best choice for CEO. Even if he had no designs on a women's line, the man could be easily distracted by recreational pursuits, which also included women.

"Business on a Saturday?" he asked his dad. He strolled to the window and stood beside his father's lounge chair.

Dressed impeccably, as was his mien, and nursing what looked like whiskey on the rocks in a cut-crystal tumbler—but which smelled more like coffee to Sebastian—his father gestured he sit. He used gestures more frequently as opposed to talking, though Elaine insisted it was important to be patient and allow Roman to speak. That was the only way he was going to improve his speech.

"What are you drinking? Doesn't smell like whiskey."

"Coffee," Roman said with a wince. "Elaine insists… less alcohol."

"Coffee has been touted to have some excellent health benefits. Though cold coffee sounds horrid, if you ask me."

Leaning over to inspect the papers on his father's lap, Sebastian watched as he pulled out a red file folder and handed it to him.

"What is this?"

Roman held up a finger to pause him from opening the file. "Important changes. Life."

"Life?" Curious, but also fearing that Roman had made those changes to the company, Sebastian didn't open the file. "Before we get into this, there's something I came here to tell you. Ask you. Well, both." He sat on the window seat before his father. "I'm in love, *mon père*. With Azalea Grace."

His father nodded. "Your...baby."

"Yes, she's the mother of my child, but that's not why I love her. I fell in love with her months ago. On the first night we met, actually. It just took my brain a while to realize what my heart has known. I know you probably can't understand..."

His father clasped his hand and squeezed. He opened his mouth to speak, so Sebastian waited to allow him to form words. "I...have loved. Do. Love."

"I know. You love your children. You love the mothers of your children. I wasn't implying... Well." To even begin to understand the intricate heart of his father could be a mad-making venture.

"I want to marry Zee," he said. "But not because of some family competition. And yet, if I ask her to marry me, she'll only believe it is because of the competition. And I thought I would come here to tell you I was out. To allow Philippe the win. But I can't do that, either. I genuinely feel I would be the best choice for heading L'Homme Mercier. And certainly, I understand how much you enjoy the work you do with the company, but you must realize it has come time for you to retire, *mon père*. You and Elaine should be spending your hours enjoying the twins."

Now his father leaned forward and slid a palm over the back of Sebastian's hand. They had never been demonstrative in their affection. Winning approval and a congratulatory nod of the old man's head had been the morsels of emotion and fondness Sebastian had learned to accept over the years. So the feel of his father's warm hand on his loosened something inside him. He clasped Roman's hand and bowed his head over it. At a loss for words. He simply wanted to experience this moment. He had almost lost him to a stroke. Twice.

Family did mean something to him. It was everything. And he could have something wondrous if only he'd step up and do it the right way. For perhaps the first time in his life, his heart was telling him which was the right way.

"I don't want to compete with my brother anymore," he said softly. "And I need to change the family dynamic that has existed for generations. It's not what I want. Can you understand?"

His father nodded. He tapped the red folder. "Wrote it. Too much to say. Mean it." He slapped a hand against his heart. "For my sons. Family."

With a heavy sigh, Sebastian opened the folder. He'd not clearly explained what he needed to his father—Zee, and nothing else.

Inside the folder were a few pages of printed text. It began with *To my sons...*

As Sebastian read his father's words tears formed. He clasped Roman's hand. The old man had had a change of heart. Elaine, and the strokes, had been the catalyst to opening his eyes. To seeing his family in a new way. He didn't want to someday pit his youngest sons against one another. He regretted doing as much with Sebastian and Philippe. It had been what he'd known. There was no way to take back the years. But he wanted to move forward in a new way. To learn a new way. He intended to ask Elaine to marry him. He would surprise her in a few days.

Sebastian nodded with joy. This really was a change for his father!

"Read the back," Roman said.

Sebastian turned over the page.

I watched you at the family dinner. The way you looked at Mademoiselle Grace. You admire her. You respect her. I've never seen you look at a woman that way.

Sebastian swallowed back a tear as he nodded, "I do admire her. Everything about her is everything to my heart. I love her."

He read the remainder.

I want to earn that same look of respect and admiration from you, my son. Someday.

Another nod. It was all he could do not to blurt, "Yes, someday, I want to look at you in that manner." It would happen. This family could change. And it would begin with this letter.

It made Sebastian's heart swell to read the next lines that detailed how Roman intended to dissolve the competition. And he wanted both his sons to agree to what he'd decided.

Sebastian stood and leaned over to hug his father. It didn't feel unnatural. Because he'd had some practice with Zee. "I love you, *mon père*. We can do this. As a family."

A week after Dahlia left, Azalea sat on the stone patio out back of the house, finishing a braided daisy crown. A pile of uprooted weeds sat to her left. The plants with the little yellow flowers remained untouched. Though she suspected they might also be weeds, they were too pretty to pull up. And she liked how they spread across the stones forming a soft carpet for her bare feet. Later, she'd surf online to find out what they were and if there were uses for them such as a natural elixir or even tea. Since settling into the château, she'd become all about using what the land gave her and DIY-ing the heck out of things. It was fun and gave her a sense of satisfaction.

She set the circlet crown on her head. "Rural princess!" she declared to the symphony of crickets. "Well, you don't have to bow, but I would appreciate a little less chirping come late night."

And thinking about noisy animals... Now, to get some chickens for the little coop that sat beside the barn. Fresh eggs every morning? She was living the life.

Sebastian had texted her this morning. He intended to stop in tomorrow and wanted to know if she needed anything. She'd given him a list of foods that she hadn't a chance to get to the grocery store for, despite the little car that had been stored in the garage for over a decade and which ran like a dream. Milk, eggs and lots of chocolate pastries. She was labeling it a pregnancy craving, but really? She just loved pastries.

She'd added "live chickens" to the list but did not expect that one to actually be fulfilled.

With a satisfied sigh, she tilted her head to take the sunshine into her pores. She could do this. She was doing this. It felt right, like the thing that had been waiting for her to finally turn around and declare, "Oh, yes, that's for me!" Her aspirations to find a job had slipped away. Supporting herself completely wasn't doable at the present moment.

In a few years, she'd revisit her goals and desires and if a job felt right then, she'd explore her options.

Yet she knew the country life was not something that Sebastian could get behind. Visits on the weekend might be all he could manage, or even want. The man had an important job that kept him at the office and in the city where he needed to meet with contacts face-to-face. He thrived on the busyness of Paris.

He might feel obligated to treat her as a girlfriend since she was having his child. But he couldn't sustain that forever. Could he? Perhaps she should tell him he should start dating so he could find a wife and win that CEO position? The competition did not stipulate the wife and baby had to be from the same person. And really, Roman Mercier should be proud his son was spreading his DNA around.

She could be okay with that.

Sighing, she shook her head. "You love him. Don't deny it. You got pregnant by the rebound guy and now he's taken over your heart."

Time to start listening to her heart.

If she was to be true to her heart, she needed to make it clear to Sebastian that she did love him. To, well, to fight for him. If they did marry it could be good. It could be real and based on love and caring for one another. It wouldn't have to be simply because of the competition. And if part of it was? Then she was going into the marriage eyes wide-open.

"I'm denying him an easy win if I insist we never marry," she said. "I want him to win. The CEO position will make him happy."

With a sense of renewed purpose, she nodded. Tomorrow she was going to ask Sebastian to marry her. Hopefully, it would be the best choice she had ever made.

CHAPTER TWENTY

SEBASTIAN WAS ARRIVING this morning. And Azalea had a plan. She'd picked wildflowers from the overgrown field behind the barn. Armloads of them. Now she stepped back from the front stoop, looking over her work. The azaleas had shed their blossoms weeks ago. She'd managed to create a bough of wildflowers cascading over the entryway. It looked lush and romantic and smelled like heaven. Here was where she'd ask him to marry her.

"It could work," she whispered with hope.

No woman was going to share her baby daddy's surname but her. Azalea Mercier had a certain ring to it.

"A ring?" A proposal wasn't a proposal without one. "Dash it. I need to find something…"

She wandered barefoot around the side of the château. The grass was soft and freshly mown thanks to the grounds crew that stopped by once every two weeks. She plucked up the daisy crown she'd made yesterday and placed it on her head.

If he said yes. Would he? She couldn't know what his answer would be. Their lives had been altered with this pregnancy. Their needs and desires had been brought to the fore, amplified. Perhaps he wouldn't be willing to commit if she demanded real love from him?

Mostly, she wished he'd just walk back into her life, kiss

her silly, make love to her until they were sated, and stake his claim to her. That was how it happened in the movies.

"Life is not a movie," she muttered. Plucking a daisy, she decapitated the white-petaled head. "This rural princess has to work a miracle if she intends to win her prince."

She busied herself with creating a ring from the stem.

When the sound of a large vehicle rolling down the drive turned her head, she dropped the daisy stem and wandered around from the backyard to see a truck backing up to the gravel side lot before the barn.

A livestock trailer? She hadn't ordered any animals. Though the barn was clean and ready to receive any stock she might wish to own. She'd already looked into finding a rescue animal, or two, in the area.

The driver got out of the truck and—

"Dad?" She rushed up to meet Oliver Grace, who sported a big smile and wrapped her in an even bigger hug. "I don't understand?"

"Hey, sweetie." He gave her tummy a pat. "You look beautiful. Wow, it's nice out here, isn't it? Diane and I will have to spend a weekend with you sometime."

"You are always welcome."

He tapped her crown, then gave her a kiss on the nose where once he'd teased that each kiss added another freckle.

"I'm glad you decided to stop in for a visit, but I don't understand why you're here? What's in the truck?"

He held up a finger. "I've brought you a few things that I know are important to you. Hang on." With that, he opened the back of the trailer and pulled down a ramp, walked up it and opened an inner gate. He then guided down a cow. And it wasn't just any cow.

"Stella?" Azalea took the reins from him as he again disappeared inside the truck, where she saw another smaller cow. "Daisy! But how? I thought you sold them, Dad?"

"I did." He shrugged. "But someone bought them back because he knew how much they meant to you. That's the other important thing I brought today." He leaned back and slapped the metal side of the truck. "Hup!"

A door slammed and from around the front of the truck walked another man, wearing sunglasses and an expensive suit perfectly fitted to accentuate his physique. On his feet were wellies. A rather stylish pair with a designer logo splashed around the tops. And he carried something she would have never thought to see a man in a suit carry. A chicken with lustrous brown feathers that gleamed blue in the sunlight.

Azalea handed the reins to her dad as she gaped at the sight of the new arrival. "Sebastian?"

"You were expecting me, yes?"

"Of course, but…. What is this?" She looked to her dad, who smiled widely but offered no explanation. But of course! She'd written *live chickens* on her grocery list. And he'd actually come through? What a guy!

"I talked to your dad days ago," Sebastian explained. "Asked him something important and…he told me *no*. It made me do a lot of thinking."

"I have no clue what you're talking about. You two are in cahoots?"

"That's a good way to put it." Sebastian pushed his sunglasses to the top of his head and winked at her dad. "That conversation with Oliver sent me to my father's doorstep and we had a long and good conversation. My dad has had a change of heart. The strokes have him viewing his life and his family with new eyes. He proposed to Elaine last night."

"Really? That's amazing. That's good, right?"

"It's incredible. She's taught an old dog a new trick. Elaine insists the twins do not grow up like Philippe and I have. Always competing. Dad agreed."

"He did? But that's…"

"That's what led him to dissolve the competition for the CEO position."

"But—Sebastian, you wanted that position. Now what happens?"

"Now Philippe is going step into the role of CEO of the new company Dad wants to form. A women's atelier. It will be completely separate from L'Homme Mercier. As it should be. And I will take the reins of L'Homme Mercier."

"You got the position!" She plunged forward for a hug but stopped abruptly as the chicken in his arms clucked. "It's what you deserve. I'm so glad your dad had a change of heart. And to celebrate you brought me the chicken I asked for."

"Actually, it's more than that."

Sebastian stroked the calm chicken. Its feathers were sheened blue and green and his strokes revealed a bright orange undertone as the soft feathers moved. The fowl was perfectly content on his arm.

It was almost too much to take in. And now she noticed his wellies had a splotch of chicken doo-doo on them. The man was out of his element. And yet, he fit in like a shiny new garden implement just waiting to be dirtied a little.

She looked to her dad, who still wasn't offering any explanation, not even a helpful gesture. The two of them had been talking? This was crazy!

"Of course, Stella and Daisy will love the field," she offered, unsure what else to say. "And there's the old chicken coop beside the barn, but…"

"But there's something more." Sebastian approached her. He held the chicken as any experienced farmer would cradle a cherished farm animal. Now he bent a knee and kneeled before her. "It's a proposal."

A pro—? But she had planned to— She'd dropped her makeshift ring upon hearing the trailer drive up. Azalea's breath gasped out as she slapped her chest. Her dad nodded, smiling widely. She wasn't sure how he was involved, but did it matter?

Sebastian, on one knee, held up the chicken in offering between them and said, "Azalea Grace, you've changed my world and my heart. I don't want to spend a day without you. I want you in my life because I love you. Because we have fun together. Because I want to dance with you until our knees creak and we can no longer move. I asked your dad permission to ask you to marry me and he said no."

With a gape, she looked to her dad.

Oliver shrugged. "He was going to refuse the CEO position and concede to his brother. I knew he loved you, and you loved him, but I also knew he wouldn't be happy. I couldn't let him ask you if it meant he wouldn't be happy."

"That's why I talked to my dad," Sebastian said. "I had to make him understand that you had won my heart, but I also knew your dad was right, that I wouldn't be completely happy if L'Homme Mercier went to Philippe. I told him all that, and then he showed me the letter he'd written stating all the plans he had for dividing the company. As well, we…shared a hug."

His smile now seemed to surprise him. Azalea understood exactly what that hug must have meant to him.

"Anyway…" He held up the chicken before her, a grand gesture if there was one. "Would you accept this chicken from me and say yes to becoming my wife?"

Azalea clasped her hands over her heart. The proposal was absolutely perfect. And everything she wanted from him. And…she glanced to the flowers hanging over the entry. Like nothing she could have imagined or planned. And that her father was here to witness made it even more special.

Still holding out the chicken, Sebastian waited for her reply.

The proposal was genuine and real. It was the most enduring gesture he could have made. And she'd already decided how her best future could look.

The chicken cooed. Sebastian tilted it to look at its little face and cooed back at it. "She'll say yes. She has to." He held the bird higher for her to inspect. "Is the chicken not enough?"

"The chicken is perfect." She took it from him and it settled in the crook of her arm and on her belly as if the bird knew there was a baby inside and it needed to nest and protect it. "You know the way to my heart, Sebastian."

He embraced her gently, including the chicken. "Do you love me?" he asked.

"I do."

"And I love you. I wouldn't have worn rubber boots and traveled for an hour with a chicken in my arms for anyone but you. Will you be my wife? Will you live with me here in the château, but also in Paris? I've already figured I can work four days a week. We can make our schedules work. Maybe you'll live in Paris a few days and then back on the weekends to the country, where you can wear your rural princess crown as I see you've already begun?"

She blushed and tilted down her head. Yes, she had created the crown and wore it with pride.

"I'll do anything to be with you, Zee. Can you be okay

with me working but being home every night in your arms? Will you share our boy's life with me?"

Our boy.

Those words landed in her heart and swelled to her extremities with the most wondrous joy.

"I will." She held up her hand, pinkie crooked. He entwined his pinkie with hers. "I love you, Sebastian. And I want to make a family with you."

Their kiss was sweet, indulgent, welcoming, and laced with a thrill of desire. It was the perfect representation of the future that waited them.

The chicken crowed and leaped to the ground. Stella nudged Azalea's arm. And her dad said casually, "Well, that's a bit of all right."

Azalea's heart fluttered. "I'm going to marry you."

"That's the plan."

"Can we get married here? Next summer after the baby is born?"

Sebastian took her in his arms and spun her. "Anything for you, Zee. Oh." He patted his suit pocket. "Almost forgot." Reaching inside his coat, he pulled out and revealed a big, sparkling diamond ring. "You didn't think I'd expect you to wear a chicken on your finger, did you?"

EPILOGUE

The following summer

THE WEDDING WAS a simple affair catered by a posh restaurant for the few dozen people who had come to celebrate Sebastian and Azalea. Now four months old, Zachary Mercier had won the day by attracting the attention of everyone by simply existing. Cute baby wearing a polka-dotted onesie sleeping on a blanket under the willow tree? Haul out the cameras!

The twins were not to be outdone. They attracted as many photo opportunities and were currently tearing apart pansies and nibbling on the petals. Roman and Elaine, who had married over Christmas, were contemplating house hunting in the south of France now that Roman was completely retired. Oliver and Diane were headed almost the same direction, to Spain, for a few weeks before then trekking to Hawaii.

After most of the guests had left, and only their closest family lingered in the château—some staying the night in the guest rooms—Sebastian and Azalea danced slowly on the patio to the music of their hearts. Zachary slept quietly in his nearby cradle, rocked gently by the breeze. Sunday, the chicken—because Sebastian had proposed on a Sunday—was perched on the bow of the cradle, her favorite place to rest when the baby slept.

The moon was full and bright. The summer air just right. Sebastian had shed his suit coat and unbuttoned his collar. Azalea's pink spaghetti-strap dress dusted the grass because she'd not worn shoes all day. Her hair spilled in thick curls—thanks to Dahlia's styling—and was circled with a frothy pink crown of her namesake flower.

"You are the most beautiful woman in the world," Sebastian said as they swayed under the moonlight. "You have my heart. And so does Zachary."

"We're doing rather well at this family thing," she said as she rested her head against his shoulder.

Since taking over as CEO, Sebastian had been able to reduce his in-office hours to three days a week, then home to the country for two days day of online work, with the weekend free. Azalea and Zac commuted to Paris for two or three days midweek. She enjoyed the change of pace, which allowed her to stroll Zac around the parks and discover all the endless tourist attractions and hidden wonders of the city.

On the days she was in Paris, the neighbor girl, a sixteen-year-old with dreams of becoming a veterinarian, looked after their livestock and chickens. It was a perfect situation.

"I sometimes wonder," he said softly. "If you hadn't been such a strong and fearless woman, I might have never experienced you charging into the limo. I'm so glad you kicked the photographer and ran to me."

"I'm glad you were there to catch me."

"Always and forever, Zee."

* * * * *

MODERN

Glamour. Power. Passion.

Available Next Month

Greek's One-Night Babies Lynne Graham

Ring For An Heir Annie West

Italian's Pregnant Mistress Carol Marinelli

Unwanted Royal Wife Clare Connelly

Their Altar Arrangement Natalie Anderson

Strictly Forbidden Boss Bella Mason

Enemy's Game Of Revenge Maya Blake

Billionaire's Bride Bargain Millie Adams

Amore

Bound By The Boss's Baby Nina Singh

Accidentally Engaged To The Billionaire Cara Colter

MODERN

Glamour. Power. Passion.

MILLS & BOON

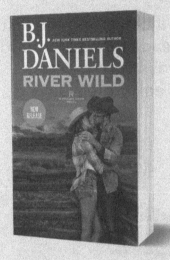

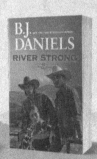

Subscribe and fall in love with a Mills & Boon series today!

You'll be among the first to read stories delivered to your door monthly and enjoy great savings.

WE SIMPLY LOVE ROMANCE

MILLS & BOON

JOIN US

Sign up to our newsletter to stay up to date with...

- Exclusive member discount codes
- Competitions
- New release book information
- All the latest news on your favourite authors

Plus...
get $10 off your first order.
What's not to love?

Sign up at **millsandboon.com.au/newsletter**